ANGELS WALKING

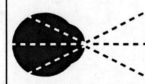

This Large Print Book carries the
Seal of Approval of N.A.V.H.

ANGELS WALKING SERIES, BOOK ONE

WITHDRAWN

ANGELS WALKING

KAREN KINGSBURY

CHRISTIAN LARGE PRINT
A part of Gale, Cengage Learning

GALE
CENGAGE Learning·

Farmington Hills, Mich • San Francisco • New York • Waterville, Maine
Meriden, Conn • Mason, Ohio • Chicago

GALE
CENGAGE Learning®

THE LIBRARY OF CONGRESS HAS CATALOGED
THE [HARDCOVER IMPRINT] EDITION AS FOLLOWS:

Kingsbury, Karen.
    Angels walking / Karen Kingsbury. — Large print edition.
        pages cm. — (Thorndike press large print basic)
        ISBN 978-1-4104-7115-4 (hardcover) — ISBN 1-4104-7115-2 (hardcover)
        ISBN 978-1-59413-791-4 (softcover) — ISBN 1-59413-791-9 (softcover)
        1. Janitors—Fiction. 2. Alzheimer's disease—Patients—Fiction. 3. Miracles—Fiction. 4. Large type books. I. Title.
        PS3561.I4873A84 2014b
        813'.54—dc23   2014028764

[CIP data for the hardcover edition without any alterations]

Published in 2015 by arrangement with Howard Books, a division of Simon & Schuster, Inc.

Printed in the United States of America
1 2 3 4 5 6 7 19 18 17 16 15

To Donald:

Do you feel it, how the years are picking up speed? Kelsey, into her second year of marriage and Tyler, racing toward college graduation. Isn't our Lord so faithful? Not just with our kids, but in leading our family where He wants us to be. I love the sign that hangs in our kitchen: "I wasn't born in the south, but I got here as fast as I could." Nothing could be more true about our new home, our new life in Nashville. It remains so very clear that God wanted us here. Not just for my writing and to be near Christian movies and music — but for our kids, and even for us. I love how you've taken to this new season of being more active in my ministry and helping our boys bridge the gap between being teenagers and becoming young men. And now that you're teaching and coaching again, we are both right where God wants us. Thank you for being steady and strong and good and kind. Hold my hand and walk with me through the coming seasons — the graduations and growing up and getting older. All of it's possible with you by my side. Let's play and laugh and sing and dance. And together we'll watch our children take wing. The ride is breathtakingly wondrous. I pray it lasts far into our twilight years. Until then, I'll enjoy not always knowing where I end and you begin. I love you always and forever.

To Kyle:

Kyle, you have become such an important part of our family. You are now and forevermore will be our son, the young man God planned for our daughter, the one we prayed and hoped for and talked to God about. Your heart is beautiful in every way: how you cherish simple moments and the way you are kind beyond words. You see the good in people and situations and you find a way to give God the glory always. I love watching you lead Kelsey, growing alongside her in faith and life and the pursuit of your dreams. Constantly I am awed by the wisdom you demonstrate, so far beyond your years. You are an example to our boys and a picture of how a husband should love his wife. Thank you for that. Even still, I am struck by the way you look at our precious Kelsey — as if nothing and no one else in all the world exists except her. In your eyes at that moment is the picture of what love looks like. This is a beautiful season, with you and Kelsey joining me at my events, your first solo Christian music project now a reality. Kyle, as God takes you from one stage to another — using that beautiful voice of yours to glorify Him and lead others to love Jesus — I pray that you always look at Kelsey the way you do today. We thank God for you, and we look forward to the beautiful seasons ahead. Love you always!

To Kelsey:

My precious daughter, I'm so happy for you and Kyle. Your dreams of acting and singing for Jesus are firmly taking shape, but even still it is your beautiful heart that best defines you. I've never known you to be so happy, and time and again I point to you and Kyle as proof of God's faithfulness. Now, as you two move into the future God has for you, as you follow your dreams and shine brightly for Him in all you do, we will be here for you both. We will pray for you, believe in you, and support you however we best can. Congratulations also on your and Kyle's first book, *The Chase: When God Writes Your Fairytale!* I pray it will reach the next generation for Jesus. Now, with that book and with Kyle's ministry of music and yours in acting, there are no limits to how God will use you both. In the meantime, you'll be in my heart every moment. I love you, sweetheart.

To Tyler:

It's hard to believe you're already well into your third year of college, ready for the next season of challenges and adventures. Watching you on stage these past years will remain one of the highlights of my life. I can imagine your papa watching from a special spot in heaven. He'd be in the front row if he could be, right next to your dad and me. But maybe my favorite moment was reading an email from one of your friends. She said she'd been gone from school for a semester abroad. When she returned, the department was different. Better. Stronger spiritually. She said it didn't take long to realize that the change had come through you. God is using you in such a great way, Ty. So many exciting times ahead, I can barely take it all in. However your dreams unfold, we'll be in the front row cheering loudest as we watch them happen. Hold on to Jesus, son. Keep shining for Him! I love you.

To Sean:

This fall you headed to Liberty University with the dream of walking onto the football team. In the journey that led to this point, you continued to put God first. For that, we're so proud of you. God will bless you for the way you're being faithful in the little things. He has such great plans for you. Sean, you've always had the best attitude, and now — even when there are hard days — you've kept that great attitude. Be joyful, God tells us. Be honest. Be a man of character. Keep working, keep pushing, keep believing. Go to bed every night knowing you did all you could to prepare yourself for the doors God will open in the days ahead. You're a precious gift, son. I love you. Keep smiling and keep seeking God's best.

To Josh:

Soccer was where you started when you first came home from Haiti, and soccer makes up much of your life now. I never for a minute doubted that you'd play NCAA Division I soccer, but watching it happen has been one of my greatest joys ever. Now I pray that as you continue to follow the Lord at Liberty University in soccer and football, He will continue to lead you so that your steps are in keeping with His. This we know: there remains a very real possibility that you'll play competitive sports at the next level. God is going to use you for great things, and I believe He will put you on a public platform to do it. Stay strong in Him, and listen to His quiet whispers so you'll know which direction to turn. I'm so proud of you, son. I'll forever be cheering on the sidelines. Keep God first in your life. I love you always.

To EJ:

EJ, it's hard to believe you're already starting college! We're so happy you could make the move to Liberty University at the same time Sean decided to transfer there. It's the best university anywhere! As you start this new season, I'm so glad you know just how much we love you and how deeply we believe in the great plans God has for you. With new opportunities spread out before you, keep your eyes on Jesus and you'll always be as full of possibility as you are today. I expect great things from you, and I know the Lord expects that too. I'm so glad you're in our family — always and forever. Thanks for your giving heart, EJ. I love you more than you know.

To Austin:

Austin, I can only say I'm blown away by your effort this past school year. You're a leader, Austin. Everyone follows your example and yes, people will want you. Schools will want you. But through it all I pray you remember you are only as strong as your dependence on Jesus. Only as brave as your tenacious grip on His truth. Your story is a series of miracles and this next chapter will be more of the same — I am convinced. Along the way, your dad and I will be in the front row cheering you on. I pray God gives you the greatest platform of all as you serve Him. Sky's the limit, Aus. The dream is yours to take. I thank God for you, for the miracle of your life. I love you, Austin.

And to God Almighty,
the Author of Life,

who has — for now — blessed me with
these.

PROLOGUE

Town Meeting — The Mission

A reverent silence defined the heavenly room as the participants took their places.

This was a new team. A new set of chosen travelers gathered for a desperate series of battles. A mission with the highest stakes. Orlon rose to his full height and took his place at the front of the room. The walls shimmered with gold and sparkling stone. The brightest possible light streamed through the windows. No one seemed to notice.

Angels were accustomed to the light.

Orlon stared at the faces before him. He could feel their concerns, their questions, their curiosity. Each of the twenty angels gathered here had been hand-picked, carefully selected for this team because together they possessed something rare and beautiful: a discernment that set them apart.

Of all heaven's angels, these compassionate beings best understood matters of the heart.

"Each of you was created for such a time as this." Orlon's voice resonated with power in the meeting space. "Our team has been given a mission to rescue the hearts of a very few sons and daughters of Adam. Humans on the precipice of history."

The angels remained silent. Their collective empathy colored the room with peace.

"The first part of our mission involves a battle for the heart and soul of a troubled man, a baseball player named Tyler Ames, who lives in Pensacola, Florida. The second centers around a young woman in Los Angeles. The girl Tyler once loved. Her name is Samantha Dawson." Orlon smiled, even beneath the weight of the mission. He felt a fondness for the two already. "Tyler called her Sami."

Orlon drew a breath. "Michael has scrutinized all angels and found you — in particular — worthy of the assignments ahead, ready for the battles that are to come."

He detailed the setup. "The situation with Tyler and his former love is complicated. Over time other people will be involved. It will take several missions to succeed. In each, we will interact with a number of humans in various earth locations." He

14

made eye contact with several angels. "We will take our assignment one stage at a time."

A slight shift came from the angels facing him. Not a restlessness. More of an anticipation. If sons and daughters of Adam were in trouble, these chosen angels were ready.

Orlon took his notes from a polished mahogany table at the front of the room. "The abandonment of faith continues unabated throughout all of earth. This is nothing new." Orlon felt a heaviness in his heart. "But Michael has learned of a child not yet conceived, not yet born. This child will grow to be a very great teacher. Like C. S. Lewis or Billy Graham. Because of him, many will change their ways and return to faith."

Angels didn't feel confusion. But the expressions on the faces in front of him showed the closest thing to it. Orlon moved a step closer. "The salvation of countless souls depends on this child."

A few of the angels nodded. Some leaned closer, intent, focused.

Orlon turned the page of his notes and his heavenly body tensed. "Tyler and Samantha are in a battle they do not know and cannot see. A battle of discouragement and defeat. A battle for their souls." Orlon sighed. "To make matters worse, these two have forgotten their potential. They have lost their way. And if" — he looked carefully around the room — "if we fail, all of history will suffer."

Every face in the room showed commitment to the fight.

Orlon steadied himself. Whatever happened, Michael had chosen correctly. These were the right angels for the mission.

"Hear me now. These two humans must not give up. For if they do, the child who would change history will never be born. In that case, people will suffer . . . and die." He paused. "You must know the name of the child. He will be called Dallas Garner. Remember that. Pray for him every day."

From the front row, an angel named Beck raised his hand. Beck was the tallest, strongest one there. He was dark-skinned with shiny brown hair and pale green eyes. If he were human, he could've easily played professional football. Instead, Beck was an angelic veteran in battles of the heart. He sat up straighter. "The child will be theirs? Tyler and Sami?"

"No." Orlon did not blink. "Those details will come. Michael stressed that we will learn about one aspect of the battle at a time." He paused. "Hours are passing. I

16

need two of you to leave now on a mission. You will be given more information along the way — where to go, when to interact."

Beck rose from his chair. "I volunteer."

"And me." Ember had been sitting at the back of the room, her long golden-red hair framing her enormous blue eyes. Ember had a strength other angels would never know. She stood, her passion for the sons and daughters of Adam palpable. "Send me, Orlon."

He thought for a long moment. "Very well." He crossed his arms. "Beck and Ember. We will send you."

Michael had told him the teams would be easy to choose. They usually were. Countless angels were on assignment from heaven to earth. Two at a time. Thousands of pairs working in tandem on missions taking place around the planet at any given moment.

Most humans never knew, never understood. Man did not need to understand for angels to do their work. The idea of an earthly assignment was familiar to all of heaven, as was the term used to describe the common phenomenon.

Angels Walking.

Beck and Ember came to the front of the room. Without a word, the others gathered around and laid hands on the two. The prayer was brief and powerful: that God's Spirit go with Beck and Ember, and that somewhere in Pensacola and Los Angeles two hearts might be rescued from destruction.

Not only for their sakes. But for the sake of a baby not yet conceived.

For the sake of all mankind.

Orlon stared into the faces of Beck and Ember. They were ready for the mission, anxious for the battle.

It was time to begin.

1

Since his fourth birthday, Tyler Ames had logged nearly twenty thousand hours training and practicing and preparing for the game of baseball. Two decades of wins and losses, warm-ups and strikeouts, game after game after game. But there was one thing Tyler had never accomplished.

He'd never been perfect.

Until now.

Tyler adjusted his Blue Wahoos cap and dug the toe of his shoe into the soft dirt of the pitcher's mound at the Pensacola Bayfront Stadium. Redemption was at hand. Bent at the waist, the ball an extension of his arm, Tyler stared down the next batter. Nearly five thousand fans screamed beneath the lights on this beautiful August evening.

Here . . . now . . . Tyler actually felt perfect.

As if tonight even the ghosts of his past were cheering for him.

19

His heart slammed around in his chest as he reeled back and released a pitch. *Ninety miles an hour,* he thought. *At least ninety.*

"Strike!" The umpire stood and pumped his right arm. "One ball, two strikes!"

One more, Tyler caught the ball from the catcher. *Just one.* A breeze blew in from the bay, but Tyler couldn't stop sweating. *Breathe, Ames. Just breathe.* They were the words he told himself every time the game got tense. He dragged his arm over his forehead, stood straight up on the mound, and took a deep breath.

One more strike. Tyler squinted at the catcher's signals. The dance was as old as the game: catcher signaling the pitch, pitcher waiting for the right signal, the pitch he wanted to throw. The signal came.

No. Tyler shook his head. Not that one. The catcher changed signals. Again Tyler shook his head. The third signal made Tyler smile. At least on the inside.

The change-up. Perfect pitch for this batter, this moment.

Tyler glanced at the stands. Four scouts from the Cincinnati Reds were here. If things went well he could bypass triple A and join the Big Leagues. As early as next week. The Majors. His dream since winning the Little League World Series twelve years

20

ago. Six years making minimum wage, trekking around down South on a bus would all be worth it after tonight. He could do it. He had never pitched like this.

Not in all his life.

Tyler wound up and released the pitch. It flew from his hands like a blazing fastball, but halfway to the plate it braked. The batter — a new third-round pick out of Texas — swung early. Way early.

"Strike three!"

Tyler jogged toward home and high-fived his catcher, William Trapnell. Six innings, eighteen straight batters. Fourteen strike-outs. Three ground-outs to first. One caught fly ball. Jep Black, the Blue Wahoos manager, met him at the dugout. "Got someone to hit for you, Tyler." He patted his back. "Rest your arm."

Tyler nodded and took a spot at the end of the bench. This was his second season with the Blue Wahoos, and though the roster changed constantly, he generally liked his teammates. Several of them shouted congratulations.

"You're perfect tonight, Ames." William swigged down a water bottle, breathless. "You own this."

Tyler gave him a thumbs-up. "Thanks. Keep it up." He volleyed a couple more

21

compliments, slid a jacket over his pitching arm, and leaned back. He could relax this inning with the designated hitter taking over.

He closed his eyes and filled his lungs with the ocean air. Hadn't he known this would happen? When he got moved up from the Dayton A team last spring he had expected great things.

Tyler blinked and stared at home plate. The first Blue Wahoos batter was up. Tyler worked the muscles in his hand, making a fist and releasing it. His team was at the top of the lineup. Plenty of time. Tyler squinted at the distant lights, the sponsor signs on the outfield walls. Like a grainy YouTube clip, the seasons ran together in his mind. Star of the 2002 Little League World Series. In high school, California's Mr. Baseball. Most recruited pitcher in the history of UCLA.

How had it all gone so wrong?

The fallout with his parents, his back injury, the public drunkenness charges, the girls. He had fallen out of grace with his fans and everyone he loved.

Sami Dawson most of all. Her name made his heart hurt. *Sami, girl . . . where are you? What happened to us?* He closed his eyes again. He had loved her more than life. But that was a hundred years ago.

Cheers interrupted his personal highlight reel. He opened his eyes and watched their centerfielder hit a triple. Blue Wahoos up, 3–0. He massaged his right arm. It was sore, but a whole lot better than usual. He had three more innings in him. Definitely.

A picture filled his mind. He and Sami, both of them seventeen, sitting together on her grandparents' roof. *Aww, Sami. We thought we had forever back then.* The stars had looked brighter that night, the silhouette of the trees like something from a dream. No one had believed in him more than Sami Dawson.

What was I thinking? How could I let you go?

Tyler gritted his teeth. Tonight was where it would all turn around. He would Google his own name tomorrow and see something different. *Tyler Ames: Perfect.* Story after story would say the same thing. He'd made it. Finally found his way. He would be perfect and everyone would know. Maybe even Sami.

Buried would be all the headlines still there at the moment.

Tyler Ames: The Kid Who Didn't Live Up to His Potential.

Minor League Purgatory: The Story of Tyler Ames.

The Sad Life of Tyler Ames: Mr. Baseball, Mr. Joke.

Tyler exhaled. The pain of his past was as close as the nearest computer. Any kid with a cell phone could read about the hero he'd been.

And the failure he'd become.

Every game, every inning of the past few years was like an act of penance now, a way to absolve himself for the sins of his past. And every single pitch had led to this.

The chance to be perfect. No hits, no walks, no one on base. Perfect.

For the first time.

What would his parents say after tonight? His father's face flashed in his mind. Funny. Whenever he thought of his dad, he thought of him angry. Correcting his pitching form, scrutinizing his weight training, questioning him.

Another run scored and the Blue Wahoos were back in the outfield. Tyler felt warm and focused. More ready than ever. Jep Black's words from earlier that day ran through his head: "Tonight's your night, Ames. Go out there and prove me right."

Indeed.

Jep had been talking to scouts from the Reds ever since the season started. Tonight, finally, the scouts were here. They actually wanted him. That's what Jep said. The Reds' director of player personnel knew his name and his numbers. Every wonderful statistic from this season. Tyler was just what they were looking for. They even knew about his past.

And they still wanted him.

Tyler set his jacket on the bench and jogged out to the mound. On the way he stopped and talked to his catcher. "More of the same." He brushed his glove against William's shoulder. "Talk to me, Trap. Keep me perfect."

"You got it."

He reached the mound and glanced up. When was the last time a guy in the AA minor leagues threw a perfect game? The Pensacola faithful were on their feet. Tyler Ames was about to make history. They could feel it. This was their night as much as it was his.

The beautiful oceanfront stadium had opened two years ago, and already it topped the list of places to see, things to do on the Florida Panhandle. The fans had bought into the Blue Wahoos, the team more than any individual player.

But tonight was different. Tonight the Blue Wahoo fans loved Tyler Ames. They knew his name. He could hear them.

Bottom of the lineup for the team from South Carolina. *Easy as the waves in the bay,* he thought. If only his parents could have been here tonight. If Sami could see how he'd made good after all. He was going to be moved up to the big show. It was actually going to happen. *Breathe, Ames . . . just breathe.* He focused on William's glove. The batter was a washed-up second baseman from the Bigs who had been sent down to the AA leagues after an injury. He couldn't swing a bat the way he once had.

Williams flashed him a signal. Tyler nodded. Yes, a fastball. That's exactly what he wanted. He lifted his knee and wound up the way he had ten thousand times. In a burst of motion he fired the ball over the plate. The batter didn't swing, didn't even have time to blink.

"Steee-rike!" The umpire was getting excited, too.

Tyler kept a straight face, but all around him it was happening. His teammates were behind him. He could feel the focus of his infield, feel the gloves of the outfield ready to react. He threw a slider and the batter connected. At the crack of the bat, Tyler's heart skipped a beat. He watched the trajectory overhead. *Get it,* he thought. *Please get it.* His teammate at centerfield responded.

Fly out.

One down. Still perfect.

A grounder to first took care of the next batter. Tyler felt stronger now than he had at the beginning of the game. He settled himself on the mound and stared at the catcher. Change-up to start the batter. Tyler liked it. He wound up and caught the guy watching. Strike one. The second pitch was outside, same with the third.

The fans at Bayfront Stadium fell to a hush. He couldn't throw another ball or the batter would walk. *Breathe, Ames.* He could be perfect. It would happen. He stared at William. His catcher signaled for a fastball. Tyler shook his head. Not for this batter. The guy had hit four home runs this month.

Next he called for a curveball. *Atta boy, William. Perfect pitch.* Tyler gave the slightest nod. This was it. A curveball would sail straight toward the plate and break hard to the inside. By then the batter would bite, and the swing would be a strike.

Another notch closer to perfection.

Tyler settled back on his heels, glove up, ball in his hand. The windup was everything it needed to be. He uncoiled himself and released the ball just as he planned, like he'd done all his life. But this time he heard something snap. Instantly fire ripped

27

through his arm and down his torso, the sort of pain Tyler had never known before.

"Steee-rike!" The umpire made the call.

Tyler was already on the ground, writhing beneath the searing pain. The noise from the stadium dimmed and the only sounds were his racing heart and his own terrible groaning. People were running to him, but he couldn't hear them, couldn't make out their faces. He felt like demons were ripping his arm from his body. The world around him faded, every voice and face.

The first uniformed medic reached him, a man Tyler had never seen before. He dropped to his knees and put his hand on Tyler's good shoulder. The guy looked like a linebacker. "You're going to be okay."

No! Tyler wanted to shout at him. But the pain was too great. *I'll never be okay again.* The man was staring at him, his eyes bright with something Tyler didn't recognize. Peace, maybe. Something otherworldly.

"This isn't the end, Tyler." The medic's hand felt warm. "It's the beginning."

Tyler shook his head. Angry tears filled his eyes. *Of course it's the end.* The name on the medic's uniform caught his attention. A name he'd never heard before.

Beck.

Figures. Brand-new medic. What would he

know? "My . . . shoulder!" The pain was killing him. Sweat dripped down his forehead and he could feel his body shaking, going into shock. Tyler lifted his eyes to the stadium lights. A strange darkness shrouded them and then gradually, everything else began to fade.

Sami would never want him now. She would blame him for making the wrong choices all those years ago. *I'm sorry, Sami. I still love you. If you only knew how much.* Two more medics with a stretcher rushed toward him, and the rest of the team gathered at a distance, silent, shocked. Tyler had one final thought before he blacked out.

He wasn't perfect.

And after tonight he never would be.

2

There were two things Sami Dawson loved most about her job as an assistant for the prestigious Finkel and Schmidt Marketing Firm in Santa Monica, California: the independence it gave her from her grandparents, and her office's breathtaking view of the Pacific Ocean.

She had another hour of work before she would meet up with Arnie for dinner at Trastevere on Third Street — their Monday night routine. Three years dating and their traditions were pretty well locked in. After dinner they would walk along the Promenade, and after an hour he would drive her home. Sometimes they would play Scrabble or watch *The Office* at her apartment. Arnie had bought her the complete DVD series two birthdays ago. Other nights they tuned in to whatever was on TV — baseball and *I Love Lucy* reruns being the exceptions. Sami didn't like baseball and Arnie couldn't stand

Lucy. Too much silliness.

Arnie left Sami's apartment by nine — weekday or not. Every time. They were early risers, both of them. Routines were rungs on the ladder to success. Her grandparents had taught her that. Arnie agreed.

"No one ever got ahead by keeping late nights," he would say. He was right. Studies showed sleep was good for the immune system — eight hours a night.

Sami's immune system was rock solid.

Her current work account was the Atlantis resort in the Bahamas and Dubai. Paradise Island's think tank was located in Pensacola, with business offices in Los Angeles and San Francisco. Sami had worked three months to get last year's *Fifteen Minutes* winner Zoey Davis to sing at the Bahamas resort. Zoey had straightened up her act in recent months and agreed to the gig last night. Today Sami expected to see news of the decision online somewhere.

Proof that Sami was doing her job.

Before she could search People.com, something on her Google feed caught her eye. A name from the past. It caught her off guard and made her heart skip a beat. Sami read the headline again and sat back in her chair. Her heart beat faster than before.

Tyler Ames Suffers Season-Ending Injury.

She leaned in closer to the screen, seeing him again, the freckle-faced boy with blue eyes who had captured her heart the summer before her senior year in high school. She saw him where she would always see him: on a pitcher's mound, ball in his glove, hat low over his pretty eyes.

Baseball was everything to Tyler. He had traded her for the game, after all.

She read the headline again. Her heart was breaking for him even before she clicked the link. A new page opened and there he was. The boy from another lifetime. A smaller headline gave her more details.

One-Time Pitching Sensation Was Almost Perfect.

Almost perfect.

Sami let the sad words play through her mind. She could still hear him saying goodbye the night before he set off to play for the Reds' rookie league. *I'll make it, Sami. I will. Then I'll come find you and we can talk about forever.*

Her eyes found the beginning of the article.

Midway through what would've been his first perfect game since being drafted six years ago, one-time pitching sensation Tyler Ames suffered a season-ending injury

Saturday night early in the seventh inning. Ames, 24, pitching for the Reds' Blue Wahoos at Pensacola's Bayfront Stadium, collapsed after the pitch. He was taken by ambulance to nearby West Florida Hospital. Team officials have said the injury will effectively end Ames' season.

With each word, Sami felt her heart sink. Tyler needed baseball the way he needed air. Now he was out for the season in some hospital in Pensacola, Florida. She kept reading.

Ames gained national fame when he won the 2002 Little League World Series for the Simi Valley Royals by striking out the side in the last inning against Japan. He went on to rack up one of the most successful prep pitching careers at baseball powerhouse Jackson High School in Simi Valley. His senior year Ames was named California's Mr. Baseball, and after graduation he was drafted in the twelfth round by the Cincinnati Reds. He turned down a UCLA scholarship for a spot in the Reds farm system.

Sami realized she was holding her breath. She slid her chair closer to the computer and exhaled. Again she looked at his photograph. The list of facts about Tyler's life did not tell the world who he had been back then. Not at all. Not the way Sami knew him. She looked intently into his eyes.

She could still hear his laugh.

The rest of the story described the part of Tyler's life that had happened since he was drafted. The quick trip from the Rookie League to the Reds' A team in Dayton, Ohio. Sami kept reading.

Ames fell from grace with his fans when he was arrested a number of times for public drunkenness after playing in games for the Dayton Dragons. One fan pressed charges against him for harassing her in a bar, and when the story ran another female fan came forward with a similar story.

This many years later the truth still hurt. Sami blinked a few times and looked out the window of her office. *Ames fell from grace.* Something her grandparents would say. Sami stared at the horizon. The ocean breathed peace into her soul. The vast sea of blue and the unchanging tide reminded her that God was in control. Even if she no longer really knew what that meant.

Once more she turned her eyes to the computer.

In 2012, things seemed to turn around for Ames. He began pitching the way he had as a kid, throwing nothing but strikes. The Reds moved him up to the Blue Wahoos, where he continued to improve. Several scouts were in attendance at Saturday's game. According to a spokesperson for the Blue Wahoos, Ames was on the brink of a move to the majors — maybe even in the next week or so.

Sami studied his face a moment longer. *We had our chance, didn't we?* She felt no ill will for Tyler Ames. He had made his choice. They both had. But Tyler hadn't tried to call her in three years. Besides, he wasn't the same person he'd been back then.

Anyone who had followed him over the last six years could see that.

Sami exhaled slowly. Looking at him was like looking backward into a dream, as if that crazy wonderful year had never happened. She searched his eyes once more. She clicked back to *People*'s home page. She had to finish up and get to the restaurant.

Arnie would be waiting for her.

Sami sent the email to the Atlantis executives, grabbed her purse, and hurried to the elevator. Their reservations were in ten minutes. She wouldn't have been late if she hadn't spent so much time on the Tyler Ames story. If she hadn't gone back to the story several times.

She didn't miss him. Not the guy he was today. She didn't even know him. Instead, she missed the girl she'd been when she was with him. That fearless girl who jumped off a rope swing into a mountain of red and yellow leaves one October night or the girl who held a conversation with a homeless man at the beach. A girl with no walls or limits or boundaries.

The girl she no longer knew.

Except for Tyler, Sami's life over the past nineteen years had been as predictable as the tide. Grandma and Grandpa Dawson had raised her since her parents died in a motorcycle wreck when Sami was five. Her grandparents were in their seventies now, good God-fearing church people who had never passed up the offering plate on Sunday morning or the chance to correct Sami if she strayed off the straight and narrow. Her grandfather ran several businesses, and he prided himself on never having missed a day of work.

Not ever.

Sami leaned against the back of the elevator and stared into the past. With her grandparents, there was a right way to do things. Period. A right way to dress — skirts below the knee. A right way to talk — she was the only girl in Southern California who said "sir" and "ma'am." There was a right way to walk — shoulders back — and a right way to visit with boys — briefly and at the Sunday afternoon dinner table. Growing up, Sami never had to wonder if she was perfect.

She was. She had no choice.

After high school, UCLA was the obvious next destination for Sami for three reasons. The school offered Sami a scholarship to write for the newspaper and of course, it took her away from her grandparents — at least during the school year. But the main reason was Tyler. He had planned to go to UCLA since he was twelve. That was his plan right up until the first week of June the year they both graduated.

The day Tyler was drafted, ten rounds earlier than he expected.

Sami stepped off the elevator and hurried to her car. But she couldn't out-pace the memories chasing her. She breathed deep the sweet ocean air and squinted through the images of yesterday.

Her first semester at UCLA, Sami's roommates drank shots of vodka before an intramural kickball game. "Come on." They passed the bottle to her. "We all have to do it!"

An exhilarating sensation had rushed through Sami's veins. She'd never so much as talked about drinking, not while living with her grandparents. Suddenly the idea of so much freedom made her feel ten feet off the ground. She was her own person, an adult. She could do what she wanted. Before she could change her mind, Sami grabbed the bottle and downed three shots.

"Perfect!" one of the girls squealed. "Let's go!"

But as the alcohol rushed into her blood, Sami's heart had begun to pound. She felt cold and clammy and her chest ached. "I . . . I don't feel good."

"You're fine." Her roommate took her hand. "Come on, it'll be fun!"

Sami had pictured her grandparents, their hands on their hips, looking at her in disappointment. Her heartbeat doubled, pounding so hard she'd wondered if it would rip through her body and fall to the floor. She caught a glimpse in the mirror that hung on the girl's dorm wall. A flaming red covered her cheeks and sweat beaded up on her forehead. She tried to draw a full breath, but she couldn't.

"I . . . I don't feel . . . okay." Sami sat down on the edge of her lower bunk. All around her the walls seemed to be closing in.

"You look sick." One of the girls came close and felt her cheek. "Maybe you're allergic to this kind?"

Sami hadn't wanted to tell them she'd never had a drink. But maybe the girl was right. Sami had dug her elbows into her knees and let her face fall in her hands. Her heart raced and nausea welled up within her. The worst nausea she'd ever felt. "I . . . think I'll stay here." She waved off her friends and when she was alone she went to the bathroom and threw up. Even then she wondered if she would die, the pain in her chest, the way she couldn't catch her breath. *How terrible,* she told herself. If she died here alone in her dorm with vodka in her system. Her grandparents would be so ashamed. Not until the morning did Sami feel like herself again.

She hadn't had a drink since.

Sami blinked back the memory. She was almost to her car. The drinking episode had convinced her she was allergic to alcohol. That's what she told her friends. The next week when they offered her a drink she

39

blamed the allergy and stayed sober. She became the responsible one, the designated driver. But the symptoms hit again later that freshman year when the girls tried to sneak out of their dorm well after curfew to meet up with some boys across campus. And again at a party when the guy she was talking to led her to a back room and started kissing her.

"No." Sami pushed him back. In the dark she could hide her sweaty forehead and racing heart. But the symptoms were gaining on her. She glared at him. "I don't even know you!"

Only then did she understand. She was having panic attacks. She wasn't allergic to alcohol or boys or breaking curfew. She was allergic to being bad. Her grandparents had so thoroughly instilled in her the right way to behave that choosing any other option made her physically sick.

Sami reached her car, but the traffic was so bad she decided to walk. She was already late. A few minutes more wouldn't make a difference. Her memories kept up with her like before. She met Arnie in the spring semester her freshman year. He was a junior, focused and determined.

Once they started dating, Sami's panic attacks disappeared.

"I like that you're a good girl," he had told her. "I don't need any trouble."

After their third date, Arnie kissed her before saying good night. A sweet, simple kiss. It felt nice. Her heart didn't race even a little. The second time, she took the lead. After a few minutes she leaned back against the door, breathless. "I won't sleep with you." She'd blurted out the words before she could change her mind. "It's a promise I made."

She didn't tell him the promise was to her grandparents, not to God. It didn't matter. Arnie only smiled and kissed her cheek. "That's fine. The last thing I need is a kid before I finish law school."

The truth was, Arnie already had his eye on politics. He had no interest in filling a closet with skeletons. The chaste arrangement was a win for both of them. Arnie turned out to be a good friend, helping her study for tests and regaling her with stories of his debate team victories. They didn't kiss often, but he made her think. Sami felt smarter around him. All her free time was spent with him. When he graduated, he moved straight into law school. She finished her bachelor's degree a week before he passed the bar.

Her life had played out like a résumé

since. She joined Finkel and Schmidt as an intern her senior year, and a month after graduation the firm brought her on full time. That summer she moved out of her grandparents' house in Woodland Hills and into a small two-bedroom walk-up with another new hire at the firm, a girl from Nashville named Mary Catherine Clark.

Sami smiled as she neared Third Street.

Mary Catherine was a red-headed free spirit who rode her bike to work along Ocean Avenue, wind-surfed the breakwaters at Will Rogers Beach, and couldn't wait for Sunday church. She ate frozen dinners and stayed up late drinking coffee past midnight. They couldn't have been more different, which was what Sami loved about her. Mary Catherine made her laugh and reminded her every day of the most wonderful truth:

She had somehow escaped the years of living with her grandparents.

Not that she didn't love them. They meant well, Sami believed that. She had just never really learned to live under their roof. They didn't mind her separation from them. In their eyes, dating Arnie Bell was the best thing Sami had ever done. By now Arnie was a third-year lawyer at a storied firm on Santa Monica Boulevard. He'd be making six figures in no time. Running the country one day, no doubt. That's what Sami's grandmother said about him.

The restaurant was just ahead. Trastevere. Sami could see Arnie sitting at their favorite corner table, looking over his shoulder, slightly irritated. Poor Arnie. He hated being off schedule. She giggled to herself, thinking about something her roommate had said the night before.

"Arnie needs a few surprises to shake him up a little." Mary Catherine had grinned at the idea. "Like maybe let a mouse loose in his Acura. You know. See what he's made of. He's too safe for you."

Despite her friend's objections, Sami liked Arnie. He was good for her. He had the same desire to be successful, the same sensible spirit. He was loyal and dependable — no weekend motorcycle trips for Arnie Bell.

No panic attacks.

Which in a world of uncertainty was a good thing for Sami. But sometimes she wondered if safe would be enough. As a kid she was terrified of two things: heights and living on her own, away from her grandparents. Now her high-rise office and her apartment were two of her favorite things.

Which sometimes made her wonder if she was missing out on something even more exciting. Something she hadn't yet considered. Like sky-diving.

Sami rushed up to the table, breathless. "Arnie, I'm sorry." She kissed his cheek and took the chair across from him. Arnie was a few inches taller than Sami, with thinning brown hair that wouldn't be around for long. He'd been a sprinter in high school, but his best athletic days were behind him now.

"I was beginning to wonder." He smiled, but his eyes held a hint of disdain. "You're never late."

"The Atlantis account." She gave a slight shrug. "I got distracted. Took longer than I thought."

"Well." He fluffed his napkin across his lap and his eyes lit up. "I have good news!"

Sami hesitated. Okay. So they were done talking about Atlantis. She slid her chair in and set her purse beside her. "Tell me."

"You won't believe this." He smiled, clearly satisfied with himself. "The senior partner told me today they're looking for me to take on a case by myself next month." He raised his brow in her direction, waiting for her response. "Can you believe it?" He leaned closer. "Samantha, this is huge. It usually takes five years of assistant work before new lawyers get their own case." He didn't give her a chance to respond. "This case is one of the most difficult in the medical malpractice division of the . . ."

Sami stopped listening. The blue sky through the front window of Trastevere distracted her and made her remember that summer. Sitting at Tyler's games his senior year, watching him pitch and believing there would never be anyone else for her as long as she lived.

"Samantha?" His tone changed. "Are you listening?"

"Yes. Definitely." She sat a little straighter.

"What did I say?"

"You're working on a big medical malpractice suit next month. You're handling it by yourself." She leaned closer to him. "That's wonderful. I'm so proud of you, Arnie. Really."

"Thank you." He looked hurt. "But I was telling you about Manny being jealous. He's been at the firm longer and he hasn't had a case of his own yet." He paused, studying her. "Did you hear any of that?"

Sami glanced around, looking for some way of escape. A nervous bit of laughter slipped between her lips. "It all sort of blends together sometimes. The law stuff."

His shoulders and face fell at the same time. "That bothers me. I mean, we're talking about my future here." He caught himself. For the first time since she sat down he reached for her hand. "*Our* future. Samantha, this is very important."

She nodded. "I'm sorry. Go ahead."

"Anyway." Arnie seemed to take longer than usual to gather his thoughts. "Manny talked to me at lunch about it and I guess he's going to the partners tomorrow morning and . . ."

Samantha. The name grated on her now. Arnie had called her that from the beginning. He thought it sounded important. Academic. She was raised with the name. Samantha was how she had thought of herself until that summer. Only two people had ever called her Sami: Mary Catherine.

And Tyler Ames.

Otherwise she was Samantha Dawson. When Tyler was in her life her grandparents frowned on the fact that he called her Sami. "It's insulting to be called something other than your given name," her grandma had told her. "Sami sounds demeaning. Especially when Samantha is such a beautiful name."

Sami had seen her grandmother's point. Back then she liked the name Samantha. It worked well with professors and her boss at Finkel and Schmidt. There was an elegance about it, a sense of success and professionalism. But it didn't fit her the way Sami did.

And while she would always introduce herself as Samantha, privately she thought of herself as Sami.

The way Tyler had seen her.

"Samantha?"

She jumped. "Hmm?"

Arnie looked shocked. "What's wrong with you?"

Before she could answer, Jean, the waiter, appeared with his perpetual smile and broken English. "Hello! How you are today?" Jean was their guy. Every time. He seemed to sense things weren't great between them. "I give you time? Yes?"

"A few minutes, Jean." Arnie's smile looked stale. "Please." Jean nodded and waved, backing up from the table and hurrying to the adjacent one. When he was out of earshot, Arnie sounded disappointed. "Could you try to listen to me? I mean, first you're late and then you're" — he waved his hand around — "I don't know, distracted. Like you don't care."

"I'm sorry." Sami gave a quick shake of her head. "Really."

"You understand how big this is, right?" His tone softened. He took her hand again. "The firm is very political. In a few years —

47

if I'm interested — there's talk of me running for office." Arnie leaned in and gently kissed her lips. "We'll be married by then, of course." Clearly, there wasn't a doubt in his mind. He touched her face and smiled. "I'll need your support, Samantha. Fully."

"Of course." She covered his hand with her own. "Just a long day at the office." Her smile came easily, even if she didn't feel it. "You have my support. You know that."

The rest of the meal she listened better, interjecting her approval or affirmation where appropriate. She was happy for Arnie and his career, his dreams, and even his political aspirations, if that's what he wanted. But every so often, despite her best efforts to stay focused, Sami caught herself looking at the blue sky and thinking about a boy who lay broken in a hospital somewhere in Pensacola, Florida. A boy who traded everything for the dream of playing baseball. Even her.

3

Cheryl Conley dreaded any call from Merrill Place Retirement Center, but especially tonight. The call came just after eight o'clock, when she and her husband had settled down in front of the TV with their granddaughters for a much-anticipated showing of Disney's *Tangled*. Saturday was their night to babysit the girls, something they looked forward to all week.

Cheryl took the call in the next room. Her mother had been in the retirement center's Alzheimer's unit for the past year. Lately she'd been on a steady decline. "Hello?" She held her breath.

"Ms. Conley, it's Harrison Myers over at Merrill Place. Sorry to bother you." He sighed. "Your mother isn't doing well. I thought I should call."

"What happened?" Cheryl sat in the nearest chair and rested her elbows on her knees. *Dear Jesus. Not again . . .*

"I found her at the front door trying to leave. She was in her nightgown and a wool coat. She was pulling an overnight bag packed with most of her things." Frustration sounded in his voice. Harrison had been manager of Merrill Place for ten years. He practically lived there. If he was worried, then things were bad.

"You really think she was going to leave?"

"Definitely. If the door hadn't been locked, she'd be halfway down the boulevard."

Heartache welled up in Cheryl. Her mother had always been so strong, the pulse of their home. Even after Dad died twenty years ago, her mom had been sharper than women half her age. How could her mind fail her like this? "Did she say anything?"

"I couldn't understand most of it. Something about finding Ben." He hesitated. "She's said that before, of course."

Cheryl closed her eyes. Ben. Her older brother. "At least that makes sense."

"You want to come down and talk to her?" The manager hesitated. "I mean, she's your mother but I understand she doesn't . . ."

"Know me?" Every time Cheryl thought about the fact, her heart broke a little more. "No. She doesn't." She stood and paced a few steps. The sentence was never easy to finish. She thought about her granddaughters in the other room. "You think it would help? If I was there?"

"Maybe. Either way we need to agree on a plan." Harrison sounded weary. "When patients get like this, we have to move them. She needs much higher-level care. There's a facility in Destin." He hesitated. "And yes. I think if you came it could help."

"Okay." They had talked about it before. Destin was nearly an hour from Pensacola. Too far for Cheryl to drop in throughout the week. Too far for a night like this. "I'll be right there."

"Thank you." Relief punctuated his words.

Cheryl walked to the back of the house where the girls were cuddled, one on each side of their grandfather. They were four and six this year. Every hour with them was priceless.

She smiled at them. "Meemaw's got to go out for a little bit. Check on Great-Gram down the street." She walked to the bookcase and pulled out Dr. Seuss's *The Sneetches and Other Stories* from the middle shelf. A quick look at Chuck, her husband of forty years, told him all he needed to know. He would help delay the start of the movie. "Papa will read while I'm gone." Cheryl patted their blond heads.

"I'll be back soon."

"You need me?" Chuck took the book, his eyes warm with empathy.

"Stay here." She leaned down and kissed his forehead. "Pray."

His eyes didn't leave hers. "Always."

The drive to Merrill Place was less than ten minutes this time of night. Most of Pensacola was at the Blue Wahoos baseball game. It's where she and Chuck would be if they weren't watching the girls. Cheryl felt her heart sink. Her poor mother.

She rolled down the window and let the ocean air clear her mind. The night was cooler than usual for August, the stars overhead brilliant. *Father, what's happening? My mother is getting worse. I'm out of ideas. Help us . . . please.*

No answer came, no immediate sense of direction or help. Cheryl prayed until she arrived and then she found Harrison Myers in his office. "I got here as fast as I could."

"She's in her room." He picked up a folder from his desk and handed it to her. "Here. Information about the center in Destin." A shadow fell over his kind brown eyes. "We can't help her much longer. Not if something doesn't change."

Cheryl took the packet. "Thank you." She nodded toward the door. "I'll go see her."

Mr. Myers folded his hands. "I'm sorry."

"It's okay." They shared a sad look and then she walked from his boxy office down the white tiled hallway to her mother's room. Room 116 at the end of the building. Cheryl never got used to the smell. Death hung in the air, the way it always did in places like this. Heaven's waiting room. A reminder that every day brought them closer to the last.

Without making a sound, Cheryl opened the door and stepped inside. Her mother was sitting on the edge of her bed. She still wore her wool coat and she looked restless. Her knuckles were white from clutching the edge of the bedspread. As soon as she spotted Cheryl her eyes immediately filled with fear. "Who are you?"

"Hello." She felt the nervousness in her smile. Some days were worse than others. Her mom might scream or even throw things at her. Tonight she looked borderline crazy. Cheryl took a few steps into the room. "It's me. Cheryl."

"What?" Her mother folded her arms tightly in front of her and looked around. "Where's Ben?"

"He's not here." She had long since stopped arguing with her mother, stopped trying to set her straight about the details of life. "He couldn't come."

"I walked to his house." Her eyes darted to the window. "Isn't this his house?"

"No." Cheryl moved slowly to the chair by her mother's bed and sat down. She used her most kind voice. "This is *your* house."

"No!" Her expression became horrified at the possibility. "This is not my house." She squinted at Cheryl. "Are you the house-keeper?"

Cheryl took a slow breath. *Help me, God . . . I need Your help.* She worked to stay calm. "Can I tell you a story?"

Some of the anxiety left her mother's tense shoulders. "A story?"

"Yes, a lovely story about Ben." Cheryl slid to the edge of the seat, her eyes locked on her mother's.

"Ben?" She relaxed a little more. "You know him?"

"I do."

Her mother nodded, her eyes distant. She eased her legs up onto the bed and slid back on the elevated stack of pillows. She seemed to consider the idea. "Yes. I'd like that." Her white hair was messier than usual, adding to the slightly deranged look in her eyes. She smoothed out the wrinkles in her sheet. "Go ahead."

"Ben was playing the baseball game of his life."

"First base." Her mother cast worried eyes in her direction. "He plays first base."

"Yes, that's right. First base." Cheryl leaned back in her chair. "It was the playoffs and this was the season's biggest game. Two outs, game tied at three apiece."

A slow smile lifted her mother's weathered cheeks. She sank a little deeper into the pillows. "Prettiest day of the year. Perfect day to be at a ball park."

"The batter up was a hot hitter from Santa Rosa Beach."

"Nothing but home runs and triples."

"Exactly." Cheryl looked toward the curtained window. "Only this day he hits a grounder to short. Shortstop bobbles it and recovers. He sweeps it into his glove and fires it to Ben at first base."

"Ben makes the out!" Her mother was staring at the air in front of her, seeing the game as if it were happening again.

"Three down, Pensacola High up to bat. Last inning. Bottom of the seventh." Cheryl could see her brother, see the determination in his face. "The first three batters get on. A walk, a hit pitch, and a single. Bases loaded."

"Ben's up next." She looked straight at

55

Cheryl. "He batted cleanup, you know. This is a true story." A few blinks and she wrinkled her face, studying Cheryl. "I'm sorry. Do I know you?"

"I'm telling you a story about Ben."

Her mother's vacant stare stayed several seconds before some sense of light returned to her eyes. She nodded barely. "That's right." She shifted her look back to the imaginary game in front of her. "Ben's up to bat."

"That's right. He walks to the plate. Six-foot-three and muscled arms. The outfield knows him."

"Yes, they do." Her mother chuckled. "They all back up. Almost to the fence."

"Yes, but Ben just knows there's nothing they can do to stop him. Not this time. His blond bangs hang just below his batting helmet. His eyes focused."

"Such beautiful eyes." Her mother's smile held a hint of sadness. "I wish he would come see me more often."

"He will. One day." Cheryl paused. "The pitcher stares Ben down, just as ready to win. The only pitcher who ever gave Ben any trouble. But not this afternoon. Ben connects with the first pitch — a fastball — right at the belly of the bat." She smiled big. "And the ball's gone. Gone over the

56

centerfield fence."

"Home run!" Her mother raised both hands and let them fall weakly back to the bed. "Pensacola Eagles win!"

"Season champs."

"Wait!" Her mother turned, suddenly startled. "We should celebrate. I'll make dinner."

Cheryl felt sick. How could she tell her mom the game had happened fifty years ago? She reached for her mother's hand. "Ben already ate dinner."

"What?" Her mom jerked her hand back and tucked it in close to her chest. "Who are you? And why won't you let Ben join us?"

"Did you like the story?" Cheryl knew better than to call her Mom. She hadn't used the name in years. "It's a good story, right?"

Again her mother relaxed, her eyes distant once more. "I like it." She glanced at Cheryl, suspicious. "You can go home now. The housekeeper goes home at the end of the day."

"You want me to go home?"

"Yes!" She pointed to the door. "I've had enough of you."

"Okay." Cheryl stood. "You can sleep now."

"I will." She worked her arms out of her coat and dropped it to the floor, all while keeping her eyes on Cheryl. She slid her feet beneath the covers and pulled the sheet and blanket close to her chin. "Tell Ben I'll be there tomorrow."

"I'll tell him." Cheryl fought tears gathering in her eyes. She held up her hand. "Good-bye."

"Go home." Her mom nodded, irritated. She made a brushing motion toward the door. "You're off work."

Cheryl turned and walked out of the room. She had no idea if she'd really helped her mother or not. But at least now the woman seemed ready to sleep. She stopped in at Mr. Myers's office on the way out. The man was sorting through a file on his desk. Cheryl found a tired smile. "She's more settled now."

"Thank you." He set the file down and stood. "Nights are the worst."

"Yes." She pulled her cell phone from her purse and held it up. "Call me if anything else happens."

"I will." Harrison Myers seemed genuinely troubled. "Call the center in Destin. Please. She'd be safer."

Cheryl tightened her hold on her purse. "I'll think about it."

"Sooner than later." He raised his brow. "For her sake."

His words ran through her head as she made the drive home and as she and Chuck and the girls watched *Tangled*. Her mother wouldn't make the move easily. She was eighty-eight years old. Moving her now would probably destroy her.

"You love watching *Tangled,* right, Meemaw?" Her oldest granddaughter looked up, innocent eyes sparkling.

"I do." She put her arm around the child's shoulders. "I love a good story."

Again she shared a quick look with her husband. They hadn't talked about it, but he would've known she had been telling her mother stories. It was the only way Cheryl had found to calm her down on nights like this. Twice this week and twice last week she'd made the trip, told the same story about Ben, and come home emotionally wrecked.

Something had to change.

When the girls left for the night, Chuck pulled her into his strong arms. "I'm sorry."

"It's so hard. She doesn't know me." The tears came now. "They want us to think about moving her."

Chuck clearly knew better than to debate the possibility. Not now anyway. Cheryl's mother couldn't stay at Merrill Place much longer. Instead her husband waited a few heartbeats and then he did the only thing he could. The only thing either of them could do.

Quietly, confidently he prayed for a miracle.

That somehow, some way, before God took her home, sweet Virginia Hutcheson might find peace.

4

Pain radiated from his shoulder up into his neck and down through his chest. The worst pain Tyler had ever known. Despite that, he was about to be discharged from the hospital — the nurse had told him. But then what? Where was he supposed to go to get help? He couldn't lift his arm, couldn't move his fingers without searing pain.

If he were a praying man, this would've been his finest hour. But prayer was part of another life. If God cared about Tyler Ames, He had never much showed it.

Tyler closed his eyes. The pain meds helped. But he had hardly slept in the last few days. His team had paid for him to stay through this afternoon. Forty-eight hours. Long enough for a complete evaluation. So far no one had told him anything except that he was going home.

"Mr. Ames?" A man entered the room.

Tyler blinked and tried to focus. It was

the doctor. He came up to the bed. "I'm Dr. Bancroft. How's the pain?" The man pushed a few buttons and raised the back of Tyler's bed.

The sitting-up position helped rouse him. "Not great." He squinted at the doctor. "What's the verdict?"

"I'm afraid it's bad news." The doctor leaned against the windowsill and crossed his arms. "You blew out your labrum. The rotator cuff is damaged, too. Can't tell from the MRI how bad it is." He let that sink in for a moment. "You need surgery."

Each sentence hit Tyler like so many cement trucks, plowing him down and running him over, leaving him flattened and unable to breathe. He pinched the bridge of his nose with his left hand, inhaled, and held it. If only he could will himself back to the start of the inning. Nine outs left, the crowd shouting his name. Pro scouts capturing every pitch for the brass in Cincinnati. Nine lousy outs.

He lowered his hand. "I was throwing a perfect game."

"I know." The doctor grimaced. "The story was on the front page of Sunday's paper." He pulled a chart from the end of Tyler's bed. "We kept you here because your heart was acting up. Skipping beats and slipping into atrial fibrillation. That's settled down now. The heart tests were negative."

Tyler exhaled. Every heartbeat sent a shockwave of pain through his torso. "What's that mean?"

"It means your heart's fine. Sometimes pain can do that — if it's intense enough."

He winced. "This probably qualifies."

Dr. Bancroft shook his head, the way people do when hope is slim. "I'm sorry."

Tyler had a hundred questions. What did the Blue Wahoos think and how about the scouts from the Reds, and when could he have surgery and what would the rehab process look like? But only one question mattered. He steeled himself. "I can play again, right? Next season?"

The doctor nodded, almost too quickly. "Yes. I think so. You need surgery, but athletes come back from this type of thing. Definitely."

"When? When's the surgery?" Tyler looked back at the door to his room. "Could we do it now? While I'm still here?"

"Actually . . . you have to book that through an orthopedic surgeon."

Tyler remembered one of his teammates needing knee surgery last season. "I think I can get the name of a good one. Someone who can get me in quickly." With his left hand he braced his right elbow against his body. "Sooner the better, right?"

"Yes. Yes, definitely." The man seemed troubled, as if he had even more bad news. "There is one thing. I'm not sure team insurance covers this type of surgery. Do you have another policy? Something . . . on your own?"

Tyler's heart bounced around inside his aching chest. "The team will cover it." He allowed a laugh that was more outrage than humor. "I was on the mound when it happened."

"True. Very true." The doctor pursed his lips and focused on the chart. "You might want to talk to management." He nodded, clearly nervous. "Just in case." He jotted something onto the chart. "Your car's still back at the stadium, is that right?"

"My car?" The haze of pain meds made it difficult to think. Saturday night felt like a lifetime ago. "I think so. Yes."

"We have a medical transport van. Someone can give you a ride." Dr. Bancroft set the chart down, took a pad of paper from his pocket, and scribbled a few lines. Then he ripped off the top sheet and handed it to Tyler. "Here's a prescription for pain medication. You'll need these for the first few weeks."

"Thanks." There wasn't much else to say.

"My family, we followed your game this fall. You were right there." The doctor clucked his tongue. "You'll get back. You're too good to hang it up now."

"Appreciate that." Even talking intensified the pain.

"The nurse will be in shortly with discharge instructions. Obviously I want you to ice it twenty minutes at a time, and take your pain medication. The thing with pain is, don't let it get ahead of you."

"Yes, sir." He still had questions, but he couldn't remember them.

"The nurse is bringing in a sling. I don't advise moving your arm until you see an orthopedic surgeon." The doctor stood to leave. "Sorry again." He paused. "Any questions?"

Tyler blinked. His mind raced but it couldn't get ahead of the searing pain. "No. No, questions." He relaxed the muscles in his right shoulder. Anything to find an edge. "Well, maybe one."

Dr. Bancroft waited.

"When are my next pain pills?"

He checked Tyler's chart once more. "Looks like you have about ten minutes." He set the chart back in the rack at the end of the hospital bed. "I'll have the nurse

65

bring them in."

And with that he was gone. Tyler tried to take a full breath, but the pain was too great. He lowered the bed back a few inches and exhaled. There was no comfortable position. Not with his shoulder on fire. Every time he looked at his right arm he expected to see it barely hanging onto his body.

The doctor's news swirled in his mind. He had destroyed his labrum and damaged his rotator cuff — so badly he couldn't move his arm without talking to a surgeon. And he'd done all that damage with a single pitch. He could see himself, winding up, getting ready to throw, and —

"Tyler." This time the voice was familiar.

He opened his eyes and stared through the pain. "Coach." As far as he could remember this was the first time someone from the club had been by. But he couldn't be sure. They'd had him on morphine until this morning.

Jep Black removed his Blue Wahoo baseball cap as he entered the room. "You don't look too good."

"Nah, I'm fine." Tyler's breathing came in short bursts. All that the excruciating pain would allow. "Got me on the lineup tonight, or what?"

The slightest smile lifted Jep's lips. But it did nothing to ease the nervousness in his expression. He made his way to the side of the bed. "I talked to your doc."

"I need a little sewing up."

Jep shook his head. "Tyler . . . I'm sorry."

His nurse entered the room holding a tray with a single small cup. The pain pills. "You're late." He tried to smile, but his body wouldn't cooperate.

"Actually . . ." The nurse checked the clock on the wall. "Right on time."

Tyler had no words. He took the pain pills with shaking hands and downed it with the water at his bedside table. "Thanks."

When she was gone, Jep stepped closer to the bed again. "I can't believe it. I mean . . . you were pitching perfect."

With his left arm, Tyler wiped the water off his mouth. "Another mountain." He raised the bed again. No matter how much he hurt, he couldn't let Jep know the extent of his pain. He was a pitcher, not damaged goods. "I'll be back next season. Better than ever."

Jep looked from Tyler's shoulder to his eyes. "The news . . . it isn't good."

"I know." He willed the pain pills to work. "Torn labrum."

"Well, that. Yes." He hesitated. "Tyler,

67

there's no easy way to say this. You've been cut from the Wahoos."

The pain screamed through his body and soul. What had Jep said? Tyler narrowed his eyes. "They cut me?"

"Yes." Jep muttered something under his breath. "I hate this part of the game." He pulled an envelope from his jeans pocket and set it on the table next to Tyler. "That's your final check." He gripped the bed rail and hung his head for a moment. When he looked up, genuine pain darkened his eyes. "This ain't right. You're an incredible pitcher, Tyler. One of the best. You work your way back to that mound. Prove 'em all wrong."

The room was spinning. Tyler grabbed the manager's hand and the bedrail at the same time, steadying himself so he wouldn't pass out. "Nothing to prove." His words came in short bursts, the best he could do. "They . . . won't cut me. . . . I'm Tyler Ames. . . . I'm their ace . . . No one can touch me, Coach . . . They'd be . . . crazy to —"

"Tyler." Jep worked his hand free and took a step back. "The decision came from the higher ups." He shook his head. "Nothing I can do."

The man's words didn't make sense. Tyler was a Blue Wahoo. He'd been the best pitcher this year and now the Bigs wanted him. That was his life just a few days ago. How could this be happening? He tried to breathe but his lungs wouldn't work right. Like he was underwater with a two-ton truck on his back. "What . . . about my surgery?"

Jep shoved his hands in his pockets and sighed. "You signed a no-injury clause two years ago in Dayton. After your third arrest, Tyler. Remember? After you hurt your back in the moped accident." He nodded toward the envelope on the table. "A copy of the clause is there with the check. Management wanted you to have it. In case you forgot."

Confusion lay like a wet blanket over the conversation. Tyler gripped his elbow. Why wouldn't the pain pills work? He clenched his teeth. "I signed . . . what?"

A drop of sweat fell off Jep's forehead onto the hospital floor. "It's all in there." He pointed to the envelope. "The injury isn't covered." He stared at Tyler for several beats. "We got new guys coming in all the time. You know that." Jep looked helpless. "It's a business. Sometimes a player's luck runs out." He started for the door and stopped. "Prove 'em wrong, Ames. No one believes in you more than me." With that he slipped his hat back on and left.

If Tyler's heartbeat was erratic Saturday after his injury he could only imagine what it was now. He held his right elbow close to his body and turned to the table next to him. The envelope was there. What had Jep said? Something about his final check? He blinked hard, forcing his mind to stay clear even for a few minutes.

He grabbed the envelope with his left hand and wedged two of his fingers beneath the flap. His heart pounded and with each beat the aching sensation spread up into his neck and down through his torso. Finally he ripped open the top and pulled out the contents. The first was a sheet of paper with small print. Jep had tried to explain it. Something about his contract.

With a snap of his wrist the paper opened all the way and he held it close to his face. The jolt caused him to cry out, but he caught himself before he might alert his nurse. If only the medication would take even the slightest edge off. Tyler tried to make out the words, but it took a while. His vision blurred the edges.

Slowly the paragraphs came into focus. He scanned the words quickly until he saw this:

Clause IV — No Injury: Due to previous

off-field injuries and arrests in the Player's past, he will at this time play without insurance coverage in case of an injury. Player assumes all responsibility for his medical costs, regardless of illness or injury obtained in future games. This clause may be renegotiated at a future date.

Tyler felt the floor beneath his bed turn liquid. As if nothing was holding him up except the bed frame, and even that was starting to fall away. A no-injury clause? Why would he have signed that? How come his agent hadn't intervened? He set the paper down on the table and squeezed his eyes shut. Somewhere in his distant memory a moment came to light.

The contract sitting on a long wooden table. The contract and a choice: sign it or walk. Take the offer or head home to California with his hat in his hands. His opportunity gone forever.

Tyler had signed it. His agent never had anything to say about it.

But until now he hadn't remembered anything about it. Two years ago? He'd done nothing but improve since then. Every week, every inning, every pitch. No more off-field craziness, no more mopeds or girls or drinking. His agent should've renegotiated the contract a year ago.

The reality of his situation began to make him shake. He might as well have been flung into a sub-zero freezer. And with each excruciating vibration his busted shoulder shot arrows through his body. Was this really happening? He had no insurance? How was he supposed to pay for his surgery? His body shook harder, the pain worse than before. Why weren't the pain pills working?

Tyler clenched his left fist and tried to see a way out. He was going to be released from the hospital, and then what? Where would he go? How would he find relief? He pursed his lips and exhaled. Over and over again. Maybe if he breathed everything out there'd be room in his lungs for air. After a few raspy breaths he settled back into the pillow.

How much money did he have? He forced himself to concentrate. His phone would have the answer. He glanced at the table next to his bed. Where was his phone? He hadn't thought about it until now. He was about to open the only drawer in the table when his nurse entered the room.

"I have your brace." She pulled something from a plastic wrapper and frowned at him. "You don't look good."

"Where's . . . my phone?"

"In here." She kept her eyes on him as she opened a cupboard at the corner of his room. The phone was on a shelf. "I'm not sure if it's charged. We turn them off when patients are admitted."

Everything felt surreal. This couldn't be happening. It was a dream. That had to be it. Maybe if he blinked a few times he would be on the mound again, ready to pitch the next inning. Nothing but perfection behind him and a contract with the Reds ahead of him. The pain pulsed through his body. Wretched pain. It wasn't a dream. It hurt too much.

The nurse handed him his phone and stepped back. Using his left hand, Tyler turned it on. He was going to pass out any second. He could feel it. His eyes narrowed and he stared at the phone's screen. What was he doing? Why did he need his phone?

"Doctor says you'll need surgery." She lowered the bed rails. "Here. Swing your legs over the side. You've been discharged."

Surgery. Yes, that was it. He tried to think around the pain. He had to pay for his surgery. No insurance meant no help from his team. His former team. He gritted his teeth. "I have to . . . move slow."

"That last dose of pain medication should take effect soon." She opened up the brace and shifted to his right side. "Turn your body toward me. You'll feel better with this."

Black dots flashed before his eyes. He gripped the edge of the bed with his good hand so he wouldn't fall to the floor. Somehow she helped him get dressed and slipped the sling over his neck and around his waist. It had built-in padding so his forearm could rest against that instead of his ribcage. Again he forced himself to relax. Maybe she was right. Maybe the pain would ease up now that he had a brace.

"Let's get you on your feet." She took a step back.

Nausea grabbed at him from every direction. Tyler held up his left hand. "Hold on. Please."

She hesitated, watching him. "How about the chair? Can we do that much?"

He didn't have enough energy to speak. His eyesight wasn't working and neither was his mind. Moving like he was in a trance, he let the nurse help him to the chair next to his bed.

"Tell you what. I'll get you something to eat. That'll help."

Tyler leaned his head back against the chair. He needed a new arm, not food. He was alone again and something was in his hand. He looked down. His phone. He tried to turn it on again but another wave of dizziness came over him. The pain was just slightly more bearable. But in its place a drunken feeling started coming over him. The buzz felt wonderful — something he hadn't felt in the past few years. An intoxicatingly sweet release. He savored the feeling for a few seconds.

The pills were working.

Tyler's phone screen lit up and he stared at the icons. What was he doing? He blinked a few times and then he remembered. His bank account. He needed to pay for the surgery so he had to check his balance. The process of signing in was nearly overwhelming, but finally the number shouted at him: *$187.32.*

Tyler didn't have two hundred dollars to his name. He sank into the chair and closed his eyes. Then he remembered the check. His eyes flew open and moving slowly, carefully, he reached for the check on the bedside table. The one Jep Black brought. His final check. He opened it up same as the copy of the page from his contract, with a snap of his wrist. He sucked in a quick breath through clenched teeth.

The number had to be wrong. He squinted through the haze of medication but the amount didn't change. One week of work with the Blue Wahoos: $312.02.

All totaled, he didn't have five hundred dollars.

The nurse returned with a tray of food. "We're going to get you home, Mr. Ames." She explained again about the icing and the pain medication. "Eat first. Otherwise the pain med will make you sick. Now listen. No driving with these pills. Have someone drive you to your orthopedic appointment. The sooner the better." She paused. "I understand your car's at the stadium."

Tyler lifted his eyes to hers. Her words were coming from at least three mouths. "Yes, ma'am."

"Okay, our driver will take you home. You can get your car later. Have your teammates bring it over."

His teammates. They would be at practice now. The truth slammed him around like a washed-up fighter on the ropes. He no longer had teammates. The Reds had cut him without a conversation. He thought about his part-time job — coaching young pitchers on off days. He couldn't do that now, either. Besides, it was a job set up for him by the Blue Wahoos. A team he no longer played for. He closed his eyes. His room was three hundred a month. Car insurance, another hundred. His phone cost fifty-something. Gas and food and now his surgery . . .

"I'm gonna . . . be sick." Tyler reached for a nearby bowl just as the nurse handed him one. He had nothing in his stomach, but the dry heaves continued until the spasms finally eased up. He handed the bowl back to the nurse and slumped forward over his arm. This was crazy. He couldn't leave here like this.

"The nausea is normal. Take deep breaths." She hesitated, watching him. "I'll get the wheelchair." She was back in a few minutes. "Come on. Hop in."

Tyler stood and pivoted, then slowly lowered himself into the wheelchair. His shoulder was killing him and his stomach was in knots. "I need . . . the bowl again." He closed his eyes and let his head fall in his good hand.

"You won't be sick. Come on. You'll feel better in your own bed."

The words wouldn't come, so with what energy he had left, Tyler shook his head. He could do nothing about the irony of her statement. His own bed? He rented a room, but he didn't own the bed. He didn't own much of anything. Some clothes, a few boxes of trophies and team photos. He had figured he'd find his own place after the season. Get through the next month, he had told himself, and he could rent an apartment. Pick up some used furniture and start clawing his way back to the top. If the Reds had brought him on, they would've given him a new contract. His medical would've been covered and he would've made six figures at least. Even for a post-season contract.

But now? He had no idea what he was going to do.

"Mr. Ames?" The nurse's tone remained kind. But clearly she was waiting. "The driver's ready."

"I don't . . . I can't . . ." Tyler stopped trying to talk. After a blur of nausea and dizziness, searing pain and desperation, he was buckled into the backseat of a van. On his lap sat a plastic bag with his pitcher's jacket, the results of his x-ray, and his discharge papers. When they reached his home, the van driver helped him to the front steps and his landlady's husband walked him to his room. Tyler lay gingerly on his rented bed. Tomorrow he'd give notice. He couldn't stay beyond the end of the week. Rent was due on the fifteenth and he was nearly out of money. How would he get a job? Where would he find the means to have the surgery? Where would he live?

And how had the golden boy from the Little League World Series wound up here?

5

The third dose of pain meds wore off around one in the morning. They must have, because that's when Tyler sat straight up and slammed his hand over his mouth so he wouldn't scream out loud. The pain sliced through his shoulder and straight across the base of his neck, along his collarbone and through his middle.

Tyler gasped for his next breath. *I can't take it . . . this has to stop,* he told himself. *Relax . . . think of something else.*

He didn't deserve this. He should still be in the hospital, with someone taking care of him and keeping him medicated and making immediate plans to put him back together. Tyler scrambled to his feet and rummaged through his top dresser drawer. Advil. He needed that, at least. His hands shook as he opened the bottle. Four pills. He grabbed a water bottle from the case on the floor.

They slid down his throat, but he knew they wouldn't help. He felt like his arm was hanging down to his knees, like his shoulder joint had been hit by a grenade. All from a single pitch. It happened, of course. Every now and then Tyler would hear of a guy losing his pitching career on a single throw. But he never thought it could happen to him.

Tyler dropped into the only chair in the room and slumped over. It hurt more to lie down. At least sitting up, gravity kept his arm in line with his shoulder.

Somehow morning came. Tyler blinked and tried to assess whether his pain was the slightest bit less than yesterday. It wasn't. It was worse. He tried to stand, but any motion made him want to throw up. He gritted his teeth. *Get up, Tyler Ames. Your feet are fine. You gotta fight this.*

He held his breath as he forced himself to stand. A few shuffling steps and he used his good arm to open his bedroom window. Sunny and warm, breezy and beautiful. The weather was a complete betrayal of the reality of Tyler's situation.

A pounding came from his burning arm, as if his heart had relocated to the place where his shoulder used to be.

He got dressed using only his left hand.

Three times he moved in a way that shot knives through his shoulder. Finally he slid his wallet in his jeans pocket and grabbed his keys. How could this have happened? He was supposed to be in Cincinnati right now, talking with management and working out with the pitching coach. Making plans for how he would help the Reds through the post-season.

Tyler moved back to his window and leaned on the frame. He flexed the muscles in his lower body. Where did the pain start and where did it stop? His feet and legs didn't hurt. His right hand felt pretty good. But if he moved too fast, his right shoulder sent a stabbing pain down his arm, through his torso, and up into his neck.

Maybe food would help. He hadn't eaten anything since yesterday afternoon. Tyler rummaged through his snack box and found a protein bar. He used his teeth and left hand to rip off the wrapper and finished it off too fast to taste it. Next he downed another bottle of water, but nothing helped.

The pain consumed him.

Tyler couldn't think of a single job he could do without the use of his right arm and while he was in this much pain. His parents' faces crossed his mind. They had said this would happen. That if he didn't go to college his life would fall apart.

For now, he needed to get his car and his pain meds. William Trapnell, his catcher, would be here any minute. *My former catcher,* he corrected himself. His new existence was more than he could comprehend all at one time. Tyler stayed by the window until he saw his friend pull up. Never mind the fact that his legs were fine. He practically limped from his room out the front door.

"Ames." William slipped his hands in his jeans pockets. "Man, I'm so sorry."

"I'll be okay." He fist-pumped his friend with his left hand. "A lot of pain, that's all."

Of course, that was hardly all. William seemed awkward, like maybe he didn't know what to say or how to say it. The whole team had to know by now that Tyler had been cut. He had a blown-out shoulder, so the Blue Wahoos didn't want him. He was out of work and running out of options.

They climbed into William's truck and started down the main road toward the stadium. "I can't believe they cut you." He glanced at Tyler and then kept his eyes on the road. "You're one of the best pitchers I've ever worked with. And the other night . . . you were crazy good."

"I'll be back." The pain made every word

difficult, but that didn't matter. Tyler was a competitor, and if there was one thing he wanted his former teammate to know it was this: he wasn't done pitching. "Doctor says I'll be back."

The unasked questions hung heavy in the car. Tyler tried to deal with them one at a time. "I'll get the surgery. I know people."

"Definitely." William nodded. "Of course."

Tyler stared at his good hand. What was he talking about? He didn't know anyone who could help put his shoulder back together. Not here or back home in California or anywhere else. This morning he should be getting in to see a surgeon. Instead he had to think about giving notice and moving.

Tyler breathed in sharp through his nose, steadying himself against the constant assault of pain. "Should be nice tonight. For the game." He wondered how long it would be before he didn't know or care about the Blue Wahoo schedule.

"Another packed house." William turned into the stadium parking lot and drove to Tyler's car. "Hey, man. If there's anything I can do." He kept his car running. Didn't even put it in park.

"Yeah. Sure." Tyler wanted to shout at him. Why was his buddy treating him this

84

way? He had a bad shoulder, but he wasn't contagious. For a long moment he stared at him until a realization hit. Without baseball, he and William had nothing in common. Nothing to talk about.

Holding his right arm against his body, Tyler climbed out and shut the door behind him. He leaned in through the open window. "Thanks for the ride."

"No problem." William nodded. "Take care of yourself."

With the ocean breeze blowing at his back, Tyler watched his friend drive away. If someone had asked him three days ago whether he had friends, Tyler would've rattled off a list of names. All teammates. Now that he no longer belonged to the Blue Wahoos, he was not only unemployed, he had no teammates. No friends.

He turned toward the stadium and read the words stretched across the front: Bayfront Stadium. Home of the Blue Wahoos. How many times had Tyler parked in this spot and walked through the player entrance of that building? Each time he had told himself the same thing: This was a chapter in his story, a steppingstone to the Big Show. Better than Dayton but still not where he expected to be six years after the draft.

His shoulder felt like flames were coming from it. Tyler gripped his right elbow and wondered if doctors ever did shoulder surgeries out of the goodness of their heart. He pulled his keys from his pocket and clicked open the door of his Dodge Charger. The car still turned heads, the wheels still among the nicest on the road.

Lot of good that did him now.

Tyler slid behind the wheel carefully, but even still he bumped his right elbow and cried out, "I can't do this!" He froze in place, squeezing his eyes shut and waiting for the white-hot pain to let up. Even a little. How was he supposed to drive without his right arm? Slowly he sank back against the leather seat and pulled his phone from his pocket. He called up Safari and searched *Cost of Shoulder Surgery.* Several figures appeared in the results. The average seemed to be around twelve thousand dollars.

The amount he made a year with the Blue Wahoos.

He stared at the steering wheel. *Okay, Tyler, you can do this. You can drive to the store and get your pills. Come on.*

All his life he had driven with his right hand. Now he felt awkward if not unsafe as he made his way to the drugstore. He paid $39.71 for the prescription of Oxycodone.

In a hurry, he struggled back to his car, found another water bottle, and downed two pills. *There.* He couldn't drive once the meds took effect, but he needed them now. In a careful move, he shut his car door and rested against the vehicle. He closed his eyes and turned his face toward the sun. How fast would the medication help? *Work fast . . . please work.* His entire body trembled from the battering effect of his shattered shoulder.

A few minutes passed and he opened his eyes. He couldn't stay here. People walking by were starting to give him strange looks. He directed his attention to the back of the store. Boxes. That's what he needed. Clutching his right elbow to his body, Tyler lumbered toward the Dumpster, grabbed half a dozen empty boxes, and managed to get them into his trunk. He had no idea what tomorrow held, but he knew he had to figure out his living situation fast. Before he ran out of money.

Back at home, he shoved the pain pills in his pocket and carried the boxes up to his room. Tyler's landlady was a woman in her fifties. She and her husband lived on the main level of the small two-story 1970s house. Tyler had the upstairs. The ceilings weren't high and both walls slanted in along the roofline. Tyler was six feet, two inches tall, so as long as he stayed in the middle of the room he had plenty of clearance. His window faced due south, toward the ocean, with a view of trees and blue sky.

The room had been home since Tyler moved to Pensacola.

He found Mrs. Cook in the front room reading. She looked up when he walked in. "Tyler, you look better than you did yesterday." She stood and moved a stack of magazines off the sofa so Tyler could sit down. "I read in the paper about your shoulder. I'm sorry."

Again he thought about praying. He needed a miracle. *If You're there, God, I could use a little help.* He steadied himself, aware of the pain pills in his left pocket as he sat down. "The Blue Wahoos . . . they cut me." Tyler looked at her, hoping for kindness. "I don't have insurance." A sad laugh came from somewhere inside his heart. "I need surgery, so yeah. Not sure what I'm going to do."

Mrs. Cook let that set in for a long moment. She lowered her brow, concerned. "That's terrible."

"I'll figure it out." He hated this, hated feeling like a victim. "Anyway, I need to talk to you about the room."

"Tyler . . ." Mrs. Cook's expression darkened. "I need rent money."

"I'm paid up through Friday. But after that . . ." He shrugged his good shoulder. What could he say? "I need to find a job. I could maybe . . . pay half the rent and then the other half after I find something?"

"I'm very sorry, Tyler." She shook her head and looked out the window for a moment. "Mr. Cook and I count on that money. We use it to pay the mortgage." She looked back at him. "We usually get four hundred for the room. You know that."

"Yes, ma'am." The pain pills weren't working. "I'm just not sure what to do."

"Me, either." Her expression filled with remorse. "I'm awful sorry."

Tyler waited, expecting some sort of compromise. He hadn't been late on rent once. But none came. "So that's it?"

"Stay till the end of the week, of course." She managed a weak smile. "No need to leave today."

"Yes, ma'am." He stood and returned to his room. By then his entire body was shaking, desperate for a way around the pain. Maybe he could take another pill. Certainly that couldn't hurt. He dropped to his chair and used his knees to brace a water bottle. Then he ripped off the top. He had to use his right hand to brace the lid while he twisted with his left. The effort killed, but one additional pill and a swig of water and he could at least know relief was on the way.

The next two days passed in a haze of medicated pain and restlessness. The pills helped, but even when they were working he couldn't get good sleep. He could only truly rest when he was sitting up, when his shoulder didn't feel detached from his body. His mind was another problem. Much as he quickly came to love the pain pills, he was clearheaded only in the morning — when the medication had worn off. That's when he would drive to Chick-fil-A for a breakfast wrap and a couple regular chicken sandwiches. Lunch and dinner for later in the day. Then he'd head back to his room. A few of the guys had called or texted. Jep had stopped by to check on him. But the team was busy with games.

Finally it was Friday, and as he walked into the house with his bag of food, Mrs. Cook was waiting. "Today's your last day, then?"

Tyler regretted not spending more time with the woman. Maybe if she'd known him better she would've been willing to help. But it was too late for any of that. "Yes, ma'am. Packing up."

She smiled, nervous. "The new tenant is a baseball player, too. Another pitcher. Just got into town."

He stared at her. What was he supposed to say to that? His heart fell to his feet and he managed a quick nod before moving past her and up the stairs to his room. His heart pounded in his aching shoulder as he sat down. Was she serious? Did she really think he would want to know that sort of information? The Blue Wahoos were bringing in a new pitcher and he was going to sleep in Tyler's old room?

So this was God's idea of a little help?

He ate his breakfast and took the pain pills. Three of them again. The only thing he had to look forward to now. As he washed them down, he stared into the bottle. Already it was half gone. He put the lid back on and set the bottle carefully on his nightstand. Couldn't let anything happen to the pills.

He stared at the empty boxes still in the middle of his floor. It was time to pack.

Tyler started in the corner of the room where a bookcase held his trophies. Whenever he moved, they were the first things he packed. Especially the big one. The single item that mattered most to him. The two-foot-tall trophy engraved with the words

91

that used to define him.

Little League World Series Most Valuable Player, 2002.

Proof that at one time he had been more than a homeless, washed-up baseball player.

He had been a champion.

6

Tyler ran his fingers over the old trophy and the years scattered like so many particles of dust. The Simi Valley Sluggers had felt it when the season began that year. If ever a team had the chance to win it all, it was that one. Surrounded by boxes and with hours left in the place he called home, Tyler closed his eyes and like a favorite movie, the memory played again.

They were a bunch of twelve-year-olds that summer, old enough to be skilled at the game and too young to be distracted by love and life and longing for something more.

There was just baseball and that was enough.

Marcus Dillinger was his best friend that year. Like Tyler, Marcus was the only boy in his family, so the two of them joked that they were twins. Never mind that Marcus was black. When people raised their eyebrows, Marcus would wink at them. "You can see the resemblance, right? We have the same pitching arm."

That much was true.

Tyler and Marcus ruled the mound from the beginning of the season through the playoffs. They were serious when they pitched and silly in the dugout — not old enough to understand the stakes. They chewed pounds of bubblegum and drank gallons of Gatorade and held contests to see who could spit sunflower seeds the farthest.

Back then all of life smiled down on Tyler and Marcus. First, they had been given the good fortune of growing up in Simi Valley, California — one of the greatest hotbeds for baseball talent in all the country. For Tyler and Marcus, it wasn't a matter of whether they would play baseball.

It was a matter of when.

Some of the greats of the game had come through Simi Valley. Long before the town's little boys turned four, most parents dreamed about their sons joining the fabled ranks. That's how old Tyler and Marcus were when they joined Simi Valley T-ball. Their parents became friends, taking turns driving to practice and bringing snacks for the team — game after game, year after year.

The boys attended different schools, but that didn't matter. They were brothers on the field and they swore they'd be best friends forever. By the time they were twelve, Tyler and Marcus could play any position. But they were money on the mound. Both of them had been clocked throwing fastballs in the high 70s, and Tyler had pitched one game where the coaches clocked him at 82 miles per hour.

"We're going pro, man, you and me!" Marcus would sling his arm over Tyler's shoulders. "We'll wind up on the same team and no one'll ever beat us."

That year it was easy to believe.

When post-season began, all of Simi Valley knew what the boys hadn't quite figured out: they really were unbeatable.

Tyler's dad and Marcus's dad were both coaches for the Sluggers. At home barely an hour passed without some sort of coaching or encouraging or reminding Tyler of how to throw and what to eat and which exercises would keep him best conditioned for the next game.

For the most part, Tyler took his father's advice. It was too soon to resent his father or accuse him of loving the athlete more than the boy. No, that year there was only baseball and winning and dreaming about tomorrow.

Nine other teams — including one from Canada, two from Mexico, and one from Japan — made up the tournament. As always, Japan was the team to beat.

Tyler took a deep breath and relaxed into the chair. The pain pills were kicking in. He could still see it all, the grassy knolls of Williamsport, the crowds that had trekked there from all over the world. He could still feel the humidity that late August, still hear the cheers from the fans.

It all came down to the final game against Japan. That day in the dugout for the first time since the season started, maybe for the first time ever, Tyler and Marcus understood the stakes.

They had a handshake back then, one they had started in coach-pitch ball, when they were only six. There in the dugout that August day before the game against Japan they did it again, their eyes locked. Opposite hands clasped, two chest thumps, a fist bump, a linking of the arms and the No. 1 symbol. All in perfect rhythm.

Tyler had grinned. "Let's go win this thing."

Breathe, he had told himself that day. *Just breathe.* He wound up and threw a strike. And then another and another and another.

Even now with his shoulder exploding from its socket and twelve seasons come and gone since, Tyler could feel the ball in his hands, smell the Pennsylvania air.

The umpire called the last strike and the Japanese players crumpled to the ground in defeat.

Marcus was the first one out to the mound. He picked Tyler up and swung him around while Tyler punched his fist in the air. Someone caught the moment on camera and it ran front page in newspapers across the nation: *Simi Valley Upsets Japan in Pitching Battle.*

The rush lasted for weeks — the team made an appearance on *The Tonight Show with Jay Leno* and Fox News. Tyler and Marcus were labeled American heroes and pundits wrote their stories as if the future was easy to see. Certainly they would dominate through high school and have unblemished pro careers. The future was theirs to take — winners both of them.

When it was all over, when summer ended and school started up, Marcus came over one Saturday and threw the ball with Tyler in his front yard. "We gotta make a pact, man. A promise." Marcus grinned at him. "Whoever gets drafted higher, the other one has to be part of the package."

Tyler liked it. "Play for the same team or not at all."

"Exactly." Before Marcus left that day, they did their special handshake, the one that had defined them and united them season after season. "Nothing separates us. Not ever."

A warm wind blew through the screen of Tyler's open window and he opened his eyes. No team or teammate could've come between them back then. Instead it was something far more insidious, something twelve-year-olds knew nothing of.

Time.

Eighth grade was social and busy and full of plans for high school. Tyler attended Jackson High and Marcus went to Royal — at the other end of town. They talked now and then, but the trophies grew dusty, and by the time they were juniors they hadn't thrown a ball together since that fabled Little League year.

Tyler clutched his elbow and tried to get comfortable.

He and Marcus were both drafted after high school. Tyler took the offer, Marcus took a scholarship to Oregon State. After graduation he played for the LA Dodgers. He got there the traditional route: through college and a year with the Chattanooga

Lookouts, a double-A team in the Dodgers' farm system. Marcus was their top pitcher now.

Marcus had called after Tyler accepted his spot in the draft their senior year of high school. "You sure?" he sounded surprised. "UCLA's a great program, man."

"I can't wait four years." Tyler had laughed. "I want the Bigs tomorrow. Soon as I can get there."

"Save me a spot."

Tyler chuckled, all of life still easy as the game. "I will. Part of my contract."

It was the last conversation he and Marcus ever had.

A few years ago when Tyler made news over the public drunkenness arrest, Marcus tweeted him. *Been too long, man. Get your game back on!* But that was it.

Marcus was making millions now, leading the Dodgers to the playoffs. Every other week he was in the news for throwing a two-hitter or improving his earned run average.

Tyler was pretty sure his childhood friend never thought of him. But if he did, it was with a passing amount of pity. Poor Tyler Ames. Never reached his potential. Messed up along the way. If he caught the current news about Tyler's blown-out shoulder, Marcus would shake his head and remember being twelve. For a minute or two. Then he'd get back to living the dream.

Tyler hadn't seen his parents since getting on the bus the summer after his senior year for Billings, Montana, where the Reds Rookie League played. Taking the draft had been a mistake. A year later he understood that. That's how long it took for Sami Dawson to tire of his mess-ups off the field. Among all the ways he'd paid for making the wrong choice after high school, that one hurt the most.

The loss of the only girl he ever loved.

7

Angie Ames saw the article in the Monday afternoon paper and wept.

Tyler had blown out his shoulder and been released from the Blue Wahoos. End of story. Now the article lay on the corner of her desk. Proof that her son was still alive. That somewhere in Florida he was suffering without her. The smell of fresh-cut wood filled her office at the front of her husband's warehouse. Bill had run Ames Fence and Deck since Tyler was a baby, but business had never been slower.

Maybe the recession or the taxes on the small businesses. Maybe people didn't have extra money for decks and fences. Whatever the reason, it wasn't Bill's work ethic or his talent. All his life Bill Ames had been expert at putting up fences.

Especially when it came to their son.

The phone on her desk rang and Angie answered it on the first ring. "Ames Fence and Deck. Can I help you?"

"Yes, I'm calling about an account. It's past due and . . ."

It was the third collector of the day and the answers left Angie exhausted. There had been times like this before, but never this bad. Sometimes she wondered if maybe Bill was weary of the business, distracted by the way he constantly missed Tyler, and always wondering how they'd gone so wrong when it came to their son.

Bill walked in and came to her desk. "I'm finished for the day." His shoulders stooped more than usual. He didn't bother to smile. "Let's get lunch."

Angie shut down her computer while Bill took the article from her desk and read it. He must've had it memorized by now, same way she did. He looked up. "Has he called?"

She stared at him. Was he kidding? Of course Tyler hadn't called. They hadn't heard from him in four years. Not since his first arrest. She shook her head. "No. He hasn't."

Bill nodded, his eyes back on the paper, distracted. "I can't imagine how badly he must hurt."

The way we all hurt, she thought. But she only sighed. "Let's lock up."

Lunch was usually at their favorite spot, a

café a few blocks from the warehouse on the north end of Simi Valley. Their favorite table was outdoors beneath a Sycamore tree. Somehow the place felt private, despite the traffic. They ordered their usual iced teas and salads and took their seats.

"It was all my fault." Bill stared over his drink at the distant mountains. "I know that now."

This wasn't the first time he'd made the confession. Angie sipped her drink. "Too much baseball."

"No one should lose his son over a game." His tone was quietly fiery. "No one."

For a long time they were quiet, and the years played over again in Angie's mind. It started with the Little League Championship, of course. That was the dividing line. Life before winning the title.

And life after.

"Things were so good when he was little." She wasn't really making conversation. It was more of a fact. Proof that life hadn't always been this way. "He was the sweetest boy when he was younger."

"He was an athlete from the time he could walk." Bill's eyes glazed over, as if he'd taken up residence some fifteen years ago.

After the championship Bill was absolutely convinced Tyler was going to reach the pros.

He used to talk about the spot on the mantle where Tyler's Cy Young Award would go. The boy wasn't even in high school yet.

"Did we talk about anything else?" Bill blinked and his eyes met hers. He set his iced tea on the small round table. "Besides baseball? Did we ever talk about God?"

Angie wanted to give him words of comfort. But she had to be honest. "It was a lot of baseball."

"Mmm." He nodded, repentant. "I read a verse this morning. 'What does it profit a man to gain the whole world and lose his soul?' "

"Powerful." Angie's words came easily. This wasn't the first time they'd talked about their regrets. It wouldn't be the last.

"The verse landed differently today." Bill narrowed his eyes. "What does it profit a man to gain the whole world and lose his son? That's how I heard it."

Tears stung Angie's eyes. If only money weren't so tight they might've flown into Pensacola this past year and seen one of Tyler's games. Surprised him afterward with a hug and a dinner out and a chance at reconciliation. Tyler had long since changed his phone number, so they couldn't call him. Early on, Angie had tried social media

— a tweet congratulating him for a winning game or a comment on Facebook. But Tyler hadn't been active on social media for years.

Nothing had sparked a response, anyway.

"He must hate us." Bill looked ten years older than his late forties, a broken man going through the motions. "Right? Don't you think?"

"I don't know." Angie ran her fingers down the cold sweat on her glass. "Hate's a strong word."

Not that she would've blamed him.

She remembered once when Tyler came home from school, his face all lit up. He had asked Sami Dawson to homecoming and she'd said yes. But Bill jumped on him before he had a chance to talk about it. "You're supposed to be at practice."

"I talked to Coach. Today was the only time I could ask Sami to —"

"Sami? You're missing practice for a girl?" Bill wore his work jeans and a denim button-up yellowed with sawdust. Angie could still see him, his scowling face. "Are you serious, Tyler? This is your senior year!"

"I'm not skipping, Dad, it was just —"

"No!" Bill wouldn't let him finish. "You can't let anything get in the way, son." He folded his arms, his expression a mix of disappointment and anger. "We've put everything into your baseball. Someone out there is working harder than you. And when it comes to earning scholarships, he'll be first in line."

"Yes, sir." Tyler didn't argue. He never did. But the light in his eyes was gone.

Bill pointed at the Little League trophy on the fireplace. "Get back to school. Don't come home until you've done your work-out."

"Yes, sir."

Angie blinked and the memory faded. She had long since forgiven Bill for pushing their son away. But it didn't change the sad fact. She turned her eyes to her husband. "You okay?"

Bill was staring at the mountains again. "I don't think I told him enough. How much I loved him."

"He knew." Angie could feel her heart breaking. "He had to know."

"I'm not sure."

They needed a miracle. In their broken-hearted state, both Bill and Angie had tried to find their faith again. They sometimes read their Bibles and on occasion they prayed. They had even talked about attending church again. But more than all that, they needed a miracle.

The café door opened and a waitress ap-

106

proached with their salads. She was new, a pretty girl with golden red hair. Angie hadn't seen her before.

"Here you go." She set the salads down and smiled at the two of them. "Sorry it took a little longer. It's my first day."

Angie looked at her nametag. "Ember." She found a smile for the young woman. "That's a beautiful name."

"Thank you." She didn't seem in a hurry to get back inside. "I moved here a few weeks ago. The weather's amazing."

"Yes." Bill seemed to remember his manners and snap out of his reminiscing. "It's the best." He looked up, his eyes softer than before. "Welcome to town."

"Thank you." Ember hesitated, and her expression grew deeper. "So . . . I heard you talking about Tyler. Your son." She stared intently at them, her eyes full of light. "I know him. I came here from Pensacola."

Angie sat a little straighter. What? How could she have heard them talk about Tyler? And how would she know which Tyler? "You . . . know our son?"

"Tyler Ames?" She slid her hands in the pockets of her apron, her tone rich with concern. "Yes. I know him well. I saw him just a few days ago."

"A few days ago?" Bill seemed confused,

too. "How did you —" He stopped short. "How is he?"

"He's hurting. Badly." The young woman frowned. "He's very alone and desperate. Baseball is all he's ever known."

Angie felt chills run down her arms. The waitress knew Tyler very well indeed. "We want to talk to him . . . but he . . ." She didn't want to say too much. "We don't have his new number."

Ember took a step closer. She exuded peace. "Do you really want to talk to him?" She looked intently at them, and Angie had the feeling they'd known her all their lives.

"Of course." Angie felt practically desperate. "It's all we can think about."

"Okay, then." Ember's tone had a calming effect. "I have a suggestion." She hesitated. "Pray." Her tone grew more serious. "When you pray, you will reach God . . . and He will reach Tyler. Pray together and pray often. Pray as if Tyler's life depends on it." She looked from Bill to Angie. "God is aware of the trouble with Tyler. But you must pray."

"We will. We've meant to do that." Bill looked as if he wanted something more, something concrete. A tangible plan — especially since Ember seemed to know so much. "Is there anything else? A way to find him?"

"Please." Angie's heart rate picked up speed. "If we had a number . . . or an address."

"I've told you what I know." Ember looked over her shoulder and then back at them. "Battles are won and lost through prayer."

Angie still couldn't believe this strange conversation. Was she dreaming? The waitress couldn't possibly have known who they were. "How did you say you knew Tyler?"

"I didn't." Ember smiled. "Let's just say I care very much for him." She put her hand on Angie's shoulder.

Bill was on his feet. "I'll leave now. I'll take a bus if I have to, sell the shop." His eyes welled up. "Whatever I have to do. He's my son. I . . . I love him."

"I know." Ember's words warmed the space between them. "Don't be discouraged. For now . . . please pray. God is in control."

Slowly, Bill settled back in his chair, his eyes never leaving Ember's.

"Thank you. For talking with us." Angie put her hand over the young woman's. She felt a empathy like none she'd ever known before. "We will pray . . . we won't give up."

"Good." Ember took a few steps back. "I

109

have to go. Don't forget. Tyler needs you."

She gave them each one more look, then turned and walked back into the café.

Angie stared at her husband. "What in the world?"

"How could she have known whose parents we are?" Bill leaned his forearms on the table on either side of his salad.

"She was inside when we were talking about him. She couldn't have heard his name." Angie picked up her fork and then set it down again. "Do you think Tyler talked to her about us? Showed her a photograph?"

"Maybe." Bill looked at his salad and then up at his wife. "She said to pray." He held his hands out to her. "Now's as good a time as any."

And so with hands joined, Bill prayed out loud for their son. That he might find help and hope. That he would not give up and that this situation might lead him home. Once and for all. Before they left, Angie and Bill stepped back in the café to find Ember again, thank her for talking to them about Tyler.

But the young woman was nowhere to be seen.

Bill shrugged as they turned to leave. "She must've gone home."

"We'll look for her next time." Angie walked beside him back to the car. "The important thing is that we pray." She looked at her husband. "The way we used to."

As they drove back to the shop, Angie felt hope work its way through her heart. This was the best breakthrough they'd had in years. A few hours later she had an idea. She could call Jep Black, the Blue Wahoos manager, and ask for Tyler's new number. Something she wouldn't have done when Tyler was playing for the team. Too pushy. But now the plan made sense, and like that, they were a step closer to reaching him.

With Bill at her side, Angie tried the number, but there was no answer. She tried again every hour on the hour. But still he didn't pick up.

Before turning in that night, Bill took her hands again. "I want to go to church this Sunday. Start being the man I used to be." He paused. "Before baseball took over."

"I'd like that." Angie rested her head on his chest and then looked in his eyes. "I want to find him, Bill. He needs to take our call. Let's pray for that."

He kissed her tenderly, the kiss of a man desperate to make things right. And with that he began to pray once more, thanking God for the chance meeting with the waitress and asking Him for a miracle. That somehow, against all odds and understanding, Tyler would do something he hadn't done in years.

Answer their call.

8

Tyler called Verizon and cut his phone service the moment he finished packing. When he could afford it, he would pick up a cheap phone at Walmart, pay by the minute. In case of emergencies. He was out of his contract, which meant his phone was worth about a hundred dollars cash. Verizon would be his first stop once his car was loaded.

Before he turned it off for the last time, he grabbed a pad of paper from his dresser drawer and scrolled through his phone book. Any number he might need he would somehow use his left hand to scribble down for later. Even if the numbers would be hard to read.

Near the top of the list were his parents. Bill and Angie Ames. He'd entered them that way, since he hadn't thought of them as Mom and Dad for years. He stared at their names. What were they doing today?

They'd be at work, of course. Trying to get ahead in the fence business. Tyler slumped over the paper, discouraged.

At least his dad could make a living.

Wasn't that what the man had warned him about? Pass up a scholarship and there'd be nothing to fall back on. Tyler wondered where he'd be now if he had a degree in communications or business. He could probably make a few phone calls to a handful of alum and have a desk job by Monday.

His dad had been right.

He'd been right back then and he was still right today.

And what about his mother? She had always taken his father's side. Tyler could picture her quiet in the background, never standing up for him. What he would've given if just one time she had told his father to back down, to lighten up. If she had reminded them both that it was just a game.

If they knew he was hurt, they were probably shaking their heads over some shared lunch, reminiscing over the fact that their son had made the wrong choice. And how that single wrong choice had ultimately led to this: a blown-out shoulder and an existence lived out between doses of pain pills.

Tyler wrote down their names and number. He wouldn't call them anytime soon.

Maybe after he had his surgery and he was back on the mound. But he wanted the option, at least. He captured Jep Black's number and the numbers of a few of his teammates. His old coach from Jackson High and a few buddies he'd gone to school with. He didn't have a number for Marcus — hadn't had one in years.

Finally, he turned off the phone and threw it in a bag. His things fit in six boxes. The first time he was actually glad for his sparse belongings. Loading the boxes into the back of his Charger with one arm wasn't easy, but it all fit. He had to clear out before dark. The new guy would be here in the morning.

The pitcher.

When his car was packed, Tyler took the cold Chick-fil-A sandwich from the bag, peeled back the foil wrapper, and ate it. He stood at the window, the same one where he'd dreamed about his future and longed for last Saturday's game. He had worked so hard to reach that point. A place in his career where everyone was watching.

He finished the sandwich in five bites and checked the bag. One more left. He would eat it later. Mrs. Cook had left the vacuum outside his door. Never mind his damaged right arm. She must've figured he could clean with his left arm just as well. The effort hurt, but he got the job done. When he was finished, he took one last look around his room and left without saying good-bye.

Mrs. Cook wouldn't miss him.

She'd have the Blue Wahoos' newest pitcher in the morning.

Verizon gave him only eighty-five bucks for his phone. They had it wiped clean before he left the store. Further proof that Tyler Ames, star pitcher, no longer existed. In no time the number would be assigned to someone else. Someone with a job and a way to pay bills.

He drove slowly along the strip, the ocean on his left side, a row of businesses on his right. Maybe Chick-fil-A was hiring. That way he could at least get free food. With an air of determination he parked his Dodge in the lot and headed inside. The manager knew him.

"Tyler!" The man was at the counter. His face lit up but fell just as quickly as he spotted Tyler's brace. "Heard about the shoulder. I'm so sorry."

"Thanks." This was one more thing Tyler hated about his new life. Everywhere he went someone was apologizing to him. He wasn't Tyler Ames. He was "poor Tyler

Ames." Broken, battered. Washed up. The manager's eyes said all of that even if his words did not. "How can I help you?"

Tyler forced a smile. At this point he couldn't afford to be seen as a victim. "I'm looking to make a little extra money while I'm rehabbing." He chuckled. "I'm here all the time anyway. Figured I'd see if you were hiring."

The man shrugged. His cheeks darkened. "You're a great guy, Tyler. I'm one of your biggest fans, you know that."

"Yes, sir."

"But I'm all full." He paused. "A few months from now I'll be needing a night manager. Come back then."

"Yeah. Okay." Tyler wasn't sure whether to laugh or cry. "Thank you."

"Just a minute." He filled a bag with six sandwiches and handed it to Tyler. "A little get-well gift."

He would've loved to tell the manager he didn't need a handout. But the truth was he needed all the help he could get. He had mailed off his car insurance before the injury. The check cleared this morning, taking half his remaining money. He needed gas in his car and he was almost out of pain pills — another forty dollars. He'd be out of money in a few weeks.

He took the bag of chicken and thanked the man.

Back in his car, Tyler slammed the steering wheel with his good hand and instantly regretted the decision. The last thing he needed was another injury.

Night manager? In a few months? The possibility made him sick to his stomach. By then he would've had his surgery and be on his way back to pitching. Making the Blue Wahoos regret the day they released him. But if Chick-fil-A wouldn't take him, Tyler wasn't sure who would.

He couldn't be picky, not now.

The strip mall next door had a Target and a Panera. A cupcake shop and a Coldstone. Someone had to be hiring. But two hours later he had a fistful of applications and a long list of no's. Managers were either not hiring or not interested as long as his arm was in a sling.

Tyler realized something as he made the rounds: he hadn't worked a real job in all his life. He was paid to pitch. Along the way, every now and then, Tyler made money coaching young pitchers, cleaning ball fields, and umping Little League games. He needed both arms for any of that. Outside of baseball he'd never made a dime.

The medication was keeping him going.

Funny how just a few days ago he was worried about driving under the influence of Oxycodone. But now . . . well, now he could only hope for the best. There was no functioning without the pills.

Two more strip malls and still, no job offer. Tyler drove to the beach, to his favorite spot just west of Bayfront Stadium. He parked his Charger, killed the engine, and opened the windows.

He could hear the announcer's voice echo across the pavement. "Ladies and gentleman, welcome to the Blue Wahoos' last home game of the season. After tonight your team will be in the playoffs. Let's give a warm welcome to the Blue Wahoos!"

The familiar music played and Tyler slid down in his seat. He grabbed his Jackson High baseball cap from the dashboard and pushed it low over his eyes. What was wrong with him, parking his car this close? Where he could hear the soundtrack of his former life playing out like a bad dream?

And what about the club paramedic who'd reached him first after that terrible pitch? The guy had said this wasn't the end. It was a beginning. Strangest thing ever. Tyler thought about calling the county and reporting the man. How dare he talk about beginnings in a moment like that! What was his name? Tyler thought back, trying to remember. Then it came to him.

Beck, right?

Yes, that was it. Beck the paramedic. Whatever the guy had meant, his words were nothing but a cruel joke now.

Tyler narrowed his eyes and stared out at the ocean. He needed this place, this moment. Needed it for inspiration. He would be back one day. Not pitching for the Blue Wahoos, but for one of their opponents. Wherever he wound up next, he'd travel here someday and pitch against the Wahoos like the star he used to be. Everyone from the top management at the Reds to the meek Jep Black would regret ever letting him go.

The sounds of the game blended together. His shoulder was killing him. Tyler pulled the pain pills from his glove box, grabbed a chicken sandwich from the bag, and ripped off the wrapper. A few bites and he was ready for the meds. He couldn't remember when he took his last dose, but it didn't matter. He needed them now. He stepped out of his car, grabbed two water bottles from the case on the backseat, and took his place behind the wheel again. One more dose of pills and he'd be out. The prescription still had a couple refills. Tyler couldn't see beyond that.

He slid the seat back and stretched out his legs. The sun was setting, casting oranges and pinks across the deep blue of the gulf. This wouldn't be bad, sleeping in his car. His shoulder felt better when he slept sitting up. He grabbed the wheel with his good hand and thought about where it all went bad.

His senior year, of course. The first time he and his father had disagreed about baseball. Even then Tyler always thought they'd come to terms, that eventually they'd see eye-to-eye. Or maybe that was just the way he felt because of Sami Dawson. Every sunrise and sunset carried her name on it back then. If there had been storm clouds on the horizon, for the most part Tyler had missed them.

He had just a few photographs of Sami now, the ones he carried with him in a box of things that had nothing to do with baseball. The trophies and plaques and team photos took up half the trunk. His clothes and shoes and baseball gear fit in the others. But one box — the one on the back seat next to the case of water — held the rest of his life.

Birthday cards from his parents and artwork he'd done in grade school. His high school yearbook and his graduation tassel and there at the top, a miniature photo album. The gift Sami had given him the last time they saw each other. Right before he took the bus to Billings.

He turned his body, ignoring the pain that shot through his arm and neck. He reached for the photo book and brought it up front with him. He no longer had a phone, so he didn't have a flashlight app. He flicked on the overhead light. He couldn't look for long without starting his engine. The last thing he could afford was a new car battery.

The book was covered in Jackson green, a dense corduroy Sami had found in a bargain bin back in the day. Across the front she'd embroidered his name and number in yellow. *Tyler Ames, No. 16.* Beneath that she had sewed on a red felt heart and near the bottom, also in yellow, she had stitched her own name: *Sami Dawson.* He smiled as he read the words.

She hadn't always been Sami.

With the sounds of the game playing in the background, Tyler ran his fingers over the worn fabric. *No one cared about me like you did, Sami. Why didn't I try harder to keep you?*

He looked out at the ocean. The colors had faded, the way they had faded from his life. He could feel the pain pills taking effect, feel the edges blurring. He might have to spend the night in his car, but he would let his mind take him somewhere else.

Back to a time when he was still sure of life and his future and his dreams of being a major leaguer. Back when his name was synonymous with success and little boys still asked for his autograph. A place where he and his parents were still close and his dad still believed he would win the Cy Young Award.

Back to the day when he first met Samantha Dawson.

9

Girls had never been part of the formula for Tyler. His parents had seen to that. It wasn't like they sat him down and told him he couldn't date. They never outlawed a student dance or a party on a Friday night. They simply kept him too busy. There were pitching clinics and tournaments and travel teams. Practice and team meetings and visits to college games.

But all that changed the summer before his senior year.

It was a tournament that took Tyler to Sami. For the first time in Tyler's life, his parents weren't able to attend the competition that summer week. His dad had been hired to build a fence around a pasture a hundred acres wide. Biggest job of the year.

"You'll stay with a host family," his dad told him before the tournament. "Your mother and I will try to make it up for a game or two."

But the tournament was in Northern California — a flight for the team. In the end his parents were too busy with the job to make the trip at all. Which left Tyler completely in the care of his host family.

The Dawsons.

A breeze off the bay swirled through his car, taking him back. The pain pills were doing their job, the blurry feeling ushering in the most wonderful of yesterdays. Tyler closed his eyes and he was there again, his coach dropping him off at a mansion in the nicest neighborhood Tyler had ever seen. And he was lugging his gear up the sidewalk to the grand front door of his host family.

Summer was thick in the air, the sky bluer than it had ever been. Tyler rang the doorbell and held his breath. Who were these people? How could they afford to live like this? He took a step back and peered up at the roofline. As he did, the door opened and there she stood. His breath caught and he felt his cheeks grow red.

"Hi." She grinned, and just as quickly she looked back over her shoulder. As if by smiling at him she was breaking some rule. "You're our player?"

He looked down at his gear and back at her. "That's me." He held out his hand. "Tyler Ames."

"Samantha Dawson." She took his fingers, the contact between them fleeting. "Come meet my grandparents."

From the beginning Tyler thought of her as Sami. She looked like a more beautiful version of Keira Knightley. Short dark hair and the prettiest features he'd ever seen. He wondered how he would catch his breath in her presence. When he finally remembered to move, he grabbed his gear bag and followed her into the house. If the outside wasn't proof, the inside certainly was.

Sami lived in a palace.

He followed her into a room that looked more like a hotel lobby than a house. Sitting across from each other reading newspapers at a glass and marble table were two older people. The man had neatly trimmed white hair, serious eyes, and a casual scowl. His wife didn't look much friendlier.

The man lowered his glasses when Samantha ushered Tyler into the room. "Who's he?"

"Grandpa, this is Tyler Ames. Our baseball player for the week." She looked back at Tyler and then secretly motioned for him to remove his baseball cap. "Tyler, this is my grandpa."

Tyler whipped off his cap and held up the other hand. "Nice to meet you, sir."

The old man managed a slight smile. He stood and held out his hand. Tyler shook it. Firm handshake. Direct eye contact. "Yes." The man seemed to sum him up. "And you."

Tyler was still shaking his hand. "Thank you . . . for having me." He finally took a step back and turned to the older woman.

"Grandma, this is Tyler." Sami stepped to the side.

"Welcome." The old woman never stood, but she nodded at Tyler, her eyes slightly warmer than before. "I trust you'll enjoy your stay with us."

"We're big baseball fans." Sami's grandfather crossed his arms. His smile came slowly. "You'll get us a copy of your game schedule."

"Yes, sir." Tyler didn't dare look at Sami.

"I can show him to his room." She practically bowed to the old man. "Is that okay?"

"Very well." He sat back down, his eyes on Tyler. "Dinner's at five o'clock sharp. If you're not on the field we'll expect you in the dining room."

"Thank you, sir."

"Let us know if you need anything." The woman returned to her newspaper.

Sami flashed him a grin and then spoke with the same formal voice she'd used with her grandparents. "Follow me."

"Right behind you." He picked up his gear and followed her up a winding staircase and down a carpeted hallway. The ceilings had to be twelve feet high. Tyler almost walked into her when they reached his room.

"Here you go." Sami's eyes shone. "This is your room. The bathroom is to the left."

Tyler stared past her, unable to believe it. He'd played more tournaments than he could count. Usually he stayed with his parents in a Motel 6 or a Best Western. "Your house . . . it's huge."

Tyler set his bag down beside the bed. It was king size, with four wooden posts like something from a showroom. It took a few minutes before he remembered his manners. He turned to her. "Sorry." He chuckled. "You actually live here?"

Her smile faded. "I do." She looked lost for a moment.

"Where are your parents?"

"They . . ." Her expression fell a little. "They died when I was five. Motorcycle accident." She looked behind her and then back at him again. "I was raised by my grandparents. They're . . . pretty strict."

"Hmmm." He looked around again. "Your grandfather owns California, I guess."

"He runs a few businesses." Sami leaned

128

against the doorframe. She still hadn't stepped foot in his room. "He's part owner of the San Francisco Giants."

"Right." Tyler nodded slowly. "I figured."

"That's why we love baseball." Her eyes started to find their way back to happy. "When's your first game?"

"Tomorrow morning." He looked out the window and then back at her. "We're on our own tonight."

She shrugged one pretty shoulder. "I have a car."

Suddenly the house was forgotten. It paled compared to Sami's eyes. "Perfect. Where should we go?"

"I know a way inside Giants Stadium." She laughed quietly. "My grandfather would kill me. He doesn't know I have a key."

"Mmm." Tyler leaned back against the windowsill. "You take all the baseball players there, is that it?"

"Actually" — she leveled teasing eyes his way — "I've never used the key. It might not even work."

"Is that right?"

"Yes." She lifted her chin. "And you're the first baseball player we've ever hosted. Just so you know."

"What about your grandparents?"

"They're asleep." She looked half terrified, half ready for adventure. "They don't have to know."

Tyler felt himself falling for her long before they drove out to the stadium that night. The Giants were on the road, and the key worked. Sami had her grandfather's credentials, which she showed to the groundskeepers on the way down to the field. They snuck into the visitors' dugout and sat on the bench, side-by-side.

"Really, Sami? This is your life?"

She laughed again. "What'd you call me?"

"Sami." He smiled at her. "Samantha's too formal."

"Like my house."

"Yeah." He chuckled. "Like your house."

The sun was setting, darkness falling around them, sprinkling stardust over the moment. "What does your girlfriend do when you're out of town?"

"Well, Sami. What makes you think I have a girlfriend?"

Her shyness combined with her spunk made her irresistible. "You just look the type." She laughed again. "And I like Sami. For the record."

He grinned. "For your information, I've never had a girlfriend." He turned and faced her. "Never had time."

"Hmm." She looked out at the field. "You

want to play at a place like this one day? That's your dream?"

"It's not a dream." He narrowed his eyes and looked out at the pitcher's mound. He could barely see it in the twilight. "I will play here one day, Sami. I already know. I made up my mind when I was twelve."

"Can I tell you something?" She pulled one knee up and hugged it to her chest. "I'm scared to death to be out here. My grandpa would send me to a boarding school straightaway if he found out."

"Great. He'll send me to jail, no doubt." Tyler laughed, but Sami's statement confused him. "Why, then? Why'd you do it?"

"I've lived nearly my whole life in that house doing everything right." She kept her voice low. "It just seemed time to have a little adventure."

Tyler couldn't possibly have liked her more. They stayed in the visitors' dugout till ten o'clock and then she took him to a park in her neighborhood where they sat on swings in the dark and talked about life. She told him how they had a second house in the San Fernando Valley. Where she attended school. "We're only here in the summer. My grandparents don't like me having too much free time around my friends."

"Sounds like my parents."

131

The longer they talked, the more they had in common. Their Southern California homes were only thirty minutes apart. And the top college courting him and his baseball skills was UCLA — the same school she'd already decided to attend. "So maybe we'll be classmates." Sami grinned, the moonlight in her eyes. "Who would've guessed?"

They laughed about all the things they'd never done. Never dated, never held hands, never kissed. Sami didn't have a curfew. Her grandparents had never had a reason to give her one. It was midnight when they pulled into the driveway, and all the lights in the house were out.

"Good." She looked relieved. "They're asleep." On their way from her car up the front walk, Tyler stopped halfway and turned to her. Then without saying a word he reached for her hand. He held it until they were inside at the base of the stairs.

"You know what I think?" He took her other hand, but he didn't look away, couldn't break eye contact.

"What?"

"I think this was the best night of my life."

She giggled and put her hand over her mouth. Her grandparents' room was at the other end of the house, but she didn't want to wake them. "You're funny. We didn't do anything."

"Yes, we did." He sounded offended, but he wasn't serious. "We shared an adventure. That has to count for something."

"True." Her eyes sparkled, but she looked suddenly shy. "Good night, Tyler."

For a moment he thought about kissing her. But that wouldn't come till the end of the week. By then — between his baseball games — they shared a bucketful of firsts. They ran barefoot across the beach, ate nothing but ice cream for dinner one night, and twice they stayed up all night talking on the floor of his bedroom.

"Just for this week, let's pretend you're my girlfriend." Tyler played with her hair as they sat in the dark that night. "Another first, okay?"

He could tell she was nervous and wanted to tell him no. Make up some funny reason why not. But she only laughed and allowed him to get lost in her eyes. "Deal."

Tyler remembered nothing of the baseball tournament that week. His coach complained that he wasn't focused. But by the time Sunday came, he knew this much: Sami Dawson had found her way into his heart. Whatever happened in the coming year, he didn't want to be without her. Their last night together, they crept outside and climbed onto the roof of her grandparents' house.

"This is crazy," she whispered as he helped her onto the lowest part of the roof, overlooking the backyard.

"Isn't that what this week is all about?" Tyler pulled her beside him, safe and secure. "Look at the stars. Up here with you, there's twice as many."

"I don't want you to go." She rested her head on his shoulder. "I won't be back in the Valley till the end of August. Six more weeks."

"We'll text. And every night when the moon comes out I'll call you and tell you to go outside and look at the stars." He angled his body so he could see her face. "So you'll remember this." Then — as if he'd done this a thousand times — he took her face gently in his hands and he kissed her. The kiss was slow and magical, like something from a dream. He drew back and searched her eyes. "There."

"There?" She was happy and startled and taken by him all at the same time. He could tell. "There what?"

"We took care of the nevers." He kissed her again. "After this week we can't say we never held hands or dated . . . or kissed."

She tilted her head back and laughed like

quiet wind chimes. Then she must've realized exactly what he said because she looked at him, her eyes wide. "Dated? Like for real?"

"Yes." He kept his hand alongside her face. "Will you be my girlfriend, Sami?"

This time she initiated the kiss. "You know what?"

She hadn't answered his question, but he played along. "What?"

"When I took you to Giants Stadium last Saturday I knew I was never going to forget this week."

"How'd you know?" He ran his fingers through her short dark hair.

"Because" — she smiled — "you're the only one who's ever called me Sami."

"So . . . does that mean you'll be my girlfriend?"

"Yes, Tyler Ames. I'll be your girlfriend."

Like that, the greatest year of Tyler's life began. It built in anticipation until Sami and her grandparents moved back to their house in the Valley and it gained ground every time they saw each other. Sami's grandparents liked that he was a baseball player and they appreciated his manners, the way he respected them and their granddaughter. But they didn't allow Sami nearly enough time to see him.

Still, she had her own car, and most weekend nights they found a way to be together. They went to Jackson High football games on Fridays and they studied together at his house on Saturdays. His parents liked her, but from the beginning his dad worried that she would distract him from baseball.

"You've made it this far," his father told him one night after Sami left. "Everyone's talking about you, Tyler. This is your year." He raised his brow. "Don't blow it. Please, son."

After that Tyler stopped talking about her to his parents. They studied at Starbucks instead. Spring came and Sami brought him the very best luck. His only loss came in an away contest she couldn't get to. "I need you, Sami. It's that simple."

Tyler made her laugh — something she hadn't done much while growing up. In the process Sami grew more beautiful. They talked about UCLA and how they couldn't wait for the next four years. But then midway through his most unbelievable senior season, the Reds sent a scout to a game.

Scouts had followed Tyler since his days in Little League, but this was different. The man hung around and pulled Tyler and his father aside after the game. "We want you, kid. We want you bad." He pulled out a list of notes and assessments, names three pages long.

Tyler was at the top.

"He's made his decision," Tyler's father told the man. "He's committed to UCLA."

"A commitment isn't a contract, Mr. Ames." The scout smiled. "You and I both know that." He looked at Tyler. "If the deal's what I think it'll be, you should take it." He pointed at Tyler as he walked off. "Isn't that the point? Play baseball for money?"

As the season continued, the scout didn't let up. A week after graduation, on the day Tyler was set to make a public announcement about playing for UCLA, the scout got word to him: the Reds were going to take him in the first few rounds.

He really was that good.

"The signing bonus better be in the high six figures," his father told him. "Otherwise we have no deal."

Tyler postponed the UCLA announcement and that night he called Sami at 11:11. "I might take it. I really might."

"The draft?" She sounded worried. "Tyler, you wouldn't start with the Reds. You know that."

"Of course. But if they take me in the first few rounds it wouldn't be long."

"Yeah, but maybe you should go to college. Take the free education and let the pros draft you later. You'll only get better." Sami paused. "That's what my grandfather said."

Tyler hated the pressure. Everywhere he turned people wanted him to play for the Bruins, take the college route. Play it safe. But Tyler wanted a chance at the Bigs sooner than that. If they paid him enough, he could play a year in Billings and move straight up through the ranks. One or two years and he'd be making half a million dollars. He could buy Sami a ring and marry her while she was still at UCLA.

That would impress everyone, right?

When draft day came, Tyler and a bunch of his teammates gathered in his parents' living room and waited. The first three rounds came and the next three went, and then another three and another. With each passing round, Tyler felt himself sink a little deeper into the sofa. Why had the Reds scout lied to him? He was about to call the coach at UCLA and tell them he was coming when the phone rang.

"Sorry, Tyler. Things got shaken up a bit at the last minute. We still want you, though. Big money if you take the offer."

Sure enough, the Reds called out his name

in the twelfth round. Tyler and his team-mates whooped and hollered and celebrated. But the next day the details of the contract came to light. His signing bonus would be $100,000 with a starting salary of just $24,000 a year.

There were a dozen incentives built in — which was what caught Tyler's eye. If he pitched half as well as he'd pitched in high school, he'd make six figures every year. Even before he reached the pros.

What happened next was the closest thing to war Tyler had ever known. He couldn't think about it, couldn't run through those details now. No pain pills were strong enough to dull the memories of what happened next, the fighting and fallout.

Tyler brought the train of memories to a halt. Enough. As he drifted off to sleep in his car to the sounds of the tide and the Blue Wahoos announcer calling another winning game, Tyler was no longer behind the wheel of his Dodge Charger. He wasn't broken or homeless or out of money. He had no regrets, no sullied past, no failed dreams.

Rather, he was seventeen and sitting on the roof of a mansion in Northern California, the summer stars close enough to touch.

And Sami Dawson at his side.

Not until he woke up the next morning, the summer sun burning through the windshield and sweat dripping down his face, did Tyler realize the whole thing had been a dream. His arm screamed for relief and he cursed himself for letting his heart go back in time. He didn't need Sami Dawson. He needed a job and a place to live and shoulder surgery. And he needed Oxycodone in a hurry.

That most of all.

10

Sami was sorting through her closet, looking for proof that she'd ever dated Tyler Ames at all, when the doorbell rang. Mary Catherine was cleaning the kitchen. "I'll get it!" When she was in a hurry Mary Catherine talked loud and fast, like a song. This was one of those times.

Sami backed out of her closet, stood, and stretched. "Who is it?" She wasn't expecting Arnie. He had a legal conference all day. The girls had decided to tackle the apartment in the morning and later walk to the Farmer's Market on Third Street.

"It's for you!" Mary Catherine held out the last part of the word "you" with more sing-song than usual. "Come here."

Sami dusted her hands on her jeans and wiped her hair back from her face. "Coming." The doorbell was a reminder. She shouldn't be going through her closet reminiscing. She had a bathroom to clean and sheets to wash. As soon as she rounded the corner she gasped. "What in the —"

"Beautiful, right?" The flowers took over the counter and stretched halfway to the ceiling. Three dozen red roses at least. Mary Catherine dug her nose in the arrangement and grinned. "Who are they from?"

"Very funny." Sami walked over and snatched the card from the center of the bouquet. They were from Arnie, of course. They had to be. Still, her heart fluttered just a little as she opened the card. Her eyes darted to the bottom. "See? They're from Arnie." She raised her brow at her roommate. "He's wonderful. I keep telling you."

"Hmmm." Mary Catherine hopped up on the counter and stared at Sami over the flowers. "What did he do wrong?"

"He didn't do anything wrong!" Indignation filled Sami's tone, but even so she started to laugh. "You always pick on poor Arnie. How come?"

"Someone has to." She jumped down and hurried to the computer. "Proof of Your Love" by For King and Country was on. "I love this song." She turned up the volume. "If I sing but don't have love . . ."

Mary Catherine couldn't carry a tune to save her life. But that didn't stop her. She grabbed the feather duster from the kitchen closet and sashayed around the room singing every word. Sami smelled the flowers. They were lovely. She looked at the card again.

These are a week late. I should've sent them after dinner the other night. I was so focused on my good news I didn't ask about your client. Forgive me. The future is ours, Samantha. Love, Arnie.

She smiled at the message just as Mary Catherine jumped on the living room sofa and held the feather duster to her mouth like a microphone. "Let my life be the proof, the proof of Your love." She closed her eyes, fully committed. "Let my love look like You and what You're made of . . ."

"I'm going back to my room." Sami held up her card. "Thanks for dusting."

Mary Catherine danced to the computer and turned the volume almost all the way down. "What's the card say?"

"It's not important." She couldn't keep a straight face around her roommate. The girl exuded pure joy.

"Come on!" Mary Catherine hurried back to the flowers and sat on the counter again, swinging her freckled legs, her eyes on Sami. "Tell me."

"He said he should've listened better last week when we had dinner." Sami smiled sweetly. "He just talked about the future. That sort of thing."

"So he *did* do something wrong."

"No, he just . . ." Sami looked at the card again and suddenly realized Mary Catherine was right. Something about that made Sami lose interest in the conversation. Enough about Arnie.

Meanwhile, Mary Catherine kept singing off-key — which made Sami start laughing. She tried to stifle her giggles at first, preserving some sense of dignity for her friend's lack of talent. But she couldn't stop herself, and after another minute, Sami fell on the couch laughing.

At first Mary Catherine looked offended. But then her voice cracked and she started laughing, too. "Okay, so I'll skip *Fifteen Minutes.*"

"Definitely."

When the song ended and they'd both caught their breath, Mary Catherine went to Sami and took the card from her fingers. After she read it she crinkled her nose. "Yuck."

"What?" Sami should've been angry with her friend for dissing Arnie, but she was laughing too hard.

" 'Love, Arnie'?" She handed the card back to Sami. "That's it?" She jumped on the coffee table and struck a dramatic pose. "Mary Catherine," she said in a baritone voice, "my darling, my everything, I will love you with all I am until my dying breath." She grinned at Sami as she jumped down from the table. "When it's my turn, I want that or nothing at all."

The thing was, Mary Catherine would get it. Never mind that she wasn't particularly striking. She had so many freckles she called them her partial tan. But that didn't matter. She was the most beautiful person Sami knew. The whole city couldn't contain her joy for life, and her love for helping others. She would find her guy yet, because she believed God would bring Him. That was the other thing.

No one could touch Mary Catherine's faith.

"Anyway." Mary Catherine smiled and twirled across the room with the feather duster. "If you want Arnie, you can have him." She stopped and for the first time since the flowers had arrived she settled down and her eyes grew soft. "I'm sorry. I don't mean it."

"Yes, you do." Sami stood, her sides sore from laughing. "It's okay. Arnie can take it."

Mary Catherine was still breathing fast from dancing and dusting and singing. "I just wish I'd known you before. When you dated that other guy. The baseball player."

"I was a kid." Sami walked back to the flowers and studied them. "He grew up and changed."

"But he called you Sami." Her eyes sparkled again. "Right?"

"He did." She uttered a tired laugh. "I need to get back to work."

How did she do that? Sami asked herself as she walked back to her bedroom, back to the old box in the closet. The one she hadn't looked at in years. It was as if Mary Catherine could read her heart. She couldn't have known Sami had been digging around her closet looking for proof of Tyler's long ago fingerprints on her heart. *But still,* Sami thought, *after Arnie sends the biggest bunch of roses ever — she asks about Tyler Ames.*

Sami understood why Mary Catherine didn't click with Arnie. He was too safe for her, too predictable. When she found her guy, he wouldn't be neat and tidy with a well-planned future. She'd probably meet him on a mission field in China or serving soup in a homeless shelter.

Sami sat on the edge of her bed and read the card from Arnie again. True, he didn't

146

actually come out and say he loved her. But by now that much was obvious, right? He talked about their future. What more could she ask? Sami set the card on her bed and returned to the closet.

So much of her childhood was stuffed in the box. Not until she reached the bottom did she find the photo album. She'd made two identical books the month they graduated from high school. One she gave to Tyler. The other she kept. She felt the corduroy cover and her heart soared. This was what she'd been looking for.

Easing it up between old papers and framed photographs that once hung in her room, Sami pulled the book free. Then slowly, like she was walking back in time, she sat on the edge of her bed again and stared at the cover. If someone had asked her back then how she pictured things ending with Tyler Ames, she would've had one answer.

She would marry him. She had no doubts.

But seeing his name in the news the other day made her wonder if she'd ever really known him. And if she had, then what changed him? Sami smiled at the photo book. The handmade cover, the carefully stitched words. The green fabric looked sort of ugly now, but not at the time.

She opened the book and smiled at the first two-page layout. Tyler in his Jackson High uniform holding a baseball with one word written across the front in Sharpie: *Prom?*

Opposite that was a picture of Sami in his embrace, her arms around his neck moments after telling him yes. Of course she would go to his prom. One of Tyler's teammates took the picture. By then their families frowned on their relationship. Tyler's parents were convinced she took away from his intensity on the mound, and her grandparents worried that he was reckless.

"Much as we like baseball, your grandfather and I never saw you dating a ballplayer," her grandmother had told her a number of times that year. "Boys like Tyler have lots of girls. They . . . expect things."

Sami laughed again at the memory. Tyler never expected anything from her. They would kiss good night, nothing more. Once in a while he would linger before he left for the evening and something in his eyes would change. He would whisper to her, "I don't ever want this to end, Sami." Or "Someday we won't have to say good night."

Sami turned the page of the scrapbook. Next was a picture of her and Tyler swinging over the edge of Castaic Lake on an old tire, both of them clinging to the rope. The picture was taken a second before they fell in the shallow water. Sami had bruises on her arms for weeks, but it didn't matter.

At least she had the memory of a rope swing. Something she wouldn't have if Tyler hadn't been in her life.

The photos took her back. Sami and Tyler, barefoot in the rain one January night. He had come to her house to take her for a walk, but then the clouds came. She could still hear herself. *"We should take an umbrella. My grandma will worry I'll catch a cold."*

Tyler only laughed. "That's the craziest thing I've ever heard. Being cold is good for you." He took her hand.

"How's that?" She glanced at the angry sky overhead.

He grinned, pulling her slowly to his side. "It makes you walk closer to me."

She tried to include only the best pictures, the ones that showed them doing something she never would've done otherwise. Roller skating at Venice Beach, sitting in the back of his friend's pick-up at the last drive-in theater known to man. Sami ran her finger over the photo. She and Tyler had snuggled under a blanket. She couldn't remember the movie they watched that night, but she remembered everything else. The other couple had made out the entire movie.

Not Sami and Tyler. He kept a running commentary going, making her laugh for reasons that wouldn't have been funny without him. She turned the pages, reliving one memory after another. The last picture was the saddest. A photo that had only made its way into her copy of the album. It was taken by a stranger minutes before Tyler stepped on the bus.

His bus to Billings was in the background.

Sami looked into the past and she could see it all again. Feel it. Hear their voices as they said good-bye. "You have to come home whenever you have a chance." She had put her hands on either side of his face. "I'll miss you too much."

"Baby, I won't be in Billings for long. I promise. It's just a stop on the way to the Bigs." He kissed her lips and then looked long into her eyes.

"I believe in you."

"I know." His smile had started in his eyes. "That's why I'm so sure I'll make it."

Sami remembered feeling helpless. The way she'd felt when her parents didn't come back home after their accident. Everyone disagreed with Tyler's decision to go with the draft. Her grandparents and his parents. His coaches. But she had wanted to believe in him. If anyone could make it through the minor leagues to the majors, it was Tyler.

But by the time he was ready to climb on the bus, he and his parents were on rocky terms. Also by then, her grandparents had unequivocally decided he wasn't the guy for her. Even the local media thought Tyler was crazy to pass up a scholarship to UCLA.

"I'll prove them all wrong," he told her before climbing on the bus. "I'll call you."

And like that, Tyler had backed away from her. He waited until the last second to turn and jog up the steps onto the bus. He took a seat by the window so he could see her, and their eyes held until the bus was too far down the road for them to see each other.

Sami could still remember how it felt, standing there in a cloud of exhaust, the summer sun beating on her shoulders and Tyler Ames moving farther away with every heartbeat. She had told him the truth. No one believed in him more than she did. He called her that night from Idaho and again when he reached Billings. He texted her all the time at first.

"Billings is great," he told her. "Nothing to do but play ball."

Tyler started out with a run of success. They worked him into the pitching rotation after a week of training and conditioning, and the wins piled up. No matter how busy, he called Sami every night. Like he said he would. Always the conversation was the same. Tyler missed her. She missed him. But life was moving faster than one of his famed pitches. Sami moved into her dorm at UCLA and suddenly they really did seem worlds away from each other. Something else happened.

For the first time since meeting a year earlier, they had nothing in common.

Sami turned the last page in the photo album. Tucked in the back was the article from the *Simi Valley Enterprise.* She opened it up, careful with the yellowed newsprint. The headline spanned the entire sports page: *Tyler Ames Makes Good on Promise.* The reporter quoted Tyler saying that only a few special people believed in him when he took the draft over the scholarship. "My game is showing them all. I'm out to prove everyone wrong," he said. "And I'll do it. I will."

Sami scanned the text to the place where the Billings coach had shared a few words. "This kid is a winner. He's unstoppable. He'll make it to the Big Leagues in record time at this rate."

The more interest baseball executives took in Tyler's pitching, the busier he became.

Sami enrolled in eighteen units at UCLA and joined an intramural volleyball team. Pretty soon the calls from Tyler came only a few times a week and then only on the weekends. He had no vacation time, no time to visit her.

When the season ended, the Reds moved Tyler to Dayton, Ohio — the club's single A team. In the media, most local sports reporters saw the move as a good thing. "If Tyler Ames keeps pitching this way, he'll be in Pensacola in a hurry," his newest coach said at a press conference.

Sami held onto every positive word. She would leave the articles out on the kitchen counter on the weekends when she visited her grandparents. Every chance she had she would tell them how Tyler was doing well and making a name for himself.

Her grandparents didn't care. A man without a college education was not one she could consider marrying. Conversation closed. "Samantha, there are a thousand handsome, intelligent boys on the campus of UCLA," her grandfather told her one weekend that spring. "Have an open mind at least."

"My mind's made up." Sami smiled at him. "I love Tyler Ames."

"Well." Her grandfather nodded slowly.

"We'll see about that."

Those were always his words: *We'll see about that.* As if he could look into the future and somehow know things weren't going to work out.

"People are watching," Tyler told her when they talked at the end of spring training in Florida. "I keep thinking they might just send me over to the Blue Wahoos. Skip single A altogether."

Sami hoped for him and believed in him and once in a while she even prayed for him. But instead of giving Tyler a promotion, the Dayton Dragons kept him in Ohio and, almost overnight, things began to unravel. It turned out Dayton had a lot more to do than Billings, and since the media had loved Tyler since he was a twelve-year-old national champion, they were always on hand to capture his victories.

And his mistakes.

"I'm bored," he told Sami a few weeks after he arrived back in Dayton. "I need more of a challenge." Almost as an after-thought he added, "I miss you. I can't believe it's almost been a year."

No one in Sami's life could believe it either. Her roommates were constantly asking her about the mystery boyfriend, the guy who was never around. Each of them had a UCLA guy they wanted her to meet, someone she could actually date and hang out with. Always she would politely tell them she wasn't interested.

But all that changed one night when Sami typed his name in the Google search line and found a headline she would never forget: *Tyler Ames Arrested for Public Drunkenness — Underage Pitching Phenom Takes a Downturn.* She read the article top to bottom five times before the truth set in.

Tyler had gone to a bar with a group of fans — mostly girls. The picture told the story. He and one of the girls had been dancing on the table at a Dayton bar when someone snapped a photo. The owner of the bar had asked Tyler to stop, but he refused. Police were called and Tyler was arrested. Minor in possession of alcohol. Public drunkenness. He was released on his own recognizance and fined a thousand dollars. The team fined him three times that.

That weekend when Sami went home the article was waiting for her on the kitchen counter. Her grandfather walked in as she spotted it, but he never said a word. Nothing about the story or the arrest or anything at all about Tyler. Instead he smiled and put his arm around her shoulder. "How are your new friends at school, Samantha?"

Like that, her grandparents clearly believed two things: that they were right about Tyler Ames and that she was over him.

She was, in some ways. She was furious with him for drinking and hanging out with the fans, and deeply disappointed that he would get himself arrested. She blocked his texts, and for the next three weeks, whenever he called she refused to answer. Finally a month after the article released, she picked up.

"Sami . . . what in the world!" Tyler sounded genuinely upset. "I've been trying to reach you!"

"Really?" She kept her tone cool. "I thought you'd be busy with lawyers and police officers."

He exhaled long and slow. "News travels fast."

"What'd you expect?" Her voice rose with the intensity of her hurt. "You're Tyler Ames. Anything you do — good or bad — will be online in an hour. Did you really think I wouldn't see?"

"No. I just . . . I wanted to tell you first." The sound of voices in the background came over the line. Someone called his name. "Look, I have to go. We're getting on the bus. Road games all week."

She stayed quiet. What could she say?

156

"You're mad?"

"Yes. At myself." It was the first time Sami had voiced her feelings on the matter. She hadn't told her roommates at school, and her grandparents had no interest talking about Tyler. "I thought I knew you." She paused. "I was wrong."

By then she'd convinced herself her grandparents were right. She was just a kid when she fell for Tyler Ames. Who wouldn't have been swept away by the magic of a summer fling? "Sami, please." Her tone probably scared him, because he sounded desperate. "I'll call you later. We have to talk."

"Don't call." The answers came to her as she spoke. "We need a break, Tyler. I need time."

A month later, when he tried again, Sami ignored his calls. Both of them. After that he stopped calling.

Even then she couldn't shake him. Whenever she had the chance she Googled his name. There were a handful of minor-in-possession charges in Dayton and another in a small Kentucky baseball town. Those were followed with a harassment claim by a female bartender in Des Moines.

Sami was sure her grandfather had seen the stories, too. But he never left articles on the kitchen counter. His way of saying the

157

Tyler Ames chapter was closed.

Which it was.

Tyler spent that season and three more in Dayton, never reaching the success he'd found in Billings. Sami checked up on him a couple times a year but the news was never good. In his third season he crashed a moped into a tree. Alcohol was suspected to have played a role in the crash.

After that the media took off its collective gloves. Editorials ran in sports pages around the country remembering who Tyler Ames had been and bemoaning the sad waste of talent and opportunity. *What was he doing on a moped, anyway?* one of them wrote. *He should be on the pitcher's mound and only the pitcher's mound.* Another reporter commented that at this rate Tyler Ames would simply be one more statistic. A story of what could've been.

Sami hated what people said about Tyler, but she could only agree. His slide to public shame and broken dreams convinced her time and again that she had been wrong. She never knew him. No matter how she felt that day when he climbed on the bus for Billings.

His final words lingered in her heart still. *I'll prove them all wrong.* His litany of bad decisions since then lined up like so many soldiers taking aim at all Sami had once believed about him.

She was putting the photo album back in the box in the closet when her cell phone rang. A quick glance told her it was Arnie — probably calling to see if the flowers had been delivered. Sami felt herself change gears. Arnie would want her full attention — he deserved it. She answered the call. She'd spent enough hours in the past.

It was time to think about her future.

11

Ember was back in Pensacola now. Beck, too.

The mission wasn't going well. Tyler was homeless and discouraged, relying on pain medication more every day. Yes, Ember's meeting with Tyler's parents had been helpful. Since then, the couple prayed several times a day for their son.

Prayer had the power to hold back all the forces of darkness.

But they needed more of it, more people praying, more sons and daughters of Adam calling out to the Father on behalf of Tyler Ames. Beck agreed with her.

For now, they had Tyler in their sights. Ember kept up with Beck as the two of them moved invisibly along, some ten feet above the roof of Tyler's car. They stayed with him as he drove through town and pulled into the YMCA parking lot.

"Why is he here?" Ember eased herself

down a few feet from the Charger.

Beck settled in beside her. They were still invisible. "He needs a shower." He stared at their subject, the one upon whom so much depended.

Ember felt suffocated by her frustration. "He doesn't need a shower as badly as he needs to get to California." She shot Beck a desperate look. "The doctor there would do his surgery at cost."

"Yes." Beck frowned. "Timing is critical. We have only a small window."

"I have an idea." She had thought of it that morning. "There's a man looking for help at a retirement home."

"I agree. The woman there — Virginia." Beck narrowed his eyes. "She's our best hope."

"Exactly." Ember wanted to will Tyler to turn around, forget this diversion. But that wasn't how angels worked. Instead she studied Tyler, his pained look and unsteady steps as he walked toward the front door. "Poor man." A terrible thought came over her. "What if he doesn't want to work there? What if —"

"Ember." Beck looked at her, his eyes blazing. "Don't. We were chosen for this mission. You must believe."

She wouldn't say it, but the thought

161

crossed her mind all the same. What if they were the wrong Angels Walking team? What if two other angels might've had better insight, better ways of intervening?

"You will, right?" Beck put his hand on her shoulder. "You will believe?"

"Yes." She forced the fears from her mind. "I will. I do."

"Let's go." Beck led the way and they slid easily through the glass wall at the front of the building. Ember knew much about Tyler Ames. She was a master in studying character. One of the reasons she was chosen for this mission.

Ember and Beck watched Tyler catch a whiff of his own stink as he approached the front desk. He hesitated, clearly hoping no one else would notice. The angels could smell him from five feet away. Smells like this were one of the strangest aspects of being here on earth. His clothes could've walked into the Y by themselves.

"Morning." The girl at the front desk was ten years older than Tyler, but that didn't stop her from flirting. She looked him up and down. "Rough night?"

"The rehab's insane." He grinned and stopped only long enough to sign in. "See ya." He headed to the large workout room.

"He can't rehab." Ember felt another

ripple of concern. "Not until after the surgery."

"It's his excuse." Beck stayed at her side, both of them still unseen. "The only way he can get a shower."

"Exercise would be good for him." Ember kept her eyes on Tyler. The two of them hovered at either side of the young man, waiting. Watching.

Tyler walked to the first stationary bike he saw, dropped his bag, and climbed on. Ember knew as she watched that his pain had settled into a constant burn, an hour-by-hour reminder that life had changed. He pedaled slowly at first, no doubt dragged down by the medication coursing through his bloodstream.

Ember's heart hurt for him. She watched him, praying. *Father, help us direct him to California. Give us wisdom.*

Tyler kept pedaling. Ten minutes became twenty, and twenty became forty. Sweat dripped down Tyler's face and into his smelly shoulder brace.

"The next hour will be critical." Beck had never looked more serious.

After his workout, Tyler finished showering, returned to his car, and turned on the engine. As he did, Ember could see the panic on his face. "He feels it," she whis-

163

pered to Beck. "The noose . . . closing in on him a little at a time."

Beck sighed. "He's running out of options."

Ember and Beck watched as Tyler drove to the gas station down the block and pulled up at the closest pump. He paid the clerk thirty dollars, enough for just half a tank, and drove away.

"He has seven dollars and fifty cents left." Ember hovered next to Beck, a few feet from Tyler.

Half a mile down the road he turned into the Winn-Dixie parking lot.

"Great." Ember couldn't see where this was going. "What's he supposed to buy with $7.50?"

Tyler stuffed his wallet in the pockets of his dirty jeans. He stared at the outdoor BBQ set-up. The sign read "Ten Dollars a Plate." Tyler didn't have that much to his name. He walked inside. Ember and Beck stayed on either side, unseen.

In the produce section one boy tugged on his mother's sleeve. "Hey, Mom . . . that's Tyler Ames!"

Tyler kept walking. He reached the refrigerator section and grabbed a single piece of string cheese. A few feet down the aisle he reached the bakery and without hesitating he took an onion bagel from the case.

He stared at the bread and string cheese for a long moment. Then he peeled back the slightest bit of wrapper.

"No!" Ember grabbed Beck's arm. "He can't steal!"

Beck didn't look worried. "God can work this out for the good."

If Tyler got arrested — if he got into trouble, he would never find his way to California. *Please, Father, intervene. Help Tyler! Please . . .*

Again Tyler stared at the bagel and the cheese and then he glanced behind him, over one shoulder and the next.

He was going to do it. Ember could feel it. She stood a few feet from him, silently pleading with him to change his mind. But even so he peeled the plastic back and bit off half the cheese at once. Keeping his back to the aisle, his face toward the bagel wall, he chewed as quickly as he could. Next, he took a bite of the bagel, as if no one would ever know, and he began walking toward the exit.

Not until he passed through the front doors did someone call out, "Hey! What are you doing?"

Ember and Beck kept up with him, one on either side. How was this going to work

165

out? Ember resisted the urge to help in any way but one — she prayed. One of the rules of Angels Walking was this: All interaction had to be covert.

Tyler seemed to set his eyes on his Charger parked in the front row. He walked quickly in front of a moving car. The woman behind the wheel slammed on her brakes and scowled at him. He nodded and at the same time someone grabbed his good shoulder.

"You need to pay for that food!" It was the manager, the same one Tyler had asked for a job two weeks ago.

"I'm sorry, I was just —"

"Give me it!" The manager glared at him. "Stealing isn't the answer. Whatever the problem."

Tyler narrowed his eyes, as if he was looking through the man to his soul. "I'm out of money. I . . . I don't know what to do."

The manager hesitated. "Fine." His expression softened some. "Take it."

"Thank you."

"You're a mess, Tyler." The man shook his head.

"Tell him about the food kitchen!" Ember hovered inches from the man, silent and invisible, but begging him all the same.

The manager started to turn to leave, but then he changed his mind. "There's a soup kitchen at Hope Community Church, end of town. They give dinner every night and canned food." He frowned. "It's a crime, the way you baseball players end up." He shook his head. "All for the love of a game."

Ember prayed the entire time until Tyler pulled into the parking lot at Hope Community. It was just after noon, probably too early for a free dinner.

"My turn," Beck pointed to the back wing of the church. "I'm about to be a volunteer."

"Go." Ember's voice sounded urgent. "Hurry."

She watched as Tyler walked through the doors and stopped, as if he might change his mind. But then his eyes locked on the cross at the front of the sanctuary. It towered from floor to ceiling.

He stood there for a long time and then slowly, gradually, Ember watched Tyler Ames fall to his knees.

And beside him, Ember did the same thing.

12

Tyler would've stayed on his knees all night. For the first time in weeks he felt peace and hope — even when there was no tangible reason.

"Hello?" A voice called to him from a few feet away. "Can I help you? Or do you need a few minutes?" The man's tone was full of something Tyler knew nothing about.

Unwarranted, undeserved, unmerited grace.

He opened his eyes and turned. The man looked vaguely familiar. He wore a button-down short-sleeve shirt and khaki pants. He took a few steps closer. "I'm Beck." He smiled. "You're Tyler Ames, right?"

Tyler struggled to his feet and tried to focus. Beck? The guy looked like a pro linebacker. "Are you — ?"

"I work with the fire department. Paramedic." He hesitated. "I was the first to reach you the night of your accident."

Of course. Tyler took a step back. Every good feeling from a moment earlier faded. "Do you . . . remember what you said that night?"

"Yes." Beck's compassion filled the space between them. "I told you this wasn't the end. It was a beginning."

Anger swept through Tyler. "Why would you say that?"

"It's true." Beck looked down the aisle to the cross. "What you felt a minute ago on your knees — that's more real than anything you ever felt on a pitching mound."

Tyler wanted to argue with him. But he was too weak. The pain pills made it difficult to turn thoughts into words.

"Anyway." Beck shook Tyler's good hand. "I'm a volunteer here at Hope Community Church." He paused. "You want to talk?"

"No." Tyler's answer was quick. He didn't want anything from the man. "I need . . . food. And a job." He couldn't look the man in the eyes. "I heard you have a soup kitchen for —"

"People in transition? Yes, we do." Beck wasn't in a hurry. He looked genuinely concerned. "Dinner's not for a few hours. But we have sandwiches." He pointed down a hallway at the end of the foyer. "Come on."

Tyler walked behind him, not sure whether he should laugh or cry. This was the best breakthrough of the day. But he didn't want to need help from Beck. Anyone who could see this as a beginning didn't understand him. No matter how kind he seemed. They reached an oversized kitchen with five refrigerators. Beck opened the first one. "We always have sandwiches ready. Pastor Roman sees to that. You never know when someone might be hungry."

Tyler held his breath. It was hard not to like the guy. Other than the Chick-fil-A guy, no one had been this nice to him since his injury.

Beck grabbed a bag and dropped in three wrapped sandwiches, an apple, and a carton of milk. "Here." He handed it to Tyler. "You said you need a job?"

"Yes, sir." Again, Tyler kept his eyes averted. The pills weren't working the way they used to. His mind was clearer but his arm killed him. How could this be his life? Begging food at a church he'd never stepped foot in? "I'll do just about anything."

Beck thought for a moment. "Pastor Roman has a friend. The guy runs a retirement center off the main boulevard." He pulled his phone from his pocket. "Here, take down this number."

Tyler reached absently into his pocket and then shook his head. "I . . . don't have my phone."

"Don't worry." Beck moved to a kitchen drawer and found paper and a pen. He wrote a number down on the pad. "Ask for Harrison Myers. Tell him Pastor Roman sent you. Harrison knows him. Pastor Roman from Hope Community."

Tyler took the paper and nodded. "Thank you." Why was the man so kind? Tyler had walked into the church starving and ashamed without a chance for a job. Now he had a bag of food and a lead on work — best lead he'd had since he'd lost his home.

Beck surveyed him, thoughtful. "Can I pray for you? For your shoulder?"

Tears welled in his eyes. He couldn't stop them. "I . . . I'm in a bad spot." He looked at the door. He needed to get out of here. He had what he wanted. If this man really knew him, he'd tell Tyler this was his own fault.

But Tyler couldn't leave. He was desperate for the man's kindness.

"It doesn't matter what got you here." Beck put his hand on Tyler's good shoulder. "I'd still like to pray with you."

Pray with me? Really? Tyler tried to remember a single time anyone had asked that. His parents had stopped praying with him when he was in the fourth grade. He pinched the bridge of his nose, holding back the tears. He couldn't talk, couldn't do anything but nod. Yes. Yes, he would like this nice man to pray for him.

Beck bowed his head and closed his eyes. Tyler did the same.

"Father, one of Your sons is in trouble. You know the details, and You know he's feeling broken." The man's voice resonated like something from heaven. "Would You show him You love him, Lord? Please help him get work and the surgery he needs. It's okay if it takes a miracle. You're the God of miracles, and we believe You. We thank You even now before it happens. In the powerful name of Jesus, amen."

Tyler opened his eyes. Peace came from the man's voice, his expression. There was a feeling around him that drew Tyler and dropped his walls. "You really think this is a beginning?"

"I do." Beck didn't hesitate.

Tyler couldn't stay much longer without breaking down. He didn't deserve anything the man had given him. He thought about the cross again and then looked back at Beck. "Thank you."

They walked together to the front door

and when they reached it, Beck shook Tyler's left hand again. "God will go with you. We already asked."

Something about the man's handshake emanated confidence. As if in this man's presence, Tyler could entertain the possibility that everything really could work out. That he might eat the lunch and get a job and find his way to the surgery he needed. That this might not be the end of his hope and future. But a beginning.

A most unlikely beginning.

Tyler's hands shook as he reached the car. He could feel Beck watching him, probably praying for him. The pain pills could wait till he was out of sight at least. At the next stoplight he shoved two pills down his throat and downed them with a bottle of water. It hadn't been long enough since his last dose at Winn-Dixie. But he couldn't go to a job interview feeling like this.

His hands shook as he put the lid back on the bottle.

What had just happened? First the cross and then Beck and the free lunch. Finally, the phone number for Harrison Myers. The slip of paper sat next to the bag of food. Tyler remembered something his mother used to say: "Good things happen to people who pray." She said it more often as he neared his senior year, always with her eyebrows raised.

Her meaning was clear: Tyler needed to eat right and condition right, he had to work out with his strength coach and his pitching coach, and he certainly needed to get the highest possible grades. But he also needed to pray.

So good things would happen.

Tyler didn't know about that, but this much was sure — Beck had prayed. And now Tyler was on his way to a job interview.

He turned into the next parking lot — a pet store and a TJ Maxx. Pulling into the first parking spot he found, he killed the engine. For a long moment he gripped the wheel with his good hand and tried to remember how he got here — homeless and desperate. Life had been so good for so long. Before high school graduation he was the boy everyone wanted. From his freshman year on he would come home and find a stack of letters from major universities.

By the time he was a senior, the letters filled three black trash bags. Tyler saved every one, and that year when the *Los Angeles Times* ran a story on him — after he was awarded California's Mr. Baseball title — Tyler pulled out the letters and dumped them across the kitchen table. The article's photo showed him sitting on the table in the middle of the pile, grinning.

Now the clipping was in one of the boxes in the trunk. The headline read: *Mr. Baseball's Tyler Ames: Still America's Favorite.*

America's Favorite.

The phrase sounded like heaven back then. It still did.

Tyler caught a whiff of his smelly brace. The heat through the windshield was warming the bag of sandwiches. He took one from the top and set the rest on the floor, in the shade. He unwrapped the plastic from the bread. Plain old peanut butter and jelly, but nothing had ever smelled so good. He ate the sandwich in just a few bites.

Just in time, since the pain pills would make him sick on an empty stomach. He finished the sandwich and opened another.

That same year, the Reds scout didn't put on the pressure until baseball season started. He wasn't the only pro scout interested. So why had Tyler been so sure that was the right choice?

Like carbon monoxide, regret filled the car, burning Tyler's eyes with tears and making each breath an effort. He set the sandwich beside him, half-eaten, and hung his head. There he was again, late April —

blue skies as far as he could see. He was tall and lean, a pitching specimen, bounding through the door with the biggest news of his life.

He had turned down the scholarship for the draft. It was official. "I'm home!"

He expected a fight, of course. But in the end he believed his parents would see it his way. As he rounded the corner his parents were sitting at the kitchen table. Waiting for him. To this day he had no idea why the Reds scout would've called them. Tyler should've been the one to break the news.

But there was no question they knew. Their disapproval was written across their faces.

"Sit down, son." His father patted the empty chair next to him. "We need to talk."

Tyler was there again. He dropped his backpack and took the seat. "You already know?"

"Yes." His father frowned at him. "You're turning down your scholarship?"

And he could feel just how he'd felt that day at the kitchen table. The hurt and embarrassment, because clearly his father thought he had chosen wrong. "I'm a man, Dad. It's my career. If I want to start this way, that's my choice."

"You're hardly a man." His father's frown

became a glare. "And you will not turn down that scholarship."

"Dad!" Tyler had felt himself losing control. "The whole point is to go pro. To be paid to play, right?"

"You've already accepted the UCLA offer." His father's tone was stern. "You can't back out."

Tyler hesitated. "I already did." Something sat heavily on Tyler's shoulders and he realized in that moment what it was. Years of being coached and pushed and prodded by his father suddenly felt like so many shackles. "Why do you care, Dad? As long as I'm successful, right — isn't that what matters? The number of strikeouts and the speed of my fastball? My wins and losses?"

"Don't take an attitude with me, young man." His father rose up out of his chair and then settled back down again. "Look, you've worked all your life for a baseball scholarship. Now you have one. A full ride, Tyler. Do you know what that means?"

"Sure." Tyler suddenly felt more like a pawn. "You want to tell your friends about how your son earned a scholarship to UCLA."

"Don't talk to your father like that." His mother's eyes were dark with disappointment. "UCLA is the only right choice. Not for us, for you. You need a degree to fall back on."

"Being drafted is out of the question." His father sat back. "End of conversation."

"It's too late. They promised me a six-figure signing bonus. You said that's what it would take." Tyler stuck out his chest. "Besides, I've made up my mind."

His father stood, towering over him, the veins at his temples pressing out from his angry face. "I said that before I knew about UCLA. It's almost impossible to get a full-ride scholarship for baseball. You know that."

Tyler wouldn't be moved. "I can always go to school."

"Tyler Ames, you listen to me." His dad's eyes narrowed. "If you take the draft, I'm done with you." His voice rose. "No son of mine will turn down a full scholarship."

And with that, the battle began.

Tyler remembered how he'd felt, how the life had drained from his body and pooled around him on the kitchen floor. He and his father didn't talk until draft day, when Tyler accepted the offer from the Reds. His father spoke to him just once after that.

Tyler could still hear every word. "When will you leave?" As if the man couldn't wait to be rid of him.

"Not soon enough." That was Tyler's response.

This many years later Tyler could only wonder. What if his dad had given him a choice? Gone over the options and applauded him for having so many offers? They could've sat down over a burger and celebrated the pluses and minuses of each direction and then his father could've patted him on the back and said, "Either way I'm proud of you, son. I'll support you whatever you decide."

Tyler squinted back at yesterday. If that had happened . . . if his dad had treated him differently . . . he might've chosen UCLA. He gripped his elbow, pressing his damaged arm to his side. Certainly if he had the choice now that's what he would do. Which could only mean one thing: His parents had been right. He should've gone to school.

If Tyler had one wish, he would be nineteen again, walking away from the Reds' offer. He would have his parents' support and Sami at his side. And his baseball uniform wouldn't say Billings.

It would say Bruins.

13

His friends the pain pills were doing their job, blurring the edges, dulling the pain inside and out. The way Tyler so desperately needed.

He picked up the piece of paper from the passenger seat. The man's name and number were all Beck had written. Now Tyler needed a payphone. He dug around his glove box and found a small handful of quarters. TJ Maxx was his best choice, so he walked there first. Sure enough, just inside next to the restrooms there was a single payphone. Almost an antique at this point. The call took all his change.

He hovered near the phone, hoping to blend in.

A man answered on the third ring. "Merrill Place. Harrison Myers."

Tyler closed his eyes. *Think, Ames . . . speak clearly.* "Uh . . . yes. Hello." He tapped his forehead with his fingers. Why had he taken pain meds before making the call? Suddenly he remembered. "Beck from Hope Community Church told me to call you. Said you might be hiring?"

"Who?" The man sounded more tired than gruff.

"Beck . . . he's a —" Suddenly he remembered. "I'm supposed to tell you Pastor Roman sent me, sir." Tyler's brain was starting to work.

"Pastor Roman. Okay. Um, yes." The man sounded distracted. "I need a maintenance man."

"I'm very interested." Adrenaline pumped through Tyler's veins. He needed this job, needed it more than he'd needed anything in all his life. "Could I . . . come in? Talk to you for a few minutes?"

The man was silent, and in that silence Tyler knew he would at least get an interview. "Do you know where we are?"

"You're off the main boulevard?"

"Two blocks north." Mr. Myers hesitated and then rattled off an address. "Be here in ten minutes. I have a lot to do."

"Thank you, sir." Tyler hung up the phone and leaned his forehead against the dirty plastic casing. He had an actual job interview! He walked back to the car, fighting through the pills and the drunken feeling that came with them. Back behind the wheel he felt the rush of panic again. How could he have a solid conversation with Mr. Myers when he felt like this?

He looked around his car. Was there anything that could sober him up? Take the edge off the effects of the pain medication? He spotted the half-empty case of water. Yes, water could help. He grabbed two bottles and drank one without stopping for a breath. The bag of food caught his eye next. Perfect. Food would definitely absorb some of this fog. He ate another sandwich and topped it off with the second bottle of water.

Tyler loosened his belt. He hadn't felt this full in a month.

He checked the time on the dashboard. Seven minutes until his interview. He felt the slow blink that came with being medicated. *Wake up, Tyler! This is important.* He shook his head and slapped his cheeks a few times. There. He felt a little more awake. For good measure he sprinkled the remaining drops of water from the second bottle onto his forehead. With the palm of his one working hand, he spread the dampness back into his hair.

Pensacola was easy to navigate. He drove with the windows open, hoping the warm breeze would help him stay awake. The medication felt more intense this time, like he could close his eyes and sleep till Sunday. He had taken too many pills too close together. *Keep your eyes open,* he ordered himself. *Sober up!* He opened his eyelids wide and kept driving. He reached Merrill Place with two minutes to spare.

His vision was cloudy as he checked the rearview mirror, but from what he could see he looked okay. As Tyler moved to open the door, he caught another wave of his stench. Never mind the shower he took that morning. He needed to wash his clothes and his brace. If he got the job, that's what he would do with his last seven dollars. For now he'd have to leave some distance between himself and Harrison Myers.

And hopefully sit downwind.

Inside, the place wasn't as bad as he expected. More of a hospital feeling — at least in the entryway. A middle-aged black man sat in an office on the other side of the entrance. He spotted Tyler, stood, and waved him in. The man looked as overworked as he had sounded on the phone, but his smile was warm.

"Have a seat." He pointed opposite his desk. "Please."

"Thank you." Tyler nearly missed the

183

chair as he introduced himself. The room seemed to tilt at an unusual angle. "I 'preciate you taking time for me."

"Yes, well." Mr. Myers didn't seem to recognize Tyler's name. He looked at a file on his desk while he talked. "I'm not sure you'll want the job. But it's yours if you do." He slid the folder to Tyler. "This is the application. I'm looking for someone to wash the floors and clean up after the residents."

"Yes, sir."

Mr. Myers looked at Tyler's brace. "Oh, man." He sounded frustrated. "I forgot about your busted shoulder."

"It won't get in the way."

Myers studied him, clearly not convinced. "I need physical labor, son. You gotta push a mop and clean tables. How you going to do that with one good arm?"

"I will, sir." The haze of medication was like the thickest fog. Tyler blinked a few times. "I'll work harder than anyone with two good arms. I promise."

"Well. We'll see," Harrison Myers muttered. He tapped the folder. "People don't last in a job like this. Cleaning up messes. Keeping things disinfected." He searched Tyler's eyes. "You have to have a heart for older people."

At this point Tyler had a heart for making

money. A heart for surviving until tomorrow. Nothing more, nothing less. Whatever Mr. Myers meant, he wasn't sure. Especially against the backdrop of Oxycodone.

Mr. Myers leaned forward. "You following me?"

"Yes, sir." Tyler chided himself. He had to remember to answer every time he was spoken to. Tyler narrowed his eyes, willing away the blurriness. "I'm sorry. It's been . . . a rough day."

For a long while Mr. Myers studied him. Then he sat back in his chair and sighed. "Look, I know who you are." He paused, thoughtful. "I followed your career since you were a kid."

Great, Tyler thought. He was done for sure. The guy would know the long, ugly résumé that came up when a person Googled his name. The job was all but lost. He was a waste of talent, a failure at every level and now —

"Tyler?"

"Yes, sir?" He looked up.

"Were you going to say something?"

"Yes, sir." Tyler blinked, desperate to focus. "I . . . disappointed a lot of people." He rubbed the bridge of his nose. "I'm sorry." He stood, his legs wobbly, and started for the office door. "I shouldn't have wasted your time."

"Tyler." The man's voice was kind but stern. "Sit back down."

He did as he was told.

"I'm offering you the job. One good arm and all. Working here . . . it isn't the dream. But all dreams have to start somewhere."

"Thank you, sir." Tears burned at the corners of Tyler's eyes. He didn't want to cry but a single tear slid down his cheek before he could swipe at it. "You . . . don't know what this means to me."

"Fill out the application." The man looked out the office door at the vast tiled entryway. "If you have time, you can start today. I needed someone last week."

"Yes. I have time, sir." A surge of hope flooded Tyler's veins. The man knew him, knew his past, and still was willing to give him a job? Even with one arm? Tyler took the application and moved to a chair in the lobby. His experience was nonexistent and he had no address. But he filled out what he could.

When he finished, Mr. Myers showed him a closet full of brooms and mops, rags and buckets, and two shelves of cleaners. "Start with the floors. Every hallway, every room. If the residents are sleeping, come back later. Most are out in the common areas."

186

He stopped short and looked at Tyler. "What'd you say the name of the guy was from Hope Community Church?"

Tyler felt more sober now. "Beck. He was a volunteer."

"Hmm." Mr. Myers shrugged. "Never heard of him." He picked up a bottle of Lysol. "Anyway, use this mixed with warm water." He looked over the floor again. "I think you get the drill."

"Yes, sir." Tyler took the cleaner, stuck it under his good arm, and grabbed a bucket. He was still badly injured, desperately broke, and homeless. But he had something now he didn't have that morning.

A chance.

14

The name on the door was Virginia Hutcheson.

It was Tyler's third day at Merrill Place and so far he hadn't been in the woman's room. She was always in her bed, always sleeping. The male nurse on staff had explained yesterday that she'd been having outbursts of terrified screaming. None of the staff could understand why.

"We keep her pretty medicated." He shrugged. "Otherwise she tries to escape."

Tyler had been through the building enough times that he didn't blame her. The place was clean, the staff was kind. But life was already over for the residents of Merrill Place. With the exception of a few card games, everywhere Tyler looked people were waiting for death. Today might be an exception for Virginia Hutcheson. Her daughter was coming and the nurse had backed off on her medication.

Which was more than Tyler could say for himself. He was going through the pain pills faster than before. Almost ready for another bottle. They were all he had to look forward to.

He knocked on the door. "Ms. Hutcheson?"

"Leave the milk on the porch!" the woman called out. She sounded pleasant.

Tyler was sober for the moment, his shoulder burning through his body, the pain pills waiting for him in the car. He needed to mop Virginia's floor before he could finish up. He opened the door and peeked in. Virginia was sitting straight up in bed, her expression slightly confused. She was thin with unruly white hair.

He gave her a nervous smile. "Hello, ma'am." He pulled the mop into sight. "Is it okay if I clean your floors?"

"What's this?" Gradually the woman's expression began to soften. "I can't believe it!" Her eyes grew soft and shiny and a smile lifted her wrinkled face. "Ben!" She put her hands to her cheeks, clearly shocked in the best possible way. "Ben, come here! I've been looking for you!"

Tyler looked behind him into the empty hall. Had someone told her his name was Ben? He entered the room with the mop

189

and bucket. "I wanted to clean your floors the other day, but you were asleep." He hesitated at the foot of her bed. "I didn't want to wake you."

Virginia waved off the possibility. "You never have to worry about waking me. You know better than that." There was an empty chair beside her bed. "Please, sit down. We need to catch up."

Merrill Place had several patients battling dementia or Alzheimer's. Tyler knew that. But so far he hadn't run into anything like this. She didn't seem to have his name wrong. It was like she thought he was someone altogether different. Tyler checked the clock on Virginia's wall. Six p.m. His hands shook. He hadn't had a pain pill since noon.

"Please, Ben! Have a seat." She pointed to the chair. "I have so much to tell you."

Clearly she hadn't noticed his name badge. Tyler tucked it into his shirt so she wouldn't be confused. He could spend a few minutes with her. Other than the volunteer at Hope Community Church, Virginia was the first person in weeks who actually wanted to talk to him.

Besides, he was getting paid by the day, not the hour. He set the mop against the floor, removed his Jackson High baseball cap, and tentatively took the seat beside her.

"Ben, my boy." Virginia shook her head, her smile taking up her whole face. "Look at you, all grown up. Sometimes I can't believe it's 1972. Where do the years go?"

Tyler wasn't sure what to say. Suddenly he felt awkward, sitting there pretending to be someone he wasn't. But his very presence made the woman so happy, what else could he do?

Virginia leaned back against her headboard, obviously more relaxed than she had been a minute ago. "I was talking to your father the other day, and he couldn't stop gushing about you." She raised her eyebrows at him. "You believe that, right?"

"I do, yes, ma'am." Tyler could play along. For a few minutes anyway.

"Sure, you've had some trouble, but who hasn't?" She tilted her head, the kindest blue eyes he'd ever seen. "You didn't mean any of the things that happened."

Tyler shifted in his seat. Maybe she recognized him after all. "No, I didn't mean them."

"It was just a car." She uttered a rusty laugh. "You were distracted. No one was hurt."

"No, ma'am."

"Here's the truth." She looked intently at

191

him, straight through him. "Your father and I forgave you that same day, Ben." A few seconds passed and she smiled. "If God can forgive me, then we can forgive you. We love you. Love always forgives."

"Yes." Tyler's heart ached for the woman. Her memory might be shot, but her recollection of times past was whole and complete.

Virginia drew a deep breath. Her increasing peace filled the room. "Don't forget that. The part about love and forgiveness. No matter what you ever did, we loved you. We forgave you." Intensity stirred in her tone. "You're our only son, Ben. You're a good boy, you always were." She reached her hand out to him. "The best son any parents ever had."

The reality hit him like a sucker punch.

Virginia Hutcheson thought he was her son. Her only son, Ben. The woman's hand trembled as she reached out to him. "It's wonderful to see you."

"Thank you." Tyler lifted his good hand and clasped her fingers. Her weathered skin felt foreign against his own. This was too weird. What was he doing? He thought about pulling away, but he couldn't hurt her.

How long had it been since he'd held his

own mother's hand? Since he'd been told he was loved?

For a long time she watched him, taking in the sight of him. "Your father should be home in an hour. We're having meatloaf." The softness in her smile seemed to come from the center of her soul. "Your favorite, Ben."

The role-playing was unfamiliar and more than a little awkward. But somehow the conversation was comforting. Again Tyler didn't know what else to do. "I love your meatloaf."

Virginia breathed in through her nose. "Smells delicious." A yawn seemed to catch her off guard. "I think I'll take a nap. Until your father comes home."

"Yes, ma'am." Tyler still had his fingers around hers. "You do that."

Already her eyes were closed. Gradually she released her hold on him and her hand fell gently to the bedspread. Tyler sat back in his chair, struck by what had just happened. Who was this sweet woman, and where was Ben? Why wasn't he here? Whatever the answers, this much was clear: Virginia loved her son.

Loved him unconditionally, whatever mistakes he'd made.

Tyler took quiet steps back to the mop,

pushing through the pain. Talking to Virginia, he had forgotten how much he hurt. Now he couldn't wait to get to the car. Without making a sound he cleaned the elderly woman's floor, glancing at her every few seconds. When he finished and left the room, she was sound asleep, the smile still on her face.

He returned the mop and bucket to the supply closet and checked out with Mr. Myers. He went to his car and pulled the pain medication from his glove box. Half a bottle left. He had no more refills, but he had a plan for when they ran out.

He would take his first check in a couple days and go to urgent care. He'd explain about his shoulder and get a refillable prescription for Oxycodone. There were four urgent care centers in Pensacola. That should keep him medicated for a while.

He wanted four pills, but he downed three of them. They needed to last until he got paid. He closed his eyes and leaned his head back. He desperately needed relief but didn't want to feel the buzz of the medication just yet. His time with Virginia was still too fresh in his heart, the feelings something he wanted to hold onto. She thought he was her son.

And for a moment he felt like he actually was.

Tyler couldn't remember the last time his parents told him they loved him.

His father had tried to reach him just once after he left for the minor leagues. It was his third season in Dayton, just after the moped accident. When he saw his father's name on Caller ID he thought about answering it. But he couldn't handle the lecture that would certainly follow. How Tyler was an idiot to choose the Reds over college, a fool to drink and drive. On and on and on.

That same week ESPN ran a story — a small story because that's all he was by then. The headline read: *Tyler Ames Proving Critics Right.* It talked about how he should've stayed in school.

After reading the article, Tyler had called his cell phone carrier. "I need to change my number." It took five minutes before he was officially cut off from his parents.

The memory screamed at him the way it always did when he let himself go back. He hadn't really thought he'd never talk to his parents again. Someday he'd call them. On his terms. When things were going well and he could be sure he'd hear approval in his father's voice.

If Tyler had been able to finish the game

that Saturday with the Blue Wahoos, if he hadn't gotten hurt, his first phone call that night would've been to his parents. He had been clean for nearly two years, away from alcohol and bars and fan girls. He'd been doing his best pitching since leaving home. A perfect game and an invitation to Cincinnati to play for the Reds? That would have been just the reason to call. What could his father say except that Tyler had made the right decision? He hadn't needed UCLA after all.

All before that single freak pitch.

The call to his parents never happened, of course. Tyler could only imagine the things his father thought about him now. The man clearly hadn't gone to the same school of faith as Virginia Hutcheson. No forgiveness for Tyler Ames — and for good reason. He was a mess. No question.

The job was the break he needed to turn things around.

He would have to work like never before to make things right, to get back on the mound. Back to a chance at the Bigs.

Then — and only then — would he call home.

Harrison had a problem.

He'd watched Tyler Ames all week, seen

him arrive early and stay late, using his one good arm to clean every floor in the building and sometimes the walls and windows for good measure. He was one of the best workers Harrison had ever hired.

But simply put, the kid reeked like a sewer.

Maybe it was his tired-looking brace or his clothes. Something definitely smelled. Yesterday Harrison could've sworn Tyler had worn a Billings Bulldogs T-shirt to work, second day in a row. The shirt had a small ketchup stain near the middle. Something that should've easily washed off. This morning when Tyler reported for work he wore the same shirt. The stain hadn't been touched.

And so while Tyler started working, Harrison sat at his desk and came up with a theory. The young man must've been dead broke. He had asked about eating leftover food in the cafeteria, and Harrison wasn't sure the kid was showering. The reality ripped at Harrison's heart.

Tyler didn't seem to have anyone.

He calculated the days the kid had worked and wrote him a check for $200. Then he ripped it up. How could he expect the kid to stay with the job if he only paid him $40 a day? He worked harder than that. Instead he wrote the check for $250. When Tyler walked by the office with the mop, Harrison called him over.

The kid looked worried. He entered the office and stood, waiting.

"Two things." Harrison rose from his chair so they were face-to-face. "First, you're doing a good job, Tyler. We needed someone like you."

Relief flooded his eyes. "Thank you, sir. I . . . I really need the work."

"Yes." Harrison nodded. "And second, you deserve a raise." He handed him the check. "This is for your first five days. After this you'll get paid every other week."

Tyler's hand shook as he took the check. "This . . . this is great, sir. Thank you."

"You're welcome." Harrison wasn't quite sure how to approach this next thing. He decided the simpler the better. "By the way. You didn't give your address on your application." He hesitated. "Do you have a place to live?"

At first the kid opened his mouth as if he might come up with an explanation. But after a few seconds his eyes found a spot near his feet. "No, sir. Not for a few weeks now."

"I thought so." Harrison dug around in the top drawer of his desk. He found a small ring of keys. "There's a room at the back of

the building. Caretaker unit. Small place —
just a bed and a chair. A bathroom. Small
kitchen."

"Thank you, but I" — Tyler shook his
head — "I couldn't afford it, sir. I'm fine.
Really. I can just —"

"Tyler." Harrison stared at the young
man. "No charge. Just keep doing a good
job around here. As long as you work here,
you can have the room. It's yours."

Tyler took the keys. He started to say
something and stopped. His eyes moved
from the keys to Harrison and back again.
Finally he managed a quiet, "Thank you.
I . . . don't know what to say."

"Turn it around, son. You've got a start,
now just turn it around."

Tyler nodded. "Yes, sir." He looked over
his shoulder. "I'll get back to work."

Something unfamiliar stirred in Harrison's heart as he sat back down at his
desk. Something new and fresh, that had
come as a direct result of helping Tyler
Ames. It took five minutes before he recognized what it was.

A sense of purpose.

Tyler needed a few minutes, a chance to
grasp what had just happened. He slipped
into the restroom just off the lobby and

locked himself in a stall. He leaned against the door, his heart pounding. Was Mr. Myers serious? Through absolutely no effort of his own Tyler now had a place to live? He closed his eyes and covered his face with his good hand.

So many things he had taken for granted were possible again. He could take a shower and go to the Laundromat and wash his clothes. He could buy milk and chicken at the store and he could sleep lying down. On his back. Like a regular person.

Tyler breathed in deep. He would take his check to the bank, open a new account, and start life over. The evening would be spent washing his clothes and his brace and then he'd stop at a market. Not the Publix where everyone knew him. Somewhere at the other end of town. He'd move out of his car and into the apartment out back.

He was going to be a winner yet.

Tyler finished up the hallway, thinking about the turn of events, the way he didn't deserve any of them. His shoulder hurt and he was dying for a few pain pills. But as he left work that day he was high on something more than Oxycodone. He was high on hope.

He could practically feel the ball in his hand again.

15

It was the third Saturday in September and Cheryl couldn't put off the phone call another moment. The grandchildren were coming over this evening, and before that she was going to Merrill Place to visit her mother. But yesterday in the mail she'd gotten an official notice.

The most serious bit of news since her mother's decline.

Cheryl had felt nervous from the moment she saw the Merrill Place envelope. The letter was from Harrison Myers. Cheryl's hands grew clammy as she opened it and quickly read:

Dear Ms. Conley,

I've been meaning to give you official notice about your mother, Virginia. This isn't a letter I ever want to write. But it's my job to inform you that if we find your mother trying to escape, or if we are forced to continue medicating her in order to keep her behavior under control, Merrill Place will no longer be an option for her housing needs. As you know, there are other facilities in Destin with more stringent safety controls.

Cheryl had lowered the letter and caught her breath. She couldn't move her mother to Destin. They would hardly ever see her. Either that or she'd have to give up time with her granddaughters. Neither option was something Cheryl wanted. She read the rest of the letter.

Since Alzheimer's is a progressive disease, I encourage you to look into those options. Please feel free to contact me if you have questions about this notice, or look me up next time you come in. I'd be happy to talk about this. Again, I'm sorry, but this letter is necessary. Your mother's contract says we must notify you in writing if it appears a move might be imminent.

Sincerely,
Harrison Myers

The letter was in the kitchen drawer now, in a pile of things that needed her attention.

This issue was easily first on the list. Chuck was at the grocery store getting spaghetti ingredients for tonight. The girls' favorite. It was their turn to babysit again — a highlight of the week for both Cheryl and Chuck.

But before she could think about that, she had to think about her mother's situation. She dialed the number for the center in Destin. The operator connected her with a serious-sounding young woman. "Yes. We've spoken to Mr. Myers at Merrill Place. Your mother would be welcome here." She paused. "Let me tell you a little about our facility."

Facility? Is that what this has come to, Lord?

The word turned Cheryl's stomach. She found paper and a pen and started taking notes. Thirty minutes later when the call ended she felt utterly defeated. She looked over what she'd written. Yes, they had a room reserved for Virginia Hutcheson — though they couldn't guarantee it without a deposit. Yes, patients at the Destin facility were often combative and hysterical. Cheryl's mother would fit right in. There were locks on the doors to each bedroom — on the outside. Locks also secured the windows and of course the main entrance.

Tie-downs were a part of every bed. Used only when necessary.

Cheryl wondered if she would survive what lay ahead. Her mother had been the most beautiful, active woman any of them ever knew.

Her mother was funny and animated, quick-witted and kind. She set a high bar for Cheryl and her brother, Ben, but gave more than enough understanding and forgiveness when either fell short. Her knees must've been calloused from how often she prayed. When Cheryl was little she was pretty sure her mother was the most fun-loving woman in all the world. She and their dad would dance in the kitchen and kiss on the couch when they thought Cheryl and Ben weren't watching.

How could she even think about sending her mom to a facility with bed tie-downs? There was only one way to handle the despair spreading through Cheryl's heart. She kept her eyes open, the sky a pure and perfect reminder of the God they served. The One who had not abandoned them even here on a day like this.

Father, we need a miracle for my mom. She's not going gently into Your arms the way we had always expected. Please, fill her heart with peace. Help her remember me and You and Ben . . . all that matters to her.

My daughter, do not be afraid. I go before

you always. The gentle whisper came on the breeze and filled her soul. As if God Himself was speaking to her through the confusion of all that lay ahead. God would go before her. Even if she had to remind herself of that truth every few minutes in the hours ahead.

The words soothed her anxious spirit and gave her strength. Strength to move into an unknown future and drive to Merrill Place today and talk to the mother who no longer knew her name. Strength to talk to Harrison Myers about his letter and the facility in Destin. And something she could never have done on her own.

Strength to consider the impossible.

Two hours later Cheryl's first stop was at Harrison Myers's office. He needed to know she took the letter seriously. The man was in the lobby helping one of the elderly residents to a seat.

"You can wait right here." He made sure the man was secure. "How's that sound?"

"The bus picks up here? You're sure?" The older gentleman looked uncertain, lost to a time gone by.

Cheryl walked in without making too much noise. She took a spot several feet away and watched. Whenever Harrison Myers left this place, there would be no write-up in the paper, no parade or mention on the Internet. But the man was a hero. Cheryl was sure of that. The problems she faced now were not his fault.

Harrison was convincing the man that the bus indeed picked up at that exact spot. A tentative peace settled in along the old man's shoulders. "Good." He nodded, his eyes distant. "I need to see my fiancée. I take the bus every Saturday."

"I tell you what." Harrison reached for a copy of one of the large-print Bibles available in every common space at Merrill Place. Harrison flipped the pages. "How about you read the book of Philippians? That's a good one."

"Yes!" The man took the Bible, suddenly more alert. Eager, almost. "I love Philippians. My grandson loves it, too."

"Perfect." Harrison took a few steps back, making sure the man's mind was settled. He spotted Cheryl and gave her a sad smile. He pointed to his office, and the two of them moved together through the lobby.

"That was very kind, the way you were with him." Cheryl looked over her right shoulder at the gentleman. He was leaning back in the sofa, reading the Bible.

"As long as I work here I'll never get used

to seeing people slowly lose their minds." Harrison pressed his lips together. "Usually all they need is someone to go along with them. If Elmer out there wants to think he's waiting for the bus to take him to see his fiancée, so be it." He glanced at the man, then back at Cheryl. "Soon enough he'll get hungry and shuffle off to dinner with everyone else." He folded his hands on the desk. "Crisis averted."

"One minute he was headed out to see his fiancée, and the next he's talking about his grandson." Cheryl set her purse down and settled into the chair. "Like yesterday is constantly stealing them away."

"Hmmm. Exactly." He reached behind him and pulled out what looked like her mother's file. "I assume you received the letter?"

"I did." Tears tried to come, but Cheryl refused them. "The place in Destin . . . It's very . . . different from this."

"It is." He looked through the chart for a moment. Then he raised his brows. "One bit of good news. Your mother's nurse said she hasn't needed as much medication. She hasn't tried to escape, either."

A single ray of hope shone through the darkness of tomorrow. "That's wonderful."

"Yes." Harrison frowned. "Unfortunately

the decline with Alzheimer's can be streaky. Sharp turn for the worse, which can last weeks or months. And then something can level it out or cause a patient to actually do better." He sighed. "If only we could bottle up whatever that is."

Cheryl understood. "She could get worse again. That's what you're saying."

"Right. Which is why we need an action plan. Not if that happens" — sadness marked his expression — "but when."

"We have a plan. The facility in Destin will take her." Cheryl picked up her purse again. "We'd like to wait as long as possible. Especially if she's doing better for now."

"That's fine."

Cheryl stood. "I think I'll go see her."

Harrison saw her to the office door. "She's a dear woman. One of my favorites." He put his hand on Cheryl's shoulder. "I'll bet she was an amazing mother back in the day."

You have no idea, she thought. Her smile was quick. "She was the best."

Cheryl left before the manager could see her tears. Time was a thief, no question. How in the world had the years brought her mother here? She reached the hallway outside her mother's room and ran her fingers across her cheeks. A few seconds to compose herself before she opened the door.

Her mother was sitting up in bed, her hair combed, hands neatly clasped on her turned down bedspread. The difference stopped Cheryl in her tracks. She took another step and closed the door behind her.

"Hello, dear." Her mother spoke first, her eyes as lucid as they'd been forty years ago.

"Hello." Cheryl could feel the promise in her smile. "How are you?"

"Oh, honey, I'm so happy." She pointed to the chair beside her bed. "Come sit for a while." She held her hands to her face. "You just missed Ben. He's been stopping by."

Adrenaline flooded Cheryl's veins. "Ben?"

Kindness eased the lines on her mother's face. "Yes, dear. Your brother, Ben." She angled her head. "I thought maybe you sent him."

"I . . ." Cheryl had to be careful. She didn't want to be the reason her mother took a turn for the worse. "Yes. I'm so glad he came by."

She nodded, clearly content. "Cheryl, what are you doing with your hair? It looks absolutely beautiful."

Nothing could stop her tears now. She pulled a tissue from the bedside table and pressed it discreetly to the corners of her eyes. Her mother remembered her. The beautiful woman who had been her best friend for most of her life remembered who she was. When she could trust her voice, she nodded. "Thank you. It's . . . I have a new girl at the salon."

"Well, tell her she's very talented."

"I will." Cheryl reached for her mother's hand. Without hesitating her mother took hold of her fingers. This moment was a gift from God, borrowed from a time Cheryl had been sure they'd never find again. "You, too, Mom. Your hair is so pretty."

"There's a new shop down the way. They took me there and pampered me." She looked slightly concerned. "I hope it doesn't cost your father too much money. He works so hard for what he makes."

So her memory wasn't perfect. So what? She was here and she was back. Cheryl had her mother again. But what did she mean, she'd spent time with Ben? Cheryl didn't want to ask. But she silently prayed God would reveal the answers — as soon as possible. "So, Mom . . . how have you been?"

"Wonderful." She shifted so she could see Cheryl better. Her look was unwavering. "I kept trying to get to Ben's house, but the guards stopped me." She rolled her eyes sweetly. "They never understand."

"No."

"So I prayed to Jesus. I asked Him to

bring my boy to me because I missed him so much."

Cheryl pressed the tissue to her eyes again.

"And you know the Lord is so good to me, Cheryl. He's so good. That very day he brought Ben here. I didn't have to go anywhere." She looked delighted at the reality. "We've had some lovely talks."

"How . . . often does he come?"

Her mother thought about that. "Seems like just about every day." She smiled. "I think he thought we were mad at him. Your father and I." She shook her head. "He doesn't think that anymore. We talked about the car accident."

"You and Ben?"

"Yes, dear." Her mother laughed, and the sound was like the most beautiful breeze from yesterday. Cheryl would've known her laugh anywhere. "I told you we've been talking every day. Of course we would talk about the accident."

"What did you tell him?"

"I told him we forgave him a long time ago." She sighed, her smile working its way from inside her heart out. "It's been three years, after all. He's twenty-three now, Ben. He needs to know we never held anything against him. We love him. Love always forgives."

"You always told us that." Cheryl searched her mother's eyes. She looked as well as she ever had.

"I have to tell you something, Cheryl." Her mom was still holding Cheryl's hand and now she patted it with her other one.

She waited. The joy of hearing her mother say her name was the greatest gift she could imagine.

"I was thinking the other day." She looked toward the window for a few seconds and then back at Cheryl. "I don't think I tell you often enough how much I love you. How much you mean to me." Her tender smile made her look half her age. "You've been such a special daughter, Cheryl. Every day I celebrate God's gift of you."

The tears came harder. Cheryl held the tissue in place beneath one eye and then the other. She smiled, waiting for her voice to cooperate. "And you've been the best mother." She worked to keep her voice even. "I was just thanking God for you today. How fun you always made every day. Especially the weekends at the lake."

"We need to go again." She jabbed her pointer finger in the air. "Maybe this weekend. I'll talk to your father. Ben and I were just chatting about our beautiful days at the lake."

Whatever dream or delusion her mother had experienced in regard to Ben, Cheryl could only be grateful. "That sounds lovely, Mom. This weekend would be perfect."

Her mother looked tired, as if the beautiful conversation had filled her heart with enough peace so she could rest. "I might take a nap, dear. Is that okay?" Her mother leaned forward and kissed the back of Cheryl's hand. "Thank you for talking with me. We'll have dinner in a few hours. Right after your father gets home."

Cheryl nodded as she used the tissue again. "I'll be there."

Her mother fell asleep easily and not until Cheryl was back out in the hallway did she let the tears come unabated. She thought about heading straight for Harrison Myers's office and telling him what had just happened. But as she reached the entryway, his office was empty.

Just as well.

She didn't want anything to interfere with the beauty of the moment God had just given her. The woman in the bed was no longer a stranger inhabiting her mother's body. She knew Cheryl's name and Ben's name and she couldn't wait to talk to their father. Never mind that she had her decades off by five or so. The woman was her mom, through and through. Maybe next weekend Chuck and the granddaughters could come to visit her.

They hadn't shared a meaningful family visit in years.

The only part that baffled Cheryl as she drove home that afternoon was the part about Ben. If Ben could've gotten there to see their mother, he would've. But Cheryl knew that wasn't the case. There was no logic in the certainty her mother felt about spending time with Ben. But this much was true: the imaginary visits with Cheryl's brother had turned things around. There could be no other answer.

It was the miracle Cheryl had prayed for.

She could hardly wait for their next visit.

16

Running was the antidote. Marcus Dillinger pounded up the bleachers at Dodger Stadium early on the last Saturday of September and tried not to think about yesterday's news. But it wasn't easy.

Conditioning, he told himself. *Think about that.* It took a few seconds, but pretty soon the image of his teammate's drug-ridden body being carted out of his apartment yesterday faded. In its place he pictured himself, his routine. His game.

Staying fit wasn't something Marcus thought about at this point in his career. Every morning he slipped on his workout shoes before his eyes fully opened. He never asked himself if he felt like getting up early and running stairs or lifting weights or working with his pitching coach. Like the famous Nike motto, he just did it.

He kept his eyes on the stairs, his pace intense. *Why'd you do it, Baldy?* His teammate had been a pitcher, a ten-year veteran trying to get his speed back. Still one of the best relievers in the major leagues. *Drugs, man? How could you? You were on top of the world, Baldy. Top of the world.*

Marcus doubled his intensity. First time around he hit every step. Second time, every other. When he reached the top he didn't hesitate before flying back down the next aisle. At the end of the aisle he jogged onto the field over to the mound and stopped just long enough to stare down an imaginary opponent. Then Marcus turned and sprinted for the stairs again.

He kept running. They were well into the playoffs now and everyone said this might be the year they won the whole thing. World Series Champions. The LA media couldn't contain their excitement over the possibility that a kid who played in the Little League World Series might soon be playing in the MLB World Series.

Something that had never been done.

By then maybe they'd stop talking about Bob "Baldy" Williams.

Marcus was aware of the enormity of the possibility. He just wished he cared more. Especially now. *Baldy's gone, Marcus. You gotta focus.* He was in his second season pitching for the Dodgers, and everything was going right. The way it always had for Marcus. From the time he was a little kid back in Simi Valley, California, back when he and Tyler Ames dominated the baseball scene. Marcus reached the top of the stadium and allowed himself ten seconds. The view was beautiful this time of the morning. Before the smog rolled in and made the mountains hazy.

Back down the steps, a thought occurred to Marcus. What had happened to Tyler Ames? His Little League buddy was a perfect distraction. They hadn't talked since high school. Tyler had chosen the minors over college — and at the time Marcus was a little jealous. Who wanted to balance chemistry and history with practice and conditioning? He figured his childhood friend would beat him to the pros easy.

But something must've sidetracked him. Marcus wasn't sure. He'd tweeted Tyler once — something about a moped accident. But for the most part Marcus had been so busy keeping up with his own career he hadn't even Googled the guy. Tyler wasn't pitching in the MLB. Marcus would've heard about him. He reached the bottom, ran out to the mound, paused in the direction of home plate, and shot straight back up the stadium stairs.

The thing was, Baldy made a million dollars a year pitching relief. A handful of innings every few days and he was set for life. He had a condo on the beach, a sports car, and any girl he wanted. His last girlfriend was a famous actress, got his picture plastered all over the magazines. Sure, he wasn't the powerhouse he'd been ten years ago, but he was thirty-five. Forever thirty-five.

Marcus reached the top and allowed fifteen seconds this time. What was the point? Work from the time you're four years old to get the dream: pro baseball. Then wash it all away on drugs. He stretched to the side one way and then the other. Then back down the steps toward the field.

Drugs had never been his thing. Marcus made $5 million a year plus endorsements. He was the spokesman for a national tire company and Dodge trucks along with a handful of vitamin firms and protein powder giants. He took care of his body every way possible — something his father had instilled in him. Drinking and drugs had been around since high school, but Marcus had always passed. Always felt good about himself for being one of the clean players.

But nothing had felt right since he'd heard the news about Baldy.

Because for all of his clean living, Marcus

hadn't made an impact on the guy, hadn't persuaded him to straighten up his act, had never asked him about his demons. Hadn't really done more than talk surface with the guy for two years straight. The question slamming around in Marcus's head like an errant pinball was this:

What did it all matter?

The money and success, the Maserati he drove to work, and the mansion on the hill in Malibu. The couple of SUVs in his garage. If it couldn't save a guy like Baldy Williams, what did it matter?

The crazy thing was his accountant had called ten minutes after Marcus heard the news. "Got a real estate deal for you." The man sounded proud of himself. "You're going to love this. Ten percent cap rate with a 40 percent return on investment. Just your kind of project."

Marcus pretended to lose the call. He still hadn't called the guy back.

Another investment wasn't the answer, the way to find meaning in this crazy pro athlete life. Marcus reached the field, ran out to the pitcher's mound, and stopped. His chest heaved, his heartbeat racing. This very spot. That's where Baldy stood just four days ago and struck out the last batter to win the game. *What happened? Were you still cel-*

ebrating, man? You should've hung out with me that night.

He had to think about something else. Back up the stadium stairs. Investments. That's what his accountant wanted him to think about. But maybe it was time to start making investments in people. Disadvantaged teens or a local reading program. Sick kids at the children's hospital. Baldy's life was over. Too late for redemption or meaning or any legacy other than sad headlines. Baldy Williams overdosed at thirty-five.

So what about his own legacy? Sure, Marcus might live to be a hundred the way he took care of his body, but for what? He was between girlfriends — models and singers, a few actresses. He wouldn't have considered spending his life with any of them.

This time at the top of the stadium he did ten squats and then took thirty seconds. Sweat streamed down the side of his face. Half a minute to remember how to breathe again. He stared at the blue sky and let the breeze dry his sweat. Nothing like September in Los Angeles. Today was gorgeous. *You're missing it, Baldy. Missing all of it.*

On the way back down darker thoughts hit him, the ones that seemed to blindside him every hour or so since yesterday's news. Where was Baldy Williams now? Like, really? Where? Were heaven and hell actual places?

He reached the field and tried to catch his breath. The idea of heaven or hell made him sick to his stomach. *Think about something else, Marcus. Forget about it. Baldy's gone. He's nowhere. He'll be in the ground. That's it.*

Suddenly out of nowhere a breeze kicked up and swirled dirt around the pitcher's mound. It formed a mini whirlwind before it dissipated somewhere near first base.

Marcus felt his heart rate pick up speed. What was that? The dirt looked like a finger. The finger of God? Was God Himself hearing his thoughts about the afterlife? Was that even possible?

He knew of God. Everyone knew of Him. Every Christmas there was talk about Jesus coming as a baby to save the world. Every Easter, the story of Jesus dying on the cross and rising to life. So that people would have the choice of heaven. Marcus had never given any of it much thought. Most people in Los Angeles didn't really talk about God — not like He was real, anyway. Life was busy, freeways were packed. The pace was intense.

When would there be time to think about God?

221

But Baldy's death had backed Marcus into a corner, a place where he had to think about what had never crossed his mind a few days ago. Heaven or hell? Here, from the pinnacle of his baseball career, he could only wonder. If the money and power and fame held no meaning, then what did? Was God real? All this time was He really here, interacting with people?

Marcus paced a few steps one way and then back again. His stomach was in cramps, tight and uneasy — like his heart. Thinking about Baldy and heaven and hell made him wish for the early days. Back when he first went to Oregon State. The campus life and the year in the minors. Back when there was still something to strive for. When life wasn't so serious.

Marcus grabbed his water bottle from the first step and downed half of it.

"Okay." He lifted his eyes to the sky again. He was still catching his breath. "If You're there . . . show me. Give me a reason to believe." He thought about his desire to invest in people, to make a difference. "If You're real . . . give me meaning. How's that?"

The breeze swirled around him again, but this time it didn't stir up the dirt. A chill ran down his arms. The field at Dodger

Stadium was one of the finest in the MLB. The dirt never did that. The groundskeeper saw to it. So what was this?

Be still, My son, and know that I am God . . .

Marcus felt his knees go weak. He sat down on the nearest step and held tight to the metal edge. "Who's there?" He asked the question out loud, and even as he did he felt like a crazy person. This was ridiculous. He glanced behind him and around the stadium walls. It was only seven in the morning. No one else was here. The voice had to have come from his imagination. He stood, collected his water and workout bag, and jogged up the steps to the concourse level.

Five minutes later he was in his car, ready for the next stage of his conditioning — weight training on the other side of the stadium. The voice haunted him. He was uneasy, that's all. Baldy's death had done this. He was overthinking his teammate's death. That's all.

Marcus thought about what he'd asked God. He still wanted a sign. A purpose for his life. If God existed, the matter was up to Him now. Still, as he headed into the weight room one question consumed him. If he died today, and if there really was something beyond the living and dying, beyond the

winning and losing of life, where would
Marcus Dillinger wind up?

Heaven or hell?

17

On the first day of October — while MLB players were heading into the second round of playoffs — Tyler woke up in his new room surrounded by his new life with one realization: the Oxycodone was becoming a problem.

With his first paycheck Tyler had gone to the local urgent care and gotten another prescription, but the doctor gave him a warning. He couldn't prescribe more unless Tyler saw an orthopedic specialist. "Pain meds are not a solution. They are a bridge, to get you from injury to recovery. If you're not working on the recovery, I can't prescribe more pain medication."

Tyler wanted to ask what he was supposed to do if recovery wasn't in sight. He had even called a hotline number for a national insurance program. But after an hour on hold he had received an explanation why his surgery couldn't be covered.

"We help people who are sick," the woman told him. "Sports-related injuries are something else — a risk you take when you play the game."

Nice, Tyler thought as he hung up. Now he was down to a final dose of pain pills. Two white tablets. He had been on the medication far too long.

The reason he knew he had a problem was this: an hour before his dose wore off, his body started shaking. His legs and arms and torso would tremble, almost like winter had landed on him all at once, and then sweat would break out across his forehead and back. Every day the shaking and sweating grew worse.

Tyler rolled onto his back and stared at the ceiling. It was just after eight in the morning. He didn't need to start work until nine. So what was he supposed to do with his time? He'd already cleaned his apartment. He was good at working with one hand now — even when his pain was at its worst.

But after a few weeks of living like this he was beginning to feel stuck. Tyler was glad for the job, grateful for the pay. The job didn't come with benefits, so at $50 a day at an hourly wage, it would take two years to save enough for his surgery. That was if he saved almost every penny.

By then his shoulder would be permanently ruined. Even now he wondered whether it was healing incorrectly. He needed a second job, another way to make money — even if that meant working through the night. In the meantime, he needed to train. He hadn't been back to the YMCA since the day he was hired at Merrill Place. His legs weren't damaged. What excuse did he have for not working them out at least? He hadn't done cardio exercise or squats or anything other than wash floors.

How could he expect to pitch for the majors one day if he didn't start his comeback now? Today? All his life he'd been putting the important things on hold. First his parents. Then Sami. Now this, his chance at a comeback. Determination grew and swelled inside him. He wasn't going to let anything stop him this time.

He looked at the clock again. His next dose of pain medication was due in ten minutes. If he didn't take it, by nine the meltdown would kick in. Signs that he needed the drug — and not just for the aching, burning pain in his shoulder. He needed it the way he needed food and water. Oxycodone had become part of his survival.

Calm down, Tyler told himself. *Relax.* His

mouth was dry, his breathing fast and erratic. Here they were — the symptoms that came around every three hours. Sweat broke out on his brow. He held his good hand in front of him and watched the shakes kick in. He felt sick to his stomach. The symptoms came like clockwork.

He slowed his breathing, willed peace into his heart and soul. If he was going to begin his comeback, the first thing he had to do was get off the pain pills. No matter what his body said about the consequences. He thought about the two lone pills sitting in the bottle by his bed. He would wait and take them tonight — since sleeping through the pain was the hardest part. And that would be that. No more trips to urgent care. No plotting for another bottle of pills.

Two more and he'd be done. For good.

The shakes and sweats and nausea would stop after a day or so, right? His forehead would eventually be dry again and he could move on. As he climbed out of bed that day, Tyler believed it with all his heart. He stretched his left arm over his head and winced at the pain even that caused in his opposite shoulder.

He had learned to make eggs with one hand, but he still wasn't good at pouring a bowl of cereal and covering it with milk.

Especially with his trembling fingers. He took the bowl to the small table and opened the laptop. It had been in the room, and when Tyler asked Mr. Myers about it, the man told him to use it.

"We have protected Wi-Fi through the building," his manager told him. "Keep it clean."

The man didn't need to worry. Tyler had dabbled in the dark side of internet life. But he felt disgusted with himself and swore off it more than two years ago. Now he took his bowl of cereal and moved to the end of the table where the computer sat open and ready.

He signed on and went to MLB.com. Ten minutes of reading about the playoffs and the home-run leaders, the best pitchers and the fastest pitches, and Tyler was ready to throw the computer across the room. Everyone was getting ahead of him. That's how the website made him feel. If he was going to make a comeback, he had to stop looking in at the majors. But before he moved on he looked up Marcus Dillinger. What he saw made him smile. His boyhood friend was killing it with the Dodgers.

Just as he went to change websites, something caught his eye. A headline about a service for Baldy Williams. Tyler leaned closer to the screen. The air in the room felt instantly thinner. Baldy Williams had died? How come he hadn't seen that? He clicked the story and raced through it. Apparently the pitcher had been found in his home. Overdosed on heroin.

Back in high school, Tyler looked up to only a handful of pitchers. Guys with speed and finesse and longevity. Baldy Williams had been one of those. Tyler stared at the story, baffled. When had the guy started taking drugs? He read further down and the answer hit him in the face like an errant baseball.

Williams became addicted to pain medication after a hip injury last year. Friends say he turned to heroin a few months later. When the pills stopped working.

Nausea slammed Tyler around until he felt like he might fall from the chair. Pain medication? Tyler knew lots of guys who existed on a pain pill now and then. A few of them had to take a season off to get clean. But heroin? Could an addiction to Oxycodone really lead to heroin?

His hands shook as he closed out of the site. Too bad about Baldy, really. But the news couldn't have come at a better time. If Tyler wanted a clean start, if he really was finished with taking pain pills, then this was

230

the day. Sweat dripped down his back beneath his T-shirt. Today, before his need for them got any stronger. His teeth chattered, his body trembling head to foot. Today, before he might even consider something as deadly as heroin. Every muscle in his body ached. He was dying for a couple pills.

But he wouldn't touch them. He couldn't.

He took a few bites of his cereal, but the nausea was too much. *Think about something else,* he told himself. *You gotta get past this.* He coursed through ESPN. But even as he surfed through one page and then another, his mind wandered to the only real distraction that could take the edge off his pain.

Sami Dawson.

Hers would've been the second phone call — right after his parents. He had promised her he'd make it in the Bigs, promised he'd prove everyone wrong. She had certainly forgotten those promises years ago. But where was she now? Still in Los Angeles? Still living with her grandparents?

Funny, both Sami and he had grown up with absolutes. She absolutely had to be perfect at life. And he absolutely had to be perfect at baseball. So had she found her perfection? With the internet at his fingers, Tyler suddenly had to know. He wiped the sweat from his forehead and started with Facebook. They'd been friends since high school. But Tyler hadn't checked her page in years.

He signed in and watched his old page come up. No one had shut it down, even though he hadn't upgraded to the new format or signed in over the last couple years. His last post was dated more than two years ago. A few weeks before he moved to Pensacola.

The comments didn't interest him. Instead, he typed "Samantha Dawson" in the search line. Her page came up, and like that, he had all the information he wanted. She lived in Los Angeles, worked at a big marketing firm, shared an apartment with a roommate, and she was in a relationship with some lawyer named Arnie Bell.

There was only one thing Tyler couldn't tell — whether Sami remembered him. The time on the computer read 8:25. Sweat dripped down the side of his face. He wiped it with his forearm. He took three quick bites of his cereal and noticed his fingers. They were trembling so badly he looked like he was having a seizure. His legs were the same way, his knees knocking together. He needed the pills. His body wasn't going down without a fight.

Tyler clenched his teeth. He wasn't giving in. Not this time.

Sami. He needed to focus on her.

He absently massaged his injured shoulder as he stared at her profile pic. She still looked like Keira Knightley. Beautiful eyes, striking cheekbones. But there was something different about her this many years later. She looked more . . . serious, maybe. More like a Samantha. He studied her, trying to see past the smile to her eyes. Her real eyes. Who was she today, the girl he used to know?

Now she was working a serious job, dating a lawyer, and living on her own. None of that reminded him of the girl clutching his arm on her grandparents' roof that summer in San Francisco. He felt his heart respond. *What happened to you, Sami? Where's the girl who wanted adventure? Did they catch you and change you? Are you like them now?*

Tyler breathed in sharp through his nose. There was only one way to find out. He had nothing to offer her, less than before he left Simi Valley. That wasn't the point. She was apparently happy in her relationship. He only wanted to see how she was. Sami had been his friend back then as he had been hers. Wasn't that the point of Facebook?

233

Connecting with friends?

He opened a private message screen and stared at it. The only reason to write her was so he could know. Had she changed — the way it looked like she had? Or was the Sami he had known and loved still living somewhere in her heart? He poised one hand over the keyboard and began plucking away at the letters.

Hey Sami, this is Tyler. It's been a long time.

His shoulder was killing him. He paused long enough to massage his aching arm. His hands shook as he returned to the task. His fingers barely stayed on the keys.

I haven't been on Facebook for a few years, but I found you here this morning and I wanted to say hello. Looks like you're doing well.

He read the words over again. How was he supposed to end a letter like this? The last time they talked they'd been fighting over the phone, over his drunken arrest.

He took a few more bites of his cereal and started typing again.

I'm still in Pensacola. Still working toward

the Big Leagues. Oh, and I got sober a few years back. Thought you'd like to know. Anyway, I think about you now and then. Just wanted to stop by. If you have a minute, let me know how you are. Take care. Tyler.

He thought about the sober line. It wasn't really true. He couldn't get through a single hour without the pain pills. He dismissed the thought and sent the message before he could change his mind, and regretted it a moment later. Sami would probably see his name and hit delete before reading it. They hadn't exactly ended things on good terms. The last time he tried to call her she never answered. So . . . yeah, she probably wouldn't be interested in anything he had to say now. But he had to try.

He closed the computer and took a shower. The whole time he wondered if he was going to lose his breakfast. He felt weak and unsteady. His breathing was uneven and he couldn't stop the sweat on his forehead and back. Three times he took steps toward the remaining pain pills, but each time he stopped himself.

By the time he had washed up, brushed his teeth, and dressed — all with his left hand — his body had taken him from freezing blizzard lows to scalding desert heat. Either way he shook. His shirt stuck to his body and he kept the towel close by so he could keep wiping his face. All told, he was a mess.

Mr. Myers would send him back to bed if he reported for work like this. Frustration churned up the cereal in his stomach a little more. Maybe if he did some cardio. He could report half an hour late. His boss only cared that he finished the work. Tyler opened the dishwasher, but bending forward did something to his damaged shoulder — even with the brace.

He cried out and turned around, falling back against the counter. He closed his eyes and breathed in short bursts, working his way through the slicing pain. After fifteen seconds the searing sensation dimmed just enough that he could open his eyes and think again. How was he going to get through the day like this? He needed to get off the medication, of course. But there had to be a better way.

Without hesitating, he took a full cup of water, went to his bedside, grabbed the last pills in the bottle, and washed them down. There. He could at least work now. The pills worked eight hours at a time. Stronger than the ones he'd used right after his injury.

Fifteen minutes later he felt the haze settle in. The sweating stopped, the shakes eased as the Oxycodone dimmed the edges of his existence, giving him permission to breathe and smile and clean the floors at Merrill Place. The pills brought so much relief, Tyler wondered if he was wrong. Maybe this was not the time to give them up. He could always quit them later.

At the end of the day, as always, he stopped by Virginia's room. She was asleep when he walked in, so he cleaned her floor first. His shoulder still hurt with every movement, but he could work past it, talk past it. The pills were that good.

Everything was possible as long as he had the Oxycodone.

He finished her floor just as she woke up. Virginia blinked a few times and then squinted through the sun-filled room. "Ben? Is that you?"

"Hi." He leaned the mop against the closed door. Again he tucked his name badge through the buttons of his work shirt. "How are you?"

"Happy." Virginia slid up in bed and smoothed out her hair. "I'm always happy when you're here. You never should've moved away." She raised hopeful eyebrows. "Can you stay and chat? Just for a few minutes?"

"Definitely." He hugged his sore arm to his body as he moved to the familiar chair. He looked over his shoulder at the window. "Beautiful day."

"You were born on a day like this. Every time God paints a sky this blue I think about the gift you've been to us."

The compliment worked its way to Tyler's heart. The dear woman might have him confused for someone else. But Tyler sometimes wondered if he maybe needed these visits as much as she did. He smiled. "Thank you."

"Remember that" — Virginia winked at him — "when you're out and about and see a blue sky. Remember that you're a gift, Ben. You always will be."

"You, too." He still hadn't called her Mom or Mother. Doing so definitely didn't feel right. She didn't seem to notice. "Can I ask you something?"

"Of course." She reached out, the way she always did.

Tyler took her fingers in his. "Can you . . . pray for me? My shoulder?"

"You know I saw that bike accident coming. I was on the front porch watching you and Cheryl, and I knew . . . I just knew you were riding too fast."

"True." He thought about his final pitch. "Much too fast."

"And there was poor Cheryl." Virginia shook her head, clearly seeing an afternoon from decades ago. "My, how that girl adored you. Soon as you were on the ground she was at your side."

Tyler had figured out that Cheryl was Ben's sister. "I'm sorry you had to see that."

"Glad I did. I grabbed the medical box and ran down the street. Cleaned up your elbow right there on the side of the road. Then me and Cheryl helped you home." Virginia's smile was as kind as he imagined it had been that day. "Your father was proud of me. I'm not usually very good with blood."

He chuckled. "Me, either."

"So yes, of course. I'll pray for your shoulder." She looked at the sling, curious. "Did the doctor give you that?"

"He did."

"Hmmm. Your father must've taken you. I remember the bandages on your forearm, but not your shoulder."

"I need an operation."

Her expression changed and she covered her mouth with her free hand. "That's terrible. I had no idea." She motioned for Tyler to lean closer. "Come here. Let me pray

239

for you now."

Tyler did as he was asked and Virginia took hold of his good shoulder. Her touch was light, her voice intense as she began to talk to God. "Lord, my son is hurt. He needs a miracle. Your healing power is the only thing we have, Father. So please . . . heal my boy. Help him get the surgery he needs. In Jesus' name, amen."

The prayer felt a little strange and Tyler felt like an imposter. But while Virginia prayed a feeling came over him that he'd felt only one other time since he was a kid.

The feeling was perfect peace.

It was the same thing he'd felt when that man at Hope Community Church prayed for him. Beck, the paramedic volunteer. Tyler wasn't sure what to make of the surge of peace, but he would take it. And certainly the Lord — if He was listening — would know Tyler needed the prayers more than Ben. Wherever Ben was.

Tyler slid back to his spot on the chair and gave Virginia's hand a slight squeeze. "Thank you."

"I'll pray every day." She looked and sounded like a woman twenty years younger, completely in her right mind. "When are you having it done?"

"That's just it." He wasn't trying to

confuse her. "I can't pay for it. I'm saving my money."

"For heaven's sake, Ben, call your sister. If you need help, she's the one to tell. Smart girl, that Cheryl. Graduated college top of her class." Virginia squeezed his hand. "Call her."

"Good idea." Tyler smiled. For a few seconds he let an easy silence settle between them. "I have a question."

"Okay." Her eyes smiled and her mouth followed. "I love times like this."

"Me, too." He allowed her happiness a polite moment. Then he felt his smile fade. "Here's the question. If I don't go to college, if I find something else I love better . . . would you . . . be angry with me?"

Surprise came slowly over her face like the sunrise. "Ben Hutcheson, of course not." She looked wounded by the possibility. "Your father and I talk about staying in school, but school is not for everyone. After all, your own father didn't take a stitch of college classwork."

Vindication came over him like the greatest gift. If his parents had been like Virginia, the war between them never would've started. "Really? You're serious?"

"Ben Alan Hutcheson, of course I'm serious." She laughed lightly. "What are you

241

thinking about doing instead?"

"Well . . ." He wondered how old Virginia thought he was. "I'm thinking about baseball."

"Baseball." She looked out the window, her expression almost dreamlike. "I love that game. Someone I know used to play baseball. I can't remember who." She turned to Tyler again. Concern flashed in her eyes. "What about your shoulder? Your surgery?"

"I mean I'd play after . . . after I'm all healed up."

"If anyone can do it, you can." Her smile grew even more tender.

Tyler wasn't sure what to say. He loved how he felt, living someone else's life even for a few moments, imagining what life might've been like if his parents had cared about him like this. The charade was wrong. It had to be. But then, he and Virginia were both benefiting.

The truth kept him here, kept him in the conversation.

"Yes, Ben." Virginia yawned. "I think baseball would be a very nice job. Your father would think so, too." She glanced at the door. "He should be home anytime."

Virginia's spells of wakefulness were never very long. Her eyelids grew heavy. "Must be nap time."

"I was just heading out." He released her fingers and stood. "Thanks for talking."

"Oh, Ben!" She held up her hand. "There is one thing. Before you go."

"Yes?" He would've done anything for the old woman.

"You used to sing worship songs for me and my church friends. Remember that?"

Tyler was quiet.

" 'Amazing Grace' . . . 'How Great Thou Art.' All the old favorites." Virginia nodded toward the door. "I'm expecting a lot of friends tomorrow morning." She thought for a few seconds. "Every morning, really. Anyway, it would be so nice if you could join us with your guitar. Play the old songs the way you used to."

Tyler felt his stomach tighten. "Ummm."

"Now, now." She waved at the air in front of her. "Don't start about how you don't have a good voice. We all love your voice. You know that."

What was he supposed to say? His heart skittered around and slid into a rapid rhythm. "Yes, ma'am. I'll . . . see if I can find the guitar."

"That's a good boy, Ben. Thank you." Virginia smiled again. "These hours with you and Cheryl and your father are my happiest of all." She radiated joy. "Jesus is so good. Giving me a family like you."

The comment stabbed at Tyler's heart — where the pain usually took a second seat to his shoulder injury. Not this time. He nodded. "I feel the same way."

He put away the broom and mop and drove west to an urgent care he hadn't visited before. An hour later he had the pain pills in his hands. If he was going to start training the rest of his body, at least this way he wouldn't have to work through pain. He would quit after this bottle. Really. The shaking had just started when he took the first two pills from the new bottle. *Better than taking three or four,* he told himself. Maybe the medicine would dull the shame he felt over needing Oxycodone. He refused to think about it.

Instead he thought about Virginia.

Was the ruse wrong? Was he unkind to let her believe the lie? Either way it was too late to stop. Virginia had found a son, and not only that.

Tyler had found a mother.

18

Ember and Beck hovered over the downtown Los Angeles Hyatt and talked in hushed tones.

"A battle is taking shape." Beck stared through the windows of the highest floor. "You see it?"

"The dinner party?"

"Yes." Beck felt anxious beside her. "The one about to start."

Ember knew the weight of the situation. They still hadn't figured out a way to get Tyler to California and time was running out.

"The humans in that room have no idea what's at stake." Beck felt the concern in his expression. "I turned up the heat."

"The heat?" Ember loved working with Beck. He was easily the most creative angel on the team. "In the building?"

"In the ballroom." He let his eyes meet Ember's. "You'll go walking. The minute

245

Sami gets too hot."

Ember didn't need to ask whether that would happen. They'd been praying for a breakthrough. If Beck had a plan, something was about to give. Which was a good thing.

They were just about out of time.

The law firm hosted the dinner several times a year. Local conservatives, politicians, and prosecutors. An accomplished crowd for sure, but Sami struggled to stay present. Dinner that Saturday night was on the top floor of the downtown Hyatt. But the room was hot and stuffy and Sami kept looking through the glass walls to the outdoors. Through two double doors was an open-air garden terrace, twenty-two floors off the ground.

Sami wanted to be out there in the worst way.

A trio of violinists played classical music from a corner near the buffet line. Prime rib at a carving station, chilled shrimp, butterflied chicken fillets. Other than the heat, the atmosphere was perfect. Like the guests — at least in her boyfriend's mind. Arnie was talking now, waxing on about the case he'd been given.

"So it turns out the drug they've been prescribing for diabetes actually makes

246

patients gain weight." He looked at the rapt faces of those at their table. A senator and a congressman and their wives, and two other lawyers from the firm. "Weight, of course, exacerbates diabetes. It raises blood sugar all on its own. It's terrible." Arnie held up his pointer finger. "Here's the clincher. I have documentation to prove that the defendants actually know their drug makes diabetes worse. But still they launched into a full marketing campaign to the contrary."

Sami stared out the window again. The sparkle of lights beyond mesmerized her. Like the stars overhead that night on her grandparents' roof with Tyler Ames. Three days had passed since she'd seen his private message. She hadn't answered him, but nothing had felt right since. She suddenly realized she wasn't listening. *Focus,* she ordered herself. *You're being rude.*

"That's terrible." The senator shook his head. "Is this a class-action suit? I mean, I know you're young, Arnie, but talk to your superiors. There's a whole generation of diabetics who need to know about this."

"Exactly." Arnie raised his brow and looked around the room. "Someone needs to turn down the heat." He didn't seem aware that Sami was even there. He smiled at the senator. "But no, this isn't class action. Not yet, anyway. The more information I find, the more damaging it is for the defendants." He sat back, clearly proud of himself. "Let's just say I feel pretty good about a win."

Sami nodded. What were they talking about? Diabetes? She nodded again. *Stay interested, Sami. Stay interested.*

The congressman leaned on his forearms, his eyes intent. "What are the parameters of the case?"

"Clear-cut." Arnie was in his glory. "The plaintiff heard about the drug through the defendants' slick marketing campaign, took it for a year, and watched her weight soar fifty pounds . . ."

Sami couldn't take another moment. "Excuse me." She stood and leaned close to Arnie. "I'll be right back."

"Samantha." Confusion creased his forehead. "We're about to eat."

"I know." She picked up her clutch purse and smiled at the others. "I won't be long."

She wore pretty black pumps and a black Rag and Bone dress for the occasion — Arnie's gift. Her hair was styled in a classic up-do — Arnie's favorite for nights like this. What had he said to her when he picked her up at her apartment? "You look like the wife of a congressman, Samantha. Beautiful and understated. Absolutely perfect."

Understated? Sami walked with practiced poise through the dining room and out into the hall. She didn't need to use the restroom. She needed air. Any means possible of clearing her mind. She quickened her pace and walked to the end of the hall. A door led to the other side of the outdoor garden. From this part of the terrace she was hidden from the dining room.

The moment she was outside she sucked in three quick breaths. Never mind the LA smog. This was the freshest air she'd had in an hour. She walked to the railing and held it with both hands, steadying herself.

Understated, really? The word rattled around in her empty heart. Did Arnie really think that was a compliment? She was twenty-four years old. Wasn't she a little young to be going for understated?

Her grandparents loved Arnie. He wasn't as perfect as they thought he was, but he came pretty close. He had even talked about getting back to church in a few years, after they married and before kids came along. Theirs would be a grounded life, safe and financially secure. No question. They would laugh at their TV shows and play board games on the weekends and pay the mortgage on time. Arnie would be a good father.

Stop, she told herself. What was she think-ing? She loved Arnie. He was kind and good and successful. They had everything in com-mon, right? They loved Italian restaurants and sitting on the beach and playing Scrabble. Of course he was the right one for her. The conversation tonight just felt a little heavy, that's all.

If only there was a way to feign sickness and go home. She and Mary Catherine could watch reruns of *The Cosby Show.* Anything but sharing a dinner table with the people here tonight. She tilted her head back and stared at the sky. Only a few stars were bright enough to compete with the lights of Los Angeles. "God . . . what am I doing?" she whispered. Not a prayer, really. Just that no one else seemed to be listening to her tonight. "How did I wind up in this life?"

Her mind settled down. She focused on taking slow breaths. Everything was going to be okay. She peered into the dark sky and tried to imagine her future with Arnie. As she did she heard the door open behind her. *Great . . . Arnie followed me.* She turned and felt herself relax. It was a woman, someone about Sami's age.

She was striking. Long blond-red hair and bright blue eyes, set off by her bright blue dress. "Beautiful out here." The woman drew a quick breath and took a spot at the railing, a few feet down from Sami.

"Yes. And quiet." Sami looked over her shoulder at the door again. "Were you at the dinner party?"

"Yes." She laughed lightly. "About to fall asleep."

"Me, too. It was hot in there." This was supposed to be a few minutes alone. But Sami liked the woman. She felt almost as if they'd met before. "I'm here with Arnie Bell." Sami hesitated. "Do I know you?"

"Ahh, Arnie Bell." The woman raised one eyebrow. "I know him. Very serious." She held out her hand. "And no. I don't think we've met. I'm Ember."

"Hi. I'm Sami." She smiled. "I like your name."

"Thanks." Ember stared out at the lights of the city. "I just needed to breathe. Needed to feel close to God. Dinner parties make that a little tough."

"Definitely." Sami studied the woman. Something about her was so familiar. "You're here with one of the lawyers?"

"Just as friends." She looked relaxed. "I learned something a long time ago. I'd rather be single than be with the wrong

251

guy." Ember smiled. "Life's too short to settle."

The woman's words seemed to cut straight through her. "You're right . . ." Sami looked back at the city lights. "I hadn't thought about that."

"Hey . . . I need to go." Ember looked at her. "God has good plans for you, Sami."

"For me?" Sami felt a chill pass over her arms and down her spine. "What does that —"

"You know. The Bible verse. Jeremiah 29:11." Ember smiled. "God has great plans for His people." She shrugged, her expression light. "I guess I was just thinking about it."

"Yeah." Sami faced the woman. "Thanks."

Ember waved. "Nice meeting you."

"You, too." Sami watched the woman walk back through the door and down the hall. Then she turned and stared into the dark sky. What a sweet person. Almost as if she had known Sami was out here.

Her words washed over Sami once more.

I'd rather be single than be with the wrong guy . . . Life's too short to settle.

Suddenly, despite the twinkling lights of the city, all Sami could see was Tyler Ames.

She had memorized his Facebook message. He was doing well. Still in Pensacola and working toward the Big Leagues. He'd stopped drinking. He still thought about her.

Every now and then, anyway.

Nothing about the injury or how it had ended his season. Nothing to tell her why he had looked her up now — after so many missed opportunities. Sami heard a plane overhead. She watched it fly east, further away from her. Where was it going? Maybe to Pensacola. It would be that easy, right? Get on a plane and go see for herself. Who was Tyler Ames today?

And how come they had lost touch?

When exactly was the last time he tried to call her? Their last conversation, of course, was after the arrest. Sure, they were Facebook friends. But Sami never looked him up. She didn't want to talk. He had hurt her. She needed to move on with her life. Which she had. Quite successfully.

If she had to guess, she doubted Tyler was eating at a place like the Hilton tonight. Sure, he'd gotten a huge signing bonus. He had paid cash for the Charger and he probably blew through the rest over the next year or so. Back then, his crazy life had to be expensive.

But wherever he was, whatever he was doing, Tyler had taken the time to write to her. She could at least respond, tell him how she was doing, talk about the job and her roommate and . . .

No! She pulled away from the railing and walked back inside. What was she thinking? If she wrote back to Tyler it would mean only one thing: she was interested. If she acted interested in Tyler, he would assume the door between them was open. Even just a crack.

Which it wasn't.

She walked quickly down the hallway. How long had she been gone? Arnie would be impatient. She absolutely would not answer Tyler's message. Better, she would delete it as soon as she got home. A group of women was leaving the dinner party as Sami entered the room. *Good,* she thought. *A distraction.* The whole room wouldn't be watching her. *Slow down. Poise over pace.* How many times had her grandmother told her that? *Young ladies don't rush into a room. They take their time. Confidence is key.*

She scanned the room for Ember. Before the night was over Sami wanted to find her and thank her for her random wisdom. She would never know the impact of her words tonight. She couldn't settle for a broken past relationship when she was dating someone so wonderful. And that was Arnie

— even on his off nights.

Instead of Ember, halfway across the dining room, Sami saw her boyfriend. He was still talking, still engrossed in telling stories. Suddenly her own pep talk on Arnie's behalf felt a little flat. *He didn't even miss me.* She thought about turning around or searching the room until she found Ember. But at the last second Arnie noticed her and he hurried to his feet. His smile remained, but as she reached him he lowered his voice so only Sami could hear it. "What took so long?"

"Sorry. I had a message . . . from work." The lie came so easily it surprised her. Samantha Dawson did not lie. She found her practiced smile, the one she used at dinners like this. "What did I miss?"

He didn't answer. Instead he pulled her chair out, and she sat down. Arnie grinned at the faces around the table. "Where were we?"

Disappointment washed over Sami. She never should've come back to the table. When it was their turn at the buffet line she took only small amounts. Her appetite wouldn't allow more. She looked again for Ember but couldn't find her. The woman's advice confused her now. Was she settling for Arnie? He was a great guy, Sami wanted to believe that. But how much did he really care for her?

Back at the table, conversation picked up with the discussion of armed administrators at public schools, after which it drifted to a talk on integrity in history books, and finally to border control. Everyone had a solution and everyone agreed that the solutions being bandied around at the table would work.

Sami constantly felt her attention drift. She thought about Ember and her timely words and the Facebook message sitting back at home on her laptop and . . .

Stay focused, she told herself. *You'll embarrass Arnie.* Sami sipped her ice water, anything to stay alert. By the time the meal ended and Arnie walked her to her apartment door, an awkward silence had taken up residence between them.

"You didn't say much at dinner." His tone didn't sound angry or frustrated. More concerned. "You're usually right there with us."

She was? Right there with them? The possibility ruffled a slight concern in the depths of her soul. She had always hated these dinners. Perfect places. Perfect people. No one seemed real.

"Samantha?"

"Yes?" A light gasp slipped from her

mouth. "Sorry. What?"

Arnie looked at her for a long time and finally he put his hand on her shoulder. "Whatever it is, sweetheart, let it go." His arms came around her waist and he eased her closer to him. "I know work's been tough. Your Atlantis account and all. But please, when you're out with me and my friends, I need you to be in the moment." He looked into her eyes. "I want to marry you, Samantha." He smiled, confident. "You might be the wife of a president one day."

"True." Sami offered a smile and a slight shrug of her shoulders. "Well. Good night, Arnie."

"I love you." They shared another hug and a quick kiss.

"You, too." She waved as she stepped inside. Arnie rarely stayed for long on a night like this. When it was after nine o'clock. Morning workouts were only hours away.

She leaned against the closed door and thought about what he'd said. How did he know her work on the Atlantis account had been tough? They never talked about it — at least not since he'd been assigned this case. The last part especially scraped at her nerves. He *needed* her to be in the moment. *His* needs. *His* moments. That's what mattered to Arnie Bell.

After all, she might be the wife of a president one day.

Sami wanted to run for her life.

She walked into the apartment just as Mary Catherine bustled out of her room. "Sami!" Her joy faded almost entirely. "Honey, what happened? You look miserable."

Her roommate's words hit home. Sami couldn't decide whether to laugh or cry, so she did both. Tears formed in her eyes even as she started giggling. "Is that normal? I come home from a night out with my serious boyfriend and I look miserable?" She tossed her hands in the air and held up her finger. "I wanna talk. I'll be right back."

In her bedroom she took off the formal dress and shoes and slipped into her favorite jeans and T-shirt. SIMI VALLEY SLUGGERS. CIRCA 2008. The words were worn. The feelings they stirred, less so. She unpinned her hair and shook it out, then she found Mary Catherine in the living room. She let out a groan as she dropped to the cushy sofa.

Mary Catherine sat cross-legged on the floor, her eyes big. "I thought you were at the law office dinner."

"Exactly." Sami shook her hands, as if that

might somehow rid her of tonight's memory. She dug her elbows into her knees. "Have you ever been so bored you thought you were stuck in a nightmare? Like you might never find your way out?"

Her roommate nodded with enthusiasm, her thick red ponytail bouncing with the effort. Then after a few seconds she slowly shook her head. "No. Actually . . . that's never happened."

Sami rolled her eyes. "Of course not. Not to you." She kicked her legs straight out and fell back against the sofa. "Ugh. How is this my life?"

"Because . . . you're dating Arnie Bell?" Mary Catherine's green eyes filled with kindness. She gave Sami a hesitant smile, maybe a little concerned she was overstepping her bounds. "I sort of saw this coming."

The weight of the situation fell squarely on Sami's shoulders. She released a tired breath. "What am I supposed to do?"

Mary Catherine winced. "How bad was it?"

"At one point we spent at least thirty minutes talking about diabetes medication. Because that's the case Arnie is working on."

"At dinner? You talked about that?" Mary Catherine's eyes got big. She brought her hand to her mouth.

"That's not all." She put her hands on either side of her head. "Integrity in history books and armed administrators at school and something the politicians were excited about, only I forgot to listen." She grabbed a quick breath. "I mean . . . I like a good conversation. I care about politics and issues and lawsuits."

Sami tossed her hands and let them fall to her lap. "But Arnie did most of the talking. Like we were his audience. And then he'd look at me like I was the worst possible girlfriend for not taking notes." As hopeless as she felt about the evening, she could sense a bout of laughter coming.

Mary Catherine must've sensed it, too, because she was definitely working to keep from smiling. "Integrity in history books is interesting." Her smile started to crack. "I mean, very interesting. I saw a documentary once on it and —" Laughter won out. She started giggling, and then laughing full force.

Sami could do nothing but join in. Mary Catherine's laugh was as contagious as spring fever. Across the room, her friend was finally getting control of her laughter. "I mean seriously? You talked about the integrity of history books?" She gave Sami a sympathetic look. "No wonder you came home looking like that."

They both laughed again and Sami shrugged. "All night I kept waiting . . . for someone to talk about thoughts or feelings. A spouse or family. What they'll be doing for the holidays. Instead it was like a formal debate. Arnie and a couple of the guys taking turns sounding important." She felt the humor leave her. "I mean, really. Those issues are great, and there's a time and place, but those people could've gone all night."

"I'm sorry." Mary Catherine giggled again.

"Yeah, well." Sami took a deep breath. "What did you do today?" She held up her hand. "Wait! Don't tell me! You swam with the dolphins off the shore of Catalina Island?"

Another fit of laughter. "Close."

Sami joined her roommate on the floor so they were sitting opposite each other. "Seriously. Tell me."

Mary Catherine's eyes lit up. "I went skydiving."

"You did not."

"I did!" She bounced up and held her arms out to her side. "Soared to the ground like an eagle. Remember? I've been planning this."

Sami thought for a second. "That's right! With the girls at your church!"

"Exactly. We took off near Castaic Lake and headed for the desert. Jumped right out of an airplane! It was crazy!" She plopped back down. "Most amazing feeling in my life."

"Weren't you scared?"

"Nah! Jesus says don't fear, so I didn't." Mary Catherine was so confident, so sure of her faith and her place in life. "YOLO, right?"

"Definitely." Sami smiled. *You only live once.* It was Mary Catherine's motto. But what about Sami? She felt her spirits fall again. "I mean . . . I guess it isn't really funny. The whole thing with Arnie." She stared at the carpet. If only she could make sense of her emotions. She lifted her eyes to her friend's. "I heard from Tyler Ames."

"What?" Mary Catherine jumped back to her feet. She paced to the window and back. "The long-lost baseball player? The one you sat on the roof with?" Once again she dropped to the floor. "What did he say? Did he call?"

"He was in the news recently. He blew out his shoulder pitching in Pensacola."

"No!" Mary Catherine sat still, taking in this new bit of information. "Is that why he contacted you?"

"I don't think so. He didn't mention it." She picked at the threads in the carpet. "He told me he was doing well, still in Florida. He got sober a few years ago. He said he still thinks about me and . . . you know, he asked how I was doing. That sort of thing."

Mary Catherine hung on every word. She really seemed to care so much. "What'd you say back?"

She hesitated. "I haven't answered. Not yet."

"What?" Her roommate wasn't trying to be rude or overly opinionated. Her shock simply spilled out. "How come?"

Sami thought for a moment. Why hadn't she answered him? No matter what impression that might give. "I don't know . . . I have Arnie."

"He found you on Facebook, right?" Mary Catherine seemed to hold back.

"Yes."

"Then he knows about Arnie." She shrugged one shoulder and made a face. "I mean, you're not engaged. I think it's okay to respond."

Her roommate had a point. Sami wasn't engaged, not yet anyway. She wasn't the wife of a lawyer or a congressman or the president. If Mary Catherine could spend

263

the day skydiving, Sami could write back to Tyler Ames, right?

"Let's do this." A sparkle started up again in her friend's eyes. "You have to answer him. I'll get your laptop." She stood and hurried to Sami's room. A few seconds later she returned and handed over the computer. "Here. Before you change your mind."

"Change my mind?" Sami laughed. She opened the laptop and stared at it. "I haven't even decided."

"See!" Mary Catherine put her hands on her hips, her eyebrows raised. "You're thinking about it! Go on . . . you have to."

Sami stared at her roommate and a quiet bit of laughter came from her confusion. "Why do you like Tyler? He messed up a whole lot more than Arnie ever did."

"Because." Mary Catherine looked straight at her. "He calls you Sami."

The answer dropped Sami's guard to the ground. She looked at the computer screen. She opened Facebook, pulled up Tyler's message, and with Mary Catherine sitting across from her she did something she swore she wouldn't do.

She wrote back to him.

The message wasn't very personal or long or particularly inviting. But she added one line she thought might make him smile.

Then she looked up at Mary Catherine and laughed. "YOLO."

Sami thought about the dinner party. The image of Ember talking to her out on the terrace earlier that night came back. Then, before she could change her mind, she sent it.

Because life was too short to settle.

19

Usually Harrison Myers took Sundays off. Not that he had anything special to do. More because his beloved wife, EmmaJean, had loved Sundays. When she was alive they would go to church every Sunday and then spend the rest of the day outdoors. A walk on the beach, a kickball game with their daughters, tennis at the park, or a stroll around the block. Weather in the Panhandle was never cold enough to keep them inside. Then they'd make Sunday supper together.

Back when EmmaJean was alive.

Now Harrison typically spent his Sundays with one of his daughters' families. Sometimes he tinkered around the house. But his family had gotten together yesterday, and today the house didn't need him.

So Harrison went in to Merrill Place.

Rain had rolled in with the tide that morning. *Even better,* Harrison thought as he locked his car and walked inside. He could spend a little time with the residents, make sure he wasn't missing anything. The sort of thing he rarely had time for during the week. He dropped his rain jacket in the office and walked to the cafeteria for a cup of coffee. Along the way he expected to see Tyler.

The guy worked seven days a week. Didn't need a break, at least that's what he said. Harrison understood the real reason. Tyler had nowhere to go, nothing else to do. Until someone could fix his shoulder, he was stuck at Merrill Place, saving his pennies. Harrison took his coffee black. He filled a mug and then walked back to his office.

First resident he wanted to see that morning was Virginia Hutcheson. On Friday he had checked with Virginia's nurse. The woman was still making progress, still peaceful and content without the heavy sedation she'd needed just a few weeks ago. Harrison sipped his coffee and sauntered down the halls. They'd never looked cleaner.

He reached Virginia's room and found the door open. Someone must've been visiting. Harrison peered in without being noticed. What he saw made his jaw drop. Tyler Ames was sitting next to Virginia, holding her hand, and listening to her. His braced arm hung against his chest and a small vase of flowers sat on her bedside table.

Harrison stayed out of sight behind the partially opened door and listened.

"Your father and I always knew you'd grow up to be a fine young man, Ben. And look at you." Virginia had never sounded happier. "I just hope that arm of yours heals up."

"Yes, ma'am. Me, too."

"How many sons bring their mothers flowers first thing Sunday morning?" The hope in her voice was a dramatic change from the desperation just weeks ago. "Prettiest flowers ever." She smiled. "Picked them from our garden, right?"

"Yes." Tyler sounded hesitant. "From the garden."

Harrison felt the shock rattle from his chest to his bones. Virginia Hutcheson thought Tyler was her son, Ben! He took a step back and leaned against the wall, breathing harder than before. His mind raced back to the warning he'd penned to Virginia's daughter. The woman had been going downhill like an errant loose tire. But lately her situation had done a complete turnaround.

Cheryl had credited God with the miracle.

Harrison glanced into the room again. Was this the miracle? God was using Tyler to lift

268

the woman's spirits? Clearly this wasn't the young man's first visit with Virginia. They seemed to have established a beautiful rapport. But why would Tyler play along with this? Suspicious thoughts rushed at Harrison. What if Tyler was trying to get money from the woman? Trying to talk her into helping him some way? He focused on the conversation.

"I was thinking about last Christmas." Virginia's voice was dreamy. "You were just fifteen. You wanted that pellet gun in the worst way."

Tyler smiled. "Yes, ma'am. A boy loves a pellet gun."

"Especially you." She laughed lightly. "But your father knew you needed a new bed." A hint of frustration colored her tone. "We didn't have enough money for both." Her smile became wistful. "You handled it so well."

"Thank you."

"Well, you did. I can see you sitting there now. Next to the tree. You opened that box with the note from me and your father. You realized you were getting a bed instead of a pellet gun and you gushed like you'd opened the prettiest pellet gun in all of Florida."

"You and Dad always knew best." Tyler's tone was sincere.

"Thank you, Ben."

Harrison moved again so he could see his employee, see the smile in the young man's eyes and how it reflected the one on Virginia's face. What was this? Nothing about Tyler's tone or mannerisms seemed sinister.

Virginia reached for Tyler's hand and he took hold of her fingers. "You make your mother so happy."

"You make me happy, too." Tyler looked completely sincere.

Harrison watched the scene and felt his defenses fall. There didn't seem to be a single motive, no reason whatsoever for Tyler to have this conversation with a woman he didn't know. Harrison kept watching, barely out of sight.

"I know you weren't perfect, Ben." Virginia tilted her head. "But no one is. Not even me."

They shared a comfortable laugh. "You make forgiveness sound . . . so easy."

"It is." She leaned back against her pillows, relaxed. "Jesus already did the hard part, Ben. You know that. If He can go to the cross for me, I guess I can forgive just about anyone."

"Hmm. I guess so."

"What does the Bible say?"

Tyler looked a little panicked. "The Bible?"

"About forgiveness?" Virginia chuckled. "Look at that. I have a better memory than you. We talked about this last month."

"Yes, ma'am."

She sat a little straighter. "In the Bible Jesus says, 'Forgive as I have forgiven you.' That means we forgive even when the person doesn't deserve forgiveness. Because none of us ever deserves it. Besides, families need to be the first to forgive. That's what love looks like."

Harrison kept watching, amazed.

Tyler nodded. "Yes. That's definitely what love looks like." He thought for a moment, then he looked intently at her. "I'm sorry. If I ever disappointed you."

Harrison wondered if he would faint from the shock. Tyler was definitely going along with Virginia, playing the role of her son like a seasoned actor.

"Disappoint me?" Virginia shook her head. Harrison wasn't sure, but she seemed to have tears in her eyes. "Ben, you've made me so happy. Just being with you. Times like this. Life's too short to be disappointed with the people you love." She patted his hand with her free one. "And I love you very much."

"I love you, too."

Harrison felt the depth of the moment. If he didn't know better he'd believe Tyler was actually Ben. The young man was that convincing.

"Okay, then." Virginia covered a yawn. "I'll take a nap and we'll see you in the living room later." A smile lifted her tired expression. "You're going to sing for us, right?"

For the first time since Harrison stumbled upon this most unbelievable scene, Tyler Ames looked nervous. "Uh . . . this afternoon?"

"Yes." She closed her eyes. "My friends are coming over so . . ." She was asleep.

Tyler carefully released her hand and stood. As he did he spotted Harrison and he froze. Fear screamed from his eyes. He held his finger to his lips and quietly retrieved the mop and bucket. He joined Harrison in the hallway and shut the door behind him without making a sound.

Harrison had never seen the kid look guilty until now. "I'll explain. Can we talk in your office?" Tyler whispered. He clearly did not want to wake Virginia.

Not until then did Harrison notice his own tears. He blinked them back and nodded. "Follow me."

They reached the office and Harrison closed the door. "What in the world was happening back there?" He didn't mean to sound angry, but he needed answers. As tender as the scene was, it was a charade. He needed to get to the bottom of the situation.

Tyler slumped in his chair. He looked tired, almost dizzy. Too much so for this early in the morning. "I'm sorry. I . . . didn't mean for it to get out of hand."

Harrison exhaled. He felt his frustration ease a bit as he leaned on his desk and squinted. "Start from the beginning. Please." His voice still sounded clipped.

Tyler gripped the arm of the chair with his good hand. "When I first started, I could never get into her room. She'd been out of control, I guess. Medicated. She was always asleep." He massaged his left temple. "I finally was able to clean her floor." He looked around as if he were grabbing at explanations. "I don't know why, but she called me Ben. She . . . she thought I was her son."

"I got that." Harrison was still hesitant, still looking for the motive.

"She asked me to sit down, so I did. Wasn't sure what else to do." Tyler sighed. "She . . . started talking to me about how it was 1970 and how my dad was almost home from work." Tyler seemed to gather a little confidence. "She was so happy, Mr. Myers. Like sitting there with her, letting her talk, was the kindest thing anyone had ever done."

"I see." Harrison felt his heart soften. He willed his tone to lighten a little. "How often have you talked to her?"

Tyler didn't blink. "Every day since then. Each time she's happier and alert. I finish my work and make her room my last stop. Sometimes I bring her flowers." He shrugged. "I guess Ben used to do that. Anyway, every afternoon she's waiting for me."

"So, she thinks you're Ben, and that you're a teenager?" Harrison's suspicions and concerns began to fall away.

"Sometimes." Tyler looked as baffled as Harrison felt. "Other times she knows I'm older. She'll talk about a car accident her son must've had. The guy wasn't hurt, but the car was damaged. She keeps saying she forgives me."

A lump formed in Harrison's throat. He had worked at Merrill Place for a long time, but he'd never seen anything like this. "First . . ." — he waited until his voice co-operated — "you should know I'm not angry. Surprised, but not angry. You did nothing to violate policy. It's just . . . nothing like this has ever happened before."

"Well, sir" — Tyler looked at his watch — "if it's all the same to you, I'd like to keep stopping in. I look forward to talking with her." His eyes betrayed a hurt he had never talked about. "She sort of, I don't know — I guess she feels like family now."

"I understand." Harrison thought for a few seconds. "I guess . . . I don't see any harm in it." He studied Tyler, wanting to be sure. "I've never met Ben. Cheryl doesn't talk about her brother." He paused again. "You really care about Virginia, is that it?"

"Yes, sir." A sad smile tugged at Tyler's lips. "Very much."

So Cheryl was right. God was using Tyler Ames to bring about the miracle in Virginia's life. The truth was more than Harrison could take in. He returned the young man's smile. "Thanks for explaining. You can get back to work."

"Yes, sir." Tyler stood, his damaged arm hanging awkwardly against his body. He hesitated. "There is one more thing."

"Go ahead."

"I saw an old guitar in the storage room when I was cleaning." He looked nervous again, the way he had when Virginia brought up singing. "Could I . . . Would you mind if I used it to sing for Virginia and the residents this afternoon? After lunch?"

Harrison raised his brow, amused and touched at the same time. "You sing?"

"No." Tyler didn't hesitate.

"You play guitar?"

"Not really." Tyler looked a little dazed. "In middle school. That's the last time."

Again Harrison was moved. The public had never seen this side of Tyler Ames. That much was certain. He glanced at Tyler's arm. "How are you going to play with one —"

"I've been asking myself the same thing. I never dreamed I'd sing again." He chuckled, and his fondness for Virginia was as obvious as his damaged shoulder. "It matters to her. What else can I do?" He shook his head. "I have to hope they're a forgiving audience."

Harrison looked at Tyler for a long time. "You can use the guitar." He smiled. "Is the sing-along in the living room?"

"I guess so." He laughed again — one of the first times Harrison had heard him sound happy. "It better not wind up on YouTube."

"You're safe here." They both laughed and Tyler left the office.

Harrison watched him go. If he hadn't

come in today he might've missed this. The truth stayed with him. Tyler Ames, former baseball star, had befriended Virginia Hutcheson, a ninety-year-old woman with Alzheimer's. And in the process Virginia was finding her way to being whole again. Harrison shook his head. He wouldn't believe it if he hadn't seen it himself.

He checked his watch. Eleven in the morning. Cheryl stopped by every Sunday after church — probably around one. Right about when Tyler planned to sing for Virginia and her friends. Harrison could hardly wait to tell the woman what he'd found out. Cheryl's mother thought Tyler was her son. Which meant Virginia had her miracle.

Now Harrison could only hope that Tyler Ames would get his.

20

The pain pills were wearing off, but Tyler didn't care. He certainly wasn't going to play the guitar and sing for Virginia and her friends high on Oxycodone. The singing mattered to Virginia, and so it mattered to Tyler. He was actually looking forward to it. How long had it been since he'd made someone else happy?

He drank extra water so the shaking wouldn't be as bad. Maybe he'd get lucky and he wouldn't feel the tremors and sweating until after he sang. He would do his best — he had to for Virginia — but his performance was bound to be a mess. Tyler knew the basic chords from band at school and at least a handful of hymns from his days at church. Before baseball became more important. Still he was pretty sure that after today Virginia would politely refrain from asking him to sing again.

Tyler finished cleaning the hallways and

bedrooms at the west wing of Merrill Place and slipped back to his apartment for lunch. *More water,* he told himself. Something to stop the incessant shaking.

On his way to the fridge, he glanced at the computer. He hadn't checked Facebook since yesterday. It didn't matter. Sami wasn't going to write back. Her Facebook page was active, up to date. Surely she'd read his message by now. No response meant Tyler never should have reached out in the first place.

He hesitated near the table. Of course, maybe she'd been away from her computer. That was possible, right? She might've just seen his message today. He flipped open the laptop, tapped a few keys with his left hand, and pulled up Facebook. A small number "1" shouted at him from the top of the screen.

One private message.

He lowered himself slowly to the seat. The message had to be from her. He hadn't talked to anyone else since his accident. The sweat on his brow grew worse. What if she was angry that he'd written to her? She went by Samantha, after all. She had probably changed. Again, she hadn't even answered his last call. Or maybe the message wasn't even from her. Her boyfriend might've written back, telling him to stay away. *Ernie something, right?*

This is crazy. He pulled a water bottle from the case on the table, ripped off the lid, and drank half of it. The pain in his shoulder grew with every passing minute. He was sick of the way his body shook, sick of feeling this way. But he couldn't take the pills. Not until after he played for Virginia. He checked the time on his computer — 12:20. The next forty minutes would feel like a year at this rate.

Just read the message, he told himself. *Get your mind off the pain.* Whatever words lay on the other side of that number, he had to read them. He clicked the notification and the hard edges of his heart melted a little. The message was from Sami. *Samantha Dawson,* it read.

He began to read.

Tyler, I can't believe it's you! What's it been, three years since we talked? Four maybe? First I have to tell you how happy I am that you're sober. I think a lot of your struggles early on came because you were drinking. So now . . . well, now you can do anything! I always believed that.

Tyler closed his eyes and held onto just

that much. Sami had always believed in him, had always known he could do any- thing. What she said was true. Their senior year of high school she had breathed confi- dence into him every time they talked. His dad would harp on him for not being focused. The man constantly pulled him aside to give him pointers. How to throw faster, cleaner, more accurately.

Not Sami.

He pictured warming up before his last home game at Jackson High. As soon as Sami parked her car she ran toward him, practically bursting with excitement. The game had been about to start, but he waved at her. From a proper distance she smiled at him, her eyes shining. "You're the best pitcher ever, Tyler Ames," she spoke loud enough so he could hear her over the sound of the infield chatter. "Go win it!"

That's exactly what he had done. He'd gone out and dominated a team that had the same win-loss record as Jackson. Later, his coach would say that game was a turn- ing point, the reason Tyler was awarded Mr. Baseball. The reason Jackson went on to be state champ.

All because Sami Dawson believed in him.

He remembered all of it. And now, no matter what the rest of the message said, he had what he needed. Confirmation. His letter to her had been the right decision. He opened his eyes and kept reading.

I heard about your injury. I guess you must be on the mend now, working toward the Big Leagues again, like you said. You'll get there. Anyway, I had to write back. Life is good and I'm happy. Most of the time — haha. I think of you every so often, too. Usually I picture you where I'll always picture you: sitting under the stars on a roof with your arm around me. Feels like a million years ago, right?

Well . . . take care. Good hearing from you. Sami.

He read the letter again, and a third time. Out of every wonderful thing she said, one line made his heart break. *Most of the time?* She was happy most of the time? So it was just like he'd feared. Her grandparents had convinced her to fall in line: Sensible job. Sensible boyfriend. But what did Sami think about when Tyler's name came up? He read her words one more time, let them soothe the emptiness inside him.

She thought about sitting on the rooftop next to him.

The news wasn't bad actually. His first love was still there in the lines of her message. She'd been honest at least — about being happy most of the time. And about her memory of him. He stared at her profile picture, the eyes that had once been so familiar. Yes, she went by Samantha now, and yes, she seemed to have settled into the life her grandparents wanted for her. But the girl he knew was definitely still in there. He was sure for one reason.

She had signed her name *Sami.*

The residents were finishing lunch when Tyler reported back to the gathering room. He had only twenty minutes, and he still needed to figure out how to play with one hand. What if he didn't remember even the easiest chords?

A small, empty room sat just off the lobby. He took the guitar there, shut the door behind him, and sat on the first chair he came to. His knees and arms shook, and he felt sick to his stomach. He never should've promised Virginia anything. What would she think if he bombed? If he couldn't carry a tune or remember how to play? Especially with one hand?

Calm down. He closed his eyes for a long moment and willed the shaking to let up.

Gradually he felt the slightest peace ease his anxiety. This wasn't about him. It was about Virginia. *God, if You're there, I need some help. Please.*

His right hand still worked — but his shoulder hurt if he used it too much or too suddenly. *All right, Tyler, let's do this.* He sat the guitar on his right knee and held the neck with his left hand. He strummed a few times and adjusted his hold, trying to find a natural position. One that didn't kill his shoulder.

The C chord. That would be a good place to start. He found the finger positions with his left hand and once he had that he strummed the strings with his right. Pain burned from his shoulder to his neck and torso. He clenched his jaw and breathed in through locked teeth. Who was he kidding about giving up the Oxycodone? He needed it more than air.

The position hurt too much to play like this. He shifted, leaning further over the guitar. That way his shoulder didn't have to support the weight of his hand. This time when he strummed there were no worsening sharp pains. But even still his body trembled and sweat dripped down the side of his face.

"Why are you doing this, Ames?" he

284

whispered. "You can't play. Virginia will know you're a fraud." He pictured the sweet old woman, her pleading face. Enough doubts. This wasn't about him. Whatever happened, he would make good on his promise to his friend.

He worked five minutes to tune the strings, and then he ran through the chords, through "Jingle Bells" and "Happy Birthday" — two songs he still remembered.

He could only hope Virginia and her friends were hard of hearing.

Tyler took his spot on a metal stool at the front of the living room at Merrill Place. An open hymnal sat on the table in front of him and around the room only a few residents filled the chairs — two of them were sleeping. No telling whether Virginia had ever made it to the lunchroom or if she'd simply forgotten about Tyler's concert.

Still he wanted to be ready in case she remembered. He had found a few hymns he could sing, songs with simpler melodies and chords he could struggle through. Now if only he could survive the pain. He clutched his right elbow to his ribs. His body was demanding relief, desperate for the pills. Everything ached, and the slightest wrong movement sent knives through his shoulder and neck. Everything in him screamed for more Oxycodone.

This is for Virginia, he thought. *I can do it for her.*

At exactly one o'clock, Virginia shuffled into the living room pushing a walker and clearly looking for him. This was the first time Tyler had seen her out of her bed.

She spotted him right away. "Ben! You're here!" She stopped and motioned back over her shoulder. Then she grinned at him. "Ethel and Roger are coming." With slow shuffling steps she came closer, a smile stretched across her face. "I've been looking forward to this for days! Ever since the last time you played for me."

"Yes, ma'am." Tyler could feel sweat beading up on his forehead, dripping down his back. He ignored it. For her, his smile came easily.

Virginia put her hand on his good shoulder. "Sing for Jesus, Ben. God loves when we sing for Him."

God again. Tyler looked down and nodded — for her benefit only. So much of his troubled life was his own fault. What would God want with him now? He lifted his eyes to hers. "You have a favorite song?"

"Ben, you make me smile." She shook her pretty white head. "We have the same favorite — you know that!" Peace filled her face as she lifted her eyes to the windows at the back of the room. "Always 'Amazing Grace.' "

"That's right." Tyler set the guitar down and stood. "Come on, let's get you a front row seat." He moved to her right side and with his left hand he kept her steady as they walked to the closest chair, just a few feet from where Tyler would sing. "How about this?"

Virginia leaned into him as they walked and when they reached the chair she smiled up at him. "You are the most thoughtful boy. Your father and I are so proud."

Tyler helped her into the seat and took his place on the metal stool again. He wondered if Virginia could see how badly he was shaking. He hadn't hurt this bad in a long time. But even as he tried to find the least painful position, even as the other residents made their way in from the lunchroom, Tyler couldn't get over what Virginia had said. Whoever Ben was and wherever he lived today, his parents were proud of him simply because he was thoughtful? Maybe he was a doctor curing diseases overseas, or a teacher or a businessman. Whatever his talents and dreams, it didn't really matter. His parents were proud of him for just being himself.

Tyler had never imagined such a thing.

He felt a little angry at Ben. Whatever took up the man's time, he needed to be here. At least once in a while. With a mother like Virginia, he was missing out. Tyler smiled at the dear woman. *Ben's loss,* he told himself. *My gain.*

Tyler positioned his guitar on his lap and leaned over. If Virginia wanted him to sing this afternoon, God would have to give him a break on the pain. For thirty minutes, anyway.

"Your father is on his way." She looked over her shoulder. "He should be here any time. Your sister, too."

If only that were true. Tyler grinned at her. "I'm not much of a singer. You know that."

"Not true! Everyone loves to hear you sing, Ben!"

A few stragglers had taken their seats. All eyes were on Tyler. He cleared his throat and looked down at the songbook. What in the world was he doing? Was this some crazy dream? He caught a few drops of sweat with his good shoulder. No. It wasn't a dream. He was about to make a fool of himself if he didn't pass out from the pain.

He caught Virginia smiling at him.

Yes, that's why he was here. For her. He forced a smile. "I'll start with 'How Great

288

Thou Art.' " He locked eyes with Virginia. "Is that okay?"

"Absolutely, dear!" She clapped a few times, her hands slow and weak. "That one's always a hit."

"Yes." Tyler managed a soft chuckle. He loved the old woman's zest for life, her enthusiasm. Her eyes remained on him as he found the first chord and began to play. "Oh Lord, my God, when I in awesome wonder . . . consider all the worlds Thy hands have made . . ."

The music flowed, and the words with it. Tyler was surprised. He hadn't sung to the radio even since long before his injury. But somehow he didn't sound half bad. He was on key or close to it, and around the room the residents turned their eyes his direction. A few of them mouthed the words.

Tyler reached the chorus. "Then sings my soul, my Savior God, to Thee . . . How great Thou art . . . how great Thou art."

Tears shone in Virginia's eyes and gradually she began to sing along, nodding and smiling. Not until he reached the end of the song did Tyler realize he hadn't once thought about the pain in his shoulder. He moved on to the next song — "Amazing Grace" — "Come Thou Fount" and "Be Thou My Vision."

The room was filling up, more residents filing in. Line by line he sang, sharing the songs these people had clearly missed. Most of the folks knew every word. Especially Virginia. As Tyler sang and played, the old hymns came back to him, too. Songs he and his parents had loved when he was a kid.

Tyler's shaking eased, his damp forehead grew dry. He kept singing. "Prone to wander, Lord, I feel it . . . prone to leave the God I love . . . Here's my heart, Lord, take and seal it, seal it for Thy courts above."

A few more lines and the song ended. Suddenly the ground beneath him seemed to shift. For the first time since this session began, the words connected at the center of his heart. *Prone to wander? Prone to leave God?* The words could've been written for him alone. He had never set out to make a mess of his life, but he had. He was prone to it, to wander from Virginia's God.

She was clapping for him, encouraging those around her to do the same. "Ben . . . you're not finished, are you?"

Tyler forced himself to focus. "No." The guitar rested easy in his hands, the pain only a distant ache. "I forgot how much I like that old song."

Virginia held up one frail hand. "I have a request."

He loved her gentle spirit, her ever-present joy. "Whatever you want."

"That's my boy." She looked at a man seated beside her, who looked to be in his nineties. "See that boy? He's my son."

"Very nice young man." The man spoke slowly, nodding at Virginia. "I'd like to buy his album."

"Me, too." Virginia's eyes sparkled. She turned back to Tyler. " 'Amazing Grace.' Can you play it again? It's our favorite."

As he began to sing the familiar hymn once more, Tyler noticed a few visitors gathered at the edge of the room, and near them, Harrison Myers. Like the residents, these people mouthed the words, their voices too soft to hear. "Amazing grace, how sweet the sound . . . that saved a wretch like me . . ."

Tears sprang to his eyes. Tyler blinked them back, his voice filling the room with the song. Gradually his surroundings faded. He was no longer singing for an audience of Virginia and her friends, but for God alone. The God Tyler had stopped believing in many years ago. For reasons Tyler couldn't grasp, let alone explain, this time around the song became personal.

"Through many dangers, toils, and snares . . . I have already come . . . 'Tis grace hath brought me safe thus far, and grace will lead me home."

A single tear slid down his cheek, but Tyler ignored it. Only the song mattered, the message and music, the way it resonated within him. What even was grace? Amazing grace? It wasn't something he had ever felt or understood.

As he sang, Tyler pictured his broken life, the last several years in the minors. Chasing sunsets from one town to the next, waiting for the chance to be perfect. At the end of the ride — when he was sitting where the residents of Merrill Place sat, he wanted more to show for it than a busted shoulder and a bagful of broken dreams.

When the impromptu concert was over, after he hugged Virginia and shook the hands of several residents, Tyler hurried to his room. The pain had subsided while he sang, but it nearly slammed him to the ground as soon as he finished. *The pills,* he told himself. *Three of them this time.*

He grabbed the bottle but as he twisted off the lid, the words of the song suddenly hit him again. *Amazing grace . . . how sweet the sound . . . that saved a wretch like me.*

Tears filled his eyes again and his hands shook worse than ever. No one had ever needed grace more than he did. Already the bottle was nearly gone. He couldn't make a comeback as a pitcher if he was addicted to pain medication. He'd wind up like Baldy Williams. *I need them bad, just a few.* But before he could take them he slammed the bottle back on his kitchen counter. He squeezed his eyes shut. There was something he wanted more than the pills.

I want to live, God. I really do. I need Your help.

He stared at the small white pills. They had been his friends day and night, bringing him countless hours of relief. But no more. When he couldn't take the pain he'd go to the workout room here at Merrill Place and do squats or crunches. Anything to distract himself.

After today, he might even sing.

The pills screamed at him from the bottle, begging him to give in. Take two or three. Relief was minutes away. *No! Not this time.* He turned and paced a few steps toward the door. *This is the first day of the rest of your life,* he told himself. He had to move on. Suddenly in a burst of motion he returned to the kitchen, grabbed the pills, dumped them down the sink, and turned on the water. The stream picked them up and swirled them out of sight. Just like that, Tyler felt both terror and peace.

He was on his own now — no more Oxycodone to get him through the nights and days. Exercise would have to take the place of the pills. He would make a chart and work out every day. Every penny would go to saving for the surgery.

He would work harder than anyone, and he would pitch again. Better than ever. Yes, he needed to tolerate the pain. He needed determination and maybe longer hours. He definitely needed to see an orthopedic doctor as soon as possible. But there was something Tyler needed more than all of that combined. Something he hadn't known he needed until he picked up the guitar and sang for Virginia Hutcheson.

God's amazing grace.

21

As Cheryl Conley watched from a distance that afternoon she couldn't decide which was the more unbelievable sight: her mother, sitting up, looking utterly in her right mind, singing hymns, or the young man playing guitar at the front of the room. Cheryl had never seen him before. It wasn't the way he played or the quality of his voice that took Cheryl's breath.

It was his uncanny resemblance to her brother, Ben.

When the young man launched into "Amazing Grace," Cheryl positioned herself so she could see her mother's face. She took a step closer, stunned. Her mother was singing a song she hadn't sung for a decade. Singing as if she hadn't missed a week of church. And the whole time her eyes were fixed on the guy with the guitar.

Cheryl watched the guy, the way he moved as he played, his expression. Just looking at him took her back to 1970. It was like looking at a family video of her brother when he was this age. The song ended and the young man put the guitar down. He went to Cheryl's mother first. He hugged her shoulders and helped her to her feet. They talked for a minute or so and then he spoke with a few of the other residents.

After the young man left, Cheryl approached her mother. She was talking with two of her friends, intent on the conversation. Cheryl almost wanted to keep the space between them, just soak in the sight of her mom. Less than a month ago Cheryl had been certain she would never see her mother like this again — social and happy, interacting with friends.

The sight was more beautiful than anything Cheryl could've dreamed.

She couldn't wait another moment. "Mom?" She came up alongside her and put her hand on her mother's shoulder. "You look wonderful!"

Her mother turned and her face lit up. "Cheryl! You're here!" Her eyes shot around the room. "You just missed Ben!"

"I . . . I saw him." Tears threatened, but Cheryl refused them. "He plays the guitar so well."

"He does!" She shook her head, her eyes

sparkling. "And that voice!"

"I love when he sings the old hymns."

"No one does it better." Her mother nodded to a nearby table. "Should we sit and talk for a bit?"

"I'd love that." Cheryl couldn't believe she was having this conversation with her mother. They linked arms as they walked. "How are you feeling?"

"Never better, dear."

Her mother moved along slowly, but she left her walker back at her chair. She took her seat at the table. "I should go get Ben. It's been too long since we've all been together."

"It has." Cheryl reached for her mother's hands across the table. Where had the young man gone, and who was he? "You look so happy, Mom."

"Ben comes home earlier these days. Before your father gets off work."

Cheryl studied her. She was clearly stuck back in the early '70s, when Ben looked like the young man leading worship, and their father worked long days at the office. Fine. Cheryl had read up on a new approach for treating Alzheimer's patients — the Past-Present Theory. Doctors were finding that patients with severe dementia responded better when they were allowed to live in whatever time period they wished. If her mom was comfortable in 1970, so be it.

They talked for another ten minutes, and then her mother's eyes grew foggy. "I'm very tired, Cheryl. I think I'll take a nap." She smiled. "Wanna be at my best when your father gets home."

"Of course." The trek to her room had been too much for her just a few weeks ago. But now even her mother's physical stamina seemed improved. Did the guy with the guitar know that her mother thought he was Ben?

Once her mom was back in bed, Cheryl kissed her cheek and left her to sleep. Her next stop was an obvious one.

The office of Harrison Myers.

He was at his desk when she knocked at the door. "Cheryl." His smile came easier than it had the last few times she stopped by. "Come in."

She took the chair opposite him. For a few seconds she only stared at him, not sure where to start. "Who was that? The young man with the guitar?"

Harrison smiled. "He's new. I had no idea he could sing."

"He knows my mother." Cheryl held her purse in her lap, unable to move or breathe until she connected the dots. "I . . . I saw

298

them talking."

"Yes." Harrison's smile faded some. "I need to talk to you about that." He leaned his forearms on the desk. "Cheryl, your mother thinks he's your brother, Ben."

"Yes!" She felt the tears again. "He looks just like him . . . the way Ben looked back then."

"The young man's name is Tyler Ames."

Something about the name sounded familiar. "He's new? I've . . . heard his name before."

"He's a baseball player. Blue Wahoos."

A soft gasp came from Cheryl. "The pitcher! That's right!" She followed the local team. Her whole family did. "Got hurt a while ago?"

"That's him. He got cut the day after the injury." Harrison pursed his lips, clearly troubled. "I'm pretty sure he was living in his car, when a pastor friend of mine sent him here." Harrison shrugged. "I needed a maintenance man."

"He's a baseball player." Cheryl was confused. "Shouldn't he be working with the team? Getting better?"

"He needs surgery on his shoulder, but my guess is he can't afford it." Harrison frowned. "I don't think the accident was covered."

Cheryl pictured Tyler, playing the guitar with the brace on his right arm. Suddenly she remembered what Harrison had said a minute ago. "How did you know? About Tyler and my mother?"

"I wasn't sure until the other day." He looked amazed and bewildered at the same time. "I walked by your mother's room and there he was, sitting beside her. Talking like he'd known her all her life."

As beautiful as that sounded, the situation didn't make sense. "Why would he? I mean, he doesn't know her."

"I wondered, too." Harrison leaned back, his brow furrowed. "He has nothing to gain." He hesitated. "He seems to enjoy talking with her as much as she does with him." He tapped his desk a few times. "It's changed her. That much is obvious."

"She's so much better." Cheryl felt the tears again, but this time she didn't try to stop them. "Ben was always so special to her. She's . . . missed him." Cheryl didn't want to get into the details, the reason why Ben hadn't been by to visit.

"You should watch Tyler with her sometime." Harrison's smile was deep. "I've never seen anything like it."

Cheryl needed to find the young man before another minute passed. She stood and thanked the manager. "Is Tyler still living in his car?"

"He has a room out back." Harrison checked the time on his phone. "He's finished work until the night shift. He's either in his apartment or in the weight room."

Harrison showed her which way to go, and Cheryl set out. The new information consumed her. Tyler Ames, onetime local baseball hero, had befriended Cheryl's mother, willingly playing the part of the 1970s version of Ben. She walked quickly down the hallway and found Tyler in the weight room. He was lying on a mat, doing sit-ups.

She stepped inside, still holding her purse, and waited until he noticed her. When he did, he stood, sweat dripping down his face. "Ma'am?"

"Hi." She wasn't sure where to start. "I'm Cheryl Conley. Virginia's daughter."

He seemed to recognize her name. "Tyler Ames." He nodded and wiped his forehead with the back of his arm. "Sorry. I'm a mess."

"That's okay." The young man's resemblance to her brother was uncanny. "I won't be long." Again she scrambled for the right words. "You look a great deal like my brother, Ben."

"Yes, ma'am. I gathered that." Kindness warmed his eyes. "Your mother is very special."

"You've been talking to her? Meeting with her?" Cheryl couldn't understand why a young man like Tyler would bother.

"First time I cleaned her floors, she seemed to recognize me. She called me Ben." His brace was off, lying on one of the weight benches. He held his right arm close to his body while he talked. "It's only ten or fifteen minutes a day." Concern darkened his expression. "I . . . hope you don't mind."

"Mind?" Cheryl felt fresh tears again. She could barely speak. "Your time with my mother, it's changed her life. She knows who I am again."

"Well, good." Tyler smiled, relieved. "It's been nice for me, too."

She didn't want to prod, didn't want to ask Tyler about the meaning of his words or the whereabouts of his own family. She'd said what she'd come to say. "I'll let you go." She had one more question. "Mr. Myers says you need shoulder surgery?"

"I'm saving for it." He looked back at the weight room. "I want to be ready when it happens."

"We've watched you play." Cheryl hoped

302

he could sense her sincerity. "You're very good. You have to get that surgery so you can get back out there."

"Yes, ma'am. Thank you."

"Could we talk some time? About your conversations with my mother?"

Tyler nodded, his eyes softer than before. "I'd like that. Maybe you could tell me about Ben." There was a depth in his eyes. "Evenings are best. I'm here all the time."

"Thank you." There were no words to convey the depth of Cheryl's gratitude. But she had to try. "What you're doing for my mother — you'll never know how much it means."

Tyler stood at his spot on the mat again. "Like I said, it's good for both of us."

"By the way." Cheryl was almost out the door when she remembered. "You're a very good singer, Tyler. The residents . . . they loved that."

"Thank you. That was for your mother."

Cheryl smiled at him through teary eyes and then headed back down the hallway toward her mother's room. She still had a hundred questions for the young man, but they would have to wait. She needed to get back to her mom. She dabbed the tears from her cheeks as she reached her mother's door.

If only she had money, a fortune stashed away somewhere. She would have paid for Tyler's surgery in a heartbeat to thank him for helping her mother. Since that wasn't possible, Cheryl did the only thing she could do, the only way she knew to help the young man get the medical care he needed.

Right there in the hallway outside her mother's room, she closed her eyes, bowed her head, and begged God for a miracle for Tyler Ames.

Tyler pounded through the rest of his workout, pushing past the pain in his shoulder. The hard work kept his mind off the burning sensation otherwise radiating from his shattered labrum. The workout was good for another reason: as long as he kept moving, he could tolerate the shakes.

Instead of thinking about how he could ease his pain, he thought about Cheryl's visit.

He had wondered about both of Virginia's grown children — whether they ever really visited. Clearly Ben would be much older now, too. Tyler wasn't sure if Virginia would remember him outside of the young man she still believed him to be. Maybe that was why he didn't seem to come around.

Either way, he looked forward to more

conversations with Cheryl. Maybe she could fill in the missing pieces of their past, the bits that Virginia alluded to. Tyler did a final set of crunches and then stood facing the mirror. Squats were next. He attacked the first set with a vengeance. He wasn't sure, but maybe God had a plan in all this. The job at Merrill Place, the conversations with Virginia, the words of "Amazing Grace," and now the moment with Cheryl Conley.

And all of it had started with a single visit to Hope Community Church and a stranger named Beck.

When Tyler finished his workout and was back in his apartment, when his shoulder pain made him wish he could crawl down the drain looking for even one more pill, he did something he should've done a long time ago. He opened the laptop and looked up the church. Then using the phone that hung on the wall of the apartment, he dialed the number.

"Hello?" The man sounded upbeat. "Hope Community, Pastor Roman."

"Hi. This is Tyler Ames." He dropped to the chair at the kitchen table. "I . . . wanted to thank you. For letting me use your name as a reference at Merrill Place." He held his elbow against his body. "I got the job. Things are working out."

The man hesitated. "I'm sorry." He seemed confused. "Do I know you?"

"We never met." Tyler felt slightly embarrassed. Clearly Beck hadn't mentioned their conversation to the pastor. "I stopped by your church a few weeks ago. A volunteer helped me out."

"I see."

Tyler felt the sweat on his forehead again. His knees were shaking. "The man . . . he told me about the job. He said I should give your name as a reference." Tyler wondered if he had dialed the wrong number. "I just wanted to thank you. And him."

"Oh." Pastor Roman sounded unaware of the situation. "I'm glad it worked out." He paused. "What did you say the volunteer's name was?"

"Beck." Tyler could picture the guy, built like a linebacker, deep concern in his eyes. "He's a paramedic in town."

"Hmmm." The pastor sounded concerned. "There's no volunteer by that name at Hope Community Church." Then it seemed to hit him. "Wait! You must mean Burt. He's a retired firefighter. Hangs out here and serves with our soup kitchen."

"You're sure? He said his name was Beck." Had the pain pills messed with his memory? Tyler squeezed his eyes shut. *Focus. Don't think about the pain,* he told himself.

"I'm positive." Pastor Roman's voice held a smile now. "Burt's always giving out information. Must've been him."

Tyler couldn't argue. There was no point. "Yes, sir. Well, tell him thank you for me."

"I will." He seemed to write something down. "Tyler Ames, right?"

"Yes." Clearly the pastor didn't follow baseball. Just as well. "Thank you."

"Okay, then. Come by anytime." Warmth filled the man's words. "The door's always open."

Again Tyler thanked him. For a long time after he hung up the phone, Tyler didn't move.

Sure, he'd been high on Oxycodone. Much about his days of being homeless was lost in the blur of medication. But he could still see the paramedic hovering over him that night at the baseball field, still see his nametag. Two things he absolutely knew for sure: the man was not old enough to be retired. And his name definitely wasn't Burt.

It was Beck.

The pastor's final words stayed with Tyler long after he hung up the phone. His parents had turned their backs on him, his team had cut him without so much as a thank you, and his landlady had kicked him out. But the new people in his life, the ones who loved God — they had open hearts and open doors. Beck . . . Burt. Whoever. People cared about Tyler now, even though he deserved none of their kindness.

Amazing grace . . . how sweet the sound.

The song played in his mind once more and a thought occurred to him, dawning somewhere in his walled-up heart. All of this had happened since he stepped foot in a church. Since he fell to his knees and stared at a rugged, wooden cross. So maybe . . . maybe Virginia's God wasn't part of her dementia.

Maybe He was real after all.

22

Sami's boss stepped into her office late that Friday, his face masked in concern. "A couple things." He paused. "Your client is very happy. That's the good news."

"Okay." Sami pictured the work she'd done for the Atlantis Resort. The property in the Bahamas especially was receiving more favorable press than she had hoped. "What's the bad news?"

"You need to fly to Florida right away. They want to go over a few ideas they have for the next stage of the campaign. They want you there in person."

She thought about the work for other clients she had lined up for next week. "How many days?"

"Fly in Sunday. Work Monday and Tuesday, then fly back Wednesday morning."

"That's fine." She would figure out the other clients later. "I'll set it up."

Sami's job included travel, but neither she

nor her boss expected this trip. Especially with so little notice. She called her contact with Atlantis and set up the details. The trip came together quickly with the first half of Monday wide open. Her heart beat faster just looking at the schedule. Her client's offices were in Pensacola.

Tyler's hometown.

The rest of the day passed slowly, but that night she and Mary Catherine had planned on pizza and a movie at the apartment. Arnie had a late meeting, and Mary Catherine had kept the evening open. "Roomies' Night," she called it. Sami waited until they were sitting in the living room around a box of pizza before she took a deep breath and looked at her friend. "I need to fly to Pensacola."

"Now?" Mary Catherine took a slice of pizza, her interest clearly piqued. "Like soon?"

"Sunday." Sami had looked forward to this moment all day. She would tell Arnie tomorrow on their date. But she needed to sort through her feelings about Tyler first. Here, with Mary Catherine.

"Pensacola." Her roommate took a bite and chewed it slowly. Then her eyes lit up and she gasped. "Wait! Isn't that where your old guy lives? The baseball player?"

"Yes. Tyler Ames." Her slice of pizza sat untouched. She was too nervous to think about eating. "I have time Monday. So should I —"

Mary Catherine dropped her pizza onto her plate and jumped to her feet. "Of course! You're supposed to see Tyler. Why else would God have brought this trip together?" She paced to the window and back, her eyes sparkling. "Are you going to tell him?"

Sami uttered a quick laugh. "I'm not sure I'll even see him."

"You have to." Her roommate returned to the floor and took a bite of pizza. "Come on. We were just talking about him."

"You were talking about him." She laughed again.

"Same thing." Mary Catherine thought for a moment. "Did he write back on Face-book?"

"No." Sami had looked every day. She had no reason to be disappointed by the fact.

"Well, then, this is perfect, Sami. Don't you see?" Her roommate's joy was contagious. "He writes you, you write him. You drop in for a surprise visit."

"Just like that." Sami was still too distracted to eat.

"Yes! Just like that." She ran her hand

through her hair. "Arnie's getting so serious. Any day now he'll probably ask you to marry him. But you can't say yes, because you still have feelings for the guy who came first. So you have to see him, Sami. You do!" She sounded set on the matter. "You have no choice, really."

Sami's stomach hurt. "I don't know."

Mary Catherine leaned back on her hands, a satisfied look on her face. "So this is why."

"Why what?" Sami faced her roommate.

"Why you wanted a night with just the two of us. So I could talk you into seeing him." As always when matters turned serious, Mary Catherine calmed down. Her craziness took a back seat when Sami's heart was involved. "If I can skydive, you can pay a visit to Tyler Ames." She leaned close again. "Look at you. You've been thinking about him all week."

"I have." Sami stared at her cold pizza. "I keep checking Facebook in case he writes again. But what would be the point?"

"He was thinking about you, we know that much." Mary Catherine's enthusiasm was building again. "But he isn't going to start some pen-pal relationship when you're clearly taken."

"True." For a while they let the facts settle around them.

Mary Catherine stood and paced again, then she sat on the arm of the sofa. "Still . . . you have to see him."

"What's the point? I mean, you're right. I'm taken." Sami was working to convince herself. "Besides, it's been over between us for a long time."

Mary Catherine looked straight to Sami's heart. "What if it's not? Can you move ahead without knowing?"

And like that, Sami had her answer. Things with Tyler might be over, yes. But maybe she needed to see him again, look in his eyes, and know for sure that somehow she hadn't missed something. She had to feel with all certainty that Tyler Ames was a no. Then — and only then — could she come back to California and do the one thing she wasn't ready to think about.

Figure out what to do with Arnie Bell.

Sami's date with Arnie that night was more sedate than usual. Or maybe she just noticed it more in light of the dizzying thoughts filling her head and heart. Either way, Arnie talked about his case, how he was gathering evidence and conducting interviews around the clock. The lawsuit could still become a class-action ordeal, in which case Arnie would become only one of a team of lawyers involved. Either way the case consumed him.

On top of that he had a trip to New York set for the first three days of next week. The exact same time Sami would be in Pensacola. Arnie held her hands as he talked, and when they finished eating they strolled along Third Street toward Santa Monica Boulevard and Ocean Avenue. "Let's walk along the pier." He put his arm around her shoulders. "I need this time with you."

"Me, too." She hesitated, waiting to see if he had more to say about his work. When he didn't, she held her breath and dropped the news. "My week was a little crazy, too. I'm flying to Pensacola on Sunday for a couple days of meetings with the Atlantis team."

"Wow . . . we'll be gone at the same time." He slowed down, his eyes on hers. "Pensacola. That's where your old boyfriend plays baseball."

"Yes." She nodded slowly. They had discussed Tyler early in their relationship. "I mean, he's hurt. But he lives there."

Arnie seemed to mull over her words as they kept walking. "How did you know he was hurt?"

"Saw it on a newsfeed somewhere. Google, maybe." She didn't want to dwell

314

on the fact that she knew what Tyler Ames was doing. "Anyway, yes. He lives there."

"Okay." Arnie nodded slowly, his eyes straight ahead again. "Will you see him?"

She didn't want to mention the private Facebook messages. One day, maybe. Not now. "I haven't told him I'm coming." She kept her tone light to cover up her guilt. After all, she'd talked with Tyler on Facebook. But how could she tell him that? "I might look him up. It's been a long time."

Again Arnie took his time processing. "Should I worry?"

"About me seeing Tyler?" Sami laughed, but it fell flat. She was being dishonest and she hated it. "There's nothing to worry about." *Not yet,* she thought.

"Okay." Arnie smiled and resumed his earlier pace. "Just making sure." They walked a few more steps. "The thing about this case is the amount of evidence. You know? Like I could take a lifetime gathering information."

Sami tried to switch gears. Apparently they were done talking about Pensacola and Tyler Ames and anything remotely related to her. She nodded. "Absolutely."

"The trick is knowing when I have enough information and making sure it's the strongest stuff I can find. All within my deadline."

He shook his head. "It's a great challenge, Samantha. Really."

"I'm sure." She volleyed feedback whenever the conversation demanded it. But her mind was no longer on a walk with her boyfriend along a moonlit boulevard toward a southern California pier. It was on a different, distant shore, two thousand miles away in Pensacola, Florida.

With a boy she had never quite forgotten.

Just after four o'clock Sunday afternoon, Sami's American Airlines flight arrived in Pensacola. Despite Mary Catherine's convincing argument and an entire day of arguing with herself, Sami still hadn't decided whether she should see Tyler. Sure, they'd talked on Facebook, and yes, he had straightened up. But that didn't mean he had found his way back to the boy he'd been the day he boarded the bus to Billings.

If she looked him up, it was because she wanted to find *that* guy, the one she'd lost along the way. And even if she found him, the real Tyler, then what? She had Arnie. A serious boyfriend who wanted to marry her — even if she wasn't quite sure how she felt about him. Either way, why seek out Tyler now?

But as soon as she completed that round

of silent arguments, Sami would look out the window at a sky full of puffy white clouds and remember the feel of Tyler's arm against hers, the way she felt in his embrace. The way she had missed him. And with the certainty of her next breath, she couldn't imagine flying to Pensacola and not finding him.

She collected her bags, exhausted from the emotional tug-of-war. Maybe if she went by the baseball stadium she would have a sense of what she should do. She had nowhere else to go, nothing else on her agenda tonight. Tyler had said he was on the mend, working toward the Big Leagues again. He might even be at the facility now.

The forecast showed high seventies and blue skies. For a moment, Sami thought about renting a convertible. The sort of car she might have driven if Tyler were still in her life. But she settled on a sensible four-door sedan. Her client might think she wasn't serious if she showed up with the top down, hair windblown. Ten minutes later, Sami pulled into the Bayfront Stadium parking lot. Only a few cars were parked near a side entrance.

The team might even be on the road. Sami used her phone to check the Blue Wahoos' schedule and what she found surprised her. Their season had ended weeks ago. She thought about the time of year. October. Yes, of course their season was over. Minor league baseball playoffs were a month before the majors. Any baseball fan should've known that.

So maybe one of the cars parked here was Tyler's. If anyone was here on a Sunday night it would be him — working around the clock to get back on the pitching mound. Sami drove slowly toward the side entrance and parked her car near the others. Her heart pounded, and the palms of her hands felt damp.

Are you here, Tyler? Still working on your dream? She cut the engine and stared at the entrance for a long time. Being here took her back, the way she knew it would. The crack of the bat, the smell of fresh-cut grass on the ball field. The stadium was beautiful and with her windows rolled down, Sami could hear the nearby surf. The view from the parking lot was spectacular.

Sami breathed in the sweet ocean air. She couldn't come this far and miss her chance. The conversation might not go anywhere. It might be as shallow and matter-of-fact as the Facebook messages. But she had to find him, had to look into his eyes and see for herself if any remnant of the old Tyler Ames remained.

Once her heart was made up, there was no turning back. She climbed out of the rental, locked the doors, and headed for the entrance. Inside she found a security guard reading a book. He looked up, uninterested. "Can I help you?"

"My friend plays for the team." Sami smiled, looking past the guard station to a hallway and a series of offices. "I'm trying to find him."

"Not many players here today. Just coaches mostly."

"That's fine. Maybe I could talk to one of them."

The man squinted. "What player you looking for?"

"Tyler Ames. He's a pitcher."

He seemed to weigh her request. "Hold on." He picked up a phone on his desk and turned his chair so she couldn't see his face. It was impossible to hear his conversation, but after a few seconds he hung up and turned to her again. "Stay here. Jep Black's coming out. He's the manager."

"Thank you." Sami leaned against the door and waited.

A minute passed and then a squat man with a Blue Wahoos jacket and baseball cap approached her. He wasn't smiling. "Can I

319

help you?"

She held out her hand. "I'm Samantha Dawson. An old friend of Tyler Ames." She smiled. "I'm in town on business. Thought I'd look him up."

"Tyler was cut. He doesn't play for us anymore." The man looked guarded. "I'm sorry."

Sami tried not to react. Tyler hadn't said anything about being cut. He was on the mend, working toward the Bigs. She scrambled for something to say. "Did that . . . happen recently?"

"He was released the day after his injury." Jep Black shook his head. He looked over his shoulder and then back at Sami. "Lousy deal. Tyler's a great pitcher."

None of this made sense. Sami chastised herself for not checking first. "Is he . . . playing somewhere else?"

"He's still in town far as I know." Jep lowered his voice. "Last I heard he was working at Merrill Place — a retirement center." He took a step back. Again he seemed careful with his words. "If you find him, tell him we're pulling for him."

"Yes. I'll tell him." She was stunned. Too shocked to do anything but find her way back to her car. "Thank you."

Sami sat behind the wheel, not moving.

Tyler was working at a retirement center? No wonder he hadn't gone into detail or written back. How could he be working on a return to the game if he'd been cut? If no one else had picked him up? Of course they hadn't. Especially after his injury. Sami used her phone to find the address. Then she punched it in her GPS.

Once Merrill Place was in sight, she parked along the curb across the street. So this was where Tyler worked. Doing what? As far as she knew he had no training in anything but baseball.

She closed her eyes and she could see him, just before he stepped on the bus that long-ago day. *I'll prove them all wrong, Sami.* The memory faded and she opened her eyes. Merrill Place was an older, low-slung building with a simple brick sign at the front of the driveway. *Tyler, what are you doing here?*

Sami pulled away and drove straight to the beach. She needed to think, to wrap her mind around what she would say if she found Tyler. She climbed out of her car and walked to a retaining wall. For a long moment she leaned against it, facing the water.

He hadn't been completely honest with her after all. He'd said nothing about being cut from the Blue Wahoos or working at Merrill Place. Was he hiding something? He could be married for all she knew.

The breeze settled her anxious heart. Maybe it was none of that. Maybe Tyler was simply at rock bottom and he hadn't wanted her to know.

For the next hour she walked along the sand, remembering her year with Tyler and the size of his dreams. They had been bigger than the Gulf of Mexico back then. So what about now?

Not until she had returned to her car was Sami sure she was ready to see him. Besides his parents, she might be the only person who remembered how badly he wanted to make it, how hard he would have to try to find his way back now that he'd been cut. She owed it to Tyler to stop in and talk to him, encourage him to fight for the chance to pitch again.

Even if it was the last conversation they ever had.

23

The shakes had stopped, but there was no escaping the prison of pain. Tyler pushed the mop over the vast floors at the front entrance of Merrill Place and tried to remember life before his torn labrum. He hummed "Amazing Grace" as he worked.

I once was lost but now am found . . .

He had a plan now. He would save his money and come spring, he would have half of what he needed for the surgery. Then he would take a few weeks off, drive to California, and visit his parents. He would explain the situation and tell them he was sorry. Virginia said apologies were free and people should use them more often. *A person can never say "I'm sorry" or "I love you" often enough.* Those were her words.

His parents might not welcome him, but Tyler was pretty certain they'd listen. At least that much. He would explain that he never should've allowed so much time to pass and then maybe they would forgive him. His parents would know where he could turn. Which doctor might take payments. That sort of thing. Certainly someone in Simi Valley would remember him and repair his labrum — if he had at least half the money.

Get the surgery by April, and he'd have a year to come back, a year to find the speed and accuracy that had always defined him. Once he was pitching like himself, he'd start with the Blue Wahoos. If they didn't want him, he'd contact every AA team in the country. Someone would take a chance on him. He was still Tyler Ames. Surely God had a plan for him. Tyler was actually beginning to believe that.

He had a million miles to go, but he was off Oxycodone and working out every day. He could never be perfect on his own — not in baseball and not in his daily interactions. He needed God's grace to get him through. It had taken meeting Virginia Hutcheson to understand that. Even on his best days before his injury, Tyler Ames had been lost.

Now he was found.

The sound of the front doors caught his attention and he turned, ready to alert whoever it was that the floors were wet. But before he could open his mouth he felt the world tilt hard to one side. Standing there, her eyes locked on his, was the only girl he'd ever loved, the one he never expected to see again.

"Sami," he whispered. He felt the blood drain from his face as he leaned the mop against the nearest wall and turned to face her.

"Tyler." She didn't move, didn't say anything else. As if words might get in the way.

It took ten seconds before Tyler saw the situation through her eyes. The great Tyler Ames, winner of the Little League World Series, was washing floors at Merrill Place, his damaged arm still in a sling nearly two months after his injury. He stood a little straighter and went to her. He hugged her, quick and awkward-like, the unconvincing embrace of distant acquaintances. He stepped back and found his smile. "Why are you here?"

"Business. I have meetings this afternoon and tomorrow." She looked embarrassed for him, like even she didn't know what to say.

"I wish —" He chuckled, too defeated to search for an explanation. "I wish you would've called." Tyler really wished he could stop the moment, rewind it, and delete it from everyone's memory. He was a broken maintenance worker, not a baseball player. The truth was as plain as the look on her face.

Before he could say anything else, something caught his eye. He turned and there was sweet Virginia, shuffling toward him, her face lit up in a smile. "Ben!"

Sami looked confused. Her eyes moved from Virginia to Tyler and back again.

"Ben, look at you cleaning house." She reached him and patted his shoulder. "Best son a mother could ever have."

There was no time to worry about Sami, what she thought, or how this looked. Tyler took Virginia's hand. "How was breakfast?"

"Wonderful. They make the best eggs. Your father's favorite."

"Good." Tyler smiled. "Glad to hear it."

Virginia seemed to notice Sami. She shuffled closer, bridging the distance between the two of them. "Are you a friend of Ben's?"

Tyler stepped closer. "Yes, ma'am." He didn't wait for Sami to answer. "She's my friend."

"Wonderful." Virginia patted Sami on the arm. "You're a good girl, then."

Sami nodded, clearly setting her curiosity aside. "Thank you."

326

"Ben is amazing." The old woman smiled. "You have yourself a real keeper."

For a moment Sami hesitated. "Yes." Then she looked straight at Tyler, as if they were the only two in the room. "I've always believed that."

Always believed? Tyler felt dizzy. Was she really here, a few feet away? And did she mean to use that word? No one had believed in him the way Sami had. But that was a lifetime ago.

Virginia turned to Tyler again. "You're coming by later?"

"Of course." He walked alongside her. "You need help to your room?"

"No, no!" She looked back at Sami. "You stay here with this pretty girl." Virginia leaned close to Tyler. "She's lovely."

"She is." Tyler walked with Virginia halfway down the hall. Sami was waiting for him back in the entryway. He suddenly realized how he must look. Old dirty jeans, a worn out T-shirt. The ratty brace keeping his shattered shoulder from too much movement.

He stood a few feet from her and shoved his good hand in his pocket. "Thanks for coming by."

Her expression changed and anger flashed in her eyes. "That's it? I come all the way from California and you're dismissing me like . . . like some stranger?"

"What do you want me to say?" His own anger caught him off guard. "You've seen me, Sami. So go. Go back to your successful life in LA. You can write me off your list now."

She looked like she might scream at him. Instead she took a quick breath and exhaled slowly. "We need to go somewhere. I can't talk here."

He wanted to tell her no. She hadn't been invited, so she could just leave. But somehow that didn't seem fair. Not after she'd come so far. "Wait here."

Tyler took the mop and bucket back to the closet and found Harrison in his office. "An old friend stopped by. Can I have an hour?"

"Take as long as you like." His boss looked relaxed. "You'll finish later. I'm not worried."

"Thank you, sir." Tyler hid his frustration as he backed out of the office.

He found Sami in the same place, still waiting for him. Fine. They would go talk so he could explain to her how he should've gone to UCLA and how his failed attempt at baseball had landed him here. He had been wrong. Everyone else had been right.

Then he would tell her good-bye.

Once and for all.

Tyler drove her to the park next to the stadium and they found a bench overlooking the beach. Along the way he asked her about her job, about the client in Pensacola and the work she had to do later today and tomorrow. Not until they were sitting opposite each other on the bench did Tyler stop looking for ways to keep the conversation going.

They sat in silence, facing the water. He tried to believe he wasn't dreaming.

"It's beautiful." Sami didn't look at him.

"Yes." Much as he tried, he couldn't keep his eyes off her. "Different from the California beaches. Gentler surf. Warmer."

More silence. Tyler was grateful for the unrushed sound of the waves. Otherwise the nothingness might've been awkward. Finally she turned to him. "I don't want to talk about the beach."

Fine, he thought. *Let's get it over with.* This was why he had brought her here, so they could say what needed to be said and let it go. Finish things between them for all time. He put one knee up on the bench and faced her. "I'm a janitor."

"I know that." She didn't look away,

didn't blink. "You think that matters? You think I'm judging you for that?"

"Of course." His voice rose. "I told you I was on the mend, working toward my shot at the majors."

"Aren't you?" She sounded frustrated. "Isn't that why you're still here in Pensacola? So you can get back to baseball?"

Tyler blinked. Why was she dragging this out? "Sami, come on." The anger left him like air from a day-old balloon. "Who are we kidding? What we had . . . it's been gone for a long time." He lifted his good hand and let it fall to his knee. "Your boyfriend . . . he's a successful lawyer. You have a great job. Your life is set." He looked out at the ocean again. "Why are we doing this? Why did you want to see me?"

"Because." The intensity in her quiet voice remained. "Tyler, look at me."

His eyes found hers. Her unforgettable, deep blue eyes. It took all his effort not to be dragged back to a time when he loved her with every breath. "Why?"

"Because I had to see for myself." With their eyes connected, Sami seemed suddenly calmer. "Who you are today."

"I told you." He felt his heart shut off. "I'm a janitor."

"The Tyler Ames I knew was a dreamer

and a doer. He would make things happen. Find a way to win." Hurt colored her tone. "After you left home, you changed. Everyone knows that. But when I got your Facebook message I thought . . . maybe that phase was over. That you'd found your way back to who you really are. The Tyler I loved."

"What does it matter?" Tyler wanted the moment to end. Nothing could come from this. "You're happy now."

"How do you know?" Her tone became more hurt. "You haven't even asked."

"Sami." he was losing the fight. A part of him wanted to take her in his arms and never let her go. If he didn't find a way to end this meeting, his heart would get the better of him. He gritted his teeth. "Let's leave it at that."

"If I'm so happy . . ." Her voice dropped so it was barely louder than the sound of the nearby surf. "Why am I here?"

He stood and walked a few feet away. For a long time he just stood there, staring at the ocean, sorting through his next words. He felt her at his side before she spoke, sensed her like his own heartbeat. "You know why I turned down UCLA?" He turned and suddenly he didn't want to argue anymore. "To make you proud of me.

All I ever wanted to do was make you proud. You and my parents."

"I always believed that."

There it was again. Her belief in him. She was only a foot away, and even though he knew better, he allowed himself to get lost in her, in the sound of her voice and the smell of her perfume. "I let you down." He worked to keep his distance. "I'm sorry."

"You let yourself down first. That's when you changed. Otherwise . . ." She folded her arms, not hiding the hurt in her eyes. "Who knows?"

Tyler clenched his jaw and turned to the beach again. How was he supposed to keep his composure with her standing so close? "There's no going back."

"I wish . . ." She moved closer so only a breeze separated them.

He turned. "What do you wish?"

She lifted her eyes to his. "I wish that when you forgot who you were, you would've come home. Even for a little while." Her eyes were impossibly familiar. The same eyes that haunted him even still. "I would've helped you remember."

For a few seconds, he let himself imagine the possibility. "I should have."

"I waited." Tears welled in her eyes. "I waited even after you changed."

The news tore into him with a pain all its own. Hadn't he always wondered whether she had held out hope that he might find his way back? Back to Simi Valley and back to the guy he'd been before he left home? "You . . . didn't take my calls."

"Of course not." She raised her chin, willing him to understand her. "I didn't want the drunken playboy Tyler Ames." A single tear slid down her cheek. "I wanted the one I lost." She struggled to finish. "The one who never came back."

He looked away and breathed in sharp through his nose. He wouldn't break down, not now, not with her standing close enough to touch. "Maybe that's why I was calling you. To tell you I'd quit all that."

"Tyler." She shook her head and brushed a tear off her cheek. "I would've known. The news about you has always been as close as Google."

His eyes found hers again. Regret consumed him and became a pain even greater than the one in his shoulder. "I'm sorry, Sami. I never meant it." He had more he wanted to say. "I thought I'd make it to the majors in a season or two. When that didn't happen, I wasn't sure how you'd feel about me. It was easy to get lost."

Sami sighed and stared at the sky for a

few beats before looking at him again. "I didn't care if you played baseball."

"Yes, you did." Tyler held his sore arm against his body. "You and my parents, your grandparents. Everyone cared." He wasn't angry anymore. Just stating a fact. "Half our time together was at one of my games."

The hurt in her expression doubled. "You know why?"

He didn't answer. Of course he knew. Sami's grandfather had been part owner of the Giants, after all. She liked that he played baseball.

She came a step closer, a whisper away, as if by doing so she could will him to understand. "I came to your games because *you* were there." Fresh tears shone in her eyes. "I would've gone wherever you were."

Like summer rain, the idea fell over him all at once. When he looked in the mirror back then — same as when he looked in the mirror now — he saw only one person: Tyler Ames, baseball player. If he wasn't playing on the biggest possible field, then all his life had turned on a single mistake. "I thought I failed you, my parents." He raked his left hand through his hair. "Everyone who ever believed in me." He shook his head. "I figured it didn't matter. I'd already lost everyone I ever loved."

Gently Sami placed her hand alongside his face. "I believed in you. Not your game." She searched his eyes. "Baseball . . . wasn't who you were to me, Tyler Ames. It was something you did. That's all."

The feel of her fingers against his face made it impossible to think clearly. But he could see in her eyes she was telling the truth. She hadn't needed him to be a perfect baseball player. He could've been a pianist or a guy on the debate team. She had needed only him. Period. The realization just about killed him. "I never knew . . ." He inched his way closer. "Come here. Please."

She came to him as if she was born to be in his arms. For the longest time they held onto each other, swaying slightly, the warm wind off the gulf swirling around them. With her this close, his blown-out shoulder almost felt normal. How could he have walked away from her?

"Tyler." She whispered near his face. "I missed you so much."

"I missed you." He ached for a way back to then. He would've gone to UCLA and he never would've spent a day away from her.

Sami lifted her eyes to his. "After you left, every night I only wanted to be sitting next to you on the roof again." She brushed her cheek against his. "Back when the stars belonged to us."

"They did." *They still could,* he wanted to say. Instead he breathed in the closeness of her, the feel of her skin against his. It would be so easy to kiss her, so wonderful to pretend the years apart had never happened.

But they had happened.

He was here. And she had moved on. They both had. He brushed his good hand along her cheek. "I'm sorry." He couldn't stay this way for long or he'd kiss her, despite every reason not to. He searched her eyes and he could see straight to her heart, to the place where she still loved him enough to find him.

"I should've taken your calls." She closed her eyes for a beat, clearly hurting.

"No." Tyler moved his hand to her shoulder and drew a slow breath. His control was slipping. "It was me. My fault."

When he was sure he couldn't take the feel of her against him one more moment, he gently pulled away. "Come on." He took her hand and led her back to the bench. When they were seated, facing each other, he did the one thing he didn't want to do.

He released her hand. "Tell me about him. Please."

For a few seconds Sami looked confused, as if she had no idea who Tyler was talking about. Then it hit her. "Arnie?"

"Yes." He needed to keep things focused on the here and now. The pain of his past actions and costly misunderstandings were enough to suffocate him. If Sami talked about her boyfriend, maybe he could find a way to move past this moment. "Tell me about him."

"No." She looked away, clearly hurt. Her eyes filled with tears again. "I don't want to talk about him."

"I saw your pictures." Tyler willed the walls to stand again, the ones that most days kept him from missing her. "You have a new life now."

"You don't know me." Another tear made its way down her cheek. She did nothing to stop it. "You thought I loved you because you could play baseball." Her eyes held a sadness he hadn't seen before. "How would you know anything about my life?"

He kept his tone kind. "Arnie — he's your reality, Sami. Maybe if you tell me about him . . ."

"I didn't come here for that." She stood and stared at him, more upset than before.

Something changed in her eyes. "I need to go."

"Sami . . . don't." He didn't understand. How could she be angry? If it were up to him, she would be single and he would slip his fingers between hers and hold her hand, pull her close. He would find his way back to the wonderful moment they'd shared a few minutes ago.

But he had to keep his distance. This crazy unexpected morning was another ending. Not a beginning. Tyler didn't go after her. "You have a boyfriend, Sami." He could hear the defeat in his voice. "That's the reality."

"I'm not sure how I feel about Arnie." Her voice was more sad than angry. "I come here to tell you how much I've missed you . . . how I never cared if you played baseball." She looked at the ocean for a few beats and then at him. "I told you . . . I want to talk about you and me. What happened to us. Not Arnie."

"He's your boyfriend."

"Yes. He is." She looked like she might cry or leave or both. Tears filled her eyes, but she blinked them away. "I have meetings, Tyler. Please, take me back to my car."

If this were a movie, they would talk about all they'd missed and the moments from yesterday when they were sure the world would stop turning if they didn't see each other, hear each other's voices. But this was not a movie. Tyler's busted shoulder and Sami's Facebook pictures told him that much. He stood and went to her. For another breathless moment he looked into her eyes — once more before the moment passed altogether — "I'll always be sorry."

"I know." Her anger eased and gradually her expression became resigned, closed off. She looked at his arm, at the brace. "Are you healing?"

"No." A quick pain sliced through his shoulder. He resisted the urge to react. "I need an operation." This part was the most difficult of all. He wasn't a kid and yet here he was without insurance, without a real home or a career. "I'm saving up."

A look of disbelief tightened her expression. "Your team isn't paying for it?"

"No. My contract didn't cover injuries." He didn't want to get into the reason why, and thankfully she didn't ask. The conversation was humiliating enough. "I'll get there. I'm not worried. Sometime this spring, probably."

"What about your parents?" Sami was still clearly shocked. "Won't they help?"

One more layer of reality he'd rather not

expose. But what did it matter now? She might as well know exactly how far he'd sunk. Then she could go back to Arnie with a full heart. A sigh rattled from his chest and he faced the ocean. "I haven't talked to my parents in years. They have no way to contact me even if they wanted to."

"Tyler!" She sounded like maybe this detail might've been the worst of all. "That's awful."

"Yeah, well." He looked at her again, the walls firmly in place. "If you could've heard how my dad talked to me last time we spoke, you would've cut ties, too. They only loved me if I could play ball. Once I messed that up, they didn't want me."

Sami folded her arms in front of her, as if her stomach hurt. "So you thought . . . I was like that, too?"

"I was wrong." He wanted to be kind, but he also wanted to wrap up the visit. "It doesn't matter now. That was a lifetime ago." He started to walk toward his car. "Come on. You have work to do."

She allowed a great deal of space between them as they headed to the car and climbed in. On the ride back, she looked out her window and didn't say a word. *Fine,* he thought. *Silence is better.* No sense making small talk. Not when he knew now that she had loved him all along. He had made a mess of every part of his life — no question.

But this most of all: losing Sami Dawson.

He drove her back to Merrill Place and pulled into an empty spot. He got out first and opened her door. It was over between them. For all time. But he wanted her to leave knowing the truth about his feelings. That much at least. She stood, leaving several feet between them. "I shouldn't have come." Her eyes met his but only briefly. "It only makes things worse." She tried to move around him, but he blocked her way.

"Sami," Tyler allowed his defenses down one last time. "Please."

She released a sad-sounding sigh but she did as he asked. "I need to go."

"I never meant to disappoint you." He put his left hand on her shoulder again. "Not now. Not ever."

She looked deep into his eyes, his face. "What happened to you, Tyler? How can you be okay with hiding here? Hiding from me . . . from your parents?"

"I'm not hiding. I'm working my way back." He pictured Virginia. "God has me here for a reason."

"God?" She narrowed her eyes, studying him. "I asked God to make things clear

341

today. Whether I had a reason to tell Arnie no." Tears gathered in her eyes again.

"I see." His voice fell to a whisper, all he could manage. "I have nothing to give you, Sami. Go back to him." He touched her face, brushed her cheek with his knuckles. "I want you to have a good life."

"You still don't know me, Tyler." She moved toward her car. "Maybe you never did."

He wanted one more hug, one more chance to hold her and remember what love felt like. But it wasn't going to happen. He took a step back and held up his hand. Then he turned and walked with fresh purpose to the front entrance of Merrill Place. Tears stung his eyes and once he was inside, he watched her through the nearest window. Watched her drive her rented sedan away from the curb and away from him.

With the back of his hand, he dried his cheeks and then finished his work. All he could think about was Sami, her eyes and her face, her voice as it filled his soul. The feel of her in his arms.

He would go see Virginia later.

First he needed to hit the gym, find a way to push through the heartache. One hour became two and two became three — more time on the stationary bike, more crunches, more squats. The longer he worked the more desperate he became to dull the ache. But there was none.

By the time he fell into bed that night, Tyler had a feeling that as long as he lived, this new pain would never go away. The pain of knowing he could've made things right, the ache of missing his opportunity, the hurt of knowing she belonged to someone else. And the painful reality of losing Sami Dawson not once.

But twice.

24

The answer came to Sami all at once, before her flight touched down in Los Angeles. Things with Tyler had been over for a long time. She had learned that much on her trip. He made no statements of love or longing, no intention of fighting for her. As much as the truth hurt, Sami would always be glad she'd looked him up, glad for their talk — no matter how sad. Because without it she wouldn't have known what to do next.

The time had come to break up with Arnie Bell.

She waited until that Friday night — because Arnie was too busy to meet sooner. That night they had an early dinner with her grandparents, and Sami wondered if maybe he would stay friends with them after tonight. Probably. The three of them had so much in common: their belief that the world's problems could be solved through politics, and that goodness and money always followed strong, proper people, educated people.

Arnie talked about his medical case over filet mignon and a $200 bottle of Bordeaux. Sami's grandparents hung on every word. Sami didn't drink, and she barely touched her steak. Her eyes kept drifting to the window and the ocean view beyond.

All she could think about was what was coming. She remembered her conversation with Mary Catherine the night she came home from Florida.

Her roommate had been doing yoga in the TV room when Sami found her. Sami took a spot on the sofa a few feet away. "I have to tell you something."

"Perfect." Mary Catherine was mid-stretch, her back arched, face toward the ceiling. "Talk to me." She settled into a cross-legged position. Her green eyes were instantly engaged. "Tell me you saw him. Yes?"

"I did."

Mary Catherine had squealed. "How did it go?"

"Not good." Sami hadn't wanted to rehash her time with Tyler. "He's moved on. There's nothing between us." It wasn't exactly the truth, but it would do. "That's not what I want to tell you."

"Okay." Her roommate blinked. "What's up?"

"It's over with Arnie. I realized it on the flight home."

"Really?" Mary Catherine leaned forward.

"I wouldn't have met with Tyler if I was happy." Sami shrugged. "If I was sure about Arnie."

"True." Mary Catherine had looked sympathetic. "I'm sorry."

"I've been doubting things with him for a long time." Sami felt peace about her decision. Then and now.

"Samantha?"

She jumped and turned her attention to Arnie. "Sorry."

"You do this all the time lately." He laughed, clearly embarrassed as he looked from Sami's grandparents back to her. "Could you try to stay focused?"

"Definitely." She sat up straighter. Her steak was getting cold. Maybe if she focused on eating she could stay with the conversation. Two bites later she gave up. She wasn't hungry. If only she could fast-forward through this dinner to the difficult conversation to come. She was ready for things to be over.

Her grandmother was looking strangely at her, a piercing sort of look. She glanced

346

down at Sami's blouse and made a subtle pointing motion. Sami looked down and saw the problem. She had a breadcrumb there. With a quick brush of her fingers she restored the perfection of her image. Her grandmother smiled and gave a slight nod.

All attention was back on Arnie. "This case could shape medical law for a generation." He looked at Sami's grandfather, his eyebrows raised. "Can you imagine? Me in charge of a case like that?"

"Absolutely." Her grandfather took his wine glass and swirled the deep red liquid in a way that showed his experience. "You'll be in greater and grander arenas every year, Arnie. I've always believed that." He gave Sami a functional smile. "Samantha is blessed to know you."

Was he serious? Sami clenched her fists beneath the table. She'd had about enough. If she could, she'd step outside and call Tyler. Just one more time. She'd tell him how grateful she was for her time with him because of one thing: his questions about Arnie had brought her to this.

Finally after a round of tiramisu, the dinner ended. Once again Arnie was looking at her, waiting for her response. Sami had no idea what she was supposed to say. "I'm tired." She smiled appropriately at her grandparents and then at Arnie. "Let's say good night."

"All right, then." Her grandfather looked ready to call it a night, too. He kissed Sami on the cheek and shook Arnie's hand. "Next week? Same place?"

"Wonderful." Arnie looked a little off-balance as he bid Sami's grandma good night. As if he could sense the trouble ahead. Not until they were both inside his car did he turn to her. His expression proved he was completely baffled. "Lately every dinner is like this. You're barely here."

"I know." She smiled, but she could feel the sadness in it. "It's my fault. Can we talk somewhere?"

He looked back at the restaurant, his tone sarcastic. "I thought we just tried that."

"I mean alone. Just the two of us." Sami didn't get angry. This was her fault. She hadn't been honest with him and now he deserved more than a quick breakup in the car.

"This late?" Arnie looked at her, his expression puzzled. As if she had suggested they go skinny-dipping at the Santa Monica pier.

"Yes." She thought for a moment. "How about the Starbucks on Third Street? The one at Barnes & Noble."

"That's fine." He turned the key in the ignition. "I'll valet."

Arnie always worried about Santa Monica at night. But it was only seven o'clock on a Friday. Hardly the most dangerous hour. They valet-parked at a hotel a block away and walked to the coffee shop. Arnie linked arms with her and walked on the outside of the sidewalk. *Always a gentleman,* she thought. *He won't have trouble finding the right girl.*

"It's nice tonight. Cooler." He smiled at her.

Sami wanted to blink and be out of this scene, finished with it. How could he make small talk when clearly she had something serious on her mind? They walked inside and headed to the counter. Arnie looked at her. "The usual, I assume?"

"Sure. Thanks." She felt colder than usual. Goosebumps rose on both her arms despite her black cashmere turtleneck. She stood to the side and watched him order.

"Two grande drips. Plain black." Arnie pulled out his wallet.

Suddenly Sami didn't want the usual. Not now. "Hold on." She stepped up. "I'll get a tall pumpkin spice latte."

"What?" He looked back at her, his brow lowered, obviously confused by her behavior. "Samantha, that's loaded with sugar."

"Actually, make it a grande." She smiled politely at the barista. "Please."

Arnie's expression changed, as if to say he wasn't going to argue but clearly he didn't agree with her choice. They took their drinks to a small table near the window. "Try not to change your order like that. It's embarrassing."

"It's fine." Sami felt herself relax. This was the right thing to do. She couldn't have been more certain. "People change their orders all the time." She wrapped her freezing fingers around her hot cup. "Thanks. For making time to talk."

"I didn't really have a choice. The way you've been acting." He sat back, his look slightly condescending. "Let's make it quick. Then we can watch *The Office* back at your apartment." He checked the time on his phone. "If it doesn't get too late."

Poor Arnie. Sami studied him. How had she ever thought the two of them had anything in common? "Here it is." She exhaled. If only her fingers would stop trembling. "Arnie . . . I don't think it's working. You and me."

For several seconds he only looked at her, as if she'd spoken in French. "That's what this is about?" He released the slightest

350

chuckle. "You're doubting us?"

"Yes." She suddenly realized that he hadn't even asked her about her time in Florida. Nothing whatsoever about her business trip. She sipped her coffee. "I saw Tyler Ames when I was in Florida."

Arnie didn't need to smirk to convey how he felt about Tyler. But he did it anyway. "I heard he got cut." He leaned his forearms on the table, his look pointed. "How's that working out for him?"

She didn't want this to get ugly. "It's working fine. Tyler doesn't need baseball."

"So that's why we're having this talk? You have feelings for your old boyfriend?"

Arnie cared a little. Otherwise he wouldn't have looked up Tyler's status since the last time they'd talked. Sami waited until the tension between them faded a little. Finally she drew a steadying breath. "This isn't about Tyler."

"Then what's the problem?" Arnie spoke louder than before. "What have I done wrong? Tell me."

"Don't raise your voice. Please." She had never seen this side of him. As if he was playing lawyer with her. "I'm not serious enough for you, Arnie. I feel like I'm acting."

That seemed to put Arnie a little at ease.

He settled back in his seat. "I'm listening."

"You're wonderful, Arnie. You're smart and accomplished. You really might be president of the United States one day." She reached one hand across the small wooden table. "I believe that."

He looked at her hand for a long moment and then finally took it. "Thank you." The fight seemed to leave him just a little. "That helps."

Sami had a suspicion that in the end this would be easier for Arnie than he thought. But she didn't want to say so. The tension between them had already faded considerably. "I just need a change. I'm sorry."

"You think serious is a bad thing?" Arnie released her hand and leaned back, putting both hands on his coffee. "Too many people aren't serious. We've talked about that."

"I know. And we do have *The Office* — which isn't exactly serious."

"Right." Arnie didn't smile. "I mean, it's okay to laugh. But people in this country are too frivolous. They're fascinated with Twitter and Facebook — dissolving their attention spans to fractions of what they once were." He took a breath. "You were never like that. It's the reason I fell in love with you."

The comment hurt. He had fallen in love

352

with her seriousness? The mere thought of that made her want to run out the door and never look back. Instead she sipped her drink and studied him. Arnie meant the words as a positive. "Thank you." She found a slight smile. "I'm glad you see me as concerned about society. Really."

"Not only that, obviously." He rolled his eyes as if he'd been trapped. "You're a beautiful girl, Samantha. Intelligent, poised. From a good family. Perfect for someone like me."

She wouldn't get angry. He was still trying to compliment her. "I appreciate that." She set her elbows on the table and leaned closer, her voice softer than before. "But I need my freedom. I feel like I'm suffocating."

His expression darkened. He brought one leg up and crossed it over his knee. "I make you feel that way?"

"Yes. You don't mean to. It's just . . ." Sami let her hands fall to her lap. At least she wasn't freezing anymore. "It's over, Arnie. I don't know what else to say."

He sipped his coffee, and for nearly a minute neither of them said anything. "If it's okay, I'd like to stay in touch with your grandparents. They're very influential. I appreciate their interest in my career."

The implied message was that her grandparents were maybe more important to Arnie than she was. But even that didn't bother Sami. She felt more relieved than angry. "I'm sure they'd love that."

"Did they know this was coming?" He seemed to doubt the possibility.

"They had no idea."

"I didn't think so." Arnie nodded slowly. "I have to believe they'll be upset with your decision."

Sami stared at him. His ugly side was appearing again. "It's a chance I'll take."

Arnie stood and tossed his empty coffee cup in the recycling bin. When he returned he offered Sami his hand. "I'll drive you back to your apartment."

She wanted to find her own way back. But she didn't want to make things worse. "Fine." When he dropped her off that night, his eyes were dry. A slight smirk stayed on the corners of his mouth, as if he could hardly believe she was really doing this. Like if Sami wanted to make this mistake, he wasn't going to stop her.

Sami couldn't breathe until she was back in her apartment. She slid down the door and fell to the floor in a heap. Only then did she let the laughter come. Not because there was anything very funny about the evening. But because she was free.

The feeling was better than anything Sami had felt in years.

Sami waded out into the Pacific Ocean trailing behind Mary Catherine. Each girl had a boogie board tethered to her wrist.

"I can't believe I'm doing this." Sami's heart pounded, the ocean water cold against her skin. She'd walked on the beach a hundred times but never, until now, had she gone in past her ankles. "You're sure it's perfectly safe?"

Mary Catherine tilted her head back, her red hair spilling down her back. She looked back at Sami. "Of course it's not perfectly safe! That's why it's fun." She waited for Sami to catch up. "God meant for us to experience life. It helps us have faith."

"Faith." Sami's teeth chattered. "If I drown, write that on my tombstone."

Again her friend laughed. "Come on. We have to get out a little ways."

"Not over our heads. You promised." The water was up to her waist now. Sami felt her breath catch in her throat. "How much further?"

"There." Mary Catherine pointed to a spot just ahead of them where smallish waves were constantly forming. "It won't be over our heads. Not this close in."

They kept walking. Sami felt panic well up, but she remembered her roommate's advice: *Pray. Have faith.* She tried to breathe. *God, be with me. Keep the sharks away. Please.* As she uttered the silent prayer, something strange happened. Her fear faded. She was standing in the Pacific Ocean, water lapping against her chest, about to ride a wave for the first time. How great was this?

"Okay. This is good." Mary Catherine slid the boogie board beneath her so she was lying on top of it. "Do this." She looked over her shoulder at the waves coming their way. "Hurry!"

Sami did as she was told. She eased herself on top of the board and pointed it toward the shore — same way Mary Catherine did. A squeal came from her. "This is crazy!"

"Here it comes!" Her friend began to paddle. "Use your arms. Come on!"

"I'm doing it! I really am!" Sami began to stroke the water, positioning herself directly in the path of the wave coming up behind them. And then — with a rush of power and force unlike anything Sami had ever felt, the wave grabbed her boogie board and propelled her toward shore.

A few feet away Mary Catherine was having the same sort of ride, laughing out loud. "Yahoooo!" she screamed as loud as she could. "I love this!"

Sami was still holding on, still trying to remember how to inhale amidst the exhilaration of the ride. But when the wave died on shore, Sami stood and raised her board in the air. "I did it! I rode a wave!" She danced around in a little circle. Then she jogged back toward the deeper water. "Let's do it again!"

Yesterday she and Mary Catherine had stayed up late talking about Sami's breakup. But instead of the conversation being sad and depressing, it was full of hope. Together they wrote a list of everything Sami needed to do. Things that weren't safe or predictable or grown-up.

Skydiving and horseback riding, hikes in the Santa Monica Mountains, and serving at the homeless mission downtown. Crazy wonderful exciting things.

Like riding the waves at Zuma Beach.

"Look at you, Sami Dawson!" Mary Catherine laughed, her voice carrying above the sound of the surf. "You're learning to live!"

It was true. Sami almost felt guilty for not being more broken up, for not allowing an appropriate amount of time to grieve the loss of her relationship with Arnie. But she couldn't bring herself to feel sad. If this was what life felt like, she could only breathe it in and savor every moment.

Life had just begun.

She could hardly wait for whatever came next.

25

Beck wore the white uniform of one of the hospital orderlies, his pace determined. He'd learned this much: when angels walked, one thing was crucial — confidence. He set his jaw and kept his eyes straight ahead.

A minute later he reached her room, stepped inside, and moved straight for the TV. Like a man on a mission.

A nurse was in the room, preparing for a patient's arrival. "Can I help you?" She narrowed her eyes at him, clearly trying to place him.

Beck smiled, his voice quiet, "Just changing the channel." He reached up and manually switched the television from a Western to ESPN. The sound was muted and Beck left it that way.

"Why?" Again the nurse looked confused.

"Request from the family." Beck nodded at the nurse and left the room. Halfway down the hall he stepped into a supply closet.

And like that he disappeared.

The call Cheryl had dreaded for most of the last decade came at three that Sunday afternoon. The one she'd expected since her mother's health began to decline. Lately her mom had been doing so well Cheryl actually stopped expecting it. As if love could prolong the life of even the most worn-out heart.

She dried her hands on a dishtowel and answered the phone on the third ring. The caller ID read Merrill Place. She leaned against the kitchen counter. "Hello?"

"Cheryl, it's Harrison Myers." He paused. "I'm sorry . . . I'm afraid your mother might've had a heart attack."

A heart attack? The room began to spin and Cheryl struggled to stay focused. She gripped the counter with one hand and pressed the phone to her ear. "Is she . . . conscious?"

"Yes. Paramedics are getting her into the ambulance now." He sounded upset. "Meet us at the hospital. Get there as fast as you can. Please."

"I will." She hung up and then closed her eyes. "Chuck! Please . . . come here!"

He was in the next room reading, but her tone must've told him something was very wrong. He was at her side immediately. "What is it?"

"It's Mom. They're taking her to the hospital. She . . . she might've had a heart attack."

"Honey." He hugged her. "I'm sorry."

She rested her forehead against his. "I've dreaded this for so long."

"We both have."

Cheryl pictured her mother the last time they talked, sitting in her room a few nights ago. She had looked so happy and healthy. But at her age a heart attack could mean the end. Cheryl waited while Chuck grabbed the keys. "We need to go."

"I'll call the girls from the car." Cheryl wasn't sure how they made it to the car. The details seemed to blur as Chuck drove to the hospital. Both their daughters wanted to meet them there. The sad thing was everyone had planned to go to Merrill Place this afternoon. "Now we won't have that time." Cheryl blinked back tears. "It's so sad. Mom would've loved it."

"Maybe she'll be awake." Chuck kept hope alive with his tone. "We need to pray." And with that Chuck spoke the most beautiful prayer, asking God to breathe life into

Cheryl's mother. "If her time is coming, Lord, please give us the chance to say good-bye. Thank You, Father. In Jesus' name, amen."

Of course they should pray. Why hadn't Cheryl thought of that? *God . . . forgive me. Go ahead of us. Please let her live. I want to say good-bye.* But before she could chastise herself any further, she thought of a thousand times when her mother had given her grace. Perfection was never expected. Peace worked its way through her, erasing her anxiety. Her mother was right.

They met one of their daughters in the hospital lobby and then quickly were led into a private room where a doctor came to them. "She's definitely had a heart attack." He looked deeply concerned. "She's stable, but critical." He hesitated. "We're watching her closely."

An hour later they were allowed back to her room, but she didn't wake up until the next day.

"She's ready to see you." The doctor smiled at Cheryl. "Your brother's already there."

Cheryl caught the surprised look on her daughters' faces. Tyler Ames must be here. "It's okay. I'll explain later. Let's go back."

When they reached her room, there he

was, sitting at her mother's side, holding her hand and talking to her. A baseball game played silently from the nearby television.

At the sound of the group at the door, Tyler looked up. His eyes were red, as if he'd been crying. He nodded at them and then turned his attention to Cheryl's mother.

She looked frail and sickly, a decade older than she had just a few days ago. She turned to them and a smile lifted the weathered corners of her mouth. "Hello." She barely motioned with her free hand. "Come in. Please."

Thank You, God. Relief flooded Cheryl's heart. *Whatever else happens, at least we have this.* She led the group into the room and took her place next to Tyler. "We're all here, Mother."

"Yes." She smiled at Tyler and then took in the entire group. "All of you."

Tyler released the old woman's hand and moved discreetly toward the wall so Cheryl could have his spot. She nodded at him, then took hold of her mother's hands and tried not to cry. "How are you feeling?"

"Mixed."

Cheryl felt Chuck's hand on her shoulder. She was thankful for his support. "How do you mean, Mom?"

"Well." Her chin quivered, her emotions gaining ground. "I'm so happy to have you all here. You and your brother. And I'm glad we're watching baseball together." She glanced at the TV and then smiled at Tyler. "But I can hear Jesus calling me home." Her eyes had never looked more lucid. "Your father's there, you know."

It was the first time in years she'd acknowledged their father's death. Tears blurred Cheryl's eyes as she nodded. "Yes. Daddy is there, waiting for you."

Her mother's smile was the sweetest thing ever, half sorrow, half joy beyond measure. "So you see" — she released a few weak coughs — "I'm mixed."

"I understand." Cheryl looked around the room. "The girls are here, Mom."

"Yes." She held out one hand toward them. "I see that. I'm so glad you could all come."

One at a time each of the girls came closer, giving Cheryl's mother the chance to acknowledge them and bid them goodbye. "But only for now," she told them. "Goodbye for now." She looked at Tyler, who remained as much out of the way as possible. "Heaven will be wonderful. Right, Ben? I feel you might know that more than the rest of us."

"Yes, ma'am. It'll be perfect." Tyler looked out of place. Cheryl motioned for him to stay. It was okay. She wanted him to be here. *What sort of warm-hearted young man he must be to stay here like this, to care about a dying ninety-year-old woman. God, remember that miracle I asked you for? Please make it happen. His kind is rare.*

"I want . . ." Cheryl's mother tried to sit up a little, but the effort fell short. Winded, she tried again from her lying-down position. "Ben?"

"I'm here." Tyler slid closer to Cheryl. "We're all here."

"Okay." Peace settled over her. "There is one thing I want to say. Especially to you, Ben."

He looked around at the others, an unspoken apology in his eyes. As if the last thing he wanted was to intrude on this private moment. Cheryl nodded in his direction, willing him to keep playing the part of Ben Hutcheson. Tyler nodded in return. He looked at Cheryl's mother. "I'm listening."

"I think about . . . our talks lately." She smiled at Cheryl and Chuck and the others. "Ben comes by every day. He brings me flowers." Her eyes turned to Ben again. "We've had the best talks."

"We have." Tyler looked at her, sincerity

365

ringing in his voice.

"Ben's shoulder is hurt and sometimes" — she looked straight at him — "sometimes you talk about your mistakes and your past like . . . like you think you need to be perfect."

"Yes." Tears filled Tyler's eyes. "I wish that. I've made a lot of mistakes."

She shook her head, though the movement was miniscule. "You have to leave room for God's grace, Ben."

Cheryl silently mouthed the next words as her mother spoke them.

"Perfect is God's job." She released Cheryl's hand and reached for Tyler's. "You'll live your life a lot happier if you stop trying to be perfect. Do your best for Jesus. When you fall short, He'll carry you." She smiled at the others. "The way He's carrying me right now."

Her eyes closed for a moment. Slowly she blinked them open. "I'm so tired." She looked from Tyler to Cheryl. "Thank you. The two of you are the best kids I could've had." Another couple slow blinks and she was asleep.

Cheryl stared at the TV. How her mother had loved baseball. Because Ben loved it. She narrowed her eyes, trying to see who was playing. It was the Dodgers. And the man on the pitcher's mound was . . .

She smiled. It was Marcus Dillinger.

How long had it been since she'd watched him pitch?

After a few minutes the doctor came in and suggested they let her rest. Once the family and Tyler Ames were out in the hallway, the doctor allowed his expression to grow grim. "Your mother's oxygen levels aren't good. Her heart's giving out."

Cheryl leaned into Chuck. "Will she go back to Merrill Place? Are we talking weeks or months?"

"We'll keep her here for now. And as for her time . . . no one can say." He checked her chart. "Could be a few days or a few weeks."

Cheryl nodded. "Thank you." She held out her arms and her daughters and husband all came close. Cheryl motioned for Tyler to join them. "This is Tyler." She looked at each of them. "I'll explain about him later. For now I need to talk to Tyler alone." A pair of empty chairs sat in the hallway outside her mother's room. "I'll meet the rest of you in the waiting room in a few minutes."

Chuck studied her. "You sure you're okay?"

"I am."

They hugged, Chuck's eyes searching hers. "I'm sorry."

"It's okay. She's not afraid."

Before he left, Chuck shook Tyler's good hand. "Thank you. Your time with Virginia . . . you'll never know how much it's meant to her. To all of us." Cheryl smiled at the young man. He had even put the ball game on in her room.

"She's a special lady." Tyler clearly meant every word. When Chuck and the rest of the family left, Tyler turned to Cheryl. "I've been looking forward to this talk." He glanced back at the hospital room. "I didn't picture it like this."

"None of us did." She sat down and Tyler did the same. "She's been so well since you came into her life."

"I have so many questions. But I guess the biggest one is about Ben." Tyler shook his head, bewildered. "Wherever he lives or whatever he does, he should be here."

"You're right." Cheryl felt fresh tears in her eyes. "Ben loved our mother very much. If he could be here, he would." She hesitated. "Tyler, Ben is dead. He was a soldier. He died in 1972, killed in Vietnam."

The news seemed to take Tyler's breath away. His head dropped and he stared at his hands. For several seconds he stayed that way before he looked at Cheryl. "I had no idea. I'm so sorry."

"Ben wasn't perfect, but he loved God . . . and he loved our family." Cheryl barely noticed the tears on her cheeks. Her heart was back in 1970 — the week before Ben left for Vietnam. "Love. That was his strong suit. He would bring my mother daisies every day. They grew wild in our backyard." Cheryl pictured her brother, tall and strapping, thoughtful to a fault. "My mother loved those daisies."

"She asked about them." Tyler looked heartbroken. "That's why I started bringing the flowers."

"You've made her so happy."

Tyler looked down again. "The loss must've just about killed her."

"Yes." Cheryl felt fresh tears in her eyes. "None of us were ever the same after we got the news. My dad's easy laugh, the sparkle in his eyes — they changed with Ben gone." Cheryl stared straight ahead, falling into that long ago yesterday. "Ben and his men were trapped. If he'd waited, he might've been rescued. The others were." The sorrow was as real as it had been back then. "But that wasn't Ben's way. He cared too much for everyone else. He set out to get help." Cheryl looked straight at Tyler.

"Two minutes later he was caught in the crossfire and killed."

Tyler shook his head. He worked the muscles in his jaw. "So sad."

"After Ben died, my father brought my mother fresh daisies every day. In honor of Ben. After Dad died, I tried to get over there and bring her daisies, but it wasn't the same. She would talk about heaven — long before she was sick. With Ben there, she could hardly wait."

"Then she lost her memory?" Tyler seemed to easily understand.

"Exactly. At first we kept photos at her bedside — the last one we had of Ben was one of her favorites. He was in uniform, so handsome." She wiped her tears. "But eventually the pictures confused her. She couldn't understand why Ben didn't visit, why no one would let her see him."

Tyler rubbed the back of his neck, clearly touched by the story. "When I came to Merrill Place, her nurse said they had to keep her medicated."

"She kept trying to escape." The hurt of those times still felt fresh. "It was so sad. She just wanted to find Ben." Cheryl brought her fingers to her face, struggling to compose herself. "Then you came into her life."

"Your mother . . . she loves so completely." Tyler stared at the closed door to her room. He looked at Cheryl again. "I definitely got the feeling Ben made some mistakes."

"He did," Cheryl could see her handsome brother again, his eyes full of life and adventure. "Crashed the family car into a tree. He never got an A in school, not once." An image flashed in her mind, Ben's face each semester when he brought his report card to her parents. "My dad wanted him to try harder. But Mom just told him he got an A-plus in the only thing that mattered — loving God and loving people."

Tears shone in Tyler's eyes. He nodded, stroking his chin. "Her words were intended for your brother, but they've helped me." He wiped the back of his hand roughly across his cheek. "I've been trying to be perfect for a long time."

Cheryl put her hand on his good one. "God works in miraculous ways. You were our answer to prayer." She paused. "Maybe she was yours."

Tyler thought for a second. "Did Ben play baseball?"

"He did." Cheryl studied the young man. He looked so much like her brother. "He was very good. If he hadn't been drafted, he might've had a shot at the pros." She thought for a moment. "Have you figured out your surgery yet?"

"I'm saving for it." He held his damaged arm closer to his body. "Sometime this spring. That's my goal."

Cheryl thought about this broken young man waiting until spring — six months or more — for his operation. He still wore the brace, and he moved carefully. "Does it hurt?"

"Yes." He hesitated. "But I'm off the pain medication. I can get through it."

Again Cheryl wished she could help. But neither she nor her mother had that sort of money. "Let's pray it happens a whole lot sooner. There has to be a way."

"Can't hurt to pray." Tyler looked at the floor, not quite confident.

"How about now." She took hold of his left hand. "My mom taught me the importance of praying. I prayed she would find peace before God took her home. That was like asking for the Lord to part the Red Sea all over again." Cheryl smiled through fresh tears. "But He did it. He brought us you. So let's ask Him about your shoulder." She closed her eyes. "Father, You are good. Above all things, You are the great I Am. There is nothing we can do to earn Your love. But You sent Jesus to rescue us, to give us the love and blessings we don't deserve and cannot earn."

As she prayed, Cheryl realized how much she sounded like her mother. The thought made her a little less sad. "So now, Lord, we lift up Tyler Ames. He needs surgery and he needs it now. He's in pain and he needs to get back out on that baseball field. We have no idea how that might happen, but You know. Please, God, work out the details. Give Tyler a miracle so he can know for sure that You see him, You love him. In the powerful name of Jesus, amen."

"Amen." They both stood and Tyler hugged her. "Thank you. For sharing your mother with me. For believing in me." He looked at the floor and then back up at her. "You'll never know how much my time with her has meant."

"You're going to get your surgery." She grinned, more hopeful than before. "I believe it."

"Thank you." Tyler pulled his car keys from his pocket. "I need to get to work. I'll come back tonight to check on her."

"We'll be here." They hugged again and she watched him leave. After he was gone, Cheryl slipped back inside her mother's room and took the chair near her bed. Her mom's breathing had slowed, but she had a slight smile on her face. Completely at peace, her sweet mother.

Cheryl leaned back in the chair. What a miracle it was that Tyler Ames had come into their lives. His kind heart and uncanny resemblance to Ben. There had to be a way to help him get the surgery. She thought for a long time, running through ideas of local charities or people of influence that she might ask.

Then she remembered something. She looked up at the game on TV and again the camera was on the young man who had rented a room from them a few years back when they lived in Tennessee. He'd been a player with the Outlooks in Chattanooga, a young man on his way up. Of course, he was in LA now playing with the Dodgers. Cheryl tried to make a point of following his career. Every Christmas they exchanged cards and she would say a prayer for the young man. That one day he would find Jesus.

Maybe she should contact him. Cheryl let the idea take root.

Yes, she would call him this afternoon. Why hadn't she thought of it sooner? At the very least he would know a doctor who might help Tyler. There had to be a surgeon somewhere who would give Tyler Ames a break, someone with a list of professional baseball clients and a love for the game. If anyone would know who that doctor might be, it was the young man who had been part of Cheryl and Chuck's family for the better part of a year. One of the top pitchers around. The one who was pitching for the Dodgers today.

Marcus Dillinger.

26

The afternoon passed slowly at Merrill Place, but as soon as Tyler finished his work, he returned to the hospital. Now as he sat beside Cheryl in Virginia's hospital room, he felt filled with a purpose that hadn't been there before today. Sure, he'd gotten off Oxycodone and he was stronger than before. But ever since his conversation with Cheryl in the hallway, he actually felt a sense of destiny.

Tyler Ames would make it back. Nothing could stand in his way. Not with people like Virginia Hutcheson and her daughter praying for him.

"It won't be long," Cheryl whispered the words, her attention on her mother.

Tyler knew he needed to say good-bye. This time was for family. He leaned forward and wrapped his fingers around the old woman's. "I'll keep you with me," he whispered, his eyes dry. He couldn't possibly be

sad for Virginia. She was about to be re-
united with her husband and her son.
Heaven would be incomparably better than
Merrill Place. Better than anything earth
could offer. Tyler believed that because of
Virginia.

She looked peaceful, her breathing slower
than it had been even an hour ago. "Before
I go" — Tyler leaned closer to her, his voice
quiet — "I have something for you."

Cheryl watched him, clearly curious.

He released the old woman's hand and
went to the grocery bag in the corner of the
room, the one he'd brought with him.

"You didn't need to get her anything."
Cheryl's tone was kind.

"I wanted to." From inside the brown bag
he pulled out a vase of flowers. Daisies.

"Tyler." Cheryl brought her hand to her
mouth.

He caught her eye. "I've brought her flowers almost every day. But never daisies." He
set them on her hospital table. "I had to.
After all she's done for me." He sat down
and took Virginia's hand again. "I brought
you daisies. Your favorite."

She already had one foot in heaven, no
doubt. But there was no mistaking the way
the corners of her mouth lifted. She gave
Tyler's hand a gentle squeeze and her lips

moved. She didn't need to say the words. Tyler knew she was thankful — the way he was thankful. He looked at Cheryl. "Do you have a phone with you?"

"Yes." Cheryl pulled her cell phone from her purse.

"Can you take our picture? Me and your mom and the daisies?" He picked up the flowers again. "You can email it to me. That would mean a great deal."

"Of course." Cheryl waited until he had positioned himself alongside her bed, his good arm on Virginia's shoulder. She took the shot and stared at it. "One day I'd like to show you photos of Ben. You really look so much like him."

Tyler gave Cheryl his email address and she sent the picture. There. He sat back down and took Virginia's hand again. This way he could remember the dear woman from Merrill Place, the grace that she had taught him so much about, and the God she loved with all her being. He kissed her hand. "Good-bye, Virginia. Ben's waiting for you."

Two hours later Tyler was in his room checking email, looking at the picture with Virginia when another email came in. This one also from Cheryl. He opened it and read the few lines it contained. Virginia was gone — home to heaven and reunited with her husband and her dear Ben. Tyler covered his face with his good hand. He didn't try to stop the tears, but they weren't for Virginia. They were for himself. For all he still had to figure out, for the long days ahead without her love and wisdom.

Tyler closed his eyes and lifted his face toward heaven. Because of Virginia he had some changes to make. His mom and dad might not understand grace, but because of Virginia, Tyler did. He would share that grace with them, and maybe they would find what they'd lost all those years ago.

Unconditional love.

He had to do one more thing before he turned in for the night. Every day since Sami's visit he had thought about her. How sincere she'd been and how much she'd cared for him. She had believed in him, not his game. He understood that now. In the last few days everything felt clearer.

Tyler pictured her again. Sami had been right there in front of him, the ocean at their side. But he had rejected her attempt to talk things out, forced himself to believe she was content with her life, better off with her boyfriend. Then he had sent her away with barely an explanation. As if every wonderful feeling they'd had and all the time they'd shared didn't matter at all.

Well, it did matter. It all mattered. And now that she was gone he wasn't going to waste another day. Not another moment. He opened his eyes and pulled the computer close again. Since Sami's visit he hadn't looked her up on Facebook. It was too hard to see her with her boyfriend — no matter how easily he had let her go last week.

He pulled up her page and was about to click the link to send her a private message when something caught his attention. First, her profile picture showed her standing in the ocean with a boogie board. She looked radiantly joyful. Tyler touched the screen. *I remember you being that happy.* He smiled despite the ache in his heart. *Good for you, Sami. You live your life.*

Then just as quickly he noticed her status. It was blank now. Tyler stared at the spot. What had happened? He scrolled down her page and through her most recent pictures. Every sign of the guy was gone.

His mind raced. Why the change? Did they break up?

He clicked the message link and thought about what he wanted to say. He began to type.

Dear Sami,
There was something I didn't tell you when you were here. I haven't only been a janitor here at Merrill Place. I was also Virginia Hutcheson's only son. You might remember her. You had just walked through the front door of the place and an older woman walked up. She called me Ben, and she told you I was a catch. She said you were pretty. That was Virginia.

He wasn't sure where this was headed, but he had to be honest. Had to tell someone who actually knew him the difference Virginia had made in his life. His fingers began to move over the keyboard again.

He told Sami the whole story. He explained that Virginia Hutcheson would stay with him always. He kept typing, recalling everything he learned since his injury.

He wasn't sure why he was telling her so much, but he couldn't stop now.

About God . . . we never talked about Him back then. But I think maybe God was there the whole time. Virginia taught me that.

Tears blurred the words on the computer screen. He missed Virginia already. He blinked so he could see what he was typing.

I guess I wanted to tell you about Virginia, but I also wanted to say I'm sorry. I didn't treat you right when you were here. You belonged to someone else, so I didn't let my heart feel anything. That's what I told myself. But that was wrong. Being with you did make me feel something.

The truth is, I miss you. More than you could ever know. Especially on nights like this. Forgive me for keeping my heart locked up. Virginia wouldn't want me to live like that. Now that she's gone, I don't want to live like that either. That's it, really. I didn't want you to think I was only a janitor at Merrill Place, when you see . . . I understand now, God doesn't define me by my job. Whatever work He gives me. Forgive me, Sami. Keep riding the waves.

Love,
Tyler

He was closing out of her page when he saw something that stopped him cold. How had he missed this a few minutes ago? His heart soared and he couldn't keep from smiling. Sure, her picture was new, and yes, she'd taken her relationship status down. But the most telling detail that something dramatic had happened in her life was this one single fact. She had changed her official name.

She was no longer Samantha Dawson.

She was Sami.

It was the third Sunday in October, the first without Virginia, and Tyler missed her more than he had ever expected. Some days he could almost feel her with him, her hand in his, her gentle voice reminding him of some life-altering truth. Today, though, would be the toughest of all.

This was Virginia's memorial service. Cheryl had decided it should take place here, in the same place where Tyler had sung for her and her friends in recent weeks. "If you would sing a few songs and share your thoughts," Cheryl had sounded weary, "I know it would mean so much to my mother."

Tyler could get through the songs more easily now. The guitar felt familiar in his broken grip and the words were etched in his heart where they would stay. But he had never played the songs without Virginia in the front row. Her sweet smile, the way she nodded, encouraging him, urging him to keep singing for her and for Jesus. He had thought he'd be nothing but happy. Virginia had her son for real now.

But what about him? Who did he have?

The residents started filing in just after one o'clock. He took his usual place on the metal stool at the front of the living room and watched them arrive. A part of him wanted to believe that somehow she would appear, that she'd walk down the hallway and step into the living room with the others. Her eyes would find his and she'd walk to the seat front and center.

Her chair was there, same as always.

As the residents took their places, they were quieter than usual. More somber. Virginia was gone. Their times were coming. No one took Virginia's seat, which was only right. When Tyler was halfway through "The Old Rugged Cross," he could look there and see her, the way she would've looked. This was one of Virginia's favorites. He'd sung it every time since the first Sunday. But this time the words hit him differently.

"So I'll cherish the old rugged cross, till my trophies at last I lay down. I will cling to the old rugged cross and exchange it one day for a crown."

A crown? Wasn't that what he'd worked all his life to find a way back to? They'd won the crown at the Little League World series, but ever since then he'd been chasing that sort of success. But that wasn't what the song meant. This crown was one of grace and peace — the crown of salvation because of Jesus on the old, rugged cross. The trophies Tyler had collected, the ones still sitting in a box in his room — he needed to lay them down. None of them mattered the way grace did.

The crown of grace.

He kept playing, looking at the faces of the men and women in their eighties and nineties. Heaven waited for all of them. If they chose the gift of God's salvation, they'd all be there one day. He sang "How Great Thou Art," and then he set down the guitar. For a long time he looked at Virginia's empty chair. Then he lifted his eyes to the residents.

At the same time he saw Cheryl and her family sitting nearby, watching. Tears streamed down her face.

Tyler found his voice. "This past week we lost our good friend Virginia Hutcheson." He worked to keep his tone clear. He let his eyes rest on Virgina's chair again. "The thing is, life is short. A hundred years is nothing." He looked at a few of the faces sitting nearby. "Right?"

A quiet chorus of murmurs and nods came in response. A few of the women quietly began to cry. One of them leaned over to the resident next to her. "Virginia died? No one told me."

Tyler picked up his guitar and began singing "Amazing Grace." "Virginia believed in Jesus and she believed in grace. She knew none of us has what it takes to make it home." His voice caught. He waited for half a minute. *Get it together, Tyler.* He was never going to be a preacher, but here — for Virginia — he had to try.

He cleared his throat. "None of us can get to heaven alone. We can't be perfect."

His eyes met Cheryl's across the room. "Perfect is God's job. He's perfect enough for all of us. You need Him and I need Him. If you haven't made peace with that, then it's time. Today." He let that settle for a few seconds. "That way when our time comes, we can find Virginia Hutcheson and sing hymns on Sunday afternoon. Forever."

That was all. Tyler finished Virginia's favorite song and as he did, he had to hope that around the room a few hearts might've heard him. Some of the women were nodding and at the back of the room a man in a wheelchair began to clap.

The clapping became contagious. While Tyler softly strummed the last few chords, three women and then another two and a couple of old men all began to clap. They clapped for Jesus and salvation and a woman who had lived out her faith.

Tyler looked at Virginia's empty chair and once more he could see her. Clapping along with her friends, tears shining in her happy eyes. Celebrating grace as only she could. He could see her and feel her presence and as he set down the guitar, he realized something he hadn't before: the words he'd told Virginia were true. She would always be with him.

As close as the song.

27

When the memorial service ended, the residents gradually made their way back to their rooms. A few of them stopped by Virginia's empty chair and touched the back of it. Just long enough to be intentional. Tyler waited, nodding and smiling. Not until they were gone did Cheryl walk up.

"It was beautiful. The songs . . . What you said. Mom would've been so proud of you."

He smiled. "She always was. No matter what."

"True." Cheryl's eyes sparkled as she studied him. "I have good news."

He sat on the stool again, appreciating the way she felt like family. "Tell me."

"Well, the other day after I prayed for you at the hospital I got to thinking." She clutched her purse in front of her. "A few years back we rented a room to a baseball player for a season. Even after he left we stayed in touch. I thought maybe I could call him and see if he knew of a surgeon who would operate on you for less money. It was worth a shot."

Tyler felt his spine stiffen. He had no idea where this was going.

"You won't believe this — or maybe you will, since we asked God for a miracle." Cheryl reached out and took hold of his left hand. "Anyway, the young man has been busy, but he called me back this morning. I told him about you, how you had loved my mother and how you needed surgery." Happy tears glistened in her eyes.

Adrenaline rushed through Tyler's veins. The floor felt liquid. "You did that?"

"I did." She made a sound that was more laugh than cry. "He told me to get you on a plane. He'd make the appointment with the team surgeon and —" Her voice broke. She shook her head, trying to speak through her emotions. "He . . . he said whatever the cost, he'd pay for it. Himself."

The words came to him all jumbled up. What had she said? She knew a baseball player who could pay for his surgery? That wasn't possible. People didn't pay for other people's operations. "How would . . . who would —"

"Here's the most amazing part." Cheryl was practically bouncing now. "You know him, Tyler. He plays for the Dodgers. He said you were on the same Little League team."

He played for the Dodgers? Tyler felt the blood leave his face. He gripped the edge of the stool and tried to keep his balance. The baseball player friend of Cheryl's could only be one person. "Marcus Dillinger?" Everything was spinning. Was this really happening? Was she really telling him this? "You called Marcus?"

"Yes." She ran her free hand over her opposite arm. "I've had chills ever since I hung up. Think about it, Tyler. We ask God for a miracle and I see the baseball game on in my mom's room. There's Marcus, pitching on TV. And because of that I feel the need to call him. In case he might know of a doctor who could help you. Only he hesitates for a second, then he tells me the thing that I never could've known: the two of you were best friends when you were twelve." She laughed again. "That's a pretty big miracle." Cheryl reached into her purse and pulled out a slip of paper. "He said you two lost track of each other. He wanted me to give you his number. He says he has a reservation on hold for you to fly to LA tomorrow!"

Tomorrow? He was going to get on a

plane and see Marcus Dillinger in the middle of the playoffs? The Dodgers were in the World Series. They'd locked their place with Saturday's win. At the busiest time in his baseball career, Marcus was making time for him?

Tyler shielded his eyes for half a minute, then he looked at Cheryl again. "You're serious?"

"We asked God for His help."

"So it's real?"

"Yes, Tyler Ames. Call Marcus." Cheryl's face beamed with joy and for a moment she looked just like her mother.

Tyler started to chuckle. The adrenaline had left him exhausted and lightheaded. He stood and pulled Cheryl into a hug. "I have no words. I mean . . . I can't believe it. The whole thing is impossible."

"It's a miracle." Cheryl stepped back and smiled at him. "The one we prayed for. Now go call your old friend."

"Yes, ma'am. Thank you."

"I've got errands to run, but I had to come here first. Tell you in person." She took a few steps toward the door. "Keep in touch, you hear?"

"I will." He pictured how his life might be in six months or a year. "If things go the way I think they will, I'll be back. I might even see if you have a spare room."

Cheryl smiled. "We'd be honored to have you." She waved before she turned around. "You're family now, Tyler. You always will be."

"You, too." He watched her leave. He wasn't sure what to do first. He decided to call Marcus. His old friend was waiting — if he could believe this wonderful miraculous turn of events. He went to his apartment and used the wall phone. Marcus answered it on the first ring. As if he was expecting the call.

"Hey, Ames! This you?"

"Marcus." He had never felt his rock-bottom place more in all his life. They were both supposed to have made it to the Bigs. They were supposed to play for the same team or meet up in the World Series. They'd had it all figured out when they were twelve. Tyler pinched the bridge of his nose, desperate for composure. "I talked to Cheryl Conley. She says —"

"We're gonna get your shoulder fixed. No time to waste." Marcus sounded happy, full of life. "It's a long story, but I think you're part of some crazy things happening."

Marcus sounded the same, as if no time had passed between them. "You're sure? I can pay you back . . . but it'll take a while."

"You always did talk too much, Ames. You know that?" He laughed. "Get your broken butt out here first thing tomorrow. I have the ticket on hold at the airport. I've got like ten million frequent flyer miles."

This was real. Marcus was on the other end of the line telling him about flight details. He was going to LA. He had an appointment with one of the top surgeons. And in a week or so, he was going to get his surgery. "I . . . I'm not sure what to say."

"Now there's a switch. Remember when Coach lit into you because you were talking when he was talking?" Marcus laughed as easily now as he had back then. "I'll give you a day, Ames. By the time you land tomorrow you'll think of something to say. I have no doubt."

Both of them laughed. Tyler could hardly wait for morning. Before the call ended, his friend's tone grew softer, more serious. "You gotta get better, Ames. You're too good to sit the bench, you hear?"

"Thanks. Remind me to tell you about Cheryl's mother tomorrow. Talk about crazy things happening."

The call ended and Tyler remembered Harrison Myers. He needed to tell the man that he was leaving. He wasn't sure when he'd be back. He held his injured arm

393

against his body, ignoring the pain as he hurried to the office. So much hope filled him he half expected to look down and see angels carrying him. God felt that close. And even if they weren't, Tyler knew this much:

Somewhere in heaven, Virginia Hutcheson was smiling.

Harrison Myers was filling out paperwork for one of the new residents at Merrill Place when Tyler Ames knocked on his door and came in. He'd never looked happier.

"Mr. Myers. Sorry — I have to talk to you. It can't wait." Tyler still wore his brace, though it was frayed at the seams now. "Is that okay?"

Harrison laughed a little. "Of course." He nodded to the chair. "Have a seat."

"I have a flight out tomorrow morning at 7:15." He was breathless. "I'm not sure when I'll be back."

Tyler explained everything. But when he finally came up for a breath Harrison thought he understood the big picture. "Are you saying this is your last day?"

Laughter shook Tyler's chest, and Harrison realized he hadn't seen this side of the young athlete. He hadn't had a reason to laugh until now. "I think so." He explained that he would come back for his things as soon as he could, or maybe he'd pay to have them shipped. "If I get everything in a few boxes, maybe you could keep them in your storage out back."

"Of course. I'll wait to hear from you." Harrison leaned his forearms on the desk and studied the young man in front of him. "I'm happy for you, Tyler. This is just what you need."

"It is." Tyler's smile faded. "None of it would've happened if it hadn't been for you. If you hadn't given me a chance. I was homeless. I hadn't showered in days and my clothes could've walked in on their own." He narrowed his eyes. "Without you, I never would've met Virginia."

"That was special, what happened between you two." Harrison slipped his glasses back on and nodded. "Never seen anything like it." Harrison stood and Tyler did the same. "I'd take you back anytime." They shook hands. "You're a hard worker and a good man, Tyler Ames. When you get back on that pitcher's mound, just know this: I'll be following your career from here. I believe in you."

"Thank you, sir." Tyler took a few steps toward the office door. "That means so much."

"Take the rest of the day off. Go pack." He sighed. "Looks like I need a new maintenance man." He pointed at Tyler. "One who can sing."

"Yes, sir." Tyler laughed again. He was at the door when he stopped and turned around. "Oh! I almost forgot. I made a phone call earlier — long distance. Ten or twelve minutes." He hesitated. "Can you take it out of my last paycheck?"

"Tyler Ames, no, I cannot." Harrison shook his head and grinned. "I think I can cover the calls. After all you've done around here."

Not until Tyler was gone did Harrison sit back down and think about what had happened.

Working at Merrill Place sometimes felt monotonous. Like he was biding time, living on cruise control. Working for a paycheck. But that wasn't true. He loved the residents here. God was using him.

He thought about Tyler walking into Hope Community Church and some volunteer remembering Pastor Roman's information about Merrill Place. Then Tyler's resemblance to Virginia Hutcheson's son and the young man's heart to take time for an old dying woman. He thought about the connection between Cheryl and Marcus

Dillinger and Tyler and he shook his head. God had allowed him to be ringside to a miracle bigger than all of them.

One that was only now beginning to play out.

28

The world series started in forty-eight hours, but Marcus Dillinger wasn't at the ballpark. He was driving to Los Angeles International Airport in his Hummer. Every other player was either at the Dodgers' training facility or working on his game. Marcus Dillinger had spoken to his coach, Ollie Wayne, and gotten permission for this diversion.

"I'm ready," he told him. "I'll deliver. I promise."

"That's fine." Ollie believed him. Always.

Marcus couldn't wait to see his old friend. Everything else was lined up. Tyler would meet with the surgeon later today. The guy had promised to do the operation at cost.

Pennies for someone with a starting pitcher's income.

He pulled off the 405 Freeway onto Airport Boulevard and worked his way to the passenger pickup area. About the same time he got a call. One ring and then it stopped. The signal they'd worked out meaning Tyler had his bags and he was headed outside.

Marcus tried to imagine not having a cell phone, not having the money to buy a plane ticket or get surgery — insurance or not. He was so far removed from the place Tyler lived in. But none of it had mattered until the call from Cheryl Conley. He had challenged God, after all. Asked Him to bring meaning to his life.

If He was real, anyway.

Baldy Williams was gone, but Marcus still had today. He wanted to make a difference.

Now he was going to get the chance.

He spotted Tyler and rolled down his window. "Ames! Over here!"

Tyler turned and lifted his good hand. The other arm was in a brace. He wore a baseball hat — proof that he still saw himself as a player. He was taking this trip to find a way back to the mound.

Marcus put his Hummer in park and jogged around to meet his friend. The two shared a hearty hug and the same handshake they'd done back when they were twelve. "Look at you!" Marcus grinned at his old friend. "I can't believe you're here."

"You don't look a day older than you did

as a senior in high school." Tyler grinned at him.

"Cross-town rivals." Marcus flicked his friend's baseball cap. "Jackson High Champs. You still have that old thing?"

"It's vintage, man. Gotta love it."

They caught up all the way back to Dodger Stadium. Marcus pulled into the player parking lot around one o'clock. His teammates were working out on their own until practice at three that afternoon. Still plenty of time to talk to Tyler, quit the jokes, and give him the back story. The unexpected way Tyler might be an answer to his own questions.

Marcus waited until they were seated in the fifth row off third base. The air was cool, the sky impossibly blue. A light breeze drifted down from the Santa Monica Mountains. Perfect LA weather.

Tyler leaned over his knees and stared at the field, at the pitcher's mound. "Can't believe this, man. You're living the dream."

"My whole life's been one lucky break." Marcus expected Tyler to laugh and say something about his being a series of unlucky breaks. Instead his friend leaned back in his seat.

"I earned my bad breaks. All of them. I was a mess long before I threw that last pitch." Tyler drew a deep breath. "I'm better now than I was when my body was perfect. I believe that."

Marcus nodded, thoughtful. "Okay . . . You want the story?"

Tyler smiled. "Every detail."

"So Baldy Williams overdosed. You heard about that?"

"I did." Tyler sighed. "Such a waste." He looked out at the mound again. "Back when we were kids, remember? We wrote a list of pitchers we wanted to be like."

Marcus could see them again, the boys they'd been that summer, sitting at Tyler's kitchen table. "I completely forgot about that."

"Yep." Tyler's smile looked sad this time. "Baldy was at the top of the list. For both of us." He shook his head. "Hit me hard, man. They had me on Oxycodone. I mean, for a long time. Read that article and not long after I quit cold. I could see things getting out of control."

"Hmmm. I didn't know that."

"Poor Baldy." Tyler lifted his face to the sunshine directly over the stadium. "I didn't want things to end like that for me."

A shudder worked its way through Marcus. How would he have felt if he'd gotten the call that the person dead from an

401

overdose was Tyler Ames? If he hadn't connected with him now and helped him like this? He would've lived with the regret all his life. "Anyway, after Baldy died I came here the next morning and pretty nearly ran myself to death. Felt like the grim reaper was chasing me up and down the stairs."

"Sounds awful." Tyler turned and looked at him, caught up in the story.

"All the money and cars and houses, the fame and play-offs. None of it mattered that morning." Marcus squinted at the distant stairs. "All I wanted was purpose. A reason for this life." He looked at Tyler again. "You know?"

"Definitely." His friend's eyes said he could relate.

"So." Marcus sat up straighter, breathing in deep. "I gave God a challenge. I told Him if He was there, He needed to show me. Give me a reason to believe. Give my life meaning."

Tyler held his damaged arm close to his body. He smiled, but his eyes remained thoughtful. "Sounds like you."

"I know . . . lotta nerve. Calling out God." Marcus chuckled, but the sound faded quickly. "That was only a few weeks ago. Since then a day hasn't gone by without some way to give back. Talking to a couple guys about converting a hotel downtown for the homeless. Maybe adding an after-school program for troubled teens." He sighed. "I've been busy writing checks. All for good things, but I never really saw God in them. If He was real I wanted better proof — something more personal."

For a long time Tyler only stared at the infield. When he looked back at Marcus, his eyes looked damp. "So God brought me."

"Exactly." He gazed at the nearby mountains. "I couldn't make this stuff up, you know? Couldn't have placed a call or had my agent figure it out." His eyes met Tyler's again. "It has to be God."

Tyler removed his baseball cap and worked his good hand through his hair. "Wait till you hear my side of the story."

"See, Ames?" Marcus grinned. "I knew you'd find your words."

For the next ten minutes Tyler told him his story. The parts Marcus couldn't possibly have known: how the blown shoulder had led to his living in a car and how a random visit to a church had opened a door for the job at Merrill Place. The way Virginia Hutcheson had thought he was her son, and the daily conversations that followed.

The way she spoke to him about God's grace.

"I mean, what are the odds you take time with an old lady and because of that, you wind up back here with me?" Marcus couldn't stop the chills that ran along his bare arms.

"That's just it. There are no odds." Tyler laughed in a way that showed his bewilderment. "Both of us needed a miracle. Both of us were backed into a corner where only God could get us out."

Tyler was right. "Cheryl . . . her mother. You."

"God tied it all together." Tyler chuckled. "So we wouldn't mistake it for something ordinary." He slipped his cap back on his head and adjusted the bill.

"Exactly." Marcus pulled his car keys and a slip of paper from his pocket. "Hey, I gotta run. Your appointment's in an hour. Here's the keys and the address."

Tyler took both and again he seemed at a loss for words. He stared at the slip of paper and hung his head. "How can I . . . ever thank you?" He shook his head. "I don't deserve this."

"I thought your friend Virginia already told you that." Marcus put his arm around his friend's good shoulder. "None of us deserve anything, right? Wasn't that it?"

"Yes, but . . ." Tyler lifted his head and

looked at Marcus. "I mean . . . my shoulder, my trouble. It isn't your problem."

"No." Marcus's heart felt lighter than it had in years. "It isn't my problem, Ames. It's my miracle." He stood and folded his arms, smiling at his friend. "How's that for a switch? I should be thanking you."

Tyler hesitated for a few seconds, but then he stood and the two of them laughed the way they had when they were kids. "You're still crazy, Marcus." They hugged like brothers and then Tyler held up the car keys. His laughter fell away. "Hey, man. After my appointment . . . can I take the car to Simi Valley? I have . . . a stop to make."

Marcus thought he understood. Tyler's parents lived in Simi Valley. They hadn't talked about it, but Cheryl Conley said they weren't in Tyler's life. "Go where you want. Take your time." He nodded toward the field. "I'll be here."

With that they parted ways. Marcus jogged down the steps through a door to the locker room. As he went, he actually felt different. Lighter in the soul, happier. As he reached his teammates he realized what the feeling was, and how God had met the challenge. More than all the fame and money the world could give him, God had given him something greater.

A purpose.

Angie Ames had a strange sense lately. She and Bill prayed every day for Tyler — the way they'd prayed since that day the waitress had talked to them. They had looked for her several times since then, but she was never there. No one seemed to know her. Of course, they were still saving money, hoping for the chance to fly to Florida and find their son. Let him know how sorry they were, how they had been wrong to let so much time pass without finding him. They had cut corners everywhere possible.

They planned to book the flight in a few weeks.

Maybe that was why lately when they prayed for Tyler, Angie felt a greater sense of hope. A greater expectancy.

But as Angie's hopes soared, Bill's seem to sink. He was more discouraged than ever. "How could Tyler forgive me? Even if we go and talk to him face-to-face?"

Angie figured they'd need to fly to Florida. Only then it would be obvious how God was working in Tyler's life. And Angie believed God was working. By now Tyler's shoulder was probably healed. He would be pitching again, working with a trainer, and finding his way back to the top. He was a fighter. She had always believed in him — even during the years of silence.

That morning she was working the front desk for the fence company when the phone rang. "Hello?"

Silence.

Angie was about to hang up when she heard something. Like the sound of a freeway. "Hello?"

"Mom?"

Her breath caught. "Tyler?" She pressed the phone to her face and closed her eyes. How many seasons had passed since she'd heard him? "Where are you?"

"I'm here in LA. It's a long story." He sounded clear-minded.

"Okay." She held onto every word. Tyler was here? In California?

"I have an appointment and then . . . I'd like to come by the house."

"We'll be there." She closed her eyes, too excited to breathe. Before the end of the day she would see her son again. She tried to focus. "What time, do you think?"

"Around four. Give or take." Again there was the sound of traffic. "Sorry. I'm at a pay phone."

"That's fine." She pictured him standing on the edge of a road somewhere. "Be careful. We'll see you in a few hours."

"Thanks, Mom." He hesitated. "I should have good news by then."

"Tyler . . ." There was so much to say, so many blown-up bridges to rebuild. "We haven't known how to reach you."

"That was my fault." The sound of traffic grew louder. "We can talk about it later. I have to go."

"All right." Her mind raced. She didn't want the phone call to end but she had to trust him. This afternoon he'd be home with some sort of news. She squeezed her eyes shut. "I love you."

Another pause, and this time she could hear the emotion in his voice. "Love you, too."

Angie hung up the phone and stared at it. The call had actually happened, right? She pressed a few buttons and saw proof of the unfamiliar number. Yes, he had called. They had talked for just under two minutes. Which meant later today their boy would be standing in the living room again. Angie shielded her eyes with her hand. She had missed him so much. Every day, every month. The seasons and years lost forever.

She pushed away the thought. Things would be different now. She could hear it in Tyler's voice. *Thank You, God . . . thank You.* The waitress had been right about Tyler and prayer and not giving up. *I knew You were doing something, God, and now this! Thank You.* She could hardly wait to find Bill in the warehouse and tell him the news.

Their son was coming home.

29

Tyler climbed back into his friend's Hummer and just sat there, not moving. Sweat beaded along his brow and his hand shook as he gripped the steering wheel. Good thing he hadn't eaten in a few hours because he would've lost it all. Of all the things he'd done in his life, placing that call was maybe the hardest.

I did it. He looked in the rear view mirror. *I actually did it. She doesn't hate me.*

He remembered to exhale. If Virginia were here, she would've cheered for him. In her world, there would be no question whether a son would call home. He would always call. If he failed a class or crashed a car or struck out in baseball, he would call.

But Tyler's life had been very different. Until now.

It took a full minute, staring at invisible memories through the windshield, before he let the relief come. He had made the call and now he was ready to face whatever came next. Instead of the yelling and criticizing and ranting about being disappointed, his mother had been kind. Happy, even.

When his breathing returned to normal he started the car and pulled back into traffic. This was the day he had longed for and dreamed about. The day he had planned during his chats with Virginia. He would talk to the surgeon about scheduling the surgery, and together they would make a plan to get him pitching again. Then he was going to drive home and see his parents.

The whole thing felt like the most wonderful dream.

As he arrived at Dr. Shawn Walsh's orthopedic office, Tyler thought about Sami. She was only an hour away. He wondered if she'd seen his message from yesterday and if she'd responded. He had no way to tell until he could get to a computer. Which wouldn't happen until tonight at Marcus's house.

Tyler parked the car, locked it, and stared at the beautiful building. *This is all You, God. Here goes!* He could picture how the next few hours would go, and he could hardly wait. This was the miracle Cheryl had prayed for! On the third floor he signed in and after a few minutes he was ushered into an MRI room.

"It's been so long since your injury, we need to do another MRI." The nurse smiled. "Besides, this is the best machine in the world. Dr. Walsh will need the clearest view of your shoulder."

Another reason to be grateful. Maybe his arm wasn't as badly damaged as the doctor at the Pensacola hospital had thought. The test took forty minutes and then Tyler spent another thirty in the waiting room before he was called back to an exam room. Something big was about to happen. Dr. Walsh would make him better than new.

This time around, he would soar through the minors.

The exam room had a wall of windows overlooking palm trees and mountains. Tyler was ready to work, ready to do whatever it took to get back in form. The surgery couldn't come soon enough. There was a knock at the door. Tyler sat up straighter, his right arm tucked in its brace again. "Yes?"

An athletic-looking man opened the door and stepped in. "I'm Dr. Walsh."

They shook hands. "Tyler Ames. Thank you . . . for seeing me on such short notice."

The man smiled. "Marcus is a friend. He

says I have to get you back in a uniform."

"Yes, sir." Tyler liked this doctor. The man didn't look a day over thirty — younger than he had expected. He'd probably played the game himself before med school.

For a few seconds, Dr. Walsh read the notes in what must've been Tyler's chart. Then he set the folder down and drew a long breath. "Let's take a look at your arm."

Tyler eased it free from the brace and undid the latches at the back of his neck and his waist. When the brace was off and on the table beside him, Dr. Walsh stepped up. "I'm sorry you're only getting help now." He shook his head "Those no-injury contracts should be illegal. If you're well enough to play ball, they should cover you. Period."

As much as Tyler agreed, there was no going back. His heart pounded in his throat, anxious for the next step.

"Can you do this?" Dr. Walsh raised his elbow out to his side. "See how far you can go."

Tyler tried. He really did. He lifted his arm an inch, maybe two, but the pain was like burning knives through his shoulder and neck. He winced. "Sorry. I think . . . my muscle isn't what it used to be."

"That's fine." The doctor tried again.

413

"Let's do this." He straightened his arm and lifted it directly in front of him. "Go ahead."

Again Tyler tried. He put his arm in the right position, but even straightening it was beyond painful. As he went to lift it he felt a pop and he cried out. Not loud or long, but he hadn't expected the sudden pain. He hadn't tried anything like this since he'd been injured. It hurt enough just getting through the day in a brace.

Dr. Walsh ran him through a few more drills, all of which Tyler failed. Basically, he couldn't move his arm more than an inch or so. It was simply too torn apart, too painful.

"This is what I was afraid of." The doctor leaned against the nearby counter. "Tyler, your shoulder's worse than you thought. I read the doctor's report from the hospital in Pensacola." He took the chart and opened it again. "The damage appears to be far more significant." He set the file down once more and came alongside Tyler. "Your labrum runs around the shoulder socket." He lightly touched Tyler's shoulder along the front and back. "We usually explain tears by varying degrees. A 30- or 60-degree tear, and sometimes — in worst-case scenarios — we might see a tear that goes halfway around. One hundred and eighty degrees."

Tyler nodded. He'd heard this before. He was ready to get to the part about fixing him.

"In your case, though, there really isn't any labrum left." Dr. Walsh pressed his lips together. "I look at baseball players' shoulders all day long. I work with college players and pros and some high school kids." He turned his eyes to Tyler. "I've never seen a case this bad."

What was he supposed to say to that? The pain was still shooting through his body from the effort of trying to move his arm. "So . . . when can you fix it?"

"Well, that's not all." The doctor gave a single shake of his head. "Looks like your rotator cuff is shot, too. Sometimes when the labrum suffers a catastrophic blow, the rotator takes the brunt of the force."

Tyler felt sick to his stomach. "So . . . a longer recovery?"

Dr. Walsh returned to his spot against the counter. He looked at Tyler for a long beat. "I'm really sorry. I don't know how else to say this." He crossed his arms. "There's no way you'll pitch again, Tyler. You'll be lucky to toss a ball to your son someday."

What? Tyler blinked. None of the doctor's words made sense. Strange ocean-type sounds crowded out Tyler's hearing. He stared at the doctor. The man's mouth was moving, but no words came. Nothing he could understand.

"Tyler? Are you tracking with me?"

"Sir?" Tyler rubbed the back of his neck. He needed his brace. That would help his recovery, right? He grabbed the brace from the table beside him and snapped it back into place. Carefully he slid his right arm safely inside. There. Everything was going to be okay.

"Tyler?" The doctor moved closer. He put his hand on Tyler's left shoulder. "Are you okay?"

Am I okay? "I'll work harder than anyone. As soon as . . . as soon as you fix my shoulder. So I can start rehab and training and —"

"I'm sorry. I don't think you heard me." The man exhaled hard. Clearly whatever he was trying to say wasn't easy. "It looks like a grenade tore through your shoulder. You're done pitching." Dr. Walsh barely paused. "I'm going to try to put you back together. I'll use cartilage and muscle and try to build you a labrum from that." He stared at Tyler. "But you will never pitch professionally again. Do you understand?"

The words were getting through now, but Tyler couldn't believe they were for him.

God had arranged this surgery. This was supposed to be his miracle. "Isn't it possible? I mean, you could go in and it might not be so bad. You repair it and I'll work harder than anyone you ever operated on. I could make it back, right? Things like that happen."

This time Dr. Walsh wasn't going to argue with him. Tyler could see it in his expression. "I haven't seen that with your kind of injury. But yes, sometimes a patient will surprise us."

"Okay, then." Tyler could breathe again. "When can you operate? I'm ready anytime."

"I have an opening in the morning. If you can be here by six-thirty. Our surgery center is on the fourth floor." He explained that the operation would take place around eight and he'd be in recovery after that. Someone could drive him back to Marcus's house late that afternoon.

Tyler didn't hesitate. "I'll be here. I'm ready now."

Hesitation shadowed the doctor's expression. "Don't get your hopes up. I can't overstate the fact: your injury . . . it's one of the worst I've seen."

"Then my recovery will be that much more of a miracle."

"I'll do what I can." The doctor excused himself to write up the orders for tomorrow.

"Thank you." Tyler watched him go. Then he stood and walked to the window. Down in the parking lot, other patients were coming and going. People with broken bones and busted dreams. Tyler clenched his teeth. None of them wanted it the way he did. He would get better and he would pitch again. He had no doubts. Not a single one.

But by the time he left the office thirty minutes later, weariness had set in. He'd be lucky to throw a ball to his son one day? Was that really what Dr. Walsh believed? *My shoulder looks that bad?* Tyler focused on the road ahead. He didn't need a map to know where he was going. The 405 to the 101 to the 118. The Simi Valley Freeway.

The miles disappeared beneath the Hummer and when Tyler began to see signs for Cochran Boulevard, a heavy cloak of doubt fell over him. He was supposed to be bringing his parents good news. He was getting his surgery. He was going to be okay. Rehab would start next week and before they knew it, he'd be back pitching again. Running hard after his dream.

Their dream.

But now . . . how could he walk in and

418

say that? Dr. Walsh had given him no hope whatsoever. So why was he going to his parents' house, anyway? *What am I going to say?* He should've gone to college. If he'd gone to UCLA he wouldn't have gotten into trouble. He would've dominated the conference and come out a champion. He would've been in the majors by now — just like Marcus Dillinger.

And he never would've been on that Blue Wahoos pitcher's mound desperate for perfection. He skipped college and now . . . now he was an out-of-work janitor who might never pitch another . . .

He let the thought die there. With the greatest determination he pictured Virginia, while he sat beside her. One of their conversations came back to him. *I don't love you for what you can do or for what you might accomplish.* He could see her smiling, feel her love still. *I love you because you're my son. That's enough.*

For Virginia Hutcheson, yes.

But would it be enough for Bill and Angie Ames? He had promised them good news. Now the best news he could give them was the fact that his surgery was in the morning. Anything beyond that would be an exaggeration. A lie even.

He took the exit and made a left turn at

419

the bottom of the off-ramp. His parents lived in a tract house in the Valley Heights subdivision. Nothing fancy, but more than enough. As Tyler turned past the sign he was struck by the way it looked older than he remembered it. Not as clean and well kept.

Nothing stays the same, he thought. *Not even home.*

By the time he pulled into his parents' driveway, his heart pounded in his throat so loud he could barely think. How long had it been since he'd seen his parents' house? The house he'd grown up in?

His stomach was in knots. Maybe he should scrap the idea, turn around, and wait another six months. Let the surgery happen, do the rehab, and figure out whether Dr. Walsh was right. If he could prove the man wrong, if he could fight his way back to a professional pitcher's mound, then . . . then he could come home.

That would be the sort of news his parents would want to hear.

Yes, that was a much better idea. He was about to put the Hummer in reverse when his mother opened the front door. She looked thinner than before, her hair shorter, grayer. Sorrow and fear seemed to tighten the lines around her eyes. She didn't stay on the doorstep. Instead she hurried down the walk to the driver's door of the Hummer.

He had no choice now so he opened the door and stepped out. His shoulder was killing him.

"Tyler." His mother held her ground, didn't rush at him or try to say too much at once. The years had created more than one kind of distance. She noticed his brace. "How are you?"

Her concern touched him. No matter how broken the trail of yesterdays, she would always be his mother, always have a connection to the condition of his soul. "I'm fine." He walked to her and slipped his good arm around her neck. The hug wasn't long or particularly full of emotion. But it was a start.

He was too distracted for anything more, too busy wondering how he would tell them this latest bad news or whether he would tell them at all. Tyler took a deep breath. He searched her anxious eyes. "Thanks for letting me come."

"Of course." Her expression showed her restraint. A smile softened her face and she linked her arm through his. "Your father's inside."

The reality made Tyler feel sick. His

father . . . his coach. His mentor. The man who had believed Tyler could be one of the best pitchers of this era. Tyler dreaded seeing him now, not because the man had believed too greatly in him. But because his father had been right. All of it had been possible — if only Tyler had done things differently.

Halfway up the walk he stopped. He swallowed hard, summoning his courage. "Mom" — he looked at her — "how's Dad?"

She looked slightly baffled by the question. "He's . . . he can't wait to see you."

"He's not mad?"

"Tyler." Shock softened her tone. "Mad at you?"

"Mom, you remember the last time we talked? I figured he would be angry with me forever. A little more every day."

"No." She looked suddenly weak, devastated even. Like she might collapse on the sidewalk and never find the strength to get up. "We've both been . . . heartsick. Every day." She hesitated, clearly wanting him to get this next part. "He wants to spend the rest of his life making it up to you. We never meant for . . ." Her voice trailed off and tears overtook her eyes.

Tyler put his arm around her shoulders

and held her. They were all so hurting, so damaged by the choices of the past. "Let's go inside."

His fears let up a little. With all that had already happened today, he wasn't sure he could face his angry father, too. He'd rather have a quick conversation with his mother here out front and then be on his way. He wouldn't mind watching Marcus and the team practice — if they'd let him. Then he had surgery in the morning.

He couldn't picture his father humbled and ready to make things right. Maybe he had only pretended so Tyler would feel welcome enough to come home. Then once he stepped inside his dad would lower the mask and light into him. Which was fine, really. Any other day Tyler could take it, receive the verbal lashing he deserved and decide whether there was a reason to ever come back home again.

Just not today.

They walked slowly together, Tyler's arm still around his mom's shoulders. How had he gone so long without his mom? He'd been so hurt by their disappointment that he'd blocked her from his heart and mind. He might've stayed away from her forever if it wasn't for Virginia. When they reached the front door he hesitated just a beat or two. He had never skydived, but he'd seen videos of people with parachute packs hovering at the open door of a plane, trying to find the will to jump.

That's how Tyler felt now. He took a deep breath and opened the door. His father was a few feet away, sitting on the edge of the sofa, elbows on his knees, hands clasped. Almost like he was praying. He looked up and their eyes met.

"Dad." Tyler steeled himself for what was certainly coming. The barrage of insults and criticisms. The deserved reminders of all he'd done wrong, all the failed choices that had broken their family and destroyed his chances at baseball.

Tyler waited. For what felt like an hour, he stood looking at the man who had once been his father, sure the words were going to come. But they never did. Instead Bill Ames stood. His eyes never left Tyler's. He had more wrinkles on his forehead and around his eyes, and he had put on a few pounds.

The real difference was in his spirit.

"Can I . . . hug you?"

His dad came to him slowly, as if the move took all his effort. The way he walked, his tentative body language felt familiar — and Tyler realized why. His father looked the way he himself must've looked a few minutes ago walking up to the front door. There was nothing natural about the hug. His dad tried to avoid Tyler's braced-up shoulder and they didn't seem to know whose arm went where.

But once he was in his father's embrace, Tyler's fears faded like April snow. Without any words at all, he was in that moment certain of things he had never expected to feel. First, his dad loved him. Without asking about how long until Tyler could pitch again and without rehashing some of the best moments in Tyler's baseball career. Love. All by itself. The kind Virginia had talked about. Tyler could feel it — and it was the strangest, most amazing feeling ever.

The other obvious truth was this: his dad was sorry. In what could only be another part of the miracle, his father clearly didn't blame him for the lost years. His hug carried with it tangible proof of his regret and remorse. Tyler's shock gave way to acceptance and finally a hope he hadn't felt before where his dad was concerned.

Tyler's mother stood nearby, her arms folded, tears on her cheeks. It was a moment that needed no words. His father's hug said it all. After a while they made their way to the sofa, all three of them. Tyler explained why he was there. He would be having surgery in the morning. He was staying with Marcus.

"I'm not sure about pitching again." Even though his parents had changed, Tyler still felt this might be the worst blow of their lives. "The doctor says we'll have to see."

His mother spoke first. "Is the operation . . . dangerous?"

Tyler blinked. Her question was the last thing he had expected. "Uh . . . I don't think so. I mean, he didn't say anything about it being risky."

His father looked relieved. "We'd like to be there. In the waiting room." He paused. "If that's okay." Even his voice was different, kinder. Quieter.

"Sure." Tyler's mind raced. This was how he had always wanted his parents to treat him, the way he had wanted them to love him.

And like that, there was no more talk about Tyler's shoulder or his pitching or his game. Instead the conversation moved on to his job at Merrill Place, and his friendship with Virginia Hutcheson.

"She sounds lovely." His mom had been on the brink of tears since he arrived. This was another of those moments. "I wish it would've been me. Giving you advice. Talking about grace."

Tyler looked at her, at the mother who had taken him to church as a little boy and cheered for him at his Little League games. "I wish that, too, Mom."

"I've been praying." Her faith shone in her eyes. Another change. "Especially after we met your friend Ember."

"Who?"

"Ember, right?" She looked at Tyler's father. "I think that was her name."

"Yes." His dad nodded. "Ember." He turned to Tyler. "She knew you in Florida."

"We saw her at lunch one day." His mom looked confused. "She definitely knew you."

Tyler had no idea who they were talking about. "She knew me?"

"Told us to pray. Not to give up." His dad shook his head. "After that, we never stopped praying."

Ember? Tyler searched his memory. Was she a fan? Someone he had met at the hospital when he was drugged up? He had no idea. Either way, he marveled at the fact. While God had brought Virginia into his life, He had brought his parents someone, too: Ember. A friend he didn't remember ever knowing.

It didn't have to make sense.

They talked for another few minutes.

Then Tyler had to get Marcus's Hummer back. He hugged his parents. This time the words came more easily for all of them. Apologies and promises that this was just the beginning.

Even his dad's hug felt more natural. "I love you, son." His emotions seemed to gain ground on him and he had to wait a few seconds. "I wasn't sure I'd ever get another chance to tell you."

"That's behind us." Tyler smiled at him and then at his mother. "I love you both."

He still had to work out forgiveness, for himself and his parents. But for now he was treating the moment the way Virginia would've treated it: Love first. Questions later. Grace beyond measure. All of it unconditional.

Because love like this was from God.

When Tyler pulled onto the freeway ten minutes later, he replayed the entire visit. Every remarkable, unexpected moment. As he did, something hit him, something he hadn't fully grasped until just now. Of all the things they'd talked about and all the ways they'd laid the foundation to a new bridge between them, one topic came up just once.

Baseball.

Which could only mean one thing. Tyler

let the truth sink deep in his heart, where it watered the dry and barren places in his soul. His parents no longer saw him as a baseball player.

They saw him as their son.

30

Beck was dressed like a janitor. Something he learned from watching Tyler. He pushed a mop bucket and a cart of cleaning supplies down a long cement corridor. Along the way, he passed a few of the grounds crew. Beck nodded briefly and kept walking.

Confidence, he told himself.

Everyone except Marcus was down on the field taking practice. The coaches, too — all of them. Including Coach Ollie Wayne.

Beck stepped inside the man's office. He glanced back once. The corridor was clear. He had time. He needed to accomplish what he'd come here for. Beck opened the top drawer at the far left side of Coach Wayne's desk. From the back, he pulled out a business card and stared at it.

Perfect. Let this work . . . Please, God.

He set the business card on the center of Coach Wayne's keyboard — where the man couldn't miss it.

Then, before Beck left the coach's office, before he returned the cleaning supplies and disappeared, he looked once more at the card and the name across it.

The name was Jep Black.

Cheryl Conley took the call from Marcus Dillinger late that Monday afternoon. Marcus had told her that this was the day for Tyler's surgery, and Cheryl had prayed all morning. This last stage of what God was doing, the miracle He was working, was the most important of all.

"The surgery just wrapped up." Marcus sounded troubled. "Doctor said it went well, better than he hoped."

"Thank God." Cheryl exhaled and dropped to the nearest chair at the kitchen table. "I've been praying."

"Well . . . the news — it wasn't all good." Marcus took what sounded like a weary breath. "The damage was even worse than the test showed. He probably had an infection after the injury. Somehow it healed on its own, but it caused significant damage. Much more than the torn labrum."

Cheryl wanted to hang up and start the conversation all over. This wasn't possible. Tyler had been given the most extraordinary chance with this surgery. He was ready to work harder than anyone in baseball to get better. She struggled to ask the one question screaming through her mind: "Was . . . the doctor able to fix it?"

"He saved Tyler's arm." Marcus sighed. "Cheryl, he'll never pitch again. He can't."

She closed her eyes and pictured the young man, the earnest way he had sat next to her mother every day. He deserved to pitch again. His story was a couple pages from a happy ending. *God . . . why?* She blinked and looked out the window. "Is there . . . if he works hard —"

"No. He'll never throw again. The doctor said he might be able to pick up his kids one day." Marcus sounded discouraged. "At least he has his arm. Seriously."

"I guess . . . I really thought God was going to —"

"Me, too."

"You did the right thing, Marcus."

"Hmmm." This time the hint of a sad smile sounded in his tone. "I know that, Miss Cheryl. I have no doubt."

Cheryl let the reality hit her. Tyler Ames was finished playing baseball. "Were you there? During the surgery?"

"I got there at the end. They let me leave practice for an hour."

"Good." Cheryl pictured Tyler being wheeled into surgery. "I hated imagining him there alone."

"He wasn't alone." His voice held a fresh sort of joy. "His parents were there the whole time."

"His parents?" Cheryl held her breath. Tyler had told her about them. "That was a good thing?"

"Yes." Marcus took a deep breath. "I told you, Miss Cheryl, God's got this. Lots of love and forgiveness happening around here."

"Wow." Cheryl leaned against the window. "Does Tyler know? About his shoulder?"

"The doctor had warned him. He's telling Tyler now." His voice was serious again. "Pray for him. He could use it."

"I will. And I'll be watching the World Series. You're going to win it all, Marcus. I believe that."

"I hope so. An LA car dealer's going to build the kids a new gym if we win."

Cheryl smiled. "Proud of you, Marcus. Really."

The call ended and for a long time Cheryl stared out the window trying to come to terms with this change of events. Out back Chuck and the granddaughters were working on a vegetable garden they planted —

in memory of their great-grandmother.

Didn't I hear You right, God? Cheryl sighed, suddenly more tired than before. *I could picture him in uniform, Lord. I could see him pitching again.* She leaned into the cool glass. *I trust You, Father. I do. But could You be with Tyler Ames right now? When he's getting the worst news of his life? Give him a reason to believe in You. Please.*

Precious daughter . . . I work all things to the good of those who love Me.

The answer whispered across Cheryl's soul, and chills ran down her arms. It was a verse from Romans she'd read that morning. Now it was as if God had spoken the words straight to her soul. He worked all things to the good for those who loved Him.

So what about Tyler Ames?

Cheryl imagined how the young man might be feeling at this moment, knowing that his dreams of pitching were over. Forever. She pictured him lying in a bed, his arm bandaged, the pain of the surgery just setting in. *Where's the rest of Tyler's miracle, Father? What happened?*

She waited, hoping for some sort of response, some spotlight of understanding so the verse from Romans would make sense in Tyler's situation. But none came. Instead, gradually, an image began to take shape in her mind. Tyler hadn't been at the hospital alone. He'd been there with his parents. The parents he hadn't talked to in years.

Nearly every conversation between her mother and Tyler was about family and staying close, forgiving one another. Tyler had told her once that the talks made him miss his mom and dad, made him see the way he was at fault for the break in their relationship. He would've done things differently if he had it to do over again. Cheryl's mother had taught Tyler that.

Now that's exactly what had happened. The course of events was uncanny, really. Tyler busts his shoulder and winds up homeless. He slips into a church and some stranger points him to Merrill Place, the retirement center where Cheryl's mother lived. At the exact time when Cheryl and Chuck were praying for healing and peace for the woman. The bedside talks, the childhood connection with Marcus, the trip to LA.

Every single one of those events had to happen for Tyler and his parents to be reunited. For a reconciliation to happen.

The light in Cheryl's soul grew brighter, the dawning more complete. Tyler wasn't going to play baseball again, but so what? They had asked God for a miracle and they had gotten one. When the reality of his situation fully hit him, he wouldn't be alone.

His parents would be there.

Which was maybe the greatest miracle of all.

Sami took the worn tray from Mary Catherine and added a scoop of salad and a couple of cookies to the plate. She passed it to the person on her left and took another one from Mary Catherine. The LA Freedom Mission was where Sami spent a great deal of her social time lately. Volunteers staffed the place, serving dinner to the city's homeless every day of the week.

Mary Catherine had heard that the mission was going to be short a few volunteers for the next two weeks. The two of them didn't hesitate. A week into the work and they knew most of the regulars on a first-name basis.

"Don't like the cookies. I'm a diabetic, remember?" A grizzled-looking man with a ragged plaid shirt and gray dreadlocks waved a gnarled finger at Sami.

"Gotcha, JT." Sami winked at him. "Double salad for the diabetics. Sound good?"

"Thatta girl." He returned the wink, took the tray from the end of the line, and headed for the cafeteria.

Sami didn't recognize the next few people. She swapped a smile with Mary Catherine and thought about how much her life had changed. Arnie hadn't called once — though her grandparents still shared dinner with him every week or so.

"He's a good man, Samantha," her grandfather had told her when he called yesterday. "You're walking out on a great opportunity."

Love could never be an opportunity. The very idea made Sami slightly nauseous. She loved her grandparents; she always would. They had cared for her and raised her and they deserved her respect. But she could never agree with their view of life. The way good things seemed earned and opportunities were meant to be exploited.

Sami would never go back to that thinking again. She had her Bible now. That was what she relied on. She had pulled it out of the box in her closet and dusted it off. Every night she became a little more familiar with Jesus. The way He lived and loved. The way He forgave and served people.

His grace.

"Connie, hello! No salad, right?" Sami flashed a smile at the woman in her late sixties, next in line. "Extra cookies?"

"You remembered!" The woman gave

Sami a thumbs-up and limped to the end of the counter for her tray.

Sami watched her go. This was love. Sami wasn't used to it or good at it, but she was trying and she liked how it felt. This weekend a few of the volunteers were going to paint a home for some foster kids.

It was after nine by the time she and Mary Catherine got back to their apartment. Her roommate was seeing a guy now, someone she met at church. He was the chief fundraiser for a ministry that worked to rescue kids from sex trafficking. Oh, and he loved to laugh. They'd been going to church together for the past three weeks.

"Nothing like talking about a sermon to see if the guy you're starting to like is real."

Real. Sami loved that. It was Mary Catherine's way of describing people who lived their faith. Broken, regular people who had discovered grace and wanted to spend the rest of their lives acting it out. Real people. Living in hope that other people would become real, too.

They were both tired, so they turned in early. Something Sami rarely did anymore. Alone in her room she spotted her laptop on a chair in the corner. Her room was a mess and she hadn't been online in a week. Not since the night after Mary Catherine took her boogie-boarding. There was no time for Facebook now. Sami was fast falling in love with life. It didn't matter if her clothes piled up or if she didn't know the latest Fox News stories. Twitter was all but forgotten.

Sami was living.

And she loved every minute.

While she brushed her teeth, she thought about Mary Catherine and her views on love. "God's all for romance," her friend had said the other night. "I'm the most hopeless romantic there is." She had twirled her coat in front of her, as if it belonged to the man of her dreams. "Romance is easy. It's the other part that can be a struggle." She let go of the coat. "Which is why I'll probably never get married." She had dropped to the floor, pensive.

Mary Catherine rarely took herself too seriously, but she was serious about only dating guys who understood love. A guy who was real about his faith. Someone who would roll up his sleeves and serve dinner at a homeless mission or let his heart get lost in a Chris Tomlin praise song. Romantic love would come only after she and her guy — whoever he turned out to be — had first experienced that kind of love.

God's kind.

The divorce of Mary Catherine's parents had shaped her, even changed her. She would never settle for the easy existence her mom and dad had shared before their split. Not that Mary Catherine talked about it much. But sometimes it seemed everything she did, her views on faith and her thoughts about life and love and God, all came from watching her own parents fail at it.

Sami looked a moment longer at her face in the bathroom mirror. God had brought Mary Catherine into her life, no question. She ran her hand over the smooth leather Bible on her bed stand. God was Sami's friend now, close enough to talk to, always available. He was the only one who knew her deepest thoughts.

How much she still thought about Tyler Ames.

The trip to Pensacola had been a disappointment, but that didn't change the past. And it didn't change the way he'd looked at her that morning in the park with the gulf a few feet away.

A sigh escaped her. The Tyler she had known had been real — or at least on his way to becoming real. But a game had gotten in the way. Winning and losing and the ocean of pressure that came with it. More than anyone could take.

She sat on the edge of her bed and again her laptop caught her attention. Maybe she should check her Facebook. She was a different person now, and she didn't need social media to validate her life. But it could be fun to see what her friends thought about her body-surfing pictures. She hurried across the room, grabbed the computer, and brought it back to the edge of her bed.

It took a few minutes to power up, but then she found her way to Facebook. There were two private messages and as she stared at the notices, her heart skipped a beat. What was this? Who would message her? She opened them and felt a rush of shock. One of them was from Arnie Bell.

The other was from Tyler.

She stared at the names long enough to believe what she was seeing. *What in the world, Lord?* She took a slow breath and opened Arnie's first. It was brief.

Samantha,

I have a favor to ask. You may have thought I was joking when I said I planned to be the president of the United States one day. But I wasn't. If that happens — when it happens — I plan to say our relationship ended by mutual agreement. It wouldn't be good for either of us if people think you broke up with me. The press would look for a reason. Neither of us needs that.

Please let me know if this is agreeable — if so, let's go with that story.
Thanks. Miss you.
Arnie

Her cheeks couldn't have felt hotter if Arnie had reached through the screen and slapped her. A single laugh escaped from the outraged hallways of her heart. *Really, Arnie? Really?* Of all the nerve. How dare he speak to her like that — even in a private Facebook message. And wasn't he worried that someone would find the private message years down the road? The whole matter was ridiculous. All Arnie ever cared about was —

The cover of her Bible caught her eye. Last night she'd read about how Jesus wanted people to love their enemies. To pray for those who persecuted them. Sami felt the fight leave her. *Fine, God. I'd like to pray for Arnie Bell. Help him hear Your voice — especially if he's headed into politics. I pray that one day he'll be real. Thank You, Lord.*

She wanted to delete his message. Instead she did the most loving thing she could do for Arnie. She hit the reply button and typed out her response.

That's fine with me, Arnie. The breakup was mutual. That'll be the story. Take care of yourself. I'm praying for you.
Sami

She was about to fix her name. He had never heard her call herself that, and certainly he had never imagined her as anything but Samantha. She felt a smile lift her lips. No. She would leave her name just as it was. She couldn't pray for Arnie to be real unless she was willing to be real, too.

She hit the send button and then opened Tyler's letter.

It was much longer. Sami's heart quickened as she began to read. He talked about how he wasn't only a janitor at Merrill Place. He was also a friend to a woman named Virginia Hutcheson. Sami read the whole thing and then she read it again.

In the message, Tyler talked about God — something that had never been a part of their relationship back in the day. God and grace and something more. How he was sorry. He hadn't wanted to be mean when she visited him in Pensacola, but she was with someone else and he didn't want to get hurt. Basically that's what the message said. She read the last part once more, though this time the letters were hard to read through her tears.

The truth is, I miss you. More than you could ever know. Especially on nights like this.

Sami let that sink in. Tyler Ames missed her. Especially at night. She smiled even as two tears trickled down her cheeks. Hadn't she known that all along? Of course he missed her. Who else knew him the way she had known him — that short time in his life when baseball wasn't his entire existence? She kept reading, drinking in the words like a person desperate for water.

Forgive me for keeping my heart locked up. Virginia wouldn't want me to live like that. Now that she's gone, I don't want to live like that either. That's it really. I didn't want you to think I was only a janitor at Merrill Place, when you see . . . I understand now, God doesn't define me by my job. Whatever work He gives me. Forgive me, Sami. Keep riding the waves.

Love,
Tyler

Yes, Tyler was so much more. Sami sniffed

and dried her eyes with her fingertips. Then she began to move her fingers across the keys. There were no walls for her either, not this time. Life was too short to hide true feelings of the heart. She had no idea when she'd be in Pensacola again or whether anything would come of this exchange with Tyler. But she had to write back, even if only for one reason.

Tyler Ames was becoming real.

31

Tyler's meeting with the Dodgers' head coach was in twelve minutes. Marcus had several cars, so he had loaned the Hummer to him indefinitely. He checked the time on the dashboard as he pulled into the stadium parking lot. He was early. Of all the twists and turns his life had taken since he'd blown out his shoulder, Tyler had a feeling today might be the craziest of all.

He took a spot near the player entrance and killed the engine.

The whirlwind of events and emotions was still more than he could believe. His surgery had been nearly two weeks ago. He had stayed on the pain pills just two days this time around. Already the ache in his shoulder was much less than what he'd walked around with for months before the operation.

He was working with a physical therapist, getting better, stronger. He had split his time since the surgery at his parents' house and then staying with Marcus. He had much to be thankful for — Tyler understood that to the center of his soul. The renewed friendship with Marcus, his mom and dad back in his life, and the handful of messages he and Sami had swapped. These were the happiest parts of his new life.

The one where he was no longer a baseball player.

He checked the time on his phone. His parents had given him one of their old ones and set it up with a basic plan. All they could afford. Tyler was careful not to use it often, and one day soon — when the brace was finally off his arm — he would look for a job and get on his feet financially. All in time.

Amazing. Now that he understood grace, he realized how much had been showered on him. So much that he didn't deserve. Tyler walked up to the entrance and for just a moment he thought about his shoulder. The doctor's words rang in his mind again the way they still did several times a day. *You will never pitch again, Tyler. I'm sorry.*

Never pitch again.

For a few seconds he stopped just shy of the entrance and lifted his eyes. The sign read OFFICIAL PLAYER ENTRANCE — LOS

ANGELES DODGERS. Right up until his trip to Los Angeles, Tyler had believed he would walk through a door like this one day. Not for some curious meeting with a coach, but to suit up for a game.

For whole seasons of games.

He nodded slowly and focused on the task ahead. Whatever it was. God could see him — He wasn't finished with him. He smiled and headed through the door. It took another two minutes to make his way to the coach's office. The man stood and introduced himself. "I'm Ollie Wayne. I coach the pitchers."

Tyler knew who he was. "Nice to meet you." He sat across from the coach. So far the meeting was like something from a dream. For the life of him, Tyler couldn't possibly understand why the man wanted to see him. Especially ten hours before what could be the last game of the World Series, with the Dodgers leading 3–2.

"I brought you in because last week I had a random talk with Jep Black — manager of the Blue Wahoos. He and I go way back, friends from our college days."

Tyler felt his expression go blank. Jep Black knew Ollie Wayne? From college?

A twinge of regret hit Tyler, the one that would always come when successful baseball players and coaches talked about their college days. Tyler let it go. He tried to focus on what Coach Wayne was saying. He still couldn't think of a single reason why he was here.

"So Jep and I got to talking and you came up. I told him you had your surgery and . . ." The coach frowned, clearly struggling with the reality of Tyler's situation. "I told him you were done playing."

"Yes, sir." Tyler couldn't grasp where this was headed. "I haven't talked to him yet."

"I figured." Another frown. "Before I say anything else, Tyler, you should know this: I've followed your pitching career ever since the Little League World Series. You're a tremendous talent. What happened with your shoulder —" He shook his head. "It's the worst kind of terrible." He paused, clearly troubled. "I'm sorry."

"Thank you." Tyler believed the words he was about to say. He felt them in his heart as he spoke: "God must have other plans for me. I'm working to figure it out."

A slight smile lifted Coach Wayne's expression. "That's why I called you in."

He had to be dreaming. The pitching coach for the Los Angeles Dodgers couldn't think Tyler would pitch again. The idea was without even the slightest degree of possibility. Tyler shifted. "Yes, sir."

"I need to hire a pitching coach for our intern program, someone we can bring along in the off-season." He leaned back in his chair. "Jep says I'd be crazy to hire anyone but you. Best young pitching coach he's ever worked with." Coach Wayne looked at a sheet of notes on his desk. "Jep said you worked with his pitchers in the off-season. Made every one of them better. Right before his eyes."

This couldn't be happening. Tyler had decided he couldn't coach if he couldn't pitch. But now . . . he had to hold onto the arms of the chair and squeeze hard to be sure he wasn't floating. A week from now he might've given up on finding work in LA — too expensive without a real job. He could've even headed back to Merrill Place. He took a few subtle deep breaths and forced himself to listen.

"Of course, the other endorsement is the one that really matters." Coach Wayne picked up a second piece of paper. "Here's what it says: 'I learned everything about pitching by the time I was in high school. Tyler Ames taught me. He was just a kid himself, but he had tricks and techniques even experienced coaches couldn't teach me.' "

Who in the world would've said that? Tyler listened, his heart pounding so loud he figured the coach had to hear it across the desk.

"There's more. This player goes on to say, 'I think about that every now and then. I'll be out there on the mound pitching a winning game and his name will come up in my mind. Tyler Ames — I'll always be thankful for him.' "

Coach Wayne looked straight at Tyler. "That was written by my top pitcher. Marcus Dillinger." He smiled. "Marcus said he could guarantee we'd be known for our pitching if I hired you. How 'bout that?"

Tyler stared at the coach for a few seconds. Then he shook his head, unable to speak. Marcus had said that? Tears tried to crowd the moment, but he blinked them back. He pictured himself and Marcus, the two of them in high school, throwing pitch after pitch after pitch. Tyler could see things, that's what he told Marcus back then: Little things. Adjustments. He would tell Marcus and Marcus would change his pitching.

It worked just about every time.

But how had Marcus remembered all these years later? And when had all this happened? "Sir . . . what about my arm?"

"Marcus says you can adjust a pitcher's

451

technique from a chair."

"I don't . . . I'm not sure what to say."

"Say yes." He laughed. "Jep Black says he'll hire you to coach for them if I don't." He studied Tyler. "But this is home for you, is that right?"

Tyler thought about his parents and Marcus, his recent conversations with Sami on Facebook. "Yes, sir. It's home."

Coach Wayne sat forward and set his forearms down hard on the desk. "Then say yes." He went on for a minute or so about how the Dodgers liked to bring in a young intern coach and develop him, keep him in the franchise if he worked out. Then the coach talked about starting pay — five times what it had been at Merrill Place. "Of course that's just the intern pay. If things go well after a few seasons, you could be up in the six figures." He grinned. "I have a feeling you'll be around for a while."

"Thank you. I hope so." Tyler wondered when the adrenaline rush would stop. "Sir? Are you serious?"

The coach laughed out loud. "Jep said I'd like you." He stood and held out his hand. "I'll take that as a yes, Tyler."

"Yes." They shook and Tyler laughed this time. A laugh of shock and disbelief and pure Christmas-like joy. "Definitely yes."

Coach Wayne walked Tyler to the door. "You start today. I've set up best-seat passes for six at the player window for tonight's game." He looked confident. "A win tonight and we're World Series Champs — which will happen. After we win, well, the off-season starts tomorrow. We'll have meetings from ten to twelve each day. We'll give you time to heal up before you start working with our staff on the field."

There were a few other details, and Coach Wayne sent him away with a packet to fill out. New hire information. Tyler walked back out to Marcus's Hummer, climbed in behind the wheel, and just sat there. He couldn't believe it. Despite the odds, and though he didn't deserve anything close, the impossible had happened.

He had made it to the Bigs.

When he could finally breathe normally again, Tyler drove to his father's warehouse and spent the day with his parents. He didn't say a word about the job. Instead he helped his mother with filing in the office and not until lunchtime, at El Pollo Loco, did he tell them the news. It took that long for *him* to believe it, let alone imagine sharing it with his mom and dad.

"I'm so happy for you, son." His dad

hugged him. The embrace was almost totally natural now. The bridge was being rebuilt — one day at a time.

That afternoon he had an appointment with Dr. Walsh, who confirmed that his shoulder was healing right on schedule. Tyler went straight into rehab from the doctor's office and at just after five, he finally gave himself permission to think about the next meeting.

The one with Sami Dawson.

They had swapped private Facebook messages for the last couple weeks and finally, a few days ago, he had told her about the surgery and the fact that he wasn't in Pensacola, but here. An hour away. Tyler still wasn't sure what would come from this, whether they could find what they shared before or whether this was only another part of his healing. But he knew this:

He had to see her.

The parking lot was empty at Zuma Station 12 when he pulled up — the last and furthest north section of the popular beach. He parked in the first row and stepped out. A brick wall separated the parking lot from the expanse of sand. She wasn't there yet, which was good. He needed this time to sort through all that had happened.

Every wonderful, unbelievable detail.

He leaned against the wall and stared at the deep blue Pacific. *Breathe, Ames. Just breathe.* There was a time when every moment led to a game, a number of pitches and balls and strikeouts. From his childhood days until three months ago, he defined himself the way the press did: by the speed of his pitch, his earned-run average, his win-loss record.

He could remember what it felt like the last time he stood on the mound for the Blue Wahoos — so close to perfect. How could he have known what God had in mind?

The sound of a car caught his attention. He turned as Sami parked her car next to the Hummer. It occurred to him again that he was employed now. He was a pitching coach for the LA Dodgers. A dream job. And one day soon he could find an apartment and get his own car, his own phone. The thought made him chuckle out loud.

There were still moments he wondered if he was dreaming. But he hadn't woken up yet. So maybe all of this was actually happening.

He stood and faced her. She looked even more beautiful than before — if that was possible. Something in her eyes, her expression. The stiffness and formality were gone.

She looked eighteen again, her smile easy.

"Hi." Her eyes caught the sun as she came to him.

"Hi." Tyler waited until their toes were nearly touching. "Thanks for coming."

She didn't say anything at first, but her eyes spoke volumes. "Let's walk."

He stayed at her right side and after a few steps he got the courage to do something he'd looked forward to since they started talking. As naturally as the waves on the shore, he reached for her hand. She gave him a shy smile and his hope doubled. If she felt the way he did, then maybe this wouldn't be their last meeting. He eased his fingers between hers and breathed deep.

The ocean air helped him believe he was really here. He needed constant reminders.

When they reached the shore they took off their shoes and walked to the water. For a minute they stood there, shoulder to shoulder, staring at the ocean, holding onto the moment. Trying to believe it. Finally he felt her take a determined breath. "Mary Catherine says when a person starts to live for God, when he steps out of the box of rules and rehearsed ways of living, he becomes real."

Tyler thought about that. "Hmmm. I like that."

"She says she wouldn't date a guy unless he was real."

"Smart girl." He turned to her and she looked at him. Again he took his time. He had only one thing he wanted to say, one thing that mattered. "Sami?" He still had hold of her hand. "Can I hug you?"

Her eyes shone prettier than the sunlight on the water. She whispered just one word, "Please."

He took her in his good arm and held her with a desperate sort of longing. He wore a new brace — and would for another four weeks. But his shoulder didn't hurt. They fit together like they were born to be this way.

After a while, they pulled back enough to see each other. "I got hired by the Dodgers. I'm going to help coach the pitchers."

Her smile lit up her face. "That means you're staying!"

"Yes." Again he loved this about her. She wasn't impressed that he'd be working for a pro baseball organization. Just that he would be here. Near her. "For a very long time."

"That's amazing."

"It is." He brushed her windblown hair off her cheek and allowed himself to fall into her eyes. "More than I could ask or imagine."

"That's how good God is." She looked serious for a moment. "I never saw that when I was living with my grandparents. The God in their imagination was . . . so different."

"Yes." He was tempted to think about the time they'd lost, the months and seasons and years. The mistakes he had made along the way. "I'll never be perfect." His smile felt sad for the first time since she got out of her car. "I already tried."

"I'll trade perfect for something else." She put her hand over his.

"What?"

She brushed her cheek against his, clearly as lost in his eyes as he was in hers. "Real. That's all I want from you, Tyler. The man you are here, now. The real you."

He let that settle into his soul. The sun was setting in the distance and it occurred to him that he'd finally caught up with it. He was finished chasing his happily ever after. He didn't need to. She was standing right in front of him.

"So I'm real, is that it?" He loved this, that he could tease her, that this time they had so easily found their way back to yester-day.

"Definitely." She grinned. "Very real."

His heart felt light enough to fly them

both out over the surf. "Would it be crazy if I kissed you?"

Her laugh danced in the breeze and mixed with the sound of the water around their ankles. "It'd be crazy if you didn't."

"Good." His laughter faded and so did hers. There was no need to rush the moment. He'd waited six years for it. When he couldn't wait another heartbeat he put his hand alongside her face and brought his lips to hers. The kiss was tentative at first, filled with a hope that still held its breath. But then fear and doubt and worry fell away and all that remained were the feelings between them. Feelings that already knew what their words had not yet declared.

They were home.

A bigger wave washed up and knocked Tyler to his knees. The jarring motion didn't hurt his shoulder, but it dragged Sami to the sand beside him. They started to laugh and didn't stop, not even after they helped each other up to their feet. Suddenly he remembered the tickets waiting for him at the player's window at Dodger Stadium. His parents and Marcus's were going to use four of them. He had definite hopes for the other two.

"Hey . . ." He wiped the saltwater from his face. "Wanna be my date tonight? Game six of the World Series?" He brushed wet sand off his jeans with his good arm.

"I look a little messy." Sand stuck to her jeans as well. She kept laughing as she tried to clean herself up.

"That's okay." He looped his arm around her shoulders as they started back to the cars. "Perfect is overrated."

Sami tilted her head back and laughed again. "So true."

They left her car at Zuma and drove together to the stadium. Their seats were behind the Dodgers' dugout, and already his parents and Marcus's were there. Not until Tyler and Sami were side by side in the seats did she lean close and whisper, "I like this better."

"What?" He wanted to kiss her again, but he had a feeling there would be time. Forever, if he had it his way.

"You and me. Sitting together." She grinned. "I've watched enough games by myself."

He had never cared about her more. With his parents talking to Marcus's parents, Tyler slid his fingers between Sami's. He still wished he could've known Ben Hutcheson. A smile started in his heart. Someday he would. When they would have forever to talk about Virginia and families, love and baseball.

Life was short. Love needed to have its way while there was still time.

The Dodgers won the World Series that night, and as Marcus Dillinger pointed up after the winning pitch, Tyler was convinced that somewhere in heaven Virginia and her husband and their baseball-player son had a front-row seat. Not so much for the game.

But for the miracle.

Tyler remembered something from the day he blew out his shoulder. Something the first paramedic told him — Beck, the one who had later directed him to Merrill Place. His words at their first meeting came back to him. As they did, a sense of wonder filled Tyler's soul and chills passed over him despite the warmth of the setting Los Angeles sun. Beck had been right after all. His injury wasn't an end.

It was a beginning.

Tyler could hardly wait to see what happened next.

EPILOGUE

Town Meeting — The Next Mission

Orlon called the meeting for two reasons: to celebrate the success of Ember and Beck's mission. And to lay the groundwork for the next one — the one in which terrible things were about to happen.

His team of angels — all twenty of them — were huddled around Beck and Ember, hanging on every detail. Orlon smiled. They would need this time, this chance to revel in the greatness of God and the victories won. Joy to get them through the coming storm.

Orlon set his notes on the mahogany table at the front of the room. It was time to begin.

"Everyone sit down. Please." His tone was kind. He liked seeing the angels laughing and swapping stories. But time was short. "Beck, Ember, come to the front of the room. We'd like a full report."

Gradually the voices quieted and the

angels found their seats. Beck and Ember moved to the front of the room and sat on two tall chairs facing Orlon and the others. They looked victorious, full of life, invigorated by the mission.

"First, welcome back." Orlon smiled at them. "The rest of us stayed in constant prayer throughout your time on earth." He leaned against a shining wall and folded his arms. "You experienced great success. Congratulations." He looked at the others. "You all watched, front row, praying, calling out to our Father."

Around the room the angels nodded, their attention keen.

Orlon picked up the piece of paper from the table. "Our Angels Walking team accomplished quite a list. Remember, ultimately we seek to protect a child who has not yet been born — Dallas Garner. The one who will be a very great teacher and turn hearts back to our Father. Because of the success of this mission, the eventual birth of this baby is still possible. For now, anyway."

He rattled off a few of the highlights, then he smiled again at Beck and Ember. "Nice work on all that, by the way. Very creative." He shook his head, still amazed. "I especially liked how you put the Dodgers game on in Virginia's room."

"That was Ember's idea." Beck patted her knee. "It was a last-minute victory."

Around the room the other angels were wide-eyed, clearly impressed.

They rose to their feet clapping and shouting their enthusiasm to the Creator. Ember and Beck smiled, then joined in the applause, the praise to their Creator. He was the only true Source of victory for any of them.

When the celebration settled down, Orlon angled his head, curious. This was the part only Beck and Ember could answer. "Were any humans aware?"

Ember took the lead this time. "As you saw, we interacted with a number of sons and daughters of Adam." She looked at Beck. "Several times."

Beck's face was serious again. "There were curious moments for several of them — Tyler, Sami, Tyler's parents. Even Marcus." He exchanged a look with Ember. "But no one suspected angels."

"Good." Orlon set his notes down and faced the others. "It's a delicate balance, team. Our Father wants humans to be aware of the spiritual battle for their souls. His word reminds them that every now and then a stranger might actually be an angel."

Again a chorus of agreement came softly from those in the room.

"But we never want man to turn his worship toward us." Orlon straightened himself. This was one of the aspects of the job Orlon was most passionate about. "We are messengers, helpers. We are never to be worshipped. If that happens — though we succeed at a task — we fail at pleasing our God."

Beck looked relieved. "Our Father received credit for our work at every turn. Our Angels Walking mission went undetected."

"Perfect." Orlon searched the room. "We will need a different set of angels walking for the next mission. The stakes will be even higher." He paused. "Life will be lost."

As with all missions, Orlon did not know every detail. He took a settling breath. "Tragedy is about to strike in Los Angeles. When it does, the faith of our humans will be more than tested. It will be shaken to the breaking point." He paced the room, thoughtful. Michael had been very concerned about what was coming.

The angels nodded, some of them intimately aware of the truth.

"We act on behalf of the King of kings. The One come to bring life." He paused. "Even in the face of death." Orlon slowly studied each of the faces in the room. "Any questions?"

Jag sat in the front row. He was blond and fierce, a warrior angel accustomed to battle. He raised his hand.

"Jag?" Orlon pointed to him.

"Is there a chance . . . we could lose one of them? Will the battle be drawn out?"

Orlon didn't hesitate. "Absolutely."

Jag nodded slowly. He had suffered much in his last Angels Walking mission. His story was legend. As a result, he had been moved to this team. In many ways, Jag was the most diversely skilled angel in the room.

"Anyone else?" Orlon waited. "Okay, then. We will meet again tomorrow and choose the next team."

Long after the other angels had dispersed, Orlon remained. He would stay here praying until tomorrow's meeting. Every angel had his or her strength. But he had to choose just the right pair of Angels Walking this time around.

The real battle was about to begin.

Dear Reader Friend,

I was on a flight from Texas to Arkansas during my last book tour when God gave me the idea for the Angels Walking series. It sort of came over me all at once, like the realization of first love or an unforgettable sunrise. I pulled out my notepad and began to scribble the ideas down as quickly as they came.

Forty minutes later when the flight landed, I had written more than thirty pages of outlines and synopses and character sketches. I had the sense that God had met me there — thirty thousand feet off the ground — and that my next four books might be my best ever.

In fact, the only other time I've felt that way was when I first outlined the Baxter Family books. I was on a flight then, too.

So why Angels Walking? Why a series that gives you a glimpse of the unseen, a chance to walk where angels walk? For one reason, contemporary literature has long been fascinated with the supernatural — usually the dark side of it. Vampires, witches, dragons, zombies: these are the subjects of so much of our entertainment.

But what about the light side?

See, the Bible says the supernatural world isn't one of merely our imaginations. Rather, it is more real and lasting than anything in our tangible existence. In the Bible, 2 Corinthians 4:18 says, "So we fix our eyes not on what is seen, but on what is unseen, since what is seen is temporary, but what is unseen is eternal."

Throughout the Bible, verses discuss the very real existence of angels. My favorite is Hebrews 13:2: "Don't forget to show hospitality to strangers, for by so doing, some people have shown hospitality to angels without knowing it."

See that? Without knowing it. That's the part I love.

That's the whole point of the Angels Walking series. Most of the time when angels walk this planet we miss it. We have no idea. Sure, we might hesitate when just the right person brings us just the right message or bit of help — exactly when we need it.

But we rarely ask ourselves, *Was that an angel?*

For years I've been writing Life-Changing Fiction™. God puts a story on my heart, but He has so many other hearts in mind. I hear that from you time and again. I'm really just a small part of the process. I've also reminded you for years that God has great plans for your life. Jeremiah 29:11 tells us that.

With the Angels Walking series, I can bring both those elements together.

My prayer is that after reading this book, you'll look a little more intently for God's fingerprints in your life, His voice in your story. Maybe now you'll pay more attention to the little miracles that happen all the time. And because of this series, every once in a while when someone brings you a message or a crucial bit of help, you'll wonder if this is a case of Hebrews 13:2. And you'll thank God because He would move heaven and earth for you. He'd go to the cross for you. And sometimes He'll even send angels for you.

Angels walking.

In His light and love,
Karen Kingsbury

P.S. At the back of the next book, I'll share my own angel encounter!

ANGELS WALKING
READING GROUP GUIDE
KAREN KINGSBURY

Use these questions to go deeper into the story or to encourage discussion with your small groups.

1. Read Hebrews 13:1–5 in the Bible. These verses list several things people ought to do in order to please God. In your own words, make a list of these bits of wisdom. Which of them hits you the most?

2. In the middle of these rules to live by is the one in Hebrews 13:2. Have you ever seen this verse? What does it mean to you?

3. What are your thoughts on the angelic meeting at the beginning of the book? Have you ever considered the idea that certain angels are chosen to interact with people and to accomplish various missions? Share and discuss your feelings.

4. *Angels Walking* gives us a way to see how

angels might be working among us. Tell of a time when you or someone you know experienced what might have been an angelic encounter.

5. Did reading *Angels Walking* help open your eyes to the way God is working in your life? Explain.

6. Often the greatest enemy we face is our own discouragement and negative talk. How did discouragement threaten to destroy Tyler Ames? How have defeatist thoughts harmed you now or in the past?

7. Tyler was on a quest for perfection from the time he boarded the bus for the minor leagues. How did that work out for Tyler? How was his attempt at being perfect possibly connected to his very great failures and losses?

8. Why did Tyler want to be perfect? Do you try for perfection? How has such a goal harmed you or someone you know?

9. How and when did Tyler begin to understand grace? How is the goal of perfection connected to the need for grace? Explain.

10. Why did Sami Dawson try to be perfect?

How was her reason for perfection different from Tyler's?

11. Explain the role fear played in Sami's life. How has fear shaped your life or your behavior? Are you a people pleaser? Explain.

12. Why did Tyler define his worth according to his career? Talk about a time when you or someone you know allowed their career to define their worth.

13. Read 1 Corinthians 12. The Bible talks about everyone having a role to play. Why is this helpful for people who find their self-worth in their career? How does this speak to you?

14. How was Tyler surprised by his conversation with Sami at Pensacola Beach? He thought Sami valued him because he could play baseball. Explain how Sami really saw Tyler. How could this part of their story help you or someone you know in *your* story?

15. Explain the chain of events that led Tyler to a new life of grace. Talk about a time when a series of unusual events led to something life-changing for you or someone you know.

16. Why and how did the miracle at work in Tyler's life affect the people around him? Share a time when a miracle or answered prayer in your life touched people around you. Why do you think it's important to recognize how our stories affect the stories of others in our lives?

17. How did Tyler's miracle turn out differently from what he had hoped and expected? Talk about a time when you received a different result or answer than you had hoped or prayed for.

18. Sometimes an attitude of forgiveness can change a person's life. Explain how that happened in Tyler's life. Tell of a time when an apology changed your life or the life of someone you know.

19. Why is it important to never give up on the people you love? Discuss how Tyler's parents destroyed their relationship with their son. What was the result for his parents? For Tyler?

20. Restoration is part of life. How was Tyler's story restored in *Angels Walking*? How about Sami's story? Has your story ever experienced restoration and healing? Share it.

ONE CHANCE FOUNDATION

The Kingsbury family is passionate about seeing orphans all over the world brought home to their forever families. As a result, Karen created a charitable group called the One Chance Foundation.

This foundation was inspired by the memory of her father, Ted C. Kingsbury. Ted always said, "Life is not a dress rehearsal. We have one chance to love, one chance to truly live!"

Karen often tells her reader friends that they have "one chance to write the story of their lives!"™ Now, with Karen's One Chance Foundation, readers can join her in the belief that all of us have one chance to make a difference in the lives of orphans.

In the Bible, James 1:27 says people with pure and genuine religion care for orphans. The One Chance Foundation was created with that truth in mind.

If you are interested in giving to Karen's

One Chance Foundation and having your dedication printed in one of Karen's upcoming novels, visit www.KarenKingsbury.com. Below are dedications from some of Karen's reader friends who have contributed to the One Chance Foundation:

In honor of Edith Kemp with love forever

In memory of sweet Bella

In memory of my precious Benjamin

With love to all our Baltzly Miracles!

For my #1 mom and friend, Alice Farnworth

For the love of reading — Angela Loper

To the best sister, Peggy Joyce Roberts

The best daughter ever, Rachel Chapman

To my beautiful daughter, Ruth Anne

Grammie — Too much! Love, The Cousins

Nicole and Linny, you are Prov. 31! Hejo

Dedicated to my mom, Carol Reynolds

Teichroeb, Elias, and Reimer: I love you —
H

Merry Christmas, MawMaw! Love, Macey
and Morgan

In honor of Macey and Morgan — Love,
Mom and Dad

My precious daughter, Kelly Aylsworth
Keys — Mom

To our sweet daughter, Heather Hankins

Thanks for all the Hawaiian sunsets, Mom!

Blessed: Thank You, Jesus! N. S. Okano &
CMM

Merry Christmas, Wendy Kerstetter, Love
ya

For JoAnn Williams — Love, Jessica

To our Children and Grandchildren —
Joyce and Nath

In honor of all RNs by Juleen Henderson

Theresa Parent, follow your dreams, Babe

To Michelle Stiller, the best mom ever!

To our beloved hero, Sherilyn Kingsbury

We love and miss you, Hollis Layne Richer

Merry Christmas to the O'Connell Gang

For my best friend and mom, Lori Erickson

For Patsy Callaway and Waynetta Myers

To our miracles, Jer. 29:11 — K&S Holman

In memory of Grandma Gerry and Grandma J.

In memory of Grandpa Conaway — Love, Laura

Mama, your life, legacy, and love live on

To Kaitlyn, Hailey, Leyla, and Elton with love, Lila

The Virginia Riggers Family

In memory of Maria Javier and Rey DeLaCruz

To my angel, Dominique Zuniga — Love, Mater

In memory of Sara Blair Brakebill

In memory of Sandra Mason Vanwinkle

Ken and Melanie Stoy, James 1:17

Ruby McKay, thank you! Love you! KMZA-Pxo

Brenda Helwig, we love you!

My light and guidance, Mom and Dad Lappa

Merry Christmas Gekas/Simmons families!

Pamela L. Brown

For Melissa Senter Roberson — Love, Mom

PTL4 His gift of Riley and Vanessa Roberts

In memory of my husband, Dr. Bill Butler

Vernon and Sharon Evers and Family

To my dear sister, Dawn Johnson

Proud of Marisa Farrugia's giving heart!

Shannon Barth, two years cancer-free! Yay!

Joan Thomson, beautiful inside and out!

To my very best, Tayler and Clay

For Pat Heffelfinger and Laureen Lewis

To honor Ellen Shufflebarger

Vern and Carolyn Vaandrager, we love you!

In honor of Evelyn J. Butts

In honor of Linda J. Rouse

Besties: Jax, Alli, Bekah! Eccl. 4:12 — Whit

In memory of Danny Hawkins from his wife, the love of his life, Judy Hawkins

ABOUT THE AUTHOR

#1 *New York Times* bestselling novelist **Karen Kingsbury** is America's favorite inspirational storyteller, with almost 25 million copies of her award-winning books in print. Her last dozen books have topped bestseller charts and many of her novels are under development as major motion pictures. Karen lives in Tennessee with her husband Don and their five sons, three of whom are adopted from Haiti. Their actress daughter Kelsey is married to Christian recording artist Kyle Kupecky. You can find out more about Karen, her books, and her appearance schedule at www.KarenKingsbury.com.